THE UNWALLED CITY

A Novel of Hong Kong

1st printing *The Unwalled City*, Chameleon Press, Hong Kong, March 2001

2nd printing *The Unwalled City*, Chameleon Press, Hong Kong, April 2002

THE UNWALLED CITY

A Novel of Hong Kong

XU XI

with an afterword by Dr. Kingsley Bolton
Department of English, University of Hong Kong

CHAMELEON PRESS LTD.
Suite 23A Success Commercial Building, 245 - 251 Hennessy Road,
Wanchai, Hong Kong, S.A.R., China
www.chameleonpress.com

Portions of an earlier version of this book appeared in the Fall 2000 issue of *World Englishes* and in *Yuan Yang*, Issue No. 1, 2000.

A CHAMELEON PRESS BOOK
THE UNWALLED CITY

Distributed in the U.S. & Canada by **WEATHERHILL**
41 Monroe Turnpike, Trumbull, CT 06611 • www.weatherhill.com
tel 800.437.7840 • fax 800.557.5601

Cover design by **Julia Brown**, Orijen.

Typeset in Adobe Garamond and Optima.
Printed in Hong Kong by Elite Printing Co., Ltd.
ISBN 1-387-80214-3

FOR DAD
"man I say"

Thanks are owed to many, but especially:

Ben Camardi, my agent, for over a decade of continued support;
Nury Vittachi, for our many moveable feasts;
Kingsley Bolton, for illuminating an alternate path home;
Julia Brown, for water, wine and an eye for the signs;
and the members of AUX, in particular,
Mary Bringle, Andrejika Hough, Scott Jones, Bill McGuire, Frank Spinelli.

You gave "big space" to these lives and loves in my unwalled city.

1997 has become a focus,
A cause, a point in space,
A date to live by,
A topic for conversation.
There's always something deadly
About deadlines,
They haunt before they occur.

- LOUISE HO, New Year's Eve 1989

I am what is around me.

Women understand this.
One is not duchess
A hundred yards from a carriage.

These, then are portraits:
A black vestibule;
A high bed sheltered by curtains.

These are merely instances.

- WALLACE STEVENS, Theory

PROLOGUE

New Year's Day 1993 • Hong Kong

By three that morning, none of the taxis would go near Central. All the drivers had heard the news. Police took command while partygoers huddled, hovered. Paparazzi paralyzed the moment.

Lan Kwai Fong was completely cordoned off.

People hung out of club doorways, knowing, not quite knowing, afraid to confront or believe. Champagne rivers flowed down steep slopes, spilling beyond sidewalks. Random drunks added liquid density. Bodies decorated street corners.

Local faces everywhere.

The Hong Kong government does not require New Year's Eve partygoers to request permission to march. New Year's Eve revelers are not an official organization. Only official bodies are required to submit the proper forms for a large, peaceful, public assembly.

Furthermore, New Year's Eve is a non-Chinese "gwailo" celebration.

Over the years, the crowds had grown larger and more unruly. The *Fong,* a square smaller in area than Trafalgar or Wall Street where, they said, only "devil-folk" got drunk and rowdy on non-Chinese New Year's Eve. Non-Chinese were less than two percent of the six and half million local populace. *They* thought it wasn't their problem, these *yan,* these "humans."

At midnight, twenty, some say thirty thousand burst through the floodgates. Police protection pushed forth, and was washed away with the rest of fermented nature.

By four thirty that morning, the remaining people trickled down in rivulets, in streams of uncertain consciousness.

Chinese faces everywhere.

Over the airwaves of the taxi drivers' radio relay, changing statistics buzzed. Each detoured driver stopped to ask the barricade of cops — *Gaau mat gwai a?* What ghostly realm has been disturbed this time? Ten dead, twenty dead, no, no, more, maybe fifty dead! Mashed by the mob! Asphyxiated here, now, in the wake of unbound feet and phantom pigtails, where mad dogs follow Englishmen to make fun in midnight moonlight.

For the next twenty four hours, tiny Hong Kong flickered across TV screens and spilled ink on newsprint around the globe, unable to hide its new year's shame.

Across the harbor in Kowloon, four young *feijai* beat up a bouncer while two girlfriends stood guard. They dragged him into a doorway by the corner of Portland and Soy, near the nightclub where he worked ("only men entertained"). A former Gurkha soldier, he had earlier barred entrance to one of the thugs and his girl.

At another nightclub on Soy Street, the fire alarm tripped. Startled by the sound, the youth gang split, their victim damaged but conscious.

Sleeping neighbors awoke. While trying to silence her crying infant, a karaoke hostess called 999. Emergency operators shrugged; a larger instance of human density consumed attention over on the other side.

The baby howled. His mother paced around their box-like room, cradling, cooing, peering outside. Two migrants to this hopeful city, far from their Guangzhou home. No man-father awoke; life here promised scant support. Down below along the narrow streets, the soldier-bouncer rose, nursing his bleeding lip, his Himalayan world swallowed up by life in the city.

Here in Kowloon where *yan* lived, the tripped alarm sang to the dark. Neither anxious owner nor passing citizen heeded its voice. The siren symphony wailed on. The baby stopped, exhausted.

MARCH 1995

1

In the reception area of JB&D, Andanna You Fun Lee paced, glancing impatiently at her watch. *Gwailo* photographers, always late. Why had she accepted this assignment anyway, killing her only free day? She despised modeling and this whole ad agency scene. But the money was good, and playing hotel lobby piano gigs didn't pay the rent. Sometimes, she wished she'd stayed in Vancouver where everything was cheaper and no one complained about what she did since she was far enough away. It was just too boring there though. Despite all its transplanted Hong Kong life, it wasn't the real thing.

She glanced at the pictures adorning the walls. A section titled "FMCG's" was empty. When she'd met Jake Wu, the agency's creative director a year ago, he had called her that and laughed. Pretending to know, she had laughed along with him even though she suspected an insult. Fast Moving Consumer Goods. Every agency's rice bowl and the work the creatives hated. Andanna knew that JB&D paid the most, had the best facilities, and handled the highest profile fashion accounts. Next to the empty wall space hung a framed testament to their success: the 1994 agency of the year award for Asia. But that was last year, and this year, what she'd been hearing was that they'd lost two of their big FMCG's. Easy come easy go, just like her piano gigs. The modeling jobs, on the other hand, were there as long as she could play the part.

"Andanna?" Vince da Luca introduced himself, apologizing for his tardiness. They shook hands.

She took in the photographer, a tired-looking, middle-aged American. A bit thick around the waist, he didn't look shaved, although perhaps, she decided, he simply had too much hair.

They headed towards the studio area, past rows of open cubicles lining the window. JB&D's office was at the east end of Hong Kong island, and their premises in Taikoo Shing framed a perfect view of the airport runway across the harbor. A green and white Cathay Pacific plane rose towards the clouds. Behind it, a purple and gold Thai International aircraft waited in line for takeoff. Sunday afternoon traffic jam.

"Did you just graduate from college?"

The photographer's voice interrupted her thoughts. She had been thinking about Albert Ho, whom she'd run into last Saturday night at Club 97. He hadn't called even though he said he would. Men.

"Ages ago. Almost three years."

"Oh, what did you study?"

He didn't want to talk, did he? She hated these foreign guys who tried to draw her out. Everyone knew that all they wanted was to fuck. "Music."

"That's cool."

Mentally, her eyes rolled. But she remained polite, smiling. No point being rude. He couldn't help being old. Of course, Albert wasn't all that young either, but not only did he like her music, he was rich. Very rich. Perhaps she could get him to fund a music video or CD. It wasn't as if she were interested in him for anything else.

At the art department, Jake Wu was trying to sort out which outfit would be used for the shot. The assignment was for some Italian sounding designer brand which Andanna had never heard of. She picked up a very short, lime green dress with orange flowers that was absolutely hideous. The price tag read HK$4,500 or ¥52,000, half of almost a month's rent for the 300-foot flat she shared with her boyfriend. "That's it, put that one on," he yelled in Cantonese, gesturing towards the bathroom. She made a face and he snorted. "Women," she heard him say, "always so critical."

When she returned, the photographer was setting up. Jake was telling him about the house he was restoring in Beijing. "One of those old places with a courtyard, you know the kind? I'm preserving all the historic detail but modernizing the plumbing and putting in central air. It's not far from Tiananmen, about a ten minute taxi ride. Very convenient. You come as my guest some weekend, okay?" He gazed meaningfully at the photographer, his fingers lightly brushing the hair on his arm.

It was ludicrous, Andanna thought, the way Jake ran after Western men. She knew that was the only reason this guy had the assignment, since he wasn't one of the regulars. Couldn't Jake tell this one was straight? Jake was one of the hot directors, but for all his talent, he could be a total dope.

The photographer continued setting up. It astonished her how much time was spent lighting and preparing to get one silly shot. And the rolls of film these photographers went through! Could the creatives who hired her really see any difference in all those rows of contact sheets? In the past year, she'd turned down a couple of local art photographers who had asked her to pose. After all, they couldn't pay much and it wasn't like she was a real model.

Would they work as slowly as this guy?

He framed her through his camera. "Photogenic."

"Really?"

"Sure. Andanna's a pretty name, by the way."

"Thank you," she replied automatically, thinking, no it wasn't, now that she knew better. All her friends had made up their English names too when they were thirteen. Living in Canada, she had come to realize how ridiculous that was. Thank god she'd at least not accidentally used a real English word like her best friend Clitoris Ho — pronounced "Cly-toris" to rhyme with fly — who survived the embarrassment when they'd first got to Vancouver for grade twelve. She went by Clio now, but had thought the whole thing a big joke. Andanna would have died if it had happened to her.

"Did you go to school abroad?"

This guy didn't give up! Perhaps she should tell him she already had a boyfriend, although that probably wouldn't stop him. It didn't stop other *gwailoes*. "Yeah, Canada."

"No wonder you speak English well."

"Thanks." She smiled but knew he was just looking for an opening. When she was growing up, she hated studying English. The grammar was difficult, and no one spoke it anyway. Her father, who was in business, wanted her to master it because he believed it would be important for her future. He insisted she study abroad, saying her English would improve faster. She had wanted to go to the Academy of Performing Arts at home with her friends. If her mother hadn't begged her to go for the passport, and if Clio hadn't been going, she would have refused. Music was easier. Tones sang in her head and her fingers obeyed. Fortunately, Mother didn't give her a hard time about English, but then, she didn't speak it all that well either. As long as she knew the language, Andanna couldn't see why speaking mattered.

Over in Vancouver, it hadn't mattered, except in high school classes. She hung around with Clio all the time and spoke Cantonese. Clio liked speaking English and made Canadian friends. What was the point of making friends you'd never see again? Andanna knew she was going home. Fortunately, music teachers didn't talk a lot, even in Vancouver. Once in college, she avoided classes where speaking up contributed to the grade. Since she'd been back, however — was it *already* three years? — she found herself holding conversations in English with foreigners at her hotel gigs. So maybe the old man had a point, even if he didn't like what she did. English helped her make money.

"Vincent . . ." Jake began. He had come around from his side of the
art table and was standing right next to the photographer.

"It's Vince," he corrected, lighting a cigarette. "I'm ready, let's
work."

Jake turned towards Andanna and went all businesslike. "Over
there," he barked, "and make like Lolita."

"Lo-who?"

"Kids today. Don't know anything." Jake was huffing, hands on his
waist, disgusted.

Vince ambled over to her and pulled up a tall stool. "Here, sit-lean
on this. Legs slightly apart, one foot on the rung of the stool. Tip your
head forward and pretend you don't want your boyfriend to kiss you."

She tried to do what he asked, feeling like an idiot. It wasn't working.
Jake was becoming increasingly impatient which irritated her. But she
didn't know what he wanted. It had been much easier last time for that
sanitary napkin ad. All the brief demanded was that she look "fresh as
a morning sunrise." Vince seemed reasonable, patiently suggesting
different poses. After about thirty minutes of this, Jake finally blew up
with "oh, give me a break, what does he have to do, fuck you?" in
Cantonese, so Vince wouldn't understand.

"I don't need this shit," she said coldly, in English, and began to
walk towards the bathroom. She didn't care if Jake gave her a lot of
work or paid big bucks; it didn't give him the right to yell at her.

"Okay, time out," Vince declared. "You," he pointed at Jake. "Out
of here. I'll get this done myself."

Jake resisted, face simmering, and then flounced off. Andanna
glared at Vince. "Now what?"

"Relax. Sit a minute." He gestured at the vending machine. "Want
something?"

"Diet Coke."

He handed her one. "By the way, what was that he said?"

She tilted the popped can to her mouth. Hesitant, surprised at her own coyness, she translated Jake's remark. Vince laughed, but quickly turned it into a cough saying, "how rude of him." She felt suddenly better about being here, about doing this ridiculous assignment and smiled, genuinely happy for the first time in days.

He picked up his camera. "So what d'you think of all this?" "Borrr-ring," she said. He shot her. "And the dress?" "Want to rip it off." "Who'd buy it?" "Girls trying to be foreign, trying to be fashionable." He took more shots. "So why're you doing this?" "Need money." Andanna realized he hadn't stopped shooting. Whatever he was doing, she hoped it was right because she didn't want to have to listen to Jake grumble.

They wrapped an hour later. Vince barely looked at her as she departed, although he did wave a cursory good bye. For just a second, that bothered her. But she forgot it as soon she boarded the MTR beneath Taikoo Shing, heading back, home to Sheung Wan.

It was only March, yet the nights were already too humid. Andanna slept badly. In the morning, the trucks delivering to the market below groaned down her narrow street early, too early, interrupting her dream cycle, spoiling the last, precious hours of slumber. Her mattress was uncomfortable: leftover lumps from the previous tenant who, she was certain, didn't wash regularly. For one brief moment that morning, she longed for her bedroom in Yau Yat Chuen and freshly ironed sheets, all in a spacious home, thoroughly cleaned, each day, by her parents' Filipino maid.

A tickling sensation on her foot, and she glimpsed a large cock-roach racing off. She threw her thong at it. In the living room, Tai Jai moaned, angry at these noises. He'd shown up late last night, drunk as usual, because he'd missed the last MTR to Kowloon again. It was a pain having him around, but he was a childhood friend of Michael's, her jazz bassist boyfriend who never said no to anyone.

She sneezed. A cacophony of cackling chickens rose from the street, followed by the ducks. What was this, poultry day? The phone rang and she raced to get it, afraid Tai Jai would send a missile in its direction. He could be rude like that.

"Ma, it's only seven thirty! Why are you calling so early?"

"You mean you haven't gotten up yet?"

"I was working late last night. Have to earn a living, you know?" It was sort of true. She, Michael and the band had rehearsed till late and then gone down to Wanchai for *siuyeh* at around two in the morning.

"If you bothered to tell me your schedule, I'd know when not to call, but of course, you always forget about your poor mother."

"Ma, what d'you want?"

"*Wei! Meih fanseng, sai sengdi la!*" From Tai Jai, loud enough for her mother to hear. Andanna waved at him to shut up. That guy didn't deserve to sleep.

"Who was that?"

"What?"

"I heard a male voice."

"Men are allowed to walk on this street."

"That wasn't from outside."

"You're imagining things. Now Ma, what did you want?" Her mother thought she lived with another girl, and had never met Michael, even though they'd been going together since she was fifteen, a year before she left for Vancouver. There wasn't any point enlightening Mother now that she'd finally accepted her daughter wasn't going to live at home like everyone else's kids.

"You haven't forgotten, have you? You do have something to wear tonight, right? Don't embarrass me by turning up in anything shabby otherwise your aunt will never stop gossiping about us."

Her cousin's wedding dinner! She'd forgotten entirely about it. She'd have to find a sub for the gig tonight, but that wouldn't be too hard on a Monday. "Of course I remembered."

"Your father has taken care of the *laisee* from our family. It's very generous. In fact, I told him he was giving her too much money . . ."

Andanna blocked out the next minutes of chatter, lit a cigarette, and wondered from whom she could borrow a dress. At the last family wedding, she'd shown up in blue jeans and her mother had been scandalized, although no one else seemed bothered. By the time her mother rang off, she'd figured out the logistics of the evening.

"*Wa! Gam 'fit'!*" Clio exclaimed after Andanna had squeezed into the dress. "You're so lucky. You really have the figure." Baby fat ran in the Ho family through adulthood.

They were at Clio's home in North Point. It was already shortly past seven. Her mother expected her in less than half an hour although why she had to get there so early was beyond her. "Photos! *Lei You Fun*, you have to participate in the family photos." When her mother used her proper name, things were way beyond questioning.

"Let me put your hair up."

"Oh must I, Clio?"

"Of course. It's much more ladylike." She set to work over Andanna's objections. "I wish I had a cousin who could afford a wedding banquet at the Grand Hyatt! It'll be so elegant. Promise you'll tell me all about it."

Andanna watched her hair swoop into a nest on top of her head. "Don't use too much hair spray," she said, alarmed at the can her friend was aiming.

"Honestly, you're such a pain. Sit still a second. You don't know how lucky you are to be both rich and gorgeous. I feel sorry for your mom sometimes. Weddings are fun."

Andanna tried to stop fidgeting. Her friend didn't understand. Clio was an easy going person, and had been that way since she was a girl. Nothing bothered her, everything made her laugh. She liked her job at Citibank, smiling at customers all day long, because, she said, there was a good career path for her there. Clio even swallowed all that customer service crap about how she was "helping" people. Never mind, she was still a wonderful friend, no matter how hopeless she was.

Her hair now completely pinned up, she stared at herself, bemused. The transformation was startling: she looked old.

"I'm thinking of dropping Andanna."

Clio flicked a comb over a few stray strands. "What do you mean?"

"I'd use my Chinese name, of course, silly. What did you think I meant?"

"Won't work. *Lei You Fun* doesn't sound jazzy enough and you're supposed to be a jazz singer. You should have an English name."

"Then maybe I need a stage name? You know, the first time Albert Ho heard me sing, he said my voice was like velvet. Isn't that romantic?"

"You're the silly one. Why don't you call yourself Velvet then? That sounds musical."

Andanna clicked impatiently. "Oh Clio, haven't you learned your lesson yet about English names? Honestly, you're too much sometimes." Hairdo fully sprayed into place, she checked her watch. Only ten minutes to make it on time. She could picture her mother pretending to be calm, glancing discreetly at her watch every thirty seconds.

"Stop rushing. You'll mess up your whole look. Besides, you'll make it if you take a taxi."

Clio *didn't* understand. She lived at home and had spare cash, even if she had to give money to her family. The trouble with being connected to a rich family was that nobody believed Andanna could be broke. As long as she refused to live at home, her father didn't provide any allowance, although Mother occasionally slipped her a little extra. She was down to her last hundred and fifty dollars until Thursday and a taxi would be twenty, possibly more. But she did have her MTR card with approximately eighty left.

She wended her way out of the maze. Clio's family lived in one of the older buildings on King's Road in North Point that was built in the fifties. There were three entrances from different streets, each through a narrow passageway surrounded by small shops. Unless you knew which passageway and lift to take, you could end up way on the opposite end of the building in the wrong bank of flats. Clio told her once there were nineteen original flats per floor, from A to S, which were further complicated by the added illegal divisions listed as H-1 or M-3. Clio lived in 14-J2, the way to which Andanna knew by now with her eyes closed.

Outside, she raced to the MTR station, doing her best to protect the hairdo and dress for just a little longer in the damp evening air.

2

When Vince got back to his borrowed flat on Robinson Road, there was a voice message on the machine from his younger brother. "Hey, we've got something to tell you. Meet us for dinner at eight. Reservations in my name at Va Bene."

Efficient imperative. Not even a "happy birthday" for today, his forty-fifth. Could Don really have forgotten or was this some kind of surprise? Not that forty five was a big deal or anything but when they'd both lived back home in New York, they talked at least once a week and nothing slipped Don's mind. People changed, but his younger brother wasn't "people." Couldn't get used to the way Don had become after only five years in this city. So smug and aloof, always having to be in control.

Vince sometimes thought that he shouldn't have come to Hong Kong — was it really more than half a year ago? All because of Don's persuasive suggestion, well meant. Hell and intentions. But Don just wasn't comfortable with him here, despite his insistence on an almost cloying, fraternal connection. Too many ghosts.

Va Bene. Pricey, like all the Lan Kwai Fong places. These days, the younger Mr. da Luca could get a reservation no matter how late he called, even there.

Dinner was only a couple of hours away. Enough time to run over to Causeway Bay and look at the place Gunter owned, which would be available in another month or so. Mercifully, the shoot wrapped sooner than he'd expected, despite Jake. That model. Nice piece of . . . forget it. Celibacy was difficult, sometimes too difficult.

He rang Gunter. A Cantonese voice replied and Vince understood her to say Gunter wouldn't be back till seven. He gave only his last name — da Luca was easier on local tongues than Vince — and she managed in English, "come seven o'clock okay?" Another five minutes getting the Chinese *deihji* for the taxi, they finally settled on *Yihdung Jaudim*, Excelsior Hotel, from where he could walk to their place. Exhausting, these bilingual arrangements.

Vince put the phone down quickly, accidentally leaving it off the cradle. He had to stop at The Jazz Club first and drop off the promised contact sheets for that trombonist. The *things* he did for his fellow Americans, unpaid. No darkroom retreat today. No break, not even on Sundays.

Late afternoon sunshine held onto the day. Vince moved quickly through the streets of Central towards Admiralty. He knew he should have taken a taxi from The Jazz Club, but the sun enticed, inviting him into its luminous warmth. Light embraced the metal structures around him. In the distance, placid concrete wrapped in steel and glass — a gift from the sea gods — emerged out of harbor reclamation, anticipating completion. Softened edges, curvaceous contours. Sharp angles becoming a thing of the past.

His camera bounced uncomfortably against him. Since arriving here last summer, he carried it often. It was as if he were fifteen again, first discovering how the metal eye made sense of his world. Vince didn't know exactly why he did this. Something to do with home that wasn't. Something about being a visitor, an outsider who advertised himself as such.

Not even a call from Didi on his birthday. His wife too busy with her . . . *stud*. Joe. The kid was ten years younger than Vince, two years younger than her, unattached and content to breathe and die in

Brooklyn, like her. Desertion — worse — a year-long betrayal till she told him in May last year. Like a leech, rage improvised in its own underlife, which he contained only because of their five-year old daughter. Ran away to Hong Kong. Temporarily. Money was good, very good, thanks to Don's introductions. If nothing else, this was for Katy and college tuition, someday.

Between Central and Admiralty the city was a perpetual construction site. Back in the seventies this had been no man's land. Back when he and Ai-Lin . . . Didi on the morning of their first wedding anniversary asking — *how much longer are you going to keep dreaming about her?* — because he had sleep-spoken the name of his ex-wife, again.

Present focus. Past lives should be blurred, not sharp.

Never mind me, you never did anything for Katy. Didi's accusation last spring, the same year Dad hadn't survived the third bypass in February. "You didn't even get home in time for her last two birthday parties. What's she going to think when she's older and it really matters?"

"I don't support this family or what?"

"What do you suppose my paycheck is? Air?"

On top of everything else, '94 had started out as another potentially low income year for him, while Didi had gotten promoted with a raise. Work had been steadily drying up since '92 as the agencies abandoned Manhattan, taking their clients to the hinterland. At least that was how he rationalized things. Or maybe it had been him. One too many pack shots of FMCG's, especially his food shots, frozen into a color facsimile for yet another supermarket display or magazine recipe. Second rate work was too easy, making him lazy, sloppy. From FOOD to food, making a mockery of his business card that proclaimed his specialty in tastefully designed uppercase. And getting fat on a happy family life. Some study he'd seen said the happiest and most content people were married men and single women. Which was why married women fucked single men. Perhaps it was the right thing after all, meeting his second coming in Hong Kong. Money, not sex, was the real mid-life crisis.

In the meantime Joe, a "sanitation engineer" in the public school system was clearing as much as ninety thou a year with overtime, plus extra cash from odd jobs. *And* he had medical and retirement. Even at his best, Vince had never made that much.

But Katy was his. No janitor Didi took up with could change that.

Outside the Bank of China, a small crowd gathered around two policemen and a young guy. The cops were scrutinizing his identity card. An Englishman said to his visitor friend, "probably an illegal, from the Mainland." To Vince, he looked like a skinny, scared kid, whose only giveaway to scruffiness were the soiled, no-brandname sneakers. A Hong Kong kid wouldn't be caught dead in those. Suddenly, the kid shot off east towards Wanchai, shoving an elderly man out of the way. The old man fell, impeding police pursuit. One cop followed. No one else ran. The Englishman helped the old man up who uttered a broken, "Sankyou," and hobbled away. The crowd dispersed. Englishman looked at Vince and said, "Well, there you are then," and, indicating his camera, "missed it, didn't you?"

Vince didn't bother responding. The kid. What would happen to that kid?

"Ai-Lin and I are getting married. We wanted you to be the first to know." Don's declaration, after the Barolo had been poured. He raised his glass. "I hope you'll wish us well, Vince."

Ai-Lin gave Vince a slightly apprehensive look. "Isn't it funny how life turns out?" She suspended her glass.

Old habits. His ex-wife uttered platitudes at difficult moments, despite her intelligence. A gnawing headache. Force a smile. They needed it from him. He toasted their waiting glasses. "I'm very happy for both of you. Really. You've waited long enough to prove it works."

Relief like wildfire on their faces.

She'd come back to Hong Kong shortly after Don arrived, and that was when they started up. At least this was what Vince assumed, since they had been too embarrassed to spell things out. He had tried to reassure them, when he'd finally found out last year, that it was okay with him. *That he was okay with it.* After all, Ai-Lin had attended his and Didi's wedding.

Yet this encounter discomfited. The few times the three of them met, Don would lapse into Cantonese. Practicing, he called it. Showing off, more like. Don was born a linguist. Fluent Italian kept him in Dad's good graces; later, French, because of his ex-girlfriend; then Chinese, Mandarin at first because of work that took him into China. And now, he gloried in Cantonese, for Ai-Lin, naturally.

During appetizers, a casually elegant Chinese man stopped by, said hi to Don. Introductions. Paul something or other, solicitor. Vince was conscious of his own casual inelegance, in contrast to the world of his brother and . . . fiancée.

"I'll call about that Shanghai deal," Paul's parting words. "Nice meeting you, Vince." Light tap on his shoulder and Vince knew, as soon as he felt it, another like Jake. Always their pick up target. Too predictable, just as it had been back home. Didn't know why. Just the way things were and he had long ceased worrying.

Ai-Lin was saying, "His wife Rose went to the same school I did, only she was in Sciences and I was in Arts. *Saigaai janhaih hou sai,*" a smile from her heart for Don. "It's really a small world," translation and a polite smile at him.

Vince frowned. Had she always said things like that? Surely not. The younger woman he had fallen in love with was an original, an impassioned journalist, although these days, she seemed calmer and happier. Don and Ai-Lin. Endless talk about work, about where to go, what to do, how to invest, what the "must's" were. So Hong Kong. Did they really care about all these people they talked to and about, whose names and connections rolled so easily off their lips? All good, surely, but their prattling bugged him. He and his brother didn't even look alike anymore. Okay, so Don lived in the gym while he was giving in to the next size up in clothing. Meanwhile, Ai-Lin still didn't look a day over twenty one. Age treated people differently, was all.

Their entrees arrived. Excellent Northern Italian, as good as Mama used to make, only better, more flavors.

" . . . so we're going to look for a place on the island. It'll be easier for entertaining," Ai-Lin was saying. She was making big money as a PR consultant these days. Between her and Don, an architect, they could even afford to buy an overpriced Hong Kong flat.

Don beamed. "That way, we'll all be closer and it'll be easier to get together. In fact, you'll be our first dinner guest, how's that?"

"Great." Vince's smile turned into a choking cough, eliciting their choric solicitude. "I'm okay," he said, waving away their concern as he sipped Pellegrino, but it had been too much, hearing Don talk like that. *When* had his brother turned into such a chipmunk? Shouldn't admit to laughter though. No reason to hurt anyone's feelings.

"We're thinking about late fall for the wedding," Don continued.

Vince grinned and quipped the obvious line for this trio, "party of the season." For years a running joke in his family when they reached the social pages of the Sunday *New York Times*. Ai-Lin knew; it used to make her laugh.

Yet her deadpan response was, "We're going to try, but it'll be tough because it is right in the middle of the social season." Don gave an approving, equally humorless nod.

Their earnest expressions defeated Vince. Enough. Humor AWOL tonight, and perhaps, it was tasteless of him. Okay, talk straight, follow their lead.

"So what'll you do with Far East Mansion?" Wondered if perhaps she'd offer for him to use it, but not wanting to ask. After her father's death, Ai-Lin had moved back into her childhood home, the top floor of a thirty-year old building in Tsimshatsui. She and Don lived there now. A rent-free luxury in this city, which was as good as it got even if it was in Kowloon. The space he saw today, Gunter's place, was on a high floor. Perfect light, convenient, a 350 foot studio for over US$2,500 a month, excluding management and utilities. Painful.

"My brother will use it when he's here. It's his home too."

Vince knew if he wanted he only need ask. Her brother was out of Hong Kong most of the time. An itinerant spiritual, he didn't care about property or money, and wouldn't have minded, would in fact have welcomed Vince's presence. So what prevented? Pride? Big brother can't take from . . . Ai-Lin and Don were the same age, four years younger than him. Virtually a generation removed. Once, he had protected and cared for them. Not anymore. Time to move on. Life, and families, did.

Later, when they separated into the night, Vince congratulated them again. No one had remarked his birthday.

A persistent tooting. Phone off the hook. It rang as soon as he replaced it.

"Who in god's name have you been talking to all that time?" Deanna's accusation flung across the Pacific. "I've been trying to reach you for hours."

"Sorry. Off the hook. Been out." Nothing but apologies lately whenever they talked. "Oh." Mollified, she probably felt silly. "Anyway, I've been talking to Tony." Her lawyer cousin, never a good thing. "He recommends we sign something spelling out the terms of our separation."

Dreading this, hoping the Joe thing would pass. Everything Deanna had said or done in the past months made this seem an increasingly remote possibility. Yet. "Didi . . . no. Please."

"Vince, be reasonable. Think of Katy."

"I am thinking of her. She needs a father too."

"You're only thinking of yourself, because you . . ."

"What?"

"Nothing."

Katy, crying, when he said he was going away for awhile. Katy, saying, is it because you're going back to your wife before mom, the Hong Kong one? And he reassuring her, no honey, Daddy's just going there to work, to make money to buy you toys. She didn't know about Joe, and he wasn't going to tell her. Protect the innocent. Always.

He heard the intake of breath. Prelude to an announcement. "Joe's moving in." Into the stillness following her nervous assertion, she said. "About the house, our house. We'd like to buy you out."

Ticking overtime. Explosion. Mushroom haze. And then unerring clarity, freezing the tears. He didn't even raise his voice. "Fuck you, Didi," and hung up. For the next hour, the phone would ring until the answering machine interrupted. "Vince da Luca, pick up the phone. How dare you talk that way to me . . ." and he would cut her off. "If you ever want to see your daughter again you better talk to me . . ." More threats. "I'll take you for every cent you have . . ." Blame. "None of this would have happened if you hadn't been so wrapped up in your work, you're just selfish Vincent . . ."

Echoes of Mama, long dead before Didi entered his life. Finally, he unplugged the phone for the dark ahead.

Happy birthday, Vincent. Mama's voice. Elegant, tall, the once-talented ballerina. She would have stopped after him, the eldest pre-marital mistake, and continued dancing if she hadn't been disowned. Familial destruction of a fragile confidence. *Things were different for women then,* she used to say, invoking Catholic forgiveness. *And I believed I was in love.*

Vince's father was an honorable man, and together they left for Brooklyn, another world. That life meant seven more births, three boys and four girls. The girls especially were all unequal to her, good only for marriage and motherhood, while the other two boys tired quickly of her standards and sought their father's blessings for their chosen wives. At least some of his siblings could live the semblance of happy lives. Now, even Don was content.

Mama paid for young love with that life, a life Vince couldn't redeem, which even Vincent had no hope of ever redeeming. He was Vincent only to her, the one woman's voice that still uttered his name with tenderness and love, especially now as the night inched forward, only now after death had freed her spirit to the dance.

3

At the entrance to the ballroom of the Grand Hyatt, six women seated at a long table greeted Andanna. Unfurled before them was a swath of red paper for guests to sign and write their good wishes. Ballpoint pens and Chinese brushes were both available. Andanna selected a brush, held it up a moment, and put it down again. Being out of practice — she seldom wrote Chinese anymore — she'd make a silly mistake for sure. It would look too shameful. Picking up a pen, she scribbled a message in English for the newlyweds.

The entire ballroom was filled with round tables. On stage, her cousin Sylvie Mei Chuen was posing in her Western style wedding gown. A group of maternal relatives surrounded her. Sylvie was related from her father's side, the youngest and only daughter of the richest uncle, her father's eldest brother. Andanna's uncle had married into a Shanghainese family who was even wealthier than he. Sylvie was the last of the three children to get married, and Andanna knew her aunt would spare no expense.

"You Fun, over here. You're late. Quick, get a photo with your cousin and our family before she has to change her dress." Her mother was perpetually fearful of her aunt, and desperate, always, to make a good impression. It was sickening.

Nonetheless, Andanna climbed obediently on stage with her parents. "You look nice," she said to her cousin.

"All brides do."

The dress was cut politely low, but impolitely enough to show off a hint of cleavage. How much padding and under wiring did she use to create that B-cup effect? Her cousin was at most a 32-A, if not a double A. They had compared bra sizes when she was fourteen and Sylvie already nineteen. Even then Andanna had been a real 34B.

"Congratulations anyway," she said, but the photographer was motioning them to pose and the bustle of ceremony overwhelmed further conversation.

Excited choruses assaulted the huge hall. Andanna felt herself drawn in, reluctantly at first and then, unable to stop herself, she too was shouting along with cousins and friends as if all were equally as joyous on this day. Exhilaration overcame the crowd — attendance was in the hundreds — at the sight of Sylvie in her red wedding *pouh* decorated with phoenixes, looking as if she belonged on a palanquin. Somewhere amid the choruses, Andanna heard her own voice commenting on the room, indulging in the latest family gossip — (they say *he's* been seeing this "starlet," but that she's actually in porn films; doesn't *she* look old, the hair's dyed it's way too black and I'll bet she's got a girdle on) — joining in the privilege of a big, celebratory moment during which ordinary life could be put on hold, and where everything would be instantaneously recalled and forgotten.

Andanna's mother shepherded her towards the head tables where relatives and other VIP's were to be seated. Confusion ensued: there was no seat for her. Sylvie remained cool and pointed her towards a nearby table where, she whispered, giggling "you can get away from the old gossips," and Andanna found herself next to an older woman, elegantly dressed, whom Sylvie introduced as her *louhbaan*.

The "boss" held out her hand. "Gail Szeto, *neih hou ?*"

A voice at odds with her appearance. Andanna tried not to stare but couldn't help herself. Gail Szeto was tall. At five foot six, Andanna was used to towering over most Chinese women she met. Even taking into account her evening's hairdo, she knew the woman seated next to her had to be at least three or four inches taller. Gail also had an unusual face. High cheekbones; a nose like Princess Di; the shape of Chinese eyes with Western contours; coal-black hair cut short but with a natural body and wave that didn't come from a perm; features that hovered between Scandinavia-Mongolia and English-Shanghainese depending how the light illuminated. In profile, she might have passed for Caucasian if her hair were just a shade lighter. She wore only a little eye makeup and very pale blush and lipstick, a sandy coral-beige. Her long nails, perfectly manicured, polished to a pale pink sheen, rested against a glass tumbler of tea. She could have been a movie star, but her demeanor was that of a someone in business, formal and reserved, a little cold.

But her voice! Pitched at an alto monotone, harsh and unmusical.

Next to Gail Szeto was a young boy, about seven or eight, who held out his hand and said in polite Cantonese, "hello, my name is Chak Gu Kwun and she's my mother," pointing at Gail. He was adorable and looked completely Chinese — straight black hair and flat nose — hardly resembling his mother at all. His voice had a curiously excitable quality, like a trumpet tuning up, even though he spoke calmly. He shook Andanna's hand and continued seriously, "I look like my father but he doesn't live with us anymore. My father is a doctor."

Gail tapped a nail against her tumbler. The thick glass clinked flatly. "You must excuse my son. He likes to advertise his heritage, or lack of one."

A roar rose above the banquet. *"Yambui!"* The MC on stage prattled with the ease of a television variety show host, and everyone raised their glasses of tea or five-star cognac to toast the sacrificial couple. And then, waiters streamed from the wings, poised to carve and serve the suckling pig at each table.

Andanna watched as Gu Kwun selected a piece of the crackling served in his bowl. He nibbled a tiny bit, and then, appearing satisfied, ate the whole piece. He placed his chopsticks back on their silver holder, and sat still, gazing at the rest in his bowl.

"Aren't you going to eat up your suckling pig?" Andanna asked.

"Since this is just an appetizer, I shouldn't eat too much." He glanced at his mother who smiled approvingly at him.

"But tonight's a party, a special occasion."

He continued solemnly. "If Mummy says I can, then it's okay."

Gail nodded. "Yes, you may."

"Thank you, Mummy." He ate the second piece as deliberately as he had the first.

Gail addressed her. "Sylvie tells me you're a musician, an artist."

Her statement, delivered matter-of-factly, startled Andanna. No one had ever called her an "artist" before. Michael called himself one, but then, he was devoted to jazz, and worked all the time as a sound engineer and musician to save enough money for Berklee College of Music, where he wanted to study performance. She supposed she was an artist too, yet truthfully, it seemed a little pretentious to describe herself that way. She began to tell Gail this, and as the evening wore on, she found herself talking all about how she tried to work as a lounge pianist despite the low pay and limited opportunities, how she couldn't live at home even though she loved her parents, how she modeled even though she hated it. How Michael was teaching her jazz so that she could sing with his band. Gail interspersed questions about her family and life in Vancouver, her friends in the arts and what work they did, what music and films they liked, which clubs they went to. Gail seemed to understand her and didn't talk like someone in business. Even Clio didn't understand her sometimes and carried on endlessly about her business career, which bored Andanna.

Gail asked how she and Michael met. It'd been a long time since Andanna had thought about those early days. When she was fifteen, Michael impressed her, because, although only a couple of years older than her and still in school, he was already working as a professional musician. She began explaining his background in great detail — his family lived in a tiny, housing estate flat, and he couldn't practice at home which was why he moved out. He loved her and never dated anyone else all the time she'd been away in Vancouver. Her mother would never approve of such a boyfriend, but then, she didn't care what her parents thought. Besides, they had no appreciation for real music. "We live together now," she confided, and then suddenly thought she shouldn't have said that in case Gail mentioned it to Sylvie, but her cousin knew, as did pretty much everyone else even though they all pretended not to. Sometimes, she wondered if her mother guessed.

When the fish arrived, Gail asked, "Are you in love with your boyfriend?"

She was about to reply, of course I am, but stopped. A waiter spooned the flesh of steamed grouper into her clean bowl, sliding a slice of mushroom on top. For an instance, she wondered why Gail didn't seem rude, even though this was such a personal question; her manner was entirely unapologetic.

"I don't know."

"These things can be difficult to know," Gail remarked.

The fish slid down Andanna's throat. A hint of its gingery sweetness left an aftertaste on her tongue.

Later, stuffed to the gills, Andanna accompanied Gail and her son to the exit. While retrieving her checked-in umbrella, Gail said, "I enjoyed meeting you. Do let's stay in touch," and proffered her business card. Funny, thought Andanna, she had liked talking to Gail even though she hadn't expected to at first. Yet after some three hours of conversation, Andanna realized she knew nothing about this woman other than her name and that she was the Asia Pacific research director of the investment bank where her cousin worked. This last fact was only gleaned from her business card.

"Yes, okay." She handed Gail her own card, a colorful design on a backdrop of sharps and flats which made Gail smile. As they passed the Champagne Bar, a deep voice said, in English, "it's Andanna isn't it?" and there was that photographer guy from the shoot the other day, that ancient American.

"Oh, hi." She paused uncertainly, trying to recall his name. It came. "Vince da Luca, this is Gail Szeto and," she gestured towards the boy, "Chak Gu Kwun." The boy spoke up first, "hi, you're an American I can tell," and stuck out his hand which Vince shook.

Gail said. "We've met somewhere, haven't we?"

"I don't think so, but in Hong Kong, it's possible."

Andanna was struck by Gail and her son's English. There wasn't a hint of an accent. Up till now, they had talked in "Canto-lish," with Cantonese dominating. If she closed her eyes, she would swear that three *gwais* were conversing. What surprised her most was the timbre of Gail's voice. It was less flat, higher pitched, almost girlish in tone.

"Yes, I'm sure we have," Gail continued and named the investment bank where she worked. "The photo for the brochure. I told you I wasn't photogenic."

Vince's eyes lit up in recognition. "Of course. Your son's picture. This is him, I take it."

"And you showed me your daughter's photo. Katy, right?"

"Hey, good memory."

Andanna mentally rolled her eyes. The trouble with older folks was that they did go on in a most tedious fashion, all in the name of being polite. Why couldn't they just get to the point? She interrupted. "I've got to go, I have a rehearsal." And promising to "stay in touch" with Gail, and bidding a "see ya" to the da Luca guy, she took off.

Gail had hoped to run into Vince again. This time she made sure she'd gotten his card.

She switched off the light in her son's room. He was tired. A wedding banquet had been more excitement than he could take, even if he did have a grand time. Funny how Gu Kwun liked being around adults. Hard to believe he was already seven, as he proudly announced to anyone he met. He had conversed readily with Vince, not shy about speaking English at all. Only three years earlier, Gu Kwun would have hidden when confronted by anyone non-Chinese. International School had definitely been the right choice.

Before he'd fallen asleep, he asked, again, when his father would come see him. She'd told him he would stop by when he came back from Beijing. How much longer should she lie, or admit she simply didn't know? His last visit had been nine months ago. It was so unfair. Their divorce was hardly Gu Kwun's fault. Yet nothing she said to her ex made any difference.

The television was off in the living room. Her mother was already asleep even though it was not quite midnight. Now that she had a few precious minutes alone, Gail switched on CNN. Not that she minded watching the local Chinese channel with Mom or anything, but there were times she needed something else.

More talk of NATO air strikes in Bosnia and clips of Clinton in Moscow. Relations between Singapore and the Philippines continued to deteriorate because of that maid's hanging, the one found guilty of murdering another Filipino maid and her charge. The report saddened Gail. Poor child, only four years old.

Dinner sat like lead. Why did *anyone* throw banquets on a Monday? It would be difficult getting up for work. Marketing had wanted a seven o'clock breakfast meeting. Thank god she'd refused, pushing it back to a sensible eight fifteen. That department was neurotic, justifying its existence by proving they worked harder than anyone else, all to impress New York. If they'd slow down a bit and thought their projects through instead of setting absurd deadlines to everything, perhaps they'd only have to do things once instead of six times. Well, not her problem.

She made herself a chamomile, using up the last bag. Mom didn't like strange foreign teas, the labels of which she couldn't decipher, and filled the kitchen pantry with bundles of dried roots and fungi wrapped in newspaper from the medicine shops in Western. Gail hated the ink smears these left on her shelves but didn't complain. It made Mom happy to boil up herbal remedies. Lately though, her mother did less and less of everything and forgot a lot more.

The chamomile settled her stomach. Gail wandered out to the balcony. Hazy night. At least she had a view and a lot of space, although this couldn't compare with Boston. Comparisons were pointless, and not worth dwelling on. This flat had been a good buy for a high floor here on the south side, and well located for a quick drive into Wanchai where she worked. More important, it was near International, which made getting Gu Kwun to and from school easy. She had lived near her own school when she was growing up in Kowloon City. In secondary school, she walked to Maryknoll Convent from her home near the airport. A shame Gu Kwun couldn't walk through neighborhoods, but then, the geography around here catered to cars.

The hotel directory took over the screen, listing ad nauseum the properties that carried CNN around the world. Gail flicked off the TV, and replaced the remote in the case next to the set. On top of it, the porcelain flower bowl was off center, and she shifted it slightly to the right, pleased to see the clean surface. Conchita *was* good. When Colleen, the wife of her college buddy Kwok Po, had offered her Filipino maid because they were moving to Singapore, Gail had jumped at the opportunity to interview her. Having tasted Conchita's dinners at the Leyland-Tangs, she remembered Colleen singing her domestic's praises time and time again. What had clinched it had been seeing the woman make Gu Kwun laugh when she'd come for the interview. One year later, she couldn't imagine life without Conchita.

Gail missed the Leyland-Tangs, especially Kwok Po, even though they did meet and catch up when business took her to Singapore. She had so few close friends in Hong Kong, and none who had shared her Boston life. Kwok Po did, all the way back to their Harvard MBA study team. A lifetime ago, before families and careers claimed them. They'd both held out the longest of all their friends, not abandoning single life until they were in their mid thirties. She had missed him when he'd returned with his bride to Hong Kong to join his family's business.

A couple of years later, Black Monday descended on Wall Street and she became a pink slip victim. *Hong Kong needs people like us,* Kwok Po had said when she called to ask advice. *Besides, it is home.*

Hong Kong had beckoned insistently then. Her mother was getting too old to look after herself, and Gail wanted a child. Everyone said it was easier raising children here. Her husband finally stopped objecting when confronted by the offers she got.

It had been the right move. Asia was alive and vibrant. Her work was more challenging than anything she'd done in the U.S. From her first position in Hong Kong, she was headhunted four years ago into her present job, a big step up. She was given a large department with staff in several countries. There was plenty of travel, a bit too much at times but nothing she couldn't handle. Extra benefits, like affording a live-in domestic, made managing her responsibilities much easier. Now, being Gail Szeto, this motley, mixed up creature, was finally an asset and not a liability.

Crossing the middle age border in Hong Kong wasn't such a bad life. She had her health and the family that mattered. What more should she want?

4

The afternoon downpour had just ended. Colleen dragged the sun chair out of the shade onto the lawn of her back garden. The grass was damp under her bare feet. In less than half an hour, the damp would be gone. This short space of time was when the air was sweetest, when the afternoon wound its way into early evening.

Colleen loved this hour of tea in Singapore. When she and Kwok Po first arrived last year, she had derided the expatriate British wives and wealthy Singaporean socialites who sat around in elegant hotel lobbies sipping tea. Now, she had begun to appreciate the rhythm of the days, slower than in Hong Kong. The daily rains marked the transition from unbearable heat to the cool of twilight. Perhaps there was a point to tea time after all, even here. For a moment, she was cast back to her childhood summers in Western Massachusetts, where the stifling humidity of the Pioneer Valley occasionally relented late in the day.

"Going now, *m'aurm.*"

It annoyed her, the way Rosa mispronounced "ma'am" in her Filipino English. Kwok Po had wanted to bring their maid Conchita from Hong Kong, but the woman refused to go. "My friends are all here in Hong Kong or back home. I don't know anyone in Singapore." So she was stuck with Rosa, an efficient enough woman, but deadly dull. Colleen missed her conversations with Conchita, who had a college degree and was supporting an unemployed husband and son back in the Philippines. To hear her talk about her family, and all her friends among the Filipinos in Hong Kong, her life by contrast seemed full, especially when Colleen first came to Hong Kong and the only people she knew were Kwok Po's family.

"Don't be too long."

"I won't. Thank you very much *m'aurm*. Thank you."

"You don't have to thank me." And the other thing she disliked was Rosa's fulsome gratitude over letting her visit a friend who worked for the people next door, which she did a lot these past couple of weeks. Who could blame her? The recent hanging of Flor Contemplacion was reason enough. All the Filipino maids talked of leaving Singapore now, scared of the harsh justice here.

Colleen settled into the afternoon sunshine, sipping iced tea, pre-occupied by her kid brother's latest escapade. When she'd flown in from Hong Kong last night after her trip to Subic Bay, Kwok Po said Danny had called from somewhere in Tibet, and that he might need help. It was always like this. Long silences, and then a call from China. If only he'd stayed in Hong Kong and stuck to playing music, instead of getting involved in politics, especially during these days when her husband's family business hinged on keeping the Chinese government happy. By now though, Danny wasn't going to listen to her anymore.

She tried to forget about him. He'd call when he was ready. Sun rays tickled her stomach. If she'd dared, she would have lain naked, instead of in this bikini. The neighbors were rarely around at this hour and they weren't expecting any deliveries. But they lived in a mostly Singaporean neighborhood, not an expatriate one, by choice. If she offended anyone, they would have hell to pay. From conversations she'd overheard in her gym locker room, however, Singapore girls were a lot more daring than the innocence touted by the sweet faced poster girls for the national airline's ads. She closed her eyes and dozed.

Half an hour later the phone rang. A distant command, probably Kwok Po. Dare she ignore it? She almost called out for Rosa to get it, and then remembered. Sitting up, she pulled her batik sun dress over her head. By the ninth ring, she made it through the back door to the kitchen and into the living room.

"I almost gave up. You okay, sis?"

"Danny! Where the hell are you?"

"Beijing." Her brother's quiet intensity reached her from the distance, the way it always had. "I'm sorry if I scared you, but I'm out of trouble now. Please tell my brother-in-law I won't need his help, and that I apologize for disturbing him."

"Oh darling, Kwok Po cares about you. You know that." She said it with as much conviction as she could muster, shutting out her husband's words — *he's crazy, getting mixed up in Tibetan politics. He doesn't understand anything about it, and he'll get into real trouble someday. Why does he have to be such a martyr? What does he know about democracy anyway?*

"Sure, sure. Are you okay?"

His insistent solicitude irritated her. It suggested that something was wrong with her when in fact, he was the one with all the problems. "Of course I am. Why shouldn't I be?"

"Oh, you know. The usual."

She bristled. "I'm fine." But she felt what Danny called the tension spider spreading its web down her neck and shoulders. He just wasn't like other men. And these days, she experienced a growing distaste at his knowledge of her, not that she told him any details, but she knew he guessed, and that was enough to make her uneasy. "Look, come to Singapore and stay with us. We've got a huge four-bedroom. They like American musicians here, and they're crazy for jazz. It's not like Hong Kong at all." Even as she said it though, she heard Kwok Po's dismissal — *of course you'll always love him because he's family but your brother's a loser. He can't amount to anything because he has no ambition.*

"I'm not exactly a musician."

"Of course you are. Besides, don't you want to see me again?"

"You really like it there." It deliberately wasn't a question.

"It's the most livable city in Asia." She wanted to bite her tongue.

Danny didn't buy this kind of bull.

"Only if you believe in caning and hanging. I won't live there."

"At least try it for a little while. I'd love to see you again, spend some time together." She could feel herself pleading and told herself, stop that, it won't work.

"You mean so that you can keep an eye on me for that husband of yours. What's the matter, Colleen? Don't you believe in anything real anymore?"

"Danny, it's not like that. You know it isn't . . ." But he'd hung up. Damn him. A part of her wanted to cry in frustration the way she would when as children, her baby brother would suddenly withdraw and play by himself, whenever he felt deserted or betrayed or uncertain of her love. All the cajoling and shouting wouldn't bring him back until she went to him and hugged him or kissed his cheek. Their mother knew how to draw him out, making up for the husband who was never around. Even after his death, her father seemed almost never to have mattered in their family's life.

Colleen went to her closet, reached for a pack of Marlboro lights from the back of her underwear drawer, extracted one cigarette and replaced the pack under a pile of slips. She carried the cigarette to the kitchen where she lit it on the gas stove. Opening a window, she exhaled out to the remnants of the day, dropping ashes into the sinkhole.

Damn Danny. Would he ever grow up, ever think of anyone other than himself? Even when he asked how she was, it was only to needle, only to show her he had loftier convictions, and practiced a higher brand of morality. Yet the only times he called, it was because he needed something, because he was in trouble again, or wanted a favor for a "friend." Maybe Kwok Po was right. Maybe it was time she stopped worrying about him.

**

Vince shut Colleen's hotel room door. He had been summarily dismissed. So why did he feel he'd just been accorded a privilege?

His body was full of her, drenched in her. They hadn't slept at all, greedily devouring every second of the night. Did she always stay at the Conrad? Would she really come back to see him? And where had she learned to wind herself around a man like that? Insatiable she was, unstoppable once she got going. Thirty seven going on seventeen.

He went out the back way, past the swimming pool on the lower level, and queued at the Pacific Place taxi rank. Colleen Leyland-Tang. Colleen Leyland. His Subic Seductress. Irish spring.

Three days ago, he and Colleen had watched a black cloud of fruit bats rise above the rain forests of Subic Bay, where something startled the nocturnal flock into flight.

His trip had been for Federal Express, a recent acquisition at JB&D. An assignment to shoot the FedEx hub currently under construction in the Philippines. All because JB&D wanted to impress their new client. As long as Jake would foot the bill, it was easy money, an adventure trip. Vince had met her only a few days prior to that moment, in the Manila airport at the limo counter. She, calmly commandeering the last available vehicle and driver for the four hour ride. He, begging a ride off her — his reservation screwed up, somehow, the way all his arrangements had been since the arrival of a new "exec sec" at JB&D. Clueless about scheduling, that woman. Colleen had agreed, reluctantly at first. "Won't try anything." He mimicked a boy scout salute. She frowned a smile. Then, adding softly, surprising himself "except on you, that is." He watched her pretend not to hear. A forgotten line, used long before in another life, a genuinely single life. What on earth had sparked such daring?

All through the ride, she had been the outgoing and friendly, but hands-off, *Mrs.* Leyland-Tang, an amateur photographer on her quest for nature shots. Somehow, he had ended up offering to accompany her that one afternoon, the day the bats took flight.

He had watched her gaze at the frantic formation in awed silence, all of her swept up in their motion. Her small frame was taut. Vince could see the outline of her breasts against white muslin. A warm wind teased her hair, whipping the long, red strands into a ripple around her head. The sky was clear, a pastel blue heaven. Humidity did not overwhelm him, the way it did in Hong Kong. Vince inhaled the clean, fresh air. He wanted to run his finger against her cheek.

And then the moment was over, and she was friendly but polite, a little stand offish, the way she had been all afternoon. When she'd offered dinner that night, he assumed nothing more than graciousness, her way of thanking him.

Charming chatterbox all through the meal. A nervous flood of questions about photography. The wine. It had to be the wine. Too many tidbits of personal history. Her brother used to work as a nature photographer in Massachusetts. She danced well and had been a star gymnast in high school. Did he speak Chinese? He didn't? She'd be delighted to teach him because she was in and out of Hong Kong all the time, to go shopping, to see friends and her in-laws. Oh yes, she was fluent, more so in Mandarin, well actually *Putonghua* as they called it in China these days, because she'd studied you know, quite seriously, back in Boston, but after all this time living in Asia, how long was it now — gosh, almost ten years — she even managed Cantonese quite well. Of course, it did help that she read Chinese too. So many Americans only studied *pinyin,* which simply wasn't any good past an elementary stage, being only phonetic *sans* meaning. But she was lucky because she got to speak to her *laihlai* in Cantonese, her mother-in-law, who was just the sweetest, dearest lady.

And perhaps he couldn't tell but she was terribly attracted to him.

She had let that slip as she paid the check, without looking up, in the same chatty tone she'd used all evening.

"You weren't imagining it," she added, looking up at him with a slightly embarrassed smile.

Vince blushed uncontrollably. Like an idiot, uttered, "I don't know what to say." Felt like kicking himself.

She bit her lower lip. "That was terribly, uh, forward of me."

"Oh, no. It's just that, well, I . . ." he stopped short.

"It doesn't matter," she said.

They walked along the water that night, and the moon was full. It was full the next night, and the next, when they walked again. Began the short story of his life, and then the pain of Didi's betrayal spilled out into words he had kept to himself until that moment. She ceased her talk and listened. Embraced her in the night air of the Philippines. Warmth of a woman's body next to his, pliant and willing. Needed this, her.

But he left her at the door of her hotel room each night.

"You're married," he said.

In the jeep, their last morning in Subic, prepared for the drive back to Manila and the hour's flight to Hong Kong late that afternoon. She would be in transit for the night, her departure for Singapore scheduled out of Hong Kong early the next morning.

"I've never said otherwise." She averted her face as she stepped up into the vehicle.

Took her hand and helped her up. "Aren't you happy?" Didn't let go as she slid into the seat beside him.

Colleen withdrew her hand and looked straight ahead. Didn't turn to face him. "My husband's business is very demanding. We don't see each other much."

"So you have an 'arrangement.'" She didn't respond. "But you haven't answered my question."

"I'm not unhappy. And my marriage is my business."

He reached for her cheek, felt its supple softness. Turning her face towards him, he stared into her eyes. Large and beautiful, their green depths did not invite.

"What are you looking for?" she asked.

In answer he placed his hand on her waist and drew her towards him.

A tiny woman, just shy of five-one, her tensile strength did not yield.

"It's a long ride," she said.

"And bumpy. You need my cushioning."

"I thought you wouldn't try anything."

"I thought you wanted me to."

"Really?" She pulled away.

It had been the same all the way back on their flight where they sat next to each other. She spoke very little. *Shit.* Blown it. Why hadn't he simply . . . his fucking morality always getting in the way. Now she was hands off again, insulted probably. Gave him up as too indecisive. Or perhaps she'd decided he was still too tangled up in himself, in his own rapidly disintegrating marriage.

In their shared taxi back in Hong Kong that night, she insisted on dropping him off at his flat before going to her hotel. As they headed up Cotton Tree Drive, well past the turn off for the Conrad, he suddenly decided, what the hell might as well it was now or never, and took her firmly in his arms. "About time," she said, unresisting. The driver muttered some Cantonese curse when Colleen redirected their taxi to the Conrad. She only interrupted Vince long enough to whisper, apologetically, "it's a non smoking room, I'm afraid." A touch of mischief crossed her lips.

**

Colleen walked out of her house and flicked the cigarette ash onto the driveway. The house stood on a small knoll, and the steep driveway was tricky to negotiate in heeled sandals. She walked carefully downhill to the front gate, opened it, stubbed out her cigarette against the stone pillar and dropped the butt into the garbage can. She jostled the can so that the butt rolled into hiding under some leaves where Kwok Po couldn't possibly see it.

Back in the house, she washed her hands, scrubbing her fingers with scented soap. Then she brushed her teeth and gargled with mouthwash. Stripping off her dress and bikini, she stepped into the bathtub and turned on the lukewarm shower spray. Kwok Po would be home soon. Tonight, she would suggest he take her to dinner at the Padang place in Changi Village. She had tried it out once for lunch, and liked their reasonable prices. A long established Muslim enclave where no booze was served, it was open, airy and exceptionally clean. The food was spicy, variously curried eggplant, okra, beef, chicken or barbecued fish, all of which they could eat with their hands if they wanted, using finger rolls of white rice as a spoon base. They could also order home-made barley water or fresh lime juice. Her husband would enjoy that. He wanted her to find them new culinary adventures, the more authentically local, the better.

After her shower, she selected a short, pale pink designer dress, the casual, slightly satiny one that clashed with her coloring. It had been a present from Kwok Po. Slipping it on over her naked body, she zipped herself into its perfect fit. She slid her feet into uncomfortable matching pink stiletto sandals, completing a chic vulgarity, the way he liked her.

She began brushing out her hair in front of the full length mirror on the closet door. Should she call Vince again, or would he break down and call first? He could be discreet, maybe. On that score, the Brits and Euros were way ahead of American men. Vince was more than a little slow on the uptake; imagine trying to put the make on her in daylight, in public, on board a jeep. How gauche. Didn't he know affairs took place only in the darkness of privacy?

Water droplets glistened and vanished as she brushed. Colleen was proud of her long hair, her thick red mane inherited from her mother's family. In this climate, it dried easily, even without a hairdryer. When she was done, she laid down the brush and stepped back to take stock of her appearance one last time. For just a second, her mirror image revolted her.

5

It was half past midnight at Visage. Saturday night overflow from nearby Lan Kwai Fong spilled into the club. A young Chinese crowd and a few Western faces peppered the scene. Wall-to-wall bodies. Even the space behind the bar was filled; the barber chairs were both occupied, one by a Chinese painter visiting from Shanghai, the other by the Cuban-American correspondent for *Businessweek*. Vague improvisations had begun to emerge from the cluster of musicians and would-be musicians in the corner opposite the bar.

The proprietor unlocked the door marked "private party," letting in Clio and Andanna.

"Ugh, it's so crowded in here," Clio remarked as they maneuvered their way through the crowd. "Besides, why d'you want to hang out at a hairdresser's?"

Andanna peered around, looking for Michael. He wasn't there. "I've told you, it's a club on Saturday nights. They only cut hair during the day."

"Let's not stay." Clio tugged her friend's arm. "Let's go meet my friends down in Causeway Bay for karaoke instead."

"Oh, don't be a spoilsport. It's still early." She surged forward. The music rose in volume. "Come on," she dragged Clio behind her. "There's someone I need to talk to."

Andanna pressed towards a man with a round, youthful face and a neat-shaggy haircut. He stood apart, surveying the crowd with detached interest. Occasionally, people greeted him and he would acknowledge them with a nod and veiled smile. He seemed impervious to the smoky, inebriated talk surrounding him. Studiously dressed down in ironed jeans and a long, loose white shirt, he was contained in his own private aura.

"It's Albert Ho," Clio uttered in hushed tones to Andanna, her eyes widening at the presence of the society figure.

"I know," Andanna replied. "Albert," she called out without raising her voice. "You look lost."

The veil lifted from his smile, and his lips twitched into the mockery of a grin. *"Wei, Lei You Fun, gammaaaaaahn dim a?"* He drew out the "night" in a Cantonese opera drawl.

"Same as usual." Andanna looked him straight in the face. "You didn't call me."

He sipped his Perrier. "Drink? For you and your friend?"

Andanna knew her friend was about to shy away and say oh no, thank you very much, and rapidly nudged a discreet elbow into Clio's ribs. "But of course, we're thirsty. We'd like a bottle of red, please."

Eyes narrowed to a feline stretch, he signaled the bartender. A bottle of something other than the house red appeared. *"Leng leui, leng jau."* Beautiful girl beautiful wine. Handing them each a wineglass, he poured the silky shiraz. "Cheers," he said in English.

She and Albert made a dramatic pair, and Andanna knew it. People said he was gay, and possibly he was, but no rumors of liaisons circulated. Clio had stepped outside the circle they created around them. More than one of the patrons at Visage exchanged words with each other about their joint presence. Andanna drank half her wine, and placed the glass carefully on the island counter behind Albert.

"Must be running along. Keep your promise and call me, okay?"

He gave her a deliberate, lazy smile. "Okay, *leng leui.*"

She took Clio by the arm and led her out of Visage.

As they climbed up the cobblestone path outside the club towards

Lyndhurst Terrace, Clio stopped them in their tracks. "Will you please explain what all that was about?"

Andanna kept moving uphill. "Nothing."

"I'm not moving till you tell me."

She stopped. "You're being a big silly."

"And you're going all mysterious on me. Are you going out with him or something?"

"Michael's my boyfriend. You know that."

"Are you going to tell me or not?"

Andanna sighed, exasperated. "It's nothing. I want him to pay for a music video or a CD for me."

"You asked him for money?"

Clio's astonished look cracked her up. "Stop being so in awe of all this. He's rich, everyone knows that. And he loves to hang around the young, arty crowd so that he can be everyone's benefactor. I'm just trying to get my slice of the pie."

"But how did you meet him? At Visage?"

She hesitated, wondering whether or not to tell the truth. Albert was more or less her *tohnggo*, an "elder brother cousin" from her father's family. His mother was a sister of her aunt, Sylvie's mother, the wife of her father's eldest brother. When Andanna was growing up, Albert sometimes attended the larger family functions on special occasions. He was much older than her, the same generation as some of her younger uncles and aunts, so she had never paid attention to him although he teased her a lot when she was a girl. The family connection didn't hurt, but she didn't want Clio to get the wrong idea.

But her friend had already guessed. "You're related, aren't you?"

"It's not what you think."

"Oh sure. You're always crying poverty but you know perfectly well that's not true."

"Don't start. Come on, let's go over to *Luhksei*." She ran up to Lyndhurst Terrace and began walking east in the direction of Club 64.

Clio followed and stopped when she reached the road. "You go to *Luhksei*. I'm going to Causeway Bay to meet my friends."

Before Andanna could prevent her, Clio had hailed a taxi and hopped in. She watched the taxi drive away, not sure if she were annoyed. Her friend's idea of night life was boring, limited to karaoke and disco. But she knew Clio was impatient with her these days, although she wasn't sure why.

Well, what to do now? She glanced west towards Hollywood Road. Home was a short walk away. Perhaps she should call it quits, since the encounter with Albert had strained her theatrical energies for the night. Then, she caught sight of Tai Jai across the road, probably headed to Lan Kwai Fong. She ran after him, hoping he would know where Michael was.

At three in the morning, Tai Jai walk-dragged Andanna home.

"You shouldn't drink so much," he said as he deposited her at the doorstep.

"I'm not drunk," she declared. She fumbled with the lock and pushed open the door. The flat was empty. "Where the fuck's Michael?"

"Quit swearing. It's not ladylike. He's probably lost track of time, rehearsing. You know how he is."

Swaying slightly, she collapsed forward onto the sofa. Tai Jai nudged her towards the bedroom. "C'mon, off. I gotta sleep there."

"Fuck you," she said, "why don't you go home for a change?" The insides of her head swung like a wrecking ball, anticipating the crash. But as she tried to rise, she was suddenly overcome by dizziness. A sickening surge soured her esophagus. "Oh fuck," she heard Tai Jai say, "you're going to puke, aren't you?" And she felt herself hoisted off the sofa, his voice urging, "hold on just a little longer, can you do that?"

Andanna brought her hand to her mouth and nodded. He moved her towards the bathroom where she threw up into the sink. She pushed the hair out of her face. Her makeup felt like a layer of dirt.

Looking down at herself, she saw that her sweater and slacks were also covered with vomit. Tai Jai had his arm around her waist and was rubbing her back. "You'll feel better," he kept saying, and she leaned forward again, the night's poison erupting out of her body like some exorcised alien invader. "I've got to clean this," she groaned, after it was all over. "Never mind that," Tai Jai said. "I'll clean up. C'mon, you need sleep."

He dragged her across the flat towards the bedroom where she tried, unsuccessfully, to pull off her clothes. His hands raised the sweater over her head, and then, she was aware that he had begun unbuckling her belt, unzipping her jeans and forcing her legs out of them. A protest began but subsided. Down to only her underwear, Andanna felt Tai Jai lifting her, placing her on the bed and drawing the covers over her. A damp towel landed against her face and he cleaned her mouth and cheeks with it.

She did feel better, although the nauseous odor on her person disgusted her. "I want to take a shower," she declared.

"Get some sleep. You're still drunk."

"I am not." She tried to sit up, but her body wouldn't budge. He left the room, closing the door quietly behind him. Turning over, she shut her eyes and tried to sleep, but the thought of Michael finding her like this irritated her. He would be bound to deliver a lecture in the morning, and they'd end up quarreling again. She had to shower.

She sat up on her elbows, her head still a mess. What had possessed her to drink so much? She hated to admit it, but Tai Jai was a little bit right when he had said that she cared way too much what Michael thought, and that she should stop trying to impress him. Well, it wasn't that she cared, but she couldn't help admiring Michael because he was ambitious and knew what he wanted, and worked hard to get it. He wasn't like Tai Jai who drifted from job to job, borrowing money. Michael only helped him out because he didn't want to see his friend head back among the triads, but she figured Tai Jai was a lost cause anyway.

Forcing herself out of bed, she opened the bedroom door. Tai Jai was sleeping on the couch, fully dressed. Andanna crept past into the bathroom. It had been cleaned. She climbed into the shower. The lukewarm trickle had its effect as the soapy stream eradicated the evening's stink. What was that Tai Jai called her earlier? Oh yeah, "astronomical dark matter." It sounded awful, like human waste. When asked to explain, he replied that she was like a dense galactic mass masquerading as a lightweight universe, hiding her light in the distance. Definitely weird. The thin spray glided down her back, along her legs. The cracked drain sucked down all remaining odors. She turned off the tap. At the front door, Michael's key clicked.

**

Why did people work on Sundays, Vince wondered, as he waited in the Champagne Bar at the Grand Hyatt Hotel. It was six thirty. Where the hell was Albert? Their appointment had been for six. How much longer before giving up? Should be used to this by now. People often kept him waiting here, especially the local Chinese.

Vince sat at the island bar, cushioned on a black stool with sleek metal legs. This was a showy room. Glass and glitz under a crystal chandelier. In the center of the bar, an enormous, black porcelain vase trumpeted a white floral arrangement of roses, lilies, gladiolus and orchids against a green backdrop of palm leaves and other vegetation.

The champagne fizzed down his throat. Why the hell had he ordered it? Didn't even like the stuff, but somehow, when the bartender had said "champagne, sir?" with that polite smile, Vince hadn't thought twice about it. Why were there no outdoor places to meet? Everything took place in icy, air conditioned interiors. Hotel fragrances reminded him of Colleen. Hard to stop thinking about her. Lingering . . . lust? Imitation love.

A dapper Albert Ho sailed into the room. "Vincent, Vincent. Terribly sorry to be late." Gesturing to the bartender, "my bill, please."

Once again Vince absorbed his presence, unsure. Should he write him off or deal with him? The man had money, real money, not

Armani suit wealth. Only tailor made stuff, probably by his personal staff. Even the tie. But Vince couldn't figure him out. It wasn't the gay thing, although he'd thought so at first. Something . . . what was it that didn't sit right?

They had met at The Jazz Club. Bar chat led to this, his first China job. Albert was opening a club in Shanghai, and had asked Vince to do a photographic record of the private launch party, the exclusive one he was hosting before the big media blitz. All because he liked Vince's shot of the trombonist, a job he'd done for cost as a favor to a fellow expat American.

"So you'll still do it?" Albert asked.

"You haven't checked around, have you? There're plenty of other guys." Albert had told him he didn't know any photographers, which Vince had found hard to believe. Vince studied his expression, but it told him nothing.

"Don't need to."

He hesitated. "You're paying too much. You sure about this?" Vince waited to hear him say something stupid like "money no object," anything, so he could dismiss him. Didn't know why he felt this way. He had asked around a little, checked Albert out. Don whistled when he'd heard "no kiddin' Ho Yuet-Kan's son, how d'you meet him?" and Jake had raised his eyebrows and muttered snidely, "oh *him,* he's got more money than sense."

Albert had only described himself as "a hopeless romantic who's fortunate enough to have a little business sense," and never once let on about his background.

"Yes. You're honest and I like you. Please do it, Vincent da Luca." Neither a command nor a plea.

Why him? He was nobody, just another working photographer who landed on these shores to make money. No history, no real social connections other than Don and Ai-Lin. Nothing. And here he was being handed this plum society assignment. A private party to mark his club opening. The international and Hollywood jet set would be there. More important, the Chinese set would throng. No paparazzi invited. He was offering an exorbitant fee so that no negatives would leak.

Vince had heard talk about this job from the photographers' grapevine, months before he'd met Albert. Everyone wondering who would get it, no one admitting they wanted it. When they met, he hadn't connected the job with Albert. Son of Ho Yuet-Kan, the shipping magnate and conglomerate emperor. The name meant nothing to Vince. Just another client, with a ridiculously lucrative job. Plus a first class air ticket and two nights at a five star hotel to be a party photographer. Contribution to Katy's legacy.

"If you really want me to, I'll do it," Vince said.

The bartender poured Vince more champagne. Albert sipped his Perrier and lime. "Vincent, I'd be most grateful." Then, glancing up at the flowers, the hint of a smile tickled his lips.

"Share the joke?" Vince asked.

Albert tilted his head. "Oh, April and dull roots."

"Come again?"

"Just call it temporal . . . connections. Border crossings."

They finished their drinks.

Back at his flat, Vince glanced at the message light in anticipation. Wasn't her. Since the night with Colleen he had waited, like a lovestruck kid, hoping she'd call. He had thought about calling but resisted, afraid of being too pushy. In this situation, she had to call the shots. The only reasonable assumption.

Besides, it wasn't as if he could afford to fly to Singapore just to get laid.

He felt a fluttering hum on his cheek. Quick slap. Missed. Goddamned mosquitoes. It was the damp; the humidity hoarded moisture in the walls, in everything of this old flat. That other place, Gunter's flat, was modern and air conditioned. But $2,500! It was just too much. There was still Didi . . . What had Colleen said? *Face it, your wife doesn't need you anymore.*

Her words stung. Didi didn't need him, and she was letting him know as forcefully as she could. Neither his love nor money counted. Once his father passed away, Didi hadn't held back. Had she been waiting for that? His dad and his second wife got along well, especially after Katy was born. Another grandchild to carry the da Luca name.

But Katy needed him. Nothing Didi said or did could change that. Katy was waiting now for his call, for her "once-a-week Daddy" chat which he faithfully performed. She deserved more, but this was better than nothing, better than no daddy at all.

He picked up the phone to return the call.

6

Gail tossed Andanna's business card onto the out tray for Ariadne to file, but held onto Vince da Luca's. It was almost two weeks after Sylvie's wedding. The trouble with cards acquired at odd social events was that they sat around in the wrong purse for too long.

Was Vince handsome? She couldn't decide. Her mother wouldn't think so. What she did know was that unlike other divorced or separated men she encountered, he didn't complain about the alimony.

Men of quality, she was discovering, were difficult to meet. When her husband left her three years ago over an affair with his receptionist, a mere girl, Gail had been completely taken by surprise. For the first two years, she refused to accept it, secretly believing he would come home. Her humiliation evolved into righteous indignation. A year ago, he divorced her and married the woman, and after that, every man Gail met was either undesirable or attached.

Until Vince came along. The marketing department had commissioned him to take corporate portraits for their new brochure. When he arrived at her department, she had sighted him first through the glass panel of her office wall. Aloof and casual, he was leaning against Ariadne's desk, fooling with his camera. When she emerged from her office, she tried not to stare. Yet it seemed he would not stop staring at her, although he didn't really seem to see her. Turning abruptly, he began talking to Ariadne, asking her who was scheduled next.

That was when Gail studied him, as discreetly as possible. He was wearing a funny, mixed up outfit. Gray sneakers and burgundy sweat socks. Green-gray denims with hulking great pockets halfway up either leg. Pale gray T-shirt and a very dark gray, almost charcoal, lightweight jacket, sleeves shoved up to his elbows. The dark hairs on his arms bristled with restrained energy. He leaned forward to catch something her secretary said. Compact ass, but broad shoulders for an otherwise slim physique, he was five eleven, maybe even six feet, but at any rate, at least a little taller than her. Then, he saw her. A flash — were his eyes green? Dark, thick, wavy hair. His complexion lightly bronzed and a distinctly Mediterranean visage. The nose, large but not overwhelming, sloping to a slight hook. He was appealing in his sensuality, the way a movie star or passing stranger could be. A minute later, everything became all business until the photo session was over and they shared pictures of their children.

His business card teased her. Vince da Luca, Photographer, plus a phone and fax. Nothing else. Just as well that she had gone to her research analyst's wedding.

Quiet afternoon. She had easily demolished her in tray pile that morning. All her calls had been handled early afternoon. The boss was out of town. Work could take a back seat for a bit. She stood up to stretch, placing his card carefully on the center of her desk. From the window of her Central Plaza office, she surveyed the waterfront reclamation. Up here on 48, the mess below was contained, reassuring her that her home city was still beautiful.

The photo of her son had been disturbed from its original position. She moved it back, approximately four degrees.

Her secretary buzzed. "Your son's on the line."

"I'm home, mother." Their daily English practice session, faithfully adhered to.

"Did you have a nice day at school?"

"We learned about Columbus. He found back America."

"No sweetie, he didn't 'found back.' He 'discovered' America." She didn't understand these funny errors in English Gu Kwun made.

"Janie said he *wanfaan* America, because it wasn't lost except to people who didn't know it existed, like the Europeans. So that's why he 'found back' America."

Janie's father wrote for the editorial pages of *The Asian Wall Street Journal*. He expounded quirky ideas and was fluent in at least four languages. Janie, it appeared, took after him. "That's 'found.' You don't say 'found back' in English."

Her son considered this. "Why not?"

"Because you don't. Now listen to Conchita and do your homework like a good boy. And don't upset *pohpo*." Her mother doted on Gu Kwun. Things were working out since she'd moved out of her filthy old home and in with them. Gail would have had her move in earlier except that her ex objected.

"Okay, Mummy. I love you."

"And I love you too, sweetie."

The problem with sending him to International was that he was perpetually confused, despite the school's other merits. It wasn't the American curriculum or system that perplexed, but the mobility of the student population. Janie had been his friend for a whole year without her father being transferred. Gu Kwun was too young to understand. Yet she didn't see what choice she had. As her mother pointed out, learning Chinese wasn't the problem, but learning English was. If he were to excel in an American university later, he needed to be acclimatized now. Her own experience at Harvard after attending a local English language school, even a good one like Maryknoll, convinced her that in this matter, her mother was right.

Ariadne, her secretary, had come in quietly to clear the out tray. Gail's eye flickered over Vince's card, and she picked it up. "I'll give this to you later to put in our database."

Would it be too forward to call?

When she'd complained to Kwok Po that men just weren't interested in her, he remarked that in the nineties, it was sometimes up to women to make the first move. *Your life is without walls now Gail. Go for it.*

Her husband's voice, in all its medical wisdom, accused her of knowing nothing about the feelings of men. For just a second, her resolve wavered. And then the false echo of his words — how wonderful a wife and mother she was — exploded in her brain.

She hit the speaker button, and punched Vince's number.

"It's 2878-4879. Leave a message. I'll call back."

A short-and-to-the-point type. Gail smiled, imagining the light hearted messages she wanted to leave. Instead, what she recorded on his machine was, "Gail Szeto from," and named her company. "Please call."

Ariadne buzzed. "It's your mother."

"Uncle Mark is coming tonight," her mother said as soon as she came on the line. Whenever she was anxious, her mother's Cantonese slid off key into her native Shanghainese. "I have to get my hair done," she continued excitedly, "but I don't have enough money."

"It's okay, we'll get the money," Gail pretended calm, but it was hard when her mother invoked delusions.

"Now?"

"You have plenty of time."

"But I want to do my hair now."

Such petulant tones. Worse than a child. "I'll do it for you when I get home."

"Don't like the way you do it. Uncle Mark likes me to look pretty. You know that."

This was new. Gail considered what was safest to say. "Shall I ask one of the girls to come up and help you out?"

"Oh yes."

Gail heard her mother breathing normally again. In a few more minutes, she would start talking about something completely different. On cue, her mother launched into a description of Gu Kwun's school bag, which was torn. The earlier episode was now forgotten. They spoke a few more minutes and then Gail asked to speak to Conchita. She instructed her domestic to wash and set her mother's hair, something she knew Conchita could do well and with ease.

Her secretary buzzed again. "Mrs., I mean Ms. Szeto, your meeting is in ten minutes."

"Thank you, Ariadne." Gail wished she could get her staff to be less formal around her. Sylvie was the most relaxed, but she also was the only one who had studied and lived abroad. Her secretary and the rest of her Hong Kong professional staff were wonderful, but they kept up that local formality, creating rules of behavior she had never imposed. Ariadne was a secretarial school graduate with a couple years experience at the investment bank when Gail hired her into the department. The first time they were together as manager and staff, Gail had asked to be addressed by her first name. Ariadne had given her a shocked look and responded, "Impossible. We're not allowed to do that with any of the other directors," so Gail had let it go. At least she'd almost gotten her off the "Mrs." thing.

She flipped through the project file, collecting her thoughts for the last meeting of the day. It was an intriguing venture, a Papua gold mine in which a Taiwan company had invested that was yielding promise. Tricky business, mining, because it was hard to get an accurate fix on things. Hopefully, the meeting wouldn't drag, but the project finance director loved the sound of his own voice so the prognosis was fifty-fifty. But it was Thursday, his favorite happy hour evening. Perhaps chances weren't so bad after all.

Gail returned from her meeting with a headache. Her colleague's pushiness drove her nuts. He wanted everything yesterday. No one had a sense of urgency, he claimed. Such sanctimonious rubbish. When she'd first brought the project forward he'd pooh-poohed it, saying that the Taiwanese didn't know anything about mining. But once their boss showed interest, it was suddenly top priority, as if it had all been his idea. Men. Such utter hypocrites.

It was past seven. Her department was gone. A note from Ariadne indicated she had called Conchita to say Gail would be late. A super secretary. Her loyal and efficient staff made up for some of the nonsense at work.

The phone shattered the stillness.

"Hey, it's Vince."

She had forgotten all about calling him earlier! Once again, his deep voice set her on edge. Stop being silly, she told herself, you hardly know him. "Oh hi. I just got back to my office."

"If you'd rather call me back later . . .?"

"Oh no, this is fine. Thanks for returning my call."

"So what can I do for you?"

He flustered her. She had planned to say something like — just called to chat — but now it seemed like a stupid idea. Something, anything, quick. "Would you like to have dinner, I mean lunch?"

"When?"

"What about . . ." she flicked through the pages of her desk diary. Why had Ariadne moved the marker? "Week from tomorrow?"

"Sorry, I'm booked to shoot all day."

"Following week then?"

"No can do. I have to go to Shanghai that weekend."

And Gail knew that the week after that, she'd be out of town for at least a week. She mumbled something to that effect.

"How's your boy? Chak Gu Kwun, isn't it?"

Thank god he'd finally relented and given her some conversational space. "Oh, he's just fine. He talked about meeting you."

"Really?"

"Yeah. He liked your camera. Got quite a charge out of it."

"Cute tyke." He paused. "I'm going to try get to New York to see Katy." He paused again, and added, "my daughter."

"I remember. When did you last see her?"

Gail heard the long hesitation, and guessed his discomfort. "Almost nine months ago. When I left to come here."

No reason was good enough. She knew. "It's tough being a parent sometimes, isn't it?"

"Yeah. Real tough." There was relief in his voice.

They talked a little longer, until Gail begged off because she had to go home. Somehow, they never got around to making that lunch appointment.

Forty minutes later, Gail pulled into her parking space, headache abated. Tylenol and money, panacea for mid life. It was past eight thirty. There'd be hardly enough time to play with Gu Kwun, maybe half an hour or so, before he had to take his bath and get to bed. Also, her mother would want Gail to admire her hair, forgetting completely why she claimed she needed it done. That would take half an hour or longer if she started dragging out old dresses and trying them on.

Gail sat in her car, too tired to move. Lucky Sylvie, she suddenly thought. Her staff was from a wealthy family and had married into more wealth, affording a honeymoon in the Maldives. She was a little young though, only twenty seven. Gail had remarked that, asking what the rush was, but Sylvie had given one of those no-fault Hong Kong answers, something like *oh, you know how it is with old folks, they need a wedding,* as if this were some kind of insurance against blame. Within at most a year or two, she would get pregnant and likely give up her job. She seemed the type. What made her think of Sylvie as lucky, when she knew too many intelligent women who regretted this very decision? It was doubly a shame in Sylvie's case because she was an excellent research analyst and could have a real career if she chose.

She willed herself into motion. Why hadn't she cut Vince off and left earlier? He wasn't interested in her. Well, maybe he was. Right now, she didn't care. Stepping out, she flipped the remote to lock the car and headed for the elevator. Passing the mailbox which Conchita cleared, she wondered if a check from her ex had arrived today. His money was due. Why didn't he arrange for direct debit? Forget it, let it go. She didn't really need it. At least he paid even if he was often late, though Gu Kwun needed far more than money from his father.

At the elevator bank, her neighbor from the floor above engaged her in a building management discussion. Yes, Gail promised, she'd call her lawyer friend and ask him about the problem they were having with the contractor. All the way up, the elderly neighbor continued her demands, insisting that Gail was the best one to do this since she was young and well connected, and that their building committee was lucky they had her on their side because she understood these business matters. It was several minutes after they stopped on her floor before she could get away.

Gail stood at her front door, key poised. With luck, whatever Conchita made for dinner would taste good re-heated.

"Why don't you just get on a plane and go see her?"

Gail's question dogged Vince.

It was that simple. All obstacles of his own making and pride. What had made him go on like that? She must think him a complete moron.

The last conversation with Katy. "Daddy, don't you love Mommy anymore?" What did or didn't his wife tell her? He'd relinquished control by leaving town, by running away from the humiliating pain. Didi had been willing, even *wanted* to talk last summer. Then, perhaps, he stood a chance against Joe. But all he knew was the anger, blinding rage that offered no path towards reconciliation. Too late now. He'd lost without even putting up a fight. Only himself to blame.

Maybe Katy knew something he didn't.

Maybe Didi was right and he was too wrapped up in his work. After all, she worked too, and had responsibilities. But secretly, he held onto the notion that his responsibility was greater, that being "head of household" meant it was up to him to hold things together. What had

Poppa always said about Didi? *A sweet wife, she'll make a wonderful mother.* In his father's time, it was all that counted. Women's role in marriage clearly spelled out where children were involved. Didi seemed to go along. So why had everything fallen apart?

Maybe Don was right, when, after his first marriage broke up, his brother told him he was too bent on playing everyone's big brother, the way he had with Ai-Lin. But it had been easy to dismiss Don then. Once, only once, he and Ai-Lin had had a fling when she, upset with Vince, had ended up in Don's bed. Don had confessed, almost too willingly, giving Vince the moral edge to grant forgiveness. But edges confined the big picture, blurring reality. Forget it. Way too many years ago now, best left buried in the Siberia of memory.

His mistake was dismissing Didi too.

Enough. Time to eat. His stomach he could believe in, unlike the world around him. Gail's call surprised. What did she really want? Couldn't tell what she was — sort of American, yet local as well. Different. Sexy woman, but too rich for his blood. Pity she corrected herself about dinner. Women played those games. Would have taken her up on it tonight though. Could have used the company.

7

Unwelcome desire. No, not desire. Empty lust, best dispelled by exercise or exhaustion. Waking up from making love to . . . from fucking Colleen. She harassed his dreams, refusing to release him, demanding attention. Face it. He was her one-night stand, nothing more.

Vince propelled himself into a sitting position. Next to the "bed," a single futon on a tatami mat, was this calendar that listed public holidays worldwide. But no clock anywhere. Vince peered at his watch. Morning of April 14, around seven.

This place belonged to Don's wealthy designer-cum-photographer friend, a local man who spent winter skiing in Switzerland and the spring and summer travelling in Germany. One of Don's many, rich Hong Kong friends.

A rarely used flat in an old building with high ceilings. Sunlight in the front rooms was subdued by trees. It was huge, over 1,500 square feet, and virtually empty. The only furniture, other than the futon in the front bedroom, was a large, low Japanese table that took up much of the living room and a piano against the end wall in what he supposed was a dining area. The floor was entirely covered by tatami mats. Hardly any clothes hung in the closet. A second bedroom, in the back by the kitchen, was completely empty except for an enormous fern. That room led to a fully equipped darkroom converted out of the spare bathroom. Don said his friend didn't really need to work. When Vince had offered to pay rent, the friend, whom he'd never met, refused. He claimed it was enough that someone would look after his fern, which Vince watered religiously.

His sanctuary since last November, compliments of Don.

Vince had given himself till the end of the month to get out of this place, even though he could have stayed longer. Too many favors from Don didn't sit well.

Didi's latest accusation. "If Katy means so much to you, you wouldn't have sent her Christmas present late. They have Federal Express over there, don't they?" Still bringing that up. Some blame for all this belonged with her too, didn't it?

Katy's present. Simply lost track of time. Trying to get settled. Meeting agency deadlines — did clients really need things done on Christmas Eve? And the parties. Too many women offering themselves. When had women become hornier than men or was this the excuse of expatriation?

He had retreated from all this frightening feminine pursuit into an orgy of alcohol instead. Back home, hardly touched the stuff.

Where had nine Hong Kong months gone? Long enough for life to begin but not to find a home. Separation agreement arrived yesterday. Now, not even a house.

The calendar beckoned. The square for April 14 was busy with type, indicating a public holiday in multiple countries. Reading now, not just looking at shapes. Good Friday, of course. A holiday in Europe and much of Asia.

Seven fifteen. Katy and Didi would be sitting down to a fish dinner. Had to be fresh fish, healthy and wholesome, not even shrimp. Didi a perfect wife and mother, tolerant, patient, wonderful with all his family. Never complained. Should have seen the signs. The gym, new clothes, a constant concern over her appearance. Her renewed sexual appetite. Unlike Ai-Lin, Didi liked sex. A moment's unease at the thought of Don and Ai-Lin . . . did his brother have some magic key he lacked? But he shut out those thoughts, preferring not to enter that territory. Years of therapy with Jim had taught him that some emotions were better left unexplored.

What about his mother? She wouldn't have liked Didi, had they ever met, and only tolerated Ai-Lin as a kindred spirit. Perhaps Didi had been possible because Mama was gone.

Too much empty space to reflect. Too much time to think about everything.

Time to make some changes.

Sputtering. Never would get used to this phone.

"Vince, I didn't wake you?"

Surprise. Didi rarely called. Didn't even sound guarded. "Isn't it dinner time?"

"Yeah, but I thought I should call. Katy wants to tell you about her new Easter dress."

"Well it's better than your usual 'it's too expensive' excuse."

Silence.

Shit! What had made him say that when all he really wanted was to come home? "I'm sorry."

"Forget it."

More silence, and then. "So, what now?" she demanded.

When had her voice become cagey, wavering perpetually around this irritable periphery? Now it felt as if it had always been this way. Time cheating him of discovery, allowing only instances of revelation, too late. "I don't know."

"Did you get the agreement?"

"Arrived yesterday."

"Have you read it?"

"No, I . . ."

"Vince, you've got to read it."

"Can I talk to Katy? Please don't say no, Didi," he added, suddenly afraid of this moment, this stranger.

Hesitation hovered, but relented. "Okay."

He replied hello to the uncertain voice on the other end. His daughter waited a few minutes before continuing. "Daddy, your voice sounds so . . . big, bigger than when it comes from your telephone."

"It should. I'm big."

"Do I sound . . . a little bit big too?"

"Yes, you do. More than just a little bit."

"Oh, good." Heard her relief, the way he would when she'd ask at bedtime, would she wake up in the morning and he told her yes. Her world safe again, Katy jabbered away about her red Easter dress until Deanna's voice said, "that's enough hon, this is costing us a lot," and came back on the line.

"We can't go on like this, Vince."

"I know."

"So, what now?" Gentler this time.

The horrible sound of call waiting. Why had he ever bothered to get this, just because Don said he had to have it? "Hang on a sec, I got another call coming in."

"Vince, don't . . ." but he had flipped over.

"Hi, it's Colleen. Remember me?"

"Oh god."

"I've been called many things in my time, but never that."

"Retard-Retard" flashed on a mental neon billboard. "How are you, babes?" He ought to tell her . . . what? That he couldn't talk because he was talking to his wife?

"Wet." Honey in her voice.

No, not again, he wanted to groan. Woman was dangerous, his own appetite gluttonous. "Had a dream about you." Didi would kill him, but he couldn't let go.

"Ah. One of those. Did I pass my screen test?"

Torturer. "You in town?"

"At the airport. Just passing through, I'm afraid, on my way back from Paris."

"Paris?"

"France."

She'd completely write him off now. "What I meant was . . ."

"I know what you meant, Vince." Deep, golden honey. "I'll be in town at the end of the month."

"You can't stay a day? A morning maybe?"

"Would you like me to?"

That was it. His body he still could believe in even if life kept making objectionable noises. "Listen, can you hang on a sec? I'll get rid of my other call."

"If you must."

He clicked over, but Didi had already hung up. "They're gone."

"No one important, I hope."

"Forget about them. Can you come over?"

"It does seem a . . . waste not to, if you know what I mean?"

"I need you, babes." Wanted to swallow his words. What compelled this craving, this absurd desperation? Would scare her off. Even scaring himself.

"Let me see about changing my ticket. I'll call if I can come."

He gave her the address, and waited.

Colleen turned away from the payphone and strained her eyes toward the departure gate. Her contacts were useless, but glasses would be out of the question. Kwok Po was headed down the corridor. She came forward and waved.

"Perfect timing, darling." She kissed his cheek. "I had a lovely shopping trip. Next time, you must come with me to Paris and not work so much."

They headed together on board the plane and took their seats. Her husband began telling her all about his Shanghai trip, and seeing his father. Colleen listened with intent features, injecting the occasional "uh huh" or "really." She was thinking about her dress, the one she planned to wear at Albert's club opening. Good thing Kwok Po hadn't suggested she buy something in Hong Kong, because then he'd come along and pick out something wrong. What she'd found was absolutely right, enough to turn even Albert's androgynous head.

Her husband was saying something about expanding the family business further. Well, that was inevitable, she knew, although the timing . . . it suddenly occurred to her that they might not be welcome at Albert's party, even though she was dying to go. Albert was entertaining. What he lacked in emotional life was made up for by steeping himself in the arts, which made him excellent company. Kwok Po had improved under her tutelage, but he would never be an Albert. "Sweetheart, I'm sorry to interrupt, and I do want to hear all about your father's ideas for the Jakarta office, but are you sure Albert wants us there?"

He seemed momentarily stumped, but quickly picked up the thread of her question. "Of course. He is my partner, after all."

"Yes, but only in the real businesses. This is one of his playthings. Maybe he doesn't want to mix business with pleasure, and we'd be cramping his style."

Her husband leaned over and kissed her lips. "You're always so considerate of other people's feelings. But it's okay to play now and then. Even Albert would grant us that."

She leaned her head against his shoulder. "Now what was that your father wanted us to do?" and he continued his previous train of thought.

Men were despairingly alike, she thought, as her husband talked on. All they wanted was either some attention or to feel like they were in charge. As long as she gave them that, she could have whatever she wanted.

Their plane taxied towards flight.

By eight thirty, Vince gave up. Colleen was too good to be true. Felt like a complete jerk. She was married after all.

Jumped into the shower and resigned himself to the day.

At eleven that night he remembered. Shit. Never called Didi back.

"About time," she said. "You never change."

Deserved that. Guilty, guilty, for this and all the times he'd gotten wrapped up in work and forgotten to call, while dinner got cold, or worse, while Didi waited, hungry, because they were supposed to go out, and he couldn't be reached because he was already eating dinner with a client who called that day. Yet this resignation in her voice, devoid of anger, chilled him.

"Anyway Vince, about the agreement, what I mean is, I guess you must know it's over."

She'd said it. Finality. "It hurts, babes."

"Sorry."

"Didn't see it coming, you know."

"Yeah, I know. I should've let you know how I felt, but you know how it was."

But how was it? Five, almost six years of married life collapsed into this telephone conversation and still he didn't know, not really. "So I should sign this thing?"

"You might read it first."

Didn't matter. Nothing left to fight about. "You'll get it back Monday."

"Monday?"

"We've got Federal Express here on Saturday, babes."

Smiling? Had to be. "Thanks, Vince."

"Welcome, Didi."

Why that hesitation? "You know something I want to tell you?"

Now what? Waited, didn't say anything at first, and then, finally, reluctantly, "what?"

"I hate being called Didi."

That night, from some forgotten recess, Ai-Lin's voice insisting over and over again, "don't call me 'babes' Vince, please don't call me that." Would he never learn? Repeating mistakes. Right at the beginning Didi-Deanna had told him and he had kidded her until she gave up. "You're so damned persistent, Vince," she would say and he'd kiss her, saying "Didi, you're adorable" figuring she didn't mind, not really.

Slept in between stretches of wakefulness, each sleep daunted by monstrous women, leaping off giant photographs, canvases, murals, ceilings. Didi's face loomed, usurped occasionally by Ai-Lin as an artist's model until Don came to take her away, wrapping blankets around her nakedness. Then Didi returned, laughing, and the only way to stop her was for him to wake up. With each awakening, the futon had shifted, and he knew that his whole being was engaged in these dreams.

Finally, around five, sank into a less fitful sleep.

He was four, holding Mama's hand at baby Don's baptism. "You will have to take care of your brother, Vincent," she said. "Promise me. He'll never be as strong as you," because Don was an underweight and sickly infant, and he promised he would.

Then it was his wedding to Ai-Lin, and Mama was smiling until the bridegroom turned around and it wasn't him at all but Don at whom she smiled. In this nightmare, he had no voice although he shouted and pleaded for Mama to look at *him,* not Don, that *he* was the bridegroom, not Don, that *he* was her Vincent, *only he,* something Don could never be. Her voice began to fade. Eventually, she no longer uttered his name.

Hell was the silence that woke him, imprisoning him in a cold chill, even though warm humidity moistened the morning air. He wept, unrestrained.

8

"We will not move to Jakarta, and that's final."

Colleen stared resolutely at Kwok Po. She said this in English, to underline the seriousness of her intent. Her husband protested, but she held firm. As willing as she was to be pliable, once she knew her mind, there was simply no way she'd change her position.

He had tried to time things correctly for compliance, she knew — dinner last night at her favorite Italian place, accompanied by a velvet smooth Amarone, with light jazz in the background. Her husband knew her better than anyone, and should have been able to sway her if he wanted to badly enough. In daily life, Kwok Po ruled. But when it came to the truly important decisions, the ones that would make or break them, she took charge. This morning was one of those times.

For the last two years, Colleen had been working toward this. "You simply have to stand up to your father." The elder Mr. Tang was almost eighty, and his control on the company needed release. But he was a tough and tenacious old man, who would not willingly relinquish power. "It's a ridiculous idea and you know it. Besides, there are other people he could send."

He grimaced. She knew his inner struggle over this. During the last trip back to Hong Kong, Kwok Po had gotten into yet another argument with his father. The latter didn't want to know China, having fled in '49, and was leery of Kwok Po's forays into ventures with the mainland through both the Hong Kong operation and Singapore subsidiary. Yet

Colleen knew her husband was right. China was the future home team playing field. Hong Kong and the rest of South East Asia would be nothing more than guests, and then, only if the Chinese chose to let them play.

Colleen had given into this Singapore move because it was the first venture abroad for the family's business, a conglomerate comprising commercial real estate and the supply and export of Chinese furniture, rattan items and Asian *objets d'art*. Additional operations could launch them on an expansion path, preferably to Shanghai. Besides, she had consulted with her mother-in-law who, being ten years her husband's junior, would soon be the one calling the shots. The elder Mrs. Tang wanted expansion, and wasn't afraid to work with the Chinese, having spent the early part of her life in Beijing. Kwok Po had done well, moving quickly, quicker than either of his brothers could have done in setting up the office, developing clients and contacts and establishing liaisons that provided alternative paths into China. So Colleen didn't mind suffering her Singapore exile, and won more in-law points, keeping her husband ahead of his brothers in the succession line.

But Indonesia! Ethnic Chinese weren't welcome, and government connections were even more difficult to manage than in China. Besides, it was too far away from what mattered.

"You're right, of course," he conceded.

"So it's settled?" She had to make sure, had to know now, this instant. Her impatience caught her off balance, and for a second, she was afraid she had pushed too hard.

He looked her in the eye. "Yes."

Good, she'd won. Given that he'd agreed this readily, she knew there was still room to negotiate the more important question. She tilted her head. "Darling?"

His eyes were already going soft. "What is it, Colleen?" She heard that tiny, familiar tremor in his voice whenever he spoke to her in Chinese.

She continued. *"Ni zhidao gai zhen yang baan ma?"*

He was running his finger lightly down her spine, looking for his reward. "Tell me," he said, leaning his mouth into her neck.

She bent her body, pliant to his command. "It's time to get us back to Hong Kong." Her hand guided his under her dress.

"I will." He had begun gripping her body.

"Do it before '97, okay? We don't want to miss out. You know you have to."

"I know." He drew her into a long, passionate kiss.

She untangled their tongues. "I adore you," she whispered. *"Shizi Wang."* My lion king.

They made love on their living room floor, even though it was mid morning, even though the door was unlocked, even though Rosa might come back at any moment and catch them. It had been like this since the beginning. Kwok Po was the only man to whom she could surrender completely, without holding back, without faking her climaxes. These moments, these rare and beautiful moments, were the reason for her marriage, the only reason she needed to know why her life would always be that of a Chinese wife.

After lunch, Kwok Po disappeared for the rest of the day to the office.

Around one, Colleen dialed the number of JB&D Advertising's Singapore office. She was put through to the creative department where a twenty-something English copywriter took her call.

Colleen showered and put on a short, dark green sun dress, beige flat sandals and a pair of large sunglasses. Then, she rang for a taxi. In less than fifteen minutes, a light blue car pulled up her street and stopped outside the gate of her home.

"Rosa," she called out, "I won't be back till late. Mr. Tang and I won't be eating dinner at home tonight." Hearing Rosa's acknowledgement, she grabbed her large handbag, headed down the driveway and into the taxi which took her into the city to Chinatown.

On the way, she bundled her hair and clipped it on top of her head.

She tied a dark green scarf around it and held up a small mirror to check her handiwork. If she had walked past Kwok Po on the streets, he might not have recognized her. The dress and sandals were atypical of her wardrobe, and he had never seen these sunglasses, which usually sat in her drawer under her slips next to the pack of Marlboros.

She stopped the taxi a block away from a small hotel. Nothing distinguished it, other than a recent coat of paint. She paid the driver the exact fare. Before she disembarked, she finished the conversation they had been having about how she was visiting her sister in Singapore. Her sister, she said, told her Chinatown was a good place to shop for souvenirs to bring back as gifts to England. He wished her a safe trip home. "You're a nice English lady," he said. Idiot, she thought as she closed the taxi door. They could never tell Westerners apart.

Once the taxi had driven away, she headed down the block towards the hotel. The clerk at the desk rang the room of Mr. Wilson, and she made her own way up. In the darkened room, Colleen screwed the young advertising copywriter. In between each of his ejaculations, he told her about the trials of pleasing his creative director, a temperamental Singaporean. She listened. Her thoughts wandered to Vince, thinking, he had some nerve, putting her on hold, but wondering, would he call. When she got bored with the creative demands of diapers, milk powder and other FMCG's, she would give what's-his-name Wilson a blowjob and they could begin again, silencing his whining.

By seven that evening, she had showered, dressed in a pale yellow, flowered cocktail affair, donned white high heeled pumps, and lined her lips with pink lipstick. Colleen did all this at her gym, where she had walked in an hour and a half earlier wearing a halter top, shorts and tennis shoes. From her large handbag, she extracted a white purse into which she transferred lipstick, mirror, hairbrush, kleenex, money, keys and her Singapore identity card. The gym outfit she stuck into the handbag, in which lay her sunglasses, and left the bag in the locker. Mr. Wilson had ripped the green dress to shreds at her request, which she told him was her preferred mode of being undressed by a man. She had worn no underwear. The dress had been discarded, along with the beige sandals and green scarf, in a dumpster outside a restaurant in Chinatown.

Giving herself a final once over in the mirror of the gym dressing room, Colleen noted her private satisfaction, and headed to the Raffles Hotel to meet her husband.

"Danny? Sweetheart, it's awfully late." Colleen picked up the phone after the second ring.

Her husband grunted from his side of the bed and glanced at the clock. Colleen's eyes followed. It was past one. "Go back to sleep," she said to him. "I'll take this call outside." She slipped on a thin robe and took the portable handset out to the living room, shutting the bedroom door behind her.

"I know it's late," her brother said. "But I know something's wrong."

"Don't be silly." She tied the belt around her robe. "Hold on, I'm going outdoors," she said and went out to the back garden. "Where are you anyway?"

"Hong Kong."

If he had left China, perhaps he wasn't in trouble this time. "So why are you calling?"

"You know why."

"Cut it out, Danny," but his deadpan voice conjured up the image of those eyes, his large green eyes that would stare at her hypnotically until she would yell at him when they were children: cut that out, you're giving me the creeps!

"You're at it again, Colleen, aren't you?"

His words lashed out at her, despite his quiet voice. That pain she wanted to forget — the one that began at the back of her head, spreading upwards to encircle her cranium — commenced its trek. She raised her voice. "You don't know anything about my life."

"Get a cigarette," Danny told her. "Get one now."

"I don't smoke, you know that."

"And I know you do. Say it, Colleen. 'I smoke.' It's not so hard. Just like you can say, 'I'm a whore and proud of it' also. Really you can. I'll still love you."

"What asshole sect leader taught you that? What gave you the right to pass judgment, you spineless creep?" She was crying now, and her words choked in her throat, lowering the decibel level.

"You'll wake up your husband, and the neighbors."

"As if you gave a rat's ass. Quit following my life. Leave me alone."

"I can't help it. You know I can't."

She hung up on him.

Colleen lay on the grass. The night embraced her. After what felt like a long time, she drew herself up and went to the garden shed. The door was unlocked. Tools and unused flower pots were stacked in the right corner. Her hand ran down the side of a tower of pots, lifted the middle one under which sat four loose cigarettes and matches. She took one and lit it.

Colleen sat on a pile of wood crates in the shed, smoking. The phone rang, and she quickly answered. Danny would apologize now that he had acted like a brat.

You must, or I'll tell Father.

But the call was only an obscene one. Colleen clicked off the lewd breathing, and continued to smoke. Sometimes, she hated Danny. He could be mean, just like Father.

She tried not to think about him. The cigarette relaxed her.

Why hadn't Vince tried to call? She didn't even know why she wanted his pursuit, except that she did. International long distance would show up on the bill which Kwok Po reviewed so carefully each month, which meant she needed to go to a sufficiently unsuspicious payphone location. That was too much of a hassle. They would have to move back to Hong Kong. It would be easier cheating on her husband there because local calls were free and weren't itemized on the bills.

Vince was such a disappointing lover, but then, all these Caucasian men were. Affairs among the expats were easy in Singapore. She could initiate any one of a potential dozen. Yet she wanted Vince. He hadn't bored her as much as these younger men. In Subic, and later in Hong Kong at the Conrad, she knew she controlled him. So why hadn't he called or tried to see her? It was galling.

The cigarette burned her and she started. She ought to be more careful. Kwok Po might see that and she'd have trouble explaining. She killed it roughly.

Returning to the bedroom, she slid back under the sheets next to her sleeping husband.

On her wedding day, the real one not the one in Boston, Colleen had worn the red *pouh* of traditional bridal attire. Kwok Po itched in his monkey suit next to her. She kept her eyes downcast and her face partially veiled, hoping to present the appropriate picture of modesty. If she had dared, she would have asked for a palanquin to complete her girlhood dream of what a Chinese wedding ought to be.

Except for Kwok Po, the rest of the Tang family lived in Hong Kong, and Colleen had not met any of them until her husband brought her home. At the wedding banquet, the only guests she knew were Gail Szeto and her then husband, who had flown in especially for the occasion. Danny had refused to attend, accusing her of selling out because she had run out of money, and their mother had already been confined in a home. Gail had helped her dress, translating for her the Cantonese chatter among the family. Colleen knew she meant well, but Gail was Kwok Po's friend, not hers, and her patronizing "older sister" attitude was annoying. Colleen had resented that time, impatient for the day when her own Cantonese would be sufficiently fluent for conversation with the family she now called her own.

The banquet had not been a huge affair, but it was expensive and exclusive. Her wedding had been all about that banquet, with the eyes of the whole Tang family on her, waiting for her to make a mistake so that they could say, *you can't expect a* gwaipo *to know our customs,* so that her husband could be roundly admonished for such a poor choice of mate. Before the evening commenced Kwok Po's father had instructed, "drink tea, not brandy," as if she were a child, ignorant of how to hold her own, ignorant of the appropriate behavior for a Chinese bride. But she had humbly accepted his instructions, thanking him for his concern. He was exceptionally fit, a businessman at the exclusion of all else, who had no vices, or at least, this was how her sisters-in-law described him. Kwok Po's two elder brothers — he had no sisters — had both married Hong Kong Cantonese women from good families. They had been friendly but distant to her, their new *muihmui,* a mere girl at twenty six.

It was her husband's mother, the one she had been most nervous about meeting, who chose to engage her prior to that banquet. Her *laihlai* made no secret of the fact that Kwok Po was the "treasure" his name suggested. Colleen had been afraid, sure that she would cause her husband to fall from grace. But when they met, Colleen heard Mrs. Tang's stilted Cantonese accent, and immediately began conversing with her in fluent Mandarin Chinese at which her *laihlai's* face lit up with pleasure, gratified by this tribute to her Beijing heritage.

Just before she and Kwok Po were to begin that interminable round of toasts, smiling and standing until her feet ached as she went from table to table, while guests indulged in the feast which she wouldn't taste, her *laihlai* had suddenly whispered in her ear, *you'll be okay, I hated it too,* and from that moment on, the rest of the evening had been a breeze.

9

Damn Michael.

Andanna strode a furious pace back to their apartment.

Damn him to, to . . . oh, Vancouver!

In the maze of hilly streets slightly west of Lan Kwai Fong, she cut through every path with an angry familiarity. Between Central and Sheung Wan, this former no man's land now housed a plethora of antique stores, new office and residential buildings, small flats converted inside decaying, pre-war structures, and a growing number of restaurants and bars. It was because of the escalator. New life sprung up around it.

Andanna hated the escalator. What a lazy way to travel. It was unsightly, a stab at modernity where rats and giant cockroaches hid barely beneath the surface. She had seen them on Staunton, the street where she and Michael lived, on the side across Aberdeen Street above the markets. The Buddhist priests who controlled the neighborhood could burn all the incense and paper offerings they wanted, as could the residents who believed in traditional superstitions. They might keep the hungry ghosts away, but not the vermin. Those thrived.

At lunch, Michael had made fun of her in front of the band. All she said was she wanted to sing a few Canto-pop songs, because that would help them get more gigs. For that, he said that since she clearly had no idea what jazz was about to make such a dumb suggestion, she was fired, which made the others laugh. The all male rhythm section comprised Michael on upright and electric bass, an Australian-Chinese on drums and an American on piano. At least, that was the group this month. Andanna knew that given time, this one too would disband, the way all her boyfriend's bands disintegrated. None of the musicians wanted to play only straight ahead jazz or bebop. Michael was too old fashioned and stubbornly purist. Sometimes, he acted like he was the only person who knew jazz in all of Hong Kong.

Andanna stopped to catch her breath. She had to stop smoking. But it was difficult around Michael who was as addicted as she.

She arrived at their flat. Tai Jai was stretched on the sofa when she came in.

"Are you still sleeping? It's after lunch."

He grunted something about not having to work till four. Definitely weird.

"I'm going to take a shower," she declared.

"Oh what, you had another fight with Michael?"

"What's that supposed to mean?"

He sat up. "Just what I said. You always want to take a shower after you've had a fight with him."

"I don't 'always' do anything. Besides, how would you know?"

"I know."

He was watching her move around the tiny space. She ignored him and headed into the bathroom. The bar of soap was barely a sliver. She came back into the living room, knelt by the sofa to reach under it where Michael kept a box of extra supplies. All the time, Tai Jai's eyes never let go of her.

"Quit staring." She snapped.

"I can't." He stuck his left foot between her knees. "I just woke up."

"So?"

In answer, he straightened his left leg and tugged at her leg, locking it in a grip that threw her off balance.

Leaning forward, he bit her neck lightly.

"Don't you know what happens to guys when they just wake up?"

he whispered. "They get hard on's,"

She struggled to get up, but his grip held her leg. "Shut up!"

Tai Jai kissed her neck. "C'mon, you want it." He sat up and took hold of her waist with both hands. His hands caressed her body, circling her breasts. They tingled. She wanted to stop him, right now.

"Michael . . ."

"Forget him. You don't love him anyway." He kissed her hard on the mouth, and she felt herself giving in. He was arousing her in a way Michael never had. There was no stopping him now, and what was worse, she didn't want him to stop. Her boyfriend vanished to far beyond Vancouver.

He made love to her slowly, for the next few hours. Her body burned. Some small voice from deep within taught her what to do, how to move. Before this moment, it had all been make believe. When he got her off first, and within minutes again and again, she almost screamed because it was such a release of energies, like nothing else, not Michael, not music, not anything, until he pulled out and came all over her stomach. Then he rolled off the sofa, breathing hard. Andanna lay back, exhausted.

They didn't speak for the next five minutes.

Then, Tai Jai got dressed, while Andanna continued to lie there, unwilling to move. She wanted to say something but was at a loss to express how she felt. He walked to the door. She suddenly knew, she didn't want him to leave, but couldn't bring herself to say it.

He leaned on the handle. "Guess you're not a virgin anymore, huh?"

She sat up quickly. "What's that supposed to mean?"

"Just what I said."

"I am on the pill," she blurted.

He cocked his chin forward, his lips forming a half smile. "I wasn't sure, and I didn't have a condom."

"But Michael . . ."

"Thank him for me, will ya?" He opened the door quickly and slid out, barely missing the thong she threw after him which bounced off the shut door, ricocheting almost all the way back where it landed, upside down, by her feet.

She should tell Clio.

The shower spray trickled down her back. Water pressure was unusually low, although it never was high.

Should she tell Clio?

Andanna gave up on the shower. She dried and unpinned her hair, which fell down to her shoulders. The only mirror in the entire flat was a medium sized one she'd bought and stuck on top of the chest where they kept their clothes. Picking it up, she tried to see all of herself in it. Surely she must look different. Long legged and small waisted, with a real 34-B bustline, her figure was the envy of all her girlfriends and girl cousins, and turned men's heads wherever she went, no matter what she wore. She studied her face. Flawless skin, not a hint of a blemish, yet all she ever used was soap and water, unlike her girlfriends who scrubbed themselves raw with expensive lotions and creams. Her eyes were naturally rounded, framed by long, thick lashes. They slanted perfectly, and if she narrowed them at just the right angle, she could manufacture a sexy, feline gaze that photographed well. She traced her finger around the outline of her "lipstick ad mouth," so dubbed by some smart ass creative, and wondered about these lips that some photographer had once told her were "too hot to kiss."

Ever since they were children, Clio had said Andanna was the most beautiful girl in the world. Now, for the first time in her life, she felt it deep inside, under the surface of her face and body, the inner beauty touted by advertising for beauty centers and aides where she had often featured as the model.

The jazz standard Michael dedicated to her, teased her with since they first started going out was "You Are Too Beautiful." What would Michael do if he found out? The opening lyrics echoed: *You are too beautiful, my dear, to be true / And I am a fool for beauty.*

If only it hadn't been Tai Jai! She had to see Clio.

"Can you talk?" Andanna asked as soon as her friend answered.

"Not really. What's up?"

She knew she ought to wait, to call back later, to arrange to meet. Instead, she said, "I slept with Tai Jai."

"Hah?"

"You heard me."

"You're kidding, right?"

"No. This is for real. Can you get away from your job and meet me?"

She knew Clio was dying to hear the rest, but was fighting her instinct to stay at work. Curiosity won. "Okay. I'll pretend to be sick."

"See you in a bit. Usual place."

Twenty minutes later, they found each other at the tea shop in North Point, a few streets away from Clio's home. This had been the post lunch hideaway since their days at St. Paul's, whenever Andanna wanted to cut classes, dragging the half reluctant Clio along. Always only half reluctant; Andanna knew Clio followed her lead because she was the beautiful, cool and talented one. Money didn't have anything to do with it, which was why she loved Clio.

The restaurant was deserted except for a few tables of late diners. They ordered tea, and a steamer basket of tripe, the only *dim sum* the kitchen had left.

"*Wei,*" Clio began. "What do you think you're up to now?"

Andanna placed her pack of Virginia Slims on the table. "Don't worry, I'll wait till we've finished eating."

"Quit fooling around. What happened?"

"He grabbed me."

"You mean he raped you?"

Clio's melodramatic voice made her laugh. "Don't be ridiculous."

"Well, how would I know? He acts like such a tough guy. Are you going to tell me what happened or not?"

She tried to find the right words. Why was this so complicated to explain? "He did something to me."

"Something bad? What?"

"No, something good. Something amazing."

"Andanna, you're not making sense."

"You know all those karaoke love songs you like?"

"Yeah, what about them?"

"About how love is painful but that there's a joy in that suffering?" Andanna saw that Clio was starting to get impatient. "Well it's not like that at all. Something really powerful happened today. It makes me feel strong and good about myself. I feel like I could do anything."

"You're not in love with him, are you?" Clio's voice was incredulous.

"I don't know what it is."

And then, something changed in Clio's face, and her next reaction was not what Andanna expected. Her friend began to laugh, a long and hearty laugh until her eyes were wet. She was laughing the way she used to when they were girls, hysterically, in a kind of cathartic upheaval. Andanna lit a cigarette, feeling quite helpless. When Clio finally calmed down enough, she managed to gasp, "He's so *wahtdaht*. How could you possibly sleep with . . . him," and she laughed some more.

Andanna was stunned. How dare she describe anything about this as ugly and disgusting. "Stop laughing, for heaven's sake. Everyone's staring."

Apparently, what she'd said touched off another spark of hilarity, because Clio began again. "You're right. He looks like a monkey with muscles. Everyone would stare if you were with him."

Andanna got huffy. Being a joke wasn't at all what she intended. "You're being ridiculous. It's not that funny."

But that set her off again. Clio wiped her eyes with a tissue, trying to stop.

"Shut up or I'm leaving."

"Shut up or I'm leaving," Clio mimicked. "So you crested on a wave, did you? What was this, the first time?"

Never in Andanna's wildest imaginings had she thought Clio would know more about anything important before she did. Euphemism for an orgasm. They had giggled over this in high school. Yet what did not occur to her was that she hadn't "crested" until now. Clio's laughter suddenly made sense. She knew, which meant she already had . . . Andanna felt like a complete fool.

Her friend laid a hand on her shoulder. "Oh Andanna, why didn't you tell me you didn't know?"

She shoved Clio's hand away and got up. "You shouldn't have laughed at me," she declared angrily, and stalked out of the restaurant, leaving her friend behind.

Andanna raced towards the MTR. How dare Clio! If that was the way Clio was going to be, she didn't need her friendship. How could she? By the time she reached the main concourse, however, she'd already simmered down. She resented being such a wimp. Her quick temper got her into trouble often, although rarely with Clio. Okay, she'd apologize, but she'd let Clio suffer first for a day or so.

What now? Remembering an earlier thought, she wandered towards the bank of public phones, digging in her bag for her notebook of numbers. She had considered calling Gail Szeto for some time, and this afternoon seemed as good a day as any.

"Andanna, I was just thinking about you," Gail said.

"Oh, why?"

"There's someone I think you should meet, if you want some work, that is." Gail flipped her desk diary back to the week before, where her friend's hotel room number was scrawled on Saturday.

"What kind of work?"

"Modeling of course. Isn't that what you do for a living?"

"Yeah, I guess."

Gail wondered if this were a good idea. Young people today could be so vague! Still, there couldn't be any harm in it. The girl didn't seem like the helpless type. "Call this friend of mine who's in from Boston. She's commissioning fashion photos to use in a catalog that targets

Asian Americans, but wants to pick the model herself. I told her about you, because so far, she hasn't seen anyone she likes. She says the models all look 'too Hong Kong.' Maybe she'll like you."

"Okay, I'll do it tomorrow."

"No, call today. Her schedule's tight. She leaves this weekend."

"Will do."

Funny girl, Gail thought after the call. Quite an original, although rather too full of herself and hopelessly self absorbed. She seemed young and naive for one seemingly so sophisticated. Not at all like her cousin, who was savvy to a fault.

That nagging regret — how she would have liked a daughter — resurfaced. Oh, she loved Gu Kwun. He was a good kid, not terribly rambunctious and difficult the way boys could be. But a daughter would have made her happy the way no son could. Daughters treasured their mothers, the way she had hers, even though Mom was hardly a sympathetic parent to her needs. Gail's one dream for marriage had been to raise a girl differently from the way her mother had raised her. Her daughter would be able to be a girl, and not have to spend her life being obedient, serious and responsible. She would never have to worry about making money as if that were the only thing that mattered. Most of all, she wouldn't be boring

The buzzer interrupted her daydream. "What is it, Ariadne?"

"It's a call from New York."

"At this hour?" Although it wasn't unheard of for her boss to call at three or four in the morning from his hotel room, Gail knew he was currently still in transit.

"It's a Mr. Ashberry. He wouldn't tell me what company he's from. Do you want to take it?"

She hesitated. Gordie always gave her pause. Her secretary continued. "He sounded quite sure you'd talk to him." Gail heard the uncertainty. Ariadne was fiercely efficient, but Gordie could get to even the most unflappable personality. "He said he had 'an offer you wouldn't dare refuse if you didn't want to be blackmailed'?" The hushed question in her staff's voice made Gail smile in spite of herself. Gordie was so outrageous he succeeded in being discreet, since no one dared ask further.

"It's okay. I'll take it." It sounded like Ariadne breathed a sigh of relief. The call was put through, and she heard the familiar voice.

Later, when Gu Kwun rang for his daily English practice, Gail asked Conchita to get her mother. "Mom, Gordie called. He's stopping in Hong Kong this summer on his way to China."

Her mother sounded dazed. "Who? Who called you?"

"Gordie. Gordon Ashberry."

"He not Uncle Mark," she replied, in English.

Gail clenched her teeth, trying to squelch her impatience. Why couldn't Mom connect at least some of the time? "No, he isn't. You know who he is, Mom." She spoke in Chinese; her mother's pidgin English always grated on her nerves.

"He not Uncle Mark." The phone went dead. Gail hit the speed dial for home, but the line was busy. Her mother had hung up in her usual scattered fashion and left the phone off the hook, something she did with unfailing regularity.

She turned back to work, giving up on her mother for now. With luck, Conchita would notice and replace the receiver. That one regret nagged with greater insistence, and she experienced, again, the unwelcome fury at her ex for his cowardice, his inability to honor and cherish his family, his lies and hypocrisy after years of pretending to love her for who she was, for what she was, and then humiliating her by choosing a woman who represented everything she was not. What was the use of such exhausting anger? He was gone, and as Kwok Po and others had told her, it was good riddance. Friends she could count on.

Anger was unreasonable. She had to curb her temper. It only got in the way of thinking rationally. Taking a deep breath, she calmed down, but not before the thought flashed that the very least her husband could have done was to have given her a daughter. Now, it was too late, like everything else about her life.

Work absorbed her till dusk.

Andanna stood in the phone booth, contemplating whether or not to make the call. This was different. My friend will pay well, Gail had said.

She had fallen into modeling quite by accident because a friend of a friend had seen her and asked the friend if she wanted to try it out, or something like that. She quickly discovered that there was work for her if she chose. It wasn't as if she had to look for it. People called, because word of mouth seemed to do. Jake had told her once that he used her because she didn't care about modeling, which didn't sound like any reason at all.

If she contacted Gail's friend, it would be the first time she'd actually taken any initiative to get work for herself. The idea put her off. Even for gigs, she depended on Michael who hustled and knew everyone. Michael, and Clio, badgered her to get more work, saying she could make a lot more money if she weren't so lazy. This only pissed her off and she procrastinated, because eventually, someone would call and there'd be work. Besides, she hated begging, which was what looking for work felt like. Her friends were all obsessed with money, especially Michael, who was being really annoying these days, going on and on about Berklee, wanting her to go to Boston with him.

Yet Gail's manner had been so matter of fact that it seemed unthinkable not to call.

A man hovered behind her, waiting for a phone. Andanna turned and glared, sending him scuttling off to hover, unrepentant, behind another booth. Turning back, she picked up the receiver.

10

Over the phone, Gunter's woman said that Cannon Street was *Gingluhnggaai,* but that none of the taxi drivers would know it. Vince knew he could simply go to the familiar hotel taxi rank at *Yihdung Jaudim,* and walk. Yet he insisted on learning how to get a taxi right to the door, so she taught him to say *Gousihdadouh,* Gloucester Road, and to turn left at the first street after the hotel.

He wondered at his insistence. Surely the flat was too expensive. Don had suggested, several times, that staying on for free at the Robinson Road place was no problem, *really.* Surely it made sense to swallow pride and stay, costing him only his phone line, paying his dues by watering the fern. Think of the money he could stash away for his family.

What family?

How truly worried was he about Katy's college tuition?

The truth — family was not the problem. Didi . . . Deanna only had a junior college degree, and he himself never finished his bachelor's in fine arts. Neither had relied on parents to come up with the money for college. Besides, a degree didn't earn a living, which he'd done passably well to date. Attitude was all.

Vince knew his ability to create the paragon of food photography had once made him special back in New York. What brought in jobs, however, was more about doing whatever was required without argument than with talent. Also, he went to where the money was, like the ad agencies or the glossies. Work was about money. It wasn't about art, the way Don tried to be about as he waxed lyrical over the art of architectural design. What mattered was being nice to the right people and swallowing pride.

Had to stop wasting time and get over to Gunter's flat. Tomorrow morning, he was flying to Shanghai to do Albert's job. *Gousihdadouh, Gingluhnggaai jyun jo,* he rehearsed. If he was going to live there, he had to know how to stop a taxi right at the door if he didn't want to have to lug his equipment from the Excelsior Hotel. *Gingluhnggaai.* Of course he could do it.

Twenty minutes later, Vince was outside "Hoi Goon" Building. Yet another Anglicized misnomer; this city housed too many to amuse him. The caretaker buzzed him through a gate, rusty to the touch, and into a narrow and dingy hallway. He felt too big for the tiny lift as it rose to the sixteenth floor.

Once again, the transformation.

A microscopic place, originally a two-bedroom, now an open studio. Plate glass windows enclosed and replaced the balcony, extending the reach of space to its outer limits. Light, lots of light, the kind that made photographers salivate. Facing north, no obstruction. Godsend after the dark on Robinson. On this clear day, the blue harbor and Royal Yacht Club below, he could have been on the Mediterranean. Garbage around boats in the typhoon shelter almost invisible.

The interior worked. It was custom designed by Gunter when he bought the flat. A built-in desk and bookshelves stacked with art, design and photography books lined one wall. A queen size bed, a real bed, not some ascetic's idea of a bed, with recessed lighting in the headboard. A walk-in closet with mirrored doors, unlike the moth-eaten, ancient wall-hole on Robinson. Track lighting. Most amazing, a real bathroom with a human, not pygmy-sized tub, plus a separate shower stall and toilet. Hot and cold running water without having to light a gas heater that looked like it might blow up any minute. Civilization began in the bath, in a solo baptism.

The flat was a magical place, hiding city squalor in a building that might not pass the local fire code.

Gunter's woman — Vince hadn't figured out if this was his friend's girlfriend, mistress or what — wore a micro mini skirt and too much makeup. Coarse hair, fat legs, jelly belly, she spoke German better than English. Through their Teutonic, Canto-lish conversation, Vince conveyed his desire for a short duration lease. Apparently okay on a month-to-month. Gunter had agreed to US $2,300 if Vince could keep all the furniture and books, and would go as low as $2,000 if Vince would rent it without a lease, allowing that Gunter might need it back on short notice. Still cheaper than most serviced flats, and far more comfortable. Also, there were two phone jacks, with one line already in place. Employment lifelines. Gunter didn't mind him using the existing line to make calls, although he didn't want Vince giving out that number since it was his own business voicemail.

Vince already had a phone line. Easy enough to transfer it here, keeping the original number on his business card. Could do that, thanks to the local telephone company, no matter where in Hong Kong he moved. One up on New York.

Month-to-month was shorter than short. Temp living, until he knew what next. Should do this. If he ignored the question of price, the Robinson Road place only had size in its favor. But what mattered most was that Gunter was his, not Don's, contact.

So made the deal and plunged back into the gloom of narrow corridors reeking faintly of garbage. Didi-Deanna, safe in their-her mortgage-laden Brooklyn home would not believe, could not imagine such a lifestyle regression, especially not at this price. Even Manhattan had been too much for her.

He'd make the money somehow, the way he had when he found his first Manhattan apartment at twenty three, the rent-controlled lease he still owned. To appease Don, he'd use the Robinson Road dark-room, its one appealing feature. And water that goddamned fern.

Heading down Cannon towards the MTR, Causeway Bay crashed waves of bursting sidewalks, drowning in clashing colors. Endless noise, an indistinct, inescapable sea of sounds. On the corner, a pharmacy, a "dispensary" filled with more cosmetics than medicines, stood opposite President Theatre. Ghoulish images of bloody ghost women on the marquee heralded the current Cantonese flick. Coming attractions were also all in Chinese. No time out for him there; subtitles graced only foreign, not local movies.

Vince slowed. Make this day end early.

And there, on the corner of Jaffe Road, looking lost, was that leggy girl-woman model. Child porn, gracing pharmaceuticals.

"Need directions?" A whiff of? Neither hair spray nor cologne. Girl scent, spring charm.

"Oh, you."

"Like a bad penny."

"Wha . . . ?"

"Nothing."

"Hey, do you know where is, uh," she consulted a scrap of paper, "Can-non Street?"

"*Gingluhnggaai.* You're on it."

Disbelief glowered. "Really?"

"Scout's honor."

"Wha . . . ?"

"Forget it." He turned her round by the shoulders and pointed upwards at the street sign, lost among the advertisements, billboards and shop signs. "See." She nodded like an obedient child, that delicious mouth forming a large "oh." "Where are you headed?"

Innocence glowed. Tender skin, absurdly smooth, her complexion barely ripe. "This guy's place. It's somewhere here. He's waiting for me with a woman."

"Kinky."

Incredulity, uncertainty, a hint of accidental decadence. Priceless.
"Are you making fun at me?"

Moi? he wanted to say, but refrained. All allusions lost on her, the
way they were on most Hong Kong people he met. But her girlishness
made her too tempting not to tease. *Was* he trying to pick her up?
What the hell . . . life could begin at forty five. No virgin after all, this
one. "Want a coffee? I know this place round the corner."

"How come you know so much? Have you lived here long?"

"Long enough."

"Oh." As if about to say more, but then as if she were too fatigued,
"no, thanks. I should look at shoes before getting off," in the manner
of needing to meet an obligation, in her imperfectly cute English. "See
ya," and she disappeared.

In her wake, an aura of urgent sexuality. Probably fucked her
boyfriend last night. That body, bursting with belated puberty. The
lips half opened, tits inviting. Unending legs and a tight, round ass.
Short skirt, way too short. Forget it, almost could be, *yikes,* definitely
could be her father. But those shoes! Clunky clog-like things. Thought
they died in the sixties. Just as well she said no.

The shoe display beckoned. Andanna wandered into the shop.

It was an easy idling of time, trying on shoes she had no intention
of buying. Shop clerks sensed she came from money. They scurried
around her, like ants hauling home a dead cockroach. Clio often said it
was because of her regal manner. Andanna found all of this ridiculous.

She tried on a clear plastic sandal. Ugly and uncomfortable.

The salesgirl cooed at her ankle. *"Wa, gam 'fit.'"*

She did the foot movement thing, pretending consideration. What
to do about Michael? Tai Jai was unlikely to say anything. But
Michael. Serious Michael who wanted to take her to America so that

they could "study jazz properly." He wanted to be a "real" musician someday. What made some music more real than others anyway? As Tai Jai once remarked, music was just music, so she might as well sing Canto-pop because at least people would understand the lyrics. Made sense to her, although she'd never let on because Michael would dismiss that as ignorant. It was all too confusing. Who knew what her future should be?

Well never mind . . . the future was just that, in the future. For the present, Gail's lead paid off and she had an appointment in half an hour.

The salesgirl brought her a shoe with a multi-colored heel. Mother would die laughing if she saw that. That photographer guy. Why did she keep bumping into him? The salesgirl was saying something to her and her attention returned to shoes.

Colleen dialed Vince's number. Good, he was home. "Tracked you."

"Girl scout," he replied. "So what're you doing tonight?"

"Why don't you ask me what I'm doing right now?"

"Conrad?"

"3820."

"Be right over."

He was there in ten minutes. What did he do, fly? She did not anticipate the animal passion that followed, so unlike the first time when it was all she could do to keep him going. Midnight came and went. She had more than satisfied him this time. Another unkempt room service tray like before and an empty Tattinger, which he'd paid for in cash when she demurred about its inclusion on her room bill.

He began to get dressed. "I've got to go." His voice reluctant.

Colleen sat up. "Oh no, why?"

"Flight to catch."

She smiled. "There's a curfew at Kai Tak, or maybe you hadn't heard?"

"Tomorrow, Ms. Smart Aleck. Sorry, but I do have to go or I'll never get up in time. It's this big job, babes."

"It's sexy when you say that."

"What?"

"Babes."

"My first wife hated it."

"Oh."

He took her in his arms. "Sorry. Shouldn't have brought that up."

"It's okay."

She must have grimaced or something, because he surprised her with, "I've hurt your feelings, haven't I?"

"No, don't be silly, of course not. But I wish you didn't have to go yet. Tell me about this job."

He looked at his watch. "Okay, but then I really have to go."

It was another hour and a half before she released him.

Colleen flicked the ash off the end of her cigarette, missing the ashtray she'd hidden away earlier. She scowled.

Of all the people in the world to be hiring him, it had to be her husband's partner. Okay, associate, since the partnership was nebulous at best. Albert Ho ran in the same circles though, no question about that, plus a few other circles of his own. Now she'd have to share Vince with everyone, since he was bound to see her in Albert's club. Fortunately, fruit bats made a good story. (*"Vince da Luca, isn't it? How lovely to see you again. Kwok Po, Albert, this is my fruit bat man."*) She trusted him to keep his cool, even though he would be shocked at first. Just wouldn't do to warn him though. Paramours were best kept on their toes.

She inhaled menthol heat.

Earlier that day, after reaching Vince, she had rung her husband. "Darling, you were right as usual. I shouldn't have come to Hong Kong and should have taken the flight with you to Shanghai. No one's free for dinner on short notice, and now I'm down with this awful throat tickle. I'm just going to order in room service, down some vitamins and go to sleep early. That way, I'll get in some shopping tomorrow morning before I catch the afternoon flight."

Kwok Po had been his normal, considerate self. For an instance, she felt a pang of guilt. Her husband loved her, never stinted on anything, although of course, he could afford it. But it was more than just the money. It was his ability to endure what she dished out.

Surely he knew about the infidelities.

After all, Kwok Po was a busy husband who appreciated her self sufficiency and lack of complaints. She was a good wife, discreet, and, ultimately, loyal to him in spirit if not flesh. Colleen dismissed the thought, refusing to dwell on it.

The clear night beckoned.

She slung on the hotel's white, terrycloth bathrobe and stood by the window. Danny was out there somewhere. She was sure of it. He probably returned to reconnect with all those democracy people he'd met the first time he came and stayed with her. Why did he have to stick his nose into things that weren't his business? Studying Chinese didn't give either of them the right to speak on behalf of a foreign race. Her brother didn't share her own keen sense of their New England heritage. It was appalling, since despite everything else he may have been, their father had descended from landed gentry. That was worth something. At least she knew enough to make a somewhat socially correct albeit interracial marriage. Okay though for someone like her. Even though Kwok Po's family was only *nouveau riche,* they had some Beijing roots, although their English name was transliterated to the Cantonese "Tang" for Hong Kong. She ought to tell *laihlai* that they should consider using the *pinyin* "Deng" soon.

What would Danny do next? She wished they hadn't argued, but sometimes, he was just the limit.

For that matter, what would Vince do next?

She was smoking way too much.

When she was a teenager, her father made numerous trips to China and described the old fashioned urban societies he saw. Teenagers didn't date which he considered excellent. Prior to her teenage life, he traveled constantly to academic conferences while her mother raised her and Danny.

Her father had been a historian and philosopher, an "independent scholar" who published nothing, advanced nothing in the body of knowledge, but found ways into China long before '79 through well placed family connections. By the time he died, his once sizeable inheritance was completely gone, leaving only their grandfather's trust funds for Danny and herself, and the ghost of his passion for China.

Danny had been fascinated by all the artifacts their father returned with. She, on the other hand, had imagined the country he didn't share with his family. She wove fantasies of a beautiful Chinese emperor, with skin paler than her own, who would make her his concubine. It had all seemed mysterious and wonderfully romantic, a fairy land. One day, she told her mother, she was going to China, to the kingdom at the center of the universe. Her librarian mother had found her books to prepare her for that time. She had devoured those, continuing the quest in college, reading the great philosophers and writers, reciting the Analects, studying Tang poetry and memorizing the four-character *cheng yu,* the "set expressions" that fuelled the rhetoric of every well educated Chinese scholar.

Now, the *last* place she wanted to go to was China. The filthy toilets, urban pollution and glorification of wealth were an assault on all her senses. Shanghai and Beijing were the only tolerable places.

She needed sleep. Climbing back into bed, she allowed her senses to drift into the meditative state which had cost her a fortune to learn from that Vermont guru. About Vince, she told herself, his problem was that he was common. The sexiest guys always were. Imagine having not one but two ex-wives! No big deal these days, but that was the problem with divorce, wasn't it? It wasn't a big deal. It was marriage that was in vogue now.

Born a decade too late to live an American life. How much easier it would have been growing up in the frigid fifties so that she could have swung through the sixties with Kinsey & Company. Divorce would have been fashionable then. Now, divorce was common, even in Asia, infected as it was by global Americana. No one raised eyebrows anymore and conversations shifted quickly to alimony and custody. Single parenting was an unbearably tedious subject that was, unfortunately, the in thing.

The trouble was, these unromantic, pragmatic nineties didn't begin to match up to her own expectations for the duration of life.

And just what *did* she want for that duration?

Danny's voice in the ghostly realm lulled. "You okay, sis?"

OCTOBER 1995

11

The taxi driver had looked at Andanna as if she were crazy when she told him to go to Clearwater Bay Road, all the way to the end. He'd muttered something about the time and getting back for lunch. But the flag went down and he took off anyway, despite all the grumbling. Andanna settled back for the long ride. It irritated her the way people made a fuss about nothing instead of just getting on with what they were supposed to do.

Last night, Michael had been out late again, the way he had been all summer. He only cared about jazz and Berklee; they hardly saw each other anymore. Although it was already the end of October, the weather was still warm. Unable to sleep, she had watched some old black and white Cantonese movie about teenager-parent generation gap. Having come into it halfway, she almost turned it off because it looked too dumb. Then the scene shifted to where the road ended at Clearwater Bay, beyond the hills, and suddenly there it was, that eternal view of sea, islands and nothingness stretching out for endless miles around. It looked even emptier and more remote than in her memory. The film had been shot during the sixties, before her time. She continued watching.

This morning, after catching a few hours sleep, she decided to go there. Michael was still sound asleep when she left. A taxi would be easiest, and she resolved to spend the money. Even though she'd grown up in Kowloon, she had never learned the intricacies of the bus and minibus system out to the New Territories. It was shortly past eleven when she finally arrived.

She was shocked by how the area had changed, because it was now an official "country park." There were *way* too many trees. In the film, as in her memory, there had been a barren stretch of cliff towards land's end, no, more, like the ends of the earth itself. An expanse of elevation undulated gradually, forking into paths that appeared to lead to the sea. She had run east down one of those paths once, in pursuit of a butterfly, thinking that eventually, she'd come to an end. But the path had gone on, seemingly forever, until she was forced to give up and turn back.

Now, she felt hemmed in by the trees, by this lush forest plantation that took away the open horizon, binding the land against the sea.

Andanna headed east. Myriad colored butterflies crossed her path.

What she recalled were the picnics with all the cousins on her father's side, when grandma was still alive. A convoy of chauffeured cars would take the family on their outings. There were eighteen cousins plus parents and servants, well, nineteen, if she counted second uncle's fifth child, Siu Mei, the girl with cerebral palsy. The one who was her own age. Siu Mei sat in a wheelchair and never could do anything. Andanna used to feel sorry for her, wondering what kind of life she led, but Mother said that Siu Mei was the happiest of all and there was no need to pity her. It was true. Siu Mei always laughed to herself glee-fully. Nowadays though, no one saw her much anymore, not since grandma died.

The picnics were fun because among the cousins, there were only five girls which meant that except for Siu Mei, the other four could do anything the boys did. Andanna had scrambled up the hill with the boys; even though she was the youngest girl cousin, she made it up to the peak faster than all the other girls. Sylvie, who was the oldest girl, would stop halfway, too scared to go to the top. Because there were so many boys, Andanna had to shout really loud to make herself heard. She never had more fun as a child than here at the end of the road.

Now, the only time she ever saw her cousins were at funerals, weddings, "full month" banquets for new babies and over the new year holidays.

She accelerated her pace. Along the edge of her vision, a handful of people blurred the periphery. A flat, harsh voice cut into her reverie. "It's Andanna, isn't it?"

Startled, she turned to see that stunning woman, Sylvie's *louh bahn*, the one from the wedding. She was with her son and an elderly Chinese woman, who clearly had once been incredibly beautiful.

Oh no, Andanna thought, she'd never called her back to say that the lead panned out. How rude of her. Somehow, this woman made her want to do the right thing. What was her name again? She stared at them a moment, emptying her mind, pulling the right names to the forefront. Mother's trick. *Never panic in a social situation, You Fun, if you can't remember someone's name. It's there somewhere, and it'll come.*

It worked every time. "Gail Szeto, and Chak Gu Kwun. Out for a picnic?"

The solemn little boy looked up. "Auntie," he greeted.

"How polite and well behaved you are," Andanna replied, charmed. But it had been a mild shock, this honorific, so natural in Cantonese. For her? Surely she wasn't that old yet.

"This is my mother." Gail indicated the elderly woman. "Mrs. Szeto."

It was a Friday. Andanna remarked the weekday and Gail explained that she sometimes took a day off in between business trips to take her family out to the New Territories when there weren't as many crowds.

"Lucky you," Andanna said to Gu Kwun. "You get to miss school."

"I have been properly excused," he responded. "But I still have to study my lesson to catch up."

He was amusingly serious, but Andanna held her laughter in check. Gu Kwun reminded her of Siu Mei's little brother, the youngest of six, the one grandma nicknamed "Prince Frog" because he had bulging eyes and a most earnest manner. Yet no one openly teased him. Just like Gu Kwun, something about that kid had commanded an odd respect. In fact, if grandma hadn't coined the nickname, none of the cousins would have dared.

Gail invited her then to join them for their picnic lunch. Andanna was drawn to this family. An easy familiarity surrounded this moment, this place. As they sat around the picnic table, she found herself talking a lot, telling Gail all about the picnics of her childhood, remarking that she had been jealous of her cousins who all had siblings because she was the one cousin who was an only child. Somehow, this led to her talking about Michael and before she knew it, she was even telling Gail about Tai Jai, about what had happened — there had been no repeat incident, she emphasized — and about how guilty she was feeling.

"You like Tai Jai."

Gail's strangely flat voice interrupted her monologue. Andanna sighed. "Not exactly. He's . . . well, it's like my friend Clio says, he's not my kind of person."

"Which is?"

"I don't know. I guess what she means is that he's not educated."

It wasn't quite what she meant. Gail continued looking directly at her, and Andanna felt compelled to find the right words. "What I mean is, he's from a different kind of background. You know, not like us."

Gail appeared amused. "What kind of background do you think I'm from?"

"Oh, you know. Cultured and educated. Quite well off."

"What about your boyfriend? Isn't he from a different background?"

"Oh, but Michael's different. He's talented and ambitious. And really good looking."

"Uh huh." She looked thoughtful. "But anyway, when we last spoke, you weren't sure if you loved your boyfriend. How about now?"

Had she said that? Andanna wasn't sure. "I guess I do. He loves me very much."

Mrs. Szeto, who up till this moment had been eating quietly, suddenly exclaimed, in English, "Uncle Mark, he must go home tomorrow, but he always love me!" and then proceeded to cry quietly. Gu Kwun began to comfort her, repeating in Cantonese. "*Pohpo,* don't cry."

Andanna glanced at Gail, who didn't react to her mother at all. All the while, Mrs. Szeto muttered in Shanghainese, her presence almost ghost-like, drifting in and out of the scene. She reminded Andanna a little of her own grandma, during her last stages of senility. But this fair skinned woman was like one of the four beauties of China, whose visage commanded the universe because its superior quality brooked only the finest sensibility and an unquestionably sincere character.

Gu Kwun declared, "Old people have their own sorrows." With that, he took his grandmother's hand and led her down the path for a walk.

Andanna watched, thinking it all a bit weird, but somehow the way the child behaved made everything seem natural. Even Gail's lack of reaction, which had perturbed her at first, seemed in keeping with her mother's outburst.

"Now, where were we?" Gail began, and encouraged Andanna to continue talking about Michael and Tai Jai, which she did, in a long stream of words, surprised that she had such a lot to say and that she could say it so easily.

It was past three when Andanna realized, reluctantly, that her "family," adopted for the afternoon, had to leave.

"How will you get back?" Gail asked.

Andanna glanced towards where the road ended. Neither bus nor mini bus in sight. When she'd set out that morning, she hadn't given a thought to the return journey, trusting that at worst, she would have to walk till some form of public transport appeared.

"Let me give you a lift. There's plenty of space in the car. The only thing is, we have to take a short detour. It won't take very long, do you mind?"

She smiled at Gail. "Oh, of course not. It's really kind of you," grateful for the ride, happy that she could prolong this wonderful day just a few more hours.

The detour was downhill past Clearwater Bay Beach. They turned off down a side road which ended at a path. On the left below them was a small fishing village. Mrs. Szeto stepped out of the car and gazed at the boats. Her grandson stood a little behind her. Gail remained in the driver's seat. Andanna sat beside her.

"What's your mother looking at?"

Gail squinted against the afternoon sun at her family outside. "She's looking for one particular boat."

"How come?"

She wasn't sure, but Andanna thought she detected an unwillingness on Gail's part to tell her. Perhaps she shouldn't be so nosy. Gail didn't speak for awhile, but then said, abruptly. "She's looking for the boat she grew up on. This is her *heungha.*"

Andanna was shocked. It wasn't possible. Mrs. Szeto was obviously not Hakka. How could she be from this fish farm? Gail had stepped quickly out of the car after her revelation and was urging her mother to get back in. The older woman appeared unwilling to go at first, and then gave in, taking Gu Kwun's hand. He led her back into the car.

The drive home was quiet. Not till after she had been dropped off did Andanna realize that she never apologized for forgetting to thank Gail for that job lead.

Andanna walked away up Pedder Street. The girl had been quite insistent that she not take Gail out of her way to her home. It was more *fongbihn,* she said, to stop on Pedder in Central than to go all the way to Sheung Wan, because it was such a short walk, really. Silly euphemism this pretentious "convenience." The girl didn't want her to know where she lived, as if it mattered.

"Why did we stop?"

Her mother's query prompted Gail into switching on the ignition.

"We had to drop off Mummy's friend, Grandma," Gu Kwun said.

"Oh, I see," and she lapsed into silence again.

"Auntie You Fun is pretty."

"Yes, she is." Funny how Gu Kwun always chose to refer to people by their Chinese names. This afternoon, he had asked Andanna what her "real" name was and she had laughed and laughed when he called her "Auntie You Fun" because, she said, no one had ever addressed her that way before.

Her son was in a talkative mood. "Does Mummy like her very much?"

She replied something non-committal, and then reminded him that now she had to concentrate because the traffic was heavy at this hour, her prompt to be quiet. He obliged. Her mother, who had dozed off, let out a small snore.

Gail negotiated her way through the city streets until she reached the highway. The line of cars for the harbor tunnel irritated her. Even though she got past that "long dragon" quickly enough to shoot towards the Eastern highway, she could not contain her annoyance at the inefficiency of what she considered an unnecessary snarl that could be prevented by better planning. What was it Ariadne had remarked the other day? That Gail could "lead a revolution for efficiency." It had been such an out-of-the-blue remark, so uncharacteristic of her secretary, that for a minute, Gail thought she was trying to be funny. But the deadpan expression on the girl's face made her think otherwise. Ariadne meant it, quite seriously.

The traffic thinned and she picked up a little speed. It had been a long day, longer because of the detour to drop Andanna. Did she like her very much? Her son sometimes seemed to read her mind, because Gail had caught herself wondering, all the time Andanna talked, whether or not she did.

Such a vacuous girl, she talked constantly about herself. Hardly the type of young woman she normally took to. But she seemed to have a sincere desire to please, and a manner that compensated for her vain self-absorption. She was young, Gail reminded herself, and exemplified utterly that youth is wasted on the young. The surprise, however, was that she had let her own guard down at her mother's village. How her mother had ended up there from Shanghai was a private matter, and best left that way.

Gail lowered her window a crack, hoping to do without the A-C. The breeze was stultifying, and she shut the window almost immediately. But her mother awoke, having felt the wind.

"Uncle Mark . . ." she began.

"Go back to sleep. Gu Kwun, make your grandma comfortable."

"But Uncle Mark . . ."

Gail clenched her teeth. "Mother, don't worry about Uncle Mark."

"He's coming back soon though, you'll see. He came this summer."

"That wasn't Mark, Mom. It was Gordon."

Her mother didn't respond, acting as if she hadn't heard. Gu Kwun clutched his grandmother's hand. *"Pohpo,* you don't have to *daamsam."*

"Without Uncle Mark, I don't even have a heart to burden," she declared, and lapsed into silence again.

Gail accelerated hard, ignoring the speed limit, but conscious of the migraine that had begun to form.

When they arrived home, finally, Gu Kwun rushed to tell Conchita all about his day, babbling excitedly about Auntie You Fun who "promised to take him to Ocean Park." He had been to the marine park four times already, but never seemed to tire of it, loving any life form that swam. Conchita handed Gail the messages from her office, neatly written in a large scrawl on five sheets of paper. Gail scanned the list quickly, feeling slightly guilty for turning off her mobile all day. Forget justification; work simply didn't stop. She resigned herself to spending Saturday in the office. So much for taking a day off.

Gu Kwun began asking, when could he go to Ocean Park with

Auntie You Fun, and did Mummy have Auntie's telephone number. She assured him she did, and he demanded, again, was she sure, absolutely sure. And then, just as she had managed to calm him down, her mother started up again.

"Gail, quickly, ask A-Yi if Uncle Mark's been here while we were out. Go right now." A-Yi had lived downstairs from them when Gail had been a girl.

Conchita looked at her mistress as if to say, shall I go and pretend to check for you ma'am, and Gu Kwun ran over to his grandmother, gripping her arm hard saying, "*Pohpo,* please don't *daamsam,* it's all going to be okay," the way Gail had taught him and he looked at his mother, searching her eyes for approval at his being such a good, responsible boy.

Gail took a deep breath. "Mother, I'm tired . . ."

Her mother didn't wait. "Go NOW," her voice raised to a feverish pitch, something that hadn't happened for several months.

"Mom, please." As hard as she tried to control it, her own voice was rising. She could feel it, the frightening temper she fought to suppress.

"It's all your fault Gail if Uncle Mark doesn't come. You know that, don't you? It's all your fault. You drove him away this summer."

"That wasn't Mark. It was Gordie, Mark's son."

"You lie. Uncle Mark has no son. All your fault. Always all your fault." Her voice descended to a grumbling murmur.

And then, Gail exploded. "Mom! Uncle Mark is never coming back. My father's dead." Raising her hand, she wiped the tears from her cheek. "He's not my Uncle Mark, he's my father. Say it. My father!" Her body was shaking as she raised both arms, both fists. Gu Kwun had run to Conchita at the sound of his mother's scream, and was hiding his face against her body. Gail's mother had retreated into a chair, cowering under her daughter's wrath. Gail struggled to control herself. A rational voice told her to stop now, before she caused irreparable harm. But another voice, from where she didn't know, told her this family deserved the pain she unleashed on them, because she had suffered more than all of them put together.

That other voice screamed in her head: *this life wasn't hers!*

She wasn't Gail Szeto, the *jaahpjung* daughter of the former Flying Tigers pilot, the girl who lied all through childhood about a dead American father, brother of "Uncle" Mark Ashberry, the father who already had a wife and family in America. The girl whose mother worked in a dance hall, as a "taxi girl" for the triads. The girl who had no family she dared to acknowledge.

Miscellaneous, assorted species. *Jaahpjung.* Not like anyone else, never belonging inside the species, at least, not the species as defined by the *respectable,* family-obsessed Hong Kong *yan,* the "real Chinese," the only "humans" who counted.

In her dreams as a child, she lived outside the Great Wall, where she would knock and knock at the door to the Wall, but no one would ever let her in.

Into the uneasy silence around them, a loud buzz shattered the voice in Gail's head. The family looked around, each one wondering at the noise. And then Conchita exclaimed, "oh, the alarm clock, I forgot!" and rushed to her bedroom to turn it off. Gail's mother stood up, went into her bedroom and locked the door. Gu Kwun tentatively eyed his mother. Conchita had returned and put her arms around him, saying softly to Gail, "ma'am, I take him to his bath now, okay?"

The shaking subsided. Gail mentally kicked aside the shards of her temper. She took a deep, deep breath, gulping the air, swallowing droughts of oxygen. The earlier migraine was gone. Her arms relaxed and hung at her side. She looked at her maid, whose hand her son clutched timorously. "Yes, Conchita," she said. "Okay."

Michael was out when Andanna got home. She didn't care. The flat was quieter without him around to nag her into cleaning up. She kicked off her shoes into a corner of the living room. There, let him complain about that.

She flopped contentedly onto the sofa.

What was it Gail said? That patience, discipline and belief in herself would get her wherever she wanted to go. Oh, and self control. She was such a kind woman. Andanna didn't understand why her cousin Sylvie found Gail such a difficult boss to work for. She felt slightly guilty about lying to her, because she had slept with Tai Jai one more time, although she wouldn't dream of admitting that to a soul. So the lie to Gail didn't really count.

She got up and opened two of the windows. The sky was a superb red glow. The air had cooled. What time was it? She pulled out her notebook to search for Albert Ho's mobile number. He had given it to her the last time she'd run into him. If she persisted, she was sure he'd agree to fund a CD for her, and then Michael would shut up about his stupid jazz. Didn't Tai Jai say she could be a Canto-pop star if she wanted? Of course she could. It was better than doing what she did now.

Albert's number, where was it? She leafed through the pages, locating it at last. As she punched the number, Andanna thought that she really must get out to the New Territories more often. Tai Jai claimed he was going to buy a motorcycle. Maybe she could get him to take her.

JANUARY 1996

12

New Year's day was not cold. Vince awoke, fully dressed, to a sore throat, a hangover and a strange bed. He had no memory of getting to this place and no idea whose it was. The last thing he remembered was shouting at Didi over the phone. Something about Joe. Something about how he would kill this motherfucker, the one who had usurped his place, his rights. His manhood.

Woman beside him. Stark naked. English? Another party girl. He covered her with the sheet and looked around for the bathroom. Ten minutes later, showered and smelling less like a distillery, he worked his way out of the enormous apartment and onto the streets.

All the buildings in the neighborhood were low rise, mostly houses. There were trees on the street. That's right, he *wasn't* in Hong Kong. Hand shot to his jacket's inner pocket. Passport intact. What guardian angel watched over him? A woman surely, who insisted he check in his equipment at the airport yesterday evening, who reminded him that enduring this emotional marathon was for the good of his little angel, his precious Katy, the one reason life was still worth living.

The apartment from which he emerged had been on the second floor of a walkup. He considered, again, its size. At least twenty five hundred feet of solid concrete. At least. That was just the L-shape of the living and dining room. Even the bedroom and bathroom had been larger than most apartments. Unbelievable, so much space on this tiny, island city.

The scene with Colleen. Why had he even bothered to call her, to see her, hanging on an extra day after his job instead of going back to Hong Kong and getting drunk there instead? After the Shanghai betrayal he should have known — the woman lies, stay away. How like a canary-fed cat she'd been that night. Her "fruit-bat man." Such nerve. But the promise of? Lust led his deadly parade.

Yesterday afternoon, though, she'd lost her cool. Taken him completely by surprise. Begun with tearful desperation that he couldn't leave, mustn't leave, that only he could "rescue" her out of her awful marital prison here in Singapore. Much more than he ever bargained for, especially after Shanghai. So he left her, unceremoniously, in that Chinatown hotel room, afraid of her unexpected demands, only hours after losing his cool with Didi.

Head pounded a steady rhythm of rock and shouting laughter.

A south east Asian morning. Oven heat, humid sea breezes, the menace of mosquitoes. No people anywhere. Major thoroughfare ahead, because he heard and saw the occasional car speed past. Taxi must eventually appear. Felt for his wallet. Singapore currency? Yes. The tickle in his throat subsided to background annoyance, as did the headache. Piece of cake compared to getting beat up in Brooklyn, circa the sixties and early seventies. Physical trauma no problem. Women, on the other hand.

Resolution number one for 1996: *no more women.*

Andanna's mother had stared at her, surprised, when she showed up back home on New Year's Eve.

"But your father and I are going to the dinner dance with your uncle. We don't have a place for you."

She sat at the kitchen table while her mother stood, elegantly gowned, manipulating a stubborn earring. "Go ahead, enjoy yourself."

Her mother frowned. "The maid's off. There's nothing to eat."

"Stop worrying about me. There's plenty. We're stocked for World War III."

"Aren't you going to parties with your friends, or to Lan Kwai Fong?" Andanna rolled her eyes.

"You Fun, stop it. You know I hate it when you look like that. It's so . . . unladylike."

Her father's voice, tinged with impatience, summoned her mother. "Well, if you're sure you'll be all right."

"Mother, I'm already an adult, remember?" Andanna flicked her palm up and waved a short "bye bye" mouthing the words with a playful smile. Giving her a last, worried frown, her mother disappeared into the evening.

Thank goodness that was over. She had originally planned to come back after they'd gone, but changed her mind because she was afraid the security combination might have been altered. Good timing though, catching them on the fly, because then there wouldn't have to be too many explanations. She got up and opened a few cabinets, rooting around for a packet of instant noodles. Extracting a Diet Coke from the fridge, she popped it and drank.

This was all Michael's fault. It had been Berklee this, Berklee that, Berklee everything, right down to a premature investigation into apartments long distance. She wasn't sure she wanted to go to Boston with him. She was tired of his jazz life. It was all so pointless, running around Lan Kwai Fong and Tsimshatsui every night, trying to be cool; putting up with idiotic hotel managers who told her to wear sexier clothes for her piano lounge gigs which paid peanuts because she was only a local musician; watching drunk *gwailoes* slobbering over her tits, leaning over the piano to get a better look. It was humiliating. Michael had been furious when she had blown off her last gig, the one he worked so hard to get for her. But what did he expect?

After more than three years back, life with Michael wasn't cool anymore. It was a pain being broke, but even more of a pain trying to care about money. Also, hanging around all those foreign musician friends of his was boring. All they wanted to do was rehearse. Worst of all, it was hard pretending to care about singing jazz when she simply didn't, even if the truth would break Michael's heart.

She wandered into the living room, picked up a fashion magazine and flipped through it. Mother looked beautiful tonight. She had the right color and look for this season, and would, as usual, outclass the rest of the female relatives. Andanna knew all the aunts were jealous of Mother which was why they were so catty. Perhaps her mother hadn't come from as rich a background as them, or as educated. But she still had the figure to wear fashionable clothes well, and the ability to select the right jewelry and accessories to match an outfit, never appearing overdone or garish, the latter being a specialty of her cousin Sylvie's mom. It was a natural elegance no amount of money or breeding could buy.

She switched on the television. The annual moronic commentary about highlights of the year. Why did these commentators bother? Did they really think they were saying anything new? News flashback to Lan Kwai Fong three years ago, her first new year's eve back. The mad melee. Andanna flicked off the image.

It was better to forget. She had been there, among the mob that surged down the narrow streets of the club scene in Central. Everyone went. It was cool to get drunk on champagne and kiss strangers, even foreign ones. Michael became another person when he drank. Looser, more fun, more sexual. He would grab her ass in the middle of the street and kiss her hard on the mouth, shoving his tongue in. He was usually such a pussycat, treating her as if she were porcelain, reserving all his passion for music.

She hadn't wanted to gig that evening and he had humored her. His musician friends said they were crazy. Fees doubled and tripled on New Year's Eve. Some musicians played three or even four gigs within a twenty-four hour period, beginning with an afternoon function, moving onto the cocktail hour followed by a dinner cum dance that peaked at midnight with "Auld Lang Syne," and then brunch on January 1st, plus dinner if they hadn't collapsed from exhaustion. The lucky ones made the same money at one party in a private home or club that cycled into dawn. Foreign players, especially, went nuts for this night, bidding themselves out months in advance, negotiating for the highest bidder.

Instead, they had joined the party crowd at the Fong.

Round midnight, the human wave engulfed them. They rolled forward in one gigantic surf. She could feel people above her, below her, encircling her, clutching at her body and limbs from all sides as she struggled to free herself. *Let me go I'm standing on people I'm going to crush them* a man shouted. That was when Andanna panicked, and she screamed at the people around her to let go off her arms, let go off her legs.

I'm going to die!

The thought rang in her head as tears poured down her face. But try as she would, she couldn't articulate it, and the only words that tumbled from her mouth were to let her go. Her pleas fell on the ears of unheeding folk who continued to cling and clutch at her and each other.

I'm going to die.

She felt herself being dragged down into the depths of the mob, and suddenly, the illuminated night disappeared and only darkness surrounded her. Andanna closed her eyes.

And then, an arm grabbed her waist and she heard Michael's voice shouting her name. Michael, the one person who could rescue her from this madness, the one person she could count on during the years in Vancouver when all she wanted was to come home, knowing he was waiting, would wait, forever if he had to. His grip, like a manacle, as he pulled her to her feet. *Hang tight Andi* — ever since the beginning it had been "Andi" — *we're going to jump.* With a massive surge of effort, he had pulled them out of the center of the wave, and they both tumbled simultaneously, falling off the edge of this universe towards an empty space on Wo On Lane, a side street, where the human current was just slightly less intense.

Her parents mouthed the conventional nonsense about *gwailo* drunkenness getting out of hand. She hadn't told them, hadn't dared, that she had been part of it, except to say she'd been round earlier and left before the trouble started. A few days later, she moved in with Michael.

Better to forget. Even Michael said, forget, let it pass. But he'd get drunk and continued to plunge back into the Fong, while she remembered, nightmares recurring, even now, and would wake up, trembling. Twenty-one Hong Kong people died that night, trampled to death by the crowd. For what? At least on the Long March, they died for a cause.

Tonight, she was blowing off their gig. These pop music parties were the only times Michael invited her to play piano with his band, although never to sing. He would feel that abandonment more keenly than her threat, this afternoon, to break up.

There were four messages from Colleen when Vince returned, spaced at half hour intervals, timed before he could possibly have arrived back in Hong Kong.

"Vince, how dare you leave me like that. Don't bother me again." His sentiments exactly. "I didn't mean that, I was just upset. I'll call later." No way he'd answer his phone tonight. "You owe me a blow job." Like hell he did. He wasn't falling for her phone sex again. "Please call me, anytime. It doesn't matter if he's home." Whimpering women were surpassed only by whimpering men on top of his list of who to avoid.

He erased the messages. The woman was nuts. As if it wasn't enough that his first wife had been crazy . . . long buried memories emerged like old photographs that captured only part of the story.

Vince lit a cigarette and set a kettle to boil. Coffee, even instant, would do. He contemplated a beer to subdue the hangover. Nothing in the fridge. He suddenly missed Didi, who kept the fridge stocked, the kitchen in order, his clothes laundered and the home cleaned. Had it ever been love? Or had she just been doing her job, because he had fathered her child?

A video-memory pulled him back to Ai-Lin, to the day she disappeared from his life.

He had come back from a family dinner. She had refused to attend, and by then, he had given up trying to hold their life together. Things had been tentative for a long time, and each time they tried to talk or make love, they would end up arguing and she would cower before him begging, *stop yelling at me, please stop yelling at me,* and he would slam his way out of the house, sometimes to call or see his therapist Jim, sometimes just to be apart from her.

Her absent things told all. The apartment was a tomb. But what had cowed him, had zapped any remaining anger, was the silence. No more crazy accusations, no more whines of despair, no more self defeating utterances from the woman who told him he was too strong for her, too much for her, too everything for her.

An instance of peace.

You never stopped loving her, did you? Didi's pained voice, after he'd forgotten their third wedding anniversary, left her sitting at the restaurant alone, waiting, while he closeted himself in his darkroom, having switched off the ringer on the phone. Never forgot a single anniversary with Ai-Lin, and up till now, on that day each year, some spark, still.

The kettle's whistle shrieked, a banshee-like wail cutting into the soundtrack. Pause. Rewind with the "record" light on, blanking the tape for the present. Made coffee. Watery bitterness. Instant never the real thing, no matter what the ads promised.

He let the phone ring until the machine answered. His brother's voice, and he grabbed the receiver. "Sorry about that."

"Oh, what? You avoiding someone?"

Not the kept brother, no matter how well he called it. Owed no explanation. "Who would I need to avoid? What's up?"

"Just wanted to wish you happy new year."

"Same to you."

Vince heard the interim hesitation and anticipated what came next.

"We were wondering if you'd like to come over for dinner tonight. Nothing fancy, just a meal at home."

Should surprise him and accept, continuing Don's unrelenting self torture. Cigarette almost out, it caught his finger in a burn, and he dropped it. Swooping down to get it, he bumped his head on the edge of the desk. Swore.

Don said. "Hey, it's not that bad."

"Sorry, wasn't you. Look, forget it, okay Don? I'm kinda hungover actually."

Another silence, and then. "Again?"

If he refused to reply, Don would eventually pipe up. Vince gave him a full minute, and finally, heard his brother snap, "aren't you too old for this?" before mumbling something about "have a nice whatever," and hung up.

Stop it, stop it! Don in tears from somewhere in their childhood when Vince would maintain a stony-cold silence, sometimes for hours, refusing to play with his brother because of some quarrel, the cause of which even he might have forgotten.

Vince stared out at the wide angled expanse of harbor and light. Afternoon glare illuminated the sky. Perhaps he did drive people crazy. Perhaps women went mad through a relationship with him because of some flaw he couldn't control. Perhaps the contact alone was enough, made them run away, the way both his wives had.

His head throbbed from the bump and alcohol. He nursed the coffee cup as the brown liquid turned lukewarm. Resolution number two. Hold the booze.

Vince gazed at the rapid end to the day, watching the sun slide down its path into the beginnings of dusk. Today was now, was the only place he knew. The one thing to control was this present life. Only then could past lives blur.

Abandoned the coffee.

Andanna felt a hand shaking her.

"You Fun," her mother's voice in her ear. "You fell asleep in front of the TV."

She turned over, vestiges of a dream rimmed the edge of consciousness. Her body was heavy.

"Come on, go to your bedroom. You'll sleep better there."

She sat up reluctantly. Along the fringe of slumber, Tai Jai leered, his mouth in an "O," whispering, "d'you want more?" She shook off the dream and dragged herself towards the bedroom, her mother following. "Never mind, Mother, I can go myself." But her mother did not step away and led her to her room where she pulled the covers off the neatly made bed. "It's a little chilly, You Fun," she said, opening the closet and extracting a blanket. "You'll need this."

Through the blur, Andanna managed to undress, found her night-gown where it had always been kept under her pillow, dragged it on and climbed into bed. Her mother drew the covers over her, saying, "don't worry, You Fun, if you and your boyfriend aren't getting along. There'll always be others. Besides, you're home now," and she nodded sleepily, barely hearing her mother's words.

She sank into the pillow, in the lingering wake of her mother's perfume. Paloma Picasso. The bed was soft and comfortable, encasing her in its safety. Her mother was closing the door. It was good to be home. It was so good to be home.

As she drifted off, a thought crept around the last of her wakefulness. What made her mother talk about a boyfriend? Surely she didn't know? But the thought crept away as quietly as it first came, and she slept soundly, peacefully, into the morning of the new year.

13

Gail ran through, again, the list of things she had to pack for their Singapore visit at the Leyland-Tang's during the Chinese New Year break. It was late this year, almost at the end of February. Gu Kwun was excited. He liked the idea of spending a winter holiday on board a boat in the sun.

Her office was quiet today. The long holidays were hard to take in Hong Kong. People fled the city, especially expatriates. If she could, she would do the same. Until her ex left her, the "crossing of the year" had been a compulsory family occasion. Gail had suffered her way through those for her husband's and Gu Kwun's sake. Now, he didn't even bother to call, let alone visit his son with a *laisee* packet of money unless she insisted. How could he? All for that woman.

When Kwok Po called with the invitation, she had jumped at it. Every year, her mother visited the dance hall "girls," with whom she could stay till the holidays were over. One less worry.

Besides, her mother only cared about Christmas.

Gail's mother had cried in despair every Christmas of her girlhood because they couldn't celebrate the way she wanted — as a family with Mark. This sorrow became tedious, and Gail preferred partying with friends as soon as she was old enough to go out alone. In the U.S., she had come to enjoy Christmas, although never as much as Chinese New Year because those childhood memories were at least neutral, if not happy.

With Gu Kwun at International, however, celebrating Christmas was a must so that he wouldn't feel left out among his multinational classmates. Her mother luxuriated in these celebrations, enjoying her presents as much as Gu Kwun did his.

This morning, when she was preparing her son for school, he had asked if Auntie Colleen would make turnip cake.

"But you don't like it, sweetheart," she had replied, slightly puzzled.

"Yes I do."

She knew better than to contradict when he got into these moods. "Well, maybe she might, but you know Auntie Colleen doesn't cook."

"Will she put out melon seeds and ice candy?"

"Perhaps."

"Mummy, call her and tell her she must." His voice was getting excitable, slightly irritable, the way it did when something tugged at him and he couldn't express what he wanted.

"Take it easy. What's the matter?"

"You have to teach Auntie Colleen if she doesn't know how to do things properly."

"Gu Kwun, we're going to be guests. Of course Auntie Colleen knows how to do things properly. She's very clever."

"But she's not Chinese. She can't know." He pouted and stamped his foot in anger.

"Now stop that this instance. What a silly thing to say."

Conchita came to him and he hugged her leg, turning his face against it. Gail groaned. Why did he have to pick this morning to act up, when she had an early meeting and was in a rush? She was about to say something, but Conchita shook her head.

"It's okay, ma'am, I take him now." And Conchita bundled him off out the door.

The morning's scene replayed itself. The trouble with her maid was that she coddled Gu Kwun, instead of making him behave. It bothered her that Conchita sometimes seemed to have better control over him than she did.

But she dismissed her concern for the moment. Today, she had a lunch date to keep.

At the restaurant, Gail waited eagerly, anticipating her guest's arrival. Just a casual lunch, this was hardly a "date." It had been a long time, though, that she'd had a non-business lunch with anyone, especially a man. Even seeing old school friends invariably degenerated into business gossip and connections.

"Sorry, job ran overtime."

She waved away Vince's apologies. "Quite all right. I just got here myself," which wasn't exactly true because she had begun to get anxious, wondering if he'd stood her up. Although she'd never admit that to a soul, since as far as she knew, he might not be interested, not that she was thinking in those terms but . . . "Take your time. Would you like something to drink?"

He glanced around the peculiar surroundings. Zebra striped chairs. Reds and purples and greens in a garish — post modern? — interior. He lived next door to *this?* "A beer would be nice. Thirsty, you know."

"Of course," she signaled the waitress, disappointed. He hadn't seemed like one of *those* who drank at lunchtime.

"It's like a mild furnace out there. Is it really February?"

She smiled. "Afraid so."

He wondered. Why was he here? Long hiatus and then her call. Almost forgotten, glad she'd called. But wary, just a bit.

They digested the menus. Ritual formality, an easy conversational gap. Undemanding.

He glanced up over his menu. "Hong Kong chic?"

"*Nouveau* Asian actually. It's quite fashionable." She proceeded to tell him, then, about an article she'd recently read describing this new fashion in Asian cuisine. He seemed so interested, so curious about the mix of spices and herbs that defied tradition. Admitted he liked to cook, although "too difficult here" because kitchens were "microscopic." She wondered how he lived — his "bachelor hole" was how he'd referred to his place when she'd called — in the heart of the city, a quick taxi ride away from everything, right here in Causeway Bay. His new card, handed over almost immediately after he was seated — how Hong Kong he was — indicated an address next door to this, the Excelsior, where they were on the top floor, at TOTTS.

"How's your little girl?"

His expression warmed her. No "face," put on for the benefit of a stranger, it was unadulterated happiness. "I'm going to see her right after Chinese New Year."

"Why don't you go during the holidays? Isn't that the best time?"

"The fares go down after, real low."

Did they? But then, she always flew business class, although it wouldn't do to say so under the circumstances. "Oh, naturally."

"So why are we having lunch?"

Again, his manner made her feel that he thought she had work for him, which she didn't. The chit chat hadn't sat well. Yet she refused to believe, not after the first time when an intimacy had sprung up over shared photographs of their children. "Just to catch up." She affected a breezy air.

"What about? We hardly know each other."

"Well, I thought we might get to know each other better this way." There, she'd said it and invisibly, under the face, the one that maintained a socially safe, unperturbed expression, she blushed.

He looked embarrassed. "Listen, I . . ."

A quick glance out the window, fighting her own embarrassment. "Look it's quite all right if you'd rather not. I just thought . . ."

Shit. Not used to straightforward friendliness. Always looking for hidden motives, since Colleen. "I'm sorry, I didn't mean to be rude. It is very good of you to have called, to have bothered I mean. People in Hong Kong don't, generally."

Her relief was apparent. "No, they don't."

It was almost three when she finally got the check. At the exit, she headed for the taxi rank.

"My turn next," he said. "Maybe dinner, okay?"

He thought he saw a resurgence of confidence in her expression. "Maybe." She winked at him when she said goodbye.

Perhaps she just wasn't going about this right, Gail decided, as she stepped into the taxi. After all, she'd never dated a Caucasian guy. Were there rules to this that she'd violated somehow? She leaned back in the seat. What had he said, that she didn't "give away" much? Just because he talked about all that personal stuff didn't mean she had to immediately follow suit, did it? People talked about what they felt comfortable talking about. She answered all his questions. What more did he expect? Wasn't it enough that she'd called, invited him out, taken so much time for the meal, even paid for lunch? How much of her face was she supposed to give? And she used to think Chinese men were difficult.

A headache started as she got out of the taxi at her office.

She was faced right away with the consequences of her late return. *He's called three times,* Ariadne told her nervously, meaning the boss who was in New York. Why the heck didn't he get some sleep, she wondered, as she rang his hotel. And of all days, he would pick this one to be looking for her.

Right after the call with her boss, which had been difficult because he was grumpy and tired, the new junior analyst came in and tendered his resignation. He had been on the job four months. What's the matter, she wanted to say, couldn't you hack it, because he wasn't the most competent although he thought he knew it all. But the timing was bad because she was going away and didn't need to be short staffed. Of course, he was perfectly within his rights to give a week's notice since he'd worked under half a year and therefore had no bonus to sacrifice.

He'd want to take as much time off during the public holidays before starting his new job . . . all these details raced through her mind as she nodded indifferently and dismissed him. There was nothing to say. These things happened, and not all new hires worked out. But she was annoyed, nonetheless.

Before she knew it, it was four and her secretary announced her maid was on the line. Gail frowned. Now what? Where was Gu Kwun?

"He's asleep, ma'am, so I didn't want to wake him for the daily call."

"Why is he asleep? You know he'll be wide awake too late now and won't want to get to bed tonight on time."

"I don't know, ma'am."

Ordinarily, she would have let it go. Conchita did her best, and sometimes, her son could be troublesome. But her irritation wouldn't subside. "Wake him up."

"Please ma'am, I don't think that's a good idea. He's a little bit upset."

"At what?" she snapped. No Filipino domestic was going to tell her how to raise her own son.

"Just about this morning. He wants to see his aunt, you know."

Gail knew, of course she knew. The morning's dramatics had been all about his father, and their annual visits to his father's sister. Her husband's very Hong Kong family kept up all the traditions, and Gu Kwun loved visiting this aunt who turned her home into a child's paradise every new year's. But there was no way she would give in to that family now, not with her ex behaving the way he was. Why should she call, why should she make an effort to stay connected to his family if he didn't even care about his son?

"Yes, of course I'm aware," she snapped. Surely her maid didn't think she didn't know what was going on.

"He'll be okay tomorrow, ma'am."

From the doorway, Ariadne was gesturing that she was late for a meeting. Gail signaled that she would be there momentarily. "Oh, all right, but Conchita, you must not let this happen too often. I don't want Gu Kwun behaving so childishly. He has to learn that he can't always get his way."

"Yes, ma'am. Okay. But he is still only a child." It sounded like Conchita put down the receiver more roughly than necessary.

This simply wasn't her day. Gail picked up her meeting files and rushed towards the conference room. In her hurry, she banged her leg hard against the side of her desk, nicking her nylon in the process. She felt the run unravel down her leg. This was definitely not her day.

Vince headed out into the sun, towards the MTR.

Expensive lunch.

Funny woman. Lukewarm and cold, never hot. Can't cock tease, though she'd like to. Like a Chinese Mary Tyler Moore with a Boston accent. Hedged on her background, thought he didn't pick up. Admitted to an American father, so why the Chinese last name? Not her husband's, ex-husband. Adamant about the "ex."

Different. Might be interesting. Probably trouble. Way too rich for his blood.

The MTR station looked different, as if he were seeing it for the first time. People river, swelling to a sea as rush hour approached. Lately, the city offered new angles. Unvisited shapes and sights forming. Why now? Photographs? Not another Hong Kong coffee table photo book. His was merely a temporary perspective, without meaning or depth. Just another visitor passing time.

February 26 booked. To New York. Deanna would have papers all ready. Quick work. Woman was serious; Joe virtually moved in. During the last call, he apologized for the New Year's Eve blow up. That was the call Katy told him that Joe took her to see the "City Radio" for Christmas.

Time to see Katy. Reclaim fatherhood.

Katydid, Katydid, Katydid. Daddy games. Used to make her laugh.

He stepped into the train. Don's office four stops away at Jordan. His brother might as well have remained in Kowloon, near his office, but Don always was a hopeless snob. Ai-Lin? Didn't expect her to turn into one. That woman was dead serious these days. Didn't women laugh anymore?

Don had said something about a job. More handouts. No difference now. Just do right by Katy. Better than being back home, in the same time zone as Didi and Joe. *Bastard.* Treated him like a friend, paid him good money to redo the bathroom, bought him beers at the local. And then he turns around and steals the wife.

Don still wary. So what if he and Ai-Lin? They happened afterwards, years after the divorce. Ancient history. Better to forget. Why the self torture? Months of therapy, when Ai-Lin withdrew, went "crazy" and fled to Cincinnati. Didn't do him any good. As Jim used to say, *your problem, not hers. Deal with it.* Now again with Didi it was his problem. Always his problem.

The train doors closed.

"So you seeing anyone?" Don, meaning well, playing caretaker.

"No."

"Couldn't we introduce . . ."

"No." Too sharply. "Leave it, will you?"

Miffed, like when Vince got the bicycle first because he was older, until he took him for a ride. Always had to share everything, this kid, even pain.

"Just being helpful. It's a lonely town. The nice women like to be introduced. I know. I've been through it."

"You're doing pretty well, I thought." Watch him blush. Papa used to say they could have been twins except for Don's red face.

Sheepish, almost hang dog. "Vince, I love Ai-Lin very much. We're good for each other."

"Yes, you are." Big brother again bestowing approval, and Don happy. Always did need some kind of looking after, this kid. At forty one, though, he wasn't a kid anymore.

Don's office was on Cox Road in a bachelor pad, the one his boss' wife didn't know about. Overlooking the Kowloon Cricket Club and its green expanse. Oasis. No high rises around colonial wickets. In Hong Kong, indoor space defined the city. Home wasn't a retreat. All space was shared, with family, friends, domestic help for those who had and aspired to have. Or in Don's case, the shared office. The most private space a beeper or cell phone. Last week, a young ad executive, showing off to Vince his new hand phone, his new account, said. *Personal Space: message in the medium. It'll take over Hong Kong like wildfire. A bigger takeover than '97.*

"So," Vince continued. "What's the job?"

A record, Don called it. A photographic diary of development construction for his boss. Easy money.

"It's not very exciting, but it'll pay. And he'd rather keep it in the family so he's happy for me to get you to do it."

"Didn't say I'd do it yet."

"Come on, Vince, what have you got to lose? It's money. What's the matter? You too good for this now that you're working for Albert Ho?"

Jealous perhaps? Don hadn't been invited to the Shanghai bash, but neither had most of Hong Kong. It mattered to Don, mostly because Vince got to go, yet treated his privileged attendance as something of a joke. Truthfully, it had been sort of fun around the stars, because Albert's frivolous pursuits had style. "I did one job for him."

"It's money," Don repeated.

"So is prostitution." Slipped out, that. Don the designer, the one with the high "artistic" standards, while all Vince ever saw himself as was someone who made a living taking photographs to someone else's brief. Don, on his graduation night, dragged Vince all over Chicago saying look at this building, and this one, don't they all speak to you? Drunk on architecture and brotherly love. Yet now? Living in a city devoid of shape, where buildings sprang up like the cyclical rice harvest and beauty, demolished daily. Managing turnkey projects at breakneck speed in Guangzhou and Shanghai, sacrificing god knows what, for more money than he'd ever seen in his life. Benefiting from the overseas tax allowance as well. Low US taxes meant more money to jet off on expensive holidays. Don had become a global yuppie. And his justification — *but that's the future, Vince, and it's what China needs.*

He wasn't even fazed by Vince's comment. "Think of Katy's next birthday. She'll love you for it," Don said.

Gail's office was dead. Outside, it was dark. This day hadn't ended soon enough for her. She tossed the last of her paperwork onto her out tray. Done at last, she sat back, tired. It was almost nine. Gu Kwun would be in bed by the time she got home.

Night was the most peaceful time imaginable.

She leafed through the *South China Morning Post.* Not much news today, not that this paper ever had anything much worth reading, except the business pages. One story caught her attention. Woman doctor, aged 32, found dead at home in bed with her six year old. A suicide. She had injected her son first with the lethal dose, and then killed herself. Apparently, she and her husband divorced two years earlier. They had met a few days prior and agreed to send their son to boarding school in England. He said she behaved normally and their conversation had been amiable. No one saw this coming. Her colleagues said she was a pleasant person, but not very talkative. All she left behind was an apology to her mother, saying she could no longer cope with despair.

Gail shuddered. She slid a Chopin album into her CD-ROM drive. Nocturnes filled the silence.

Pulling a box of Pop-Pans out of her drawer, she began eating one after another.

When she was a teenager, her mother wouldn't let her eat Pop-Pans. Mom said they were greasy, and insisted she eat only imported biscuits and crackers. But Gail hadn't liked the sweet, creamy fillings of the English biscuits, and found crackers too dry. So she had saved her allowance and bought her own boxes of Pop-Pans, produced by the local Garden Bakery, and hidden them in her schoolbag, eating them only when she was out of the house. Even now, when her mother wouldn't care anymore, Gail didn't keep any at home.

The crunch of spring onion and sesame savored her tongue. Pop-Pans were her worst vice. Her secretary knew to keep them in stock. This was better than dinner. It freed her, liberated her in a way that nothing else, not alcohol, the occasional cigarette, or even sex could.

Mom had been behaving well since last fall.

Ever since her outburst, Gail felt guilty, ashamed of the way she had hurt her mother and frightened Gu Kwun. What could she say though? "Uncle" Mark was not something she could talk about easily with her mother.

As a child, even after knowing that her family was not like other families, and that Mark was really her father, she obliged her mother by calling him "Uncle." Whenever he came, he would hand her a *laisee* packet. When Mark was in town, her mother didn't go to the dance hall, and spent all her time with him. The year Gail finished Lower 6, her father died. His will included a sizeable fund for her education, and finally acknowledged her birthright, giving her both U.S. citizenship and the right to use his name. She took the first but not the second.

The problem was her self-centered mother. There, that was the truth, in all its naked ugliness.

The first time Gail recognized this, she had been about eight.

Mark was visiting that evening. Her mother had been fussing, the way she always did on those occasions, and Gail was brushing her hair. Your hair is beautiful, Mom, just like you, she remembered saying, to which her mother replied, *I already have white hairs because of you.*

Gail had asked if she could come along for dinner. Just this once, she had pleaded with her mother. She didn't know why it mattered that day, why she wanted to be there with the two of them. Her father seldom talked to her, reserving most of his time and attention for her mother.

Her mother had looked at her strangely, so strangely that Gail had been scared. Stop looking at me like that, she said, you look like a ghost. *You needn't think you can ever win Mark's affections,* her mother declared. *I'm the only Chinese girl he'll ever love,* and with that, she turned away and continued to dress.

She never saw her father that night. During subsequent visits, he came to their home less and less. Years later, she realized her mother had deliberately gotten pregnant, thinking Mark would divorce his wife and marry her, only to have the scheme backfire. .

Gail brushed the crumbs off her desk and resealed the Pop-Pan package. None of this should matter, not now, which was why she felt bad about her outburst. Obviously, she still cared, perhaps too much, that she was and would always be an unwanted child. Her parents had done the right things for her, giving her the best education and all the opportunities in the world. The will hadn't surprised her mother, who had accepted the concubine's role but insisted on her child's rights. As her ex used to say, it was a kind of love, demonstrated through sacrifice, perhaps the only kind they knew how to give. Her life was much better than her mother's. Even Gordie treated her as family, defying his own mother's wishes. And she had Gu Kwun.

She was about to leave, but suddenly remembered — she ought to call Kwok Po and Colleen tonight to confirm details, because they would be leaving for a few days to Jakarta in the morning. Flipping through her Rolodex, she located the number and was about to find her personal calling card, but stopped. What still nagged was her boss yelling that afternoon, saying she would have to go to New York right after her vacation whether she liked it or not. Yes, she'd go, because it was her job, despite the short notice and the chaos it would create in her schedule and life. Yes, he was in a foul mood because of the politics at headquarters and could almost be forgiven for his surly manner. But he still had pissed her off.

Right now, her one little act of vengeance would be to make this call at her company's expense. She punched in her office's international long distance code and the Singapore number.

The phone rang. Gail thought about the dead woman in the news. Despair was an awful thing. It was her mother's chronic condition. But the one thing she had learned from years of listening to her mother's complaints was that sometimes, bitching, like revenge, could keep you going no matter how bad life got.

Chopin's nocturnes soothed. Tonight was turning into a remedy for this day.

She heard the answering click.

14

Colleen forced as polite a tone as she could muster. Gail's voice on the phone grated. For over a month, she'd listened to her husband go on about Gail — reminiscing about their Harvard days, praising Gail for her intelligence and capability in an industry where she was one of the few, senior, Asian, women executives, going on *ad nauseum* about her "courage" as a single mother who balanced parenting and a career, especially in Hong Kong where divorce was not yet as common as in the States. What the hell was so courageous, Colleen wondered, about a woman who couldn't hang onto her husband and therefore have to support herself? Kwok Po's own mother would have declared likewise.

"It's so good of you and Kwok Po to have us," Gail was saying. "Gu Kwun's been real excited. It'll be such a treat for him."

"Oh, it's nothing. We're looking forward to it. So how's the love life these days?" There. That would shut her up. She probably hadn't had sex in years.

"Well, as a matter of fact . . ." and she told Colleen all about what she called her "sort-of date" with Vince.

Afterwards, Colleen wanted to slam the phone down. It was too much, it was all simply too much. How dare he take up with Gail of all people! She dismissed the illogic of her irritation. This anger was new, this . . . jealousy.

She lit a cigarette and slumped onto the sofa. Was she jealous because of Gail, or Vince?

Please call me, anytime. It doesn't matter if he's home. Colleen cringed at the memory of her own voice, whining. What had possessed her? What had made her so clingy, so horribly pathetic? Since New Year's, she hadn't tried to contact him again. Besides, she couldn't risk any more calls; Kwok Po would notice the same, unfamiliar number if it appeared on their bill too many times. Her husband's photographic numeric recall was a small problem in her affairs.

She allowed the deeply inhaled smoke to drift through her. Perhaps . . . perhaps it had to do with loneliness.

Colleen gazed around her palatial home. Well, not palatial, but large and spacious and private. On top of a knoll, surrounded by greenery. Around the base of the sloping grounds, a floral boundary. Birds of paradise, frangipani, hibiscus, bursting colors and fragrances tended to by their Malaysian gardener. Indoors, expensive elegance. Less than one percent of the more than billion people in Asia, even in the world, lived as well as her.

Tonight, Kwok Po was in his study working, again, in preparation for his Jakarta trip in the morning. When had this back-to-back work schedule become the norm? His comment when they'd first moved back to Hong Kong — *Think of the public holidays, Colleen, more than triple what the U.S. has! We'll have tons of time off together.* And it had been like that at first, plus all the travel and social life. Exactly the way she'd always imagined it, the privileged glamour glimpsed as a poor scholar. It had been better, much better than their Boston days when he was just another well paid slave to some investment bank. But sometime in the last five years or so, as the family business had expanded into more of Asia, things began to change and a frenetic, unrelenting pace shoved its way into their lives. This persistent frenzy, this perpetual obsession with work appeared, however, to be right in sync with all of the Asia around them.

She had dealt with the isolation in her own way for some time. Yet now, a nagging discontent, not to be solved by just another discreet affair. The smoke seeped through her, filling her insides with its soothing, sedating shimmer. Lately, even these coffin nails hadn't been able to still the noise in her head.

As a girl, Colleen talked aloud to herself all the time. These were conversations she held with imaginary visitors — she'd always known they existed only because she said they did — and they drowned out the voices of real people who were far less entertaining. It wasn't till she was eight or nine that she finally stopped, because too many remarked it. *It's okay darling, now you'll just have to do it in your head instead.* Her mother thought it was perfectly fine, and taught her to listen to her "visitors," to learn from them, to trust the instincts of her unusual intelligence.

How had her mother endured all those years of her father's selfish abandonment, raising her and Danny virtually on her own with the pittance he contributed from his fortune? Yet she had returned to work, uncomplaining, condoning his irresponsibility.

The thought of her mother alone now, aging before her time, made her sad.

Her maid was gone for the day. It was a pleasure not having a live-in domestic, the way she had in Hong Kong. What if life were more controlled here? Her Hong Kong friends wondered how she could "stand" Singapore to which she always replied, but think of the privacy, the quality of life, the space.

Lately, though, the silence was deafening.

"I am not really unfaithful to him," she said to the empty room.

Yes you are. The voice had begun to sound like Danny's, which meant she couldn't make believe anymore.

"It's the boredom," she continued.

You have a mind full of pleasures if you choose, and even the option for spirituality if you desire. You're a beautiful, sexual woman who's lucky enough to have a husband who adores you.

"But I don't do anything. I can't take anything other than okay photographs, or paint or write or sculpt or play music or dance. I didn't even finish my Ph.D. And I certainly can't earn my own living."

She got up and stood in the middle of the room. The voice had gone silent. It was like this now. Her head was full of noisy questions without answers. Once upon a time, Kwok Po had been her confidante. He never thought her "visitors" unusual, never questioned the way her brain moved, fast, leaping ahead to strategies and conclusions which took others twice as long to approach. He appreciated her immersion in a Chinese education, indulged her penchant for the arts by supporting the causes she chose, attending the charity functions she designated.

He accepted her.

You are my life partner, my only partner, he used to tell her during their most intimate moments. *I'll always love you, no matter what happens to our lives.*

It had been a long time, too long since she'd heard Kwok Po say that.

"I'm a big girl. I don't need him."

Silence.

Because it wasn't true.

When she spoke untruths she was guaranteed silence, and none of her visitors ever came.

The first time Kwok Po kissed her, he bit her lower lip till it bled.

"Damn," he said pulling away from her. "Did I really do that?"

It was at the end of winter, in the season when Boston's mud and ice demanded galoshes. They were on the stoop outside her apartment building after their first date. Colleen had been standing on the toes of her boots to reach him, and slipped. "It's nothing." She sucked in her lip to stanch the blood. "It was because I moved suddenly."

"Let me." He leaned over and licked her wound.

His tongue caressed first her lip, then her neck, and finally her ear. He had a scar on his tongue from a childhood accident. It was a long scar, she realized, when she touched its rough surface some weeks later.

But that first intimacy, the moment she felt his uneven tongue, had reached her in a way she couldn't explain.

He had just turned thirty three when they started dating. Four years prior, the United States formally opened relations with China. Kwok Po talked incessantly about China's future. As an educated overseas Chinese, he felt that responsibility to answer the call to assist the motherland's development.

But is it truly your home country, she'd demanded, *this "motherland" that exiled your father?* There was a huge cultural divide between his real home, Hong Kong, and China. He wasn't Chinese, she reminded him, not the way the people of China today were Chinese. Even she knew the country better than him. After all, she had been there as a scholar only two years earlier, whereas the only China he knew was the one of his parents' memories — he had left as a child with his mother, to follow his father and brothers five years after their flight to Hong Kong— and the rest of his life had been nothing like the world behind the bamboo curtain.

Their relationship was easy and the sex good. He could articulate the unspeakable to her, about his fear of yet need for respect from his father, about his growing understanding that he was smarter, much more capable in business than either of his two older brothers and that his *raison d'etre* was to usurp their positions in the family hierarchy, however difficult that would prove to be.

You really understand this stuff, don't you? He'd stopped suddenly, once, in the middle of a long outpouring, three months into their relationship. It was after lovemaking, at the instance when words could be found for the heart. *You really give a damn about all this Chinese family stuff.* And she had smiled at him, secure in the knowledge that their lives belonged together.

"Be my partner," he asked her after they had been together a little over a year. "I can do it with you."

"Are you proposing marriage?" She wanted to know.

"No."

"Then I can't help you. I won't be your white girl concubine."

He stared hard at her, trying to fight her mentally. His mother lined up several, eligible Chinese women each time he came home.

She read his mind. "It's not going to go away."

"Give me time, *Hong Qi*. Give me time. I don't have the guts."

"You will. And you've got time."

He needed her. She spoke *Putonghua* well; he spoke badly, and she corrected his Cantonese accent. She knew who all the players were, and could recite the recent historical, cultural and political developments of China in her sleep. He was only now becoming fully aware of all their implications. She was, at twenty four, still a student, steeped in ideas and learning, able to argue ideals. He had left behind the urgency of intellectual excitement in favor of the pragmatism of an MBA, and after that, for his apprenticeship in the world of global business and finance.

Most important of all, by listening to him talk about the politics of his family, she knew what it would take to ensure his succession. Kwok Po was at a disadvantage as the youngest even though he was his mother's favorite.

What Colleen wanted, what enticed her, was the entree he could offer into an authentic Chinese life. Very deliberately, calculatedly, in a manner worthy of a future empress dowager, she set out to make him fall deeply, inextricably in love with her.

It worked. They were married two years later.

What she hadn't counted on was how hard she would fall for him.

Kwok Po emerged from his study. He looked fatigued. "Who was that on the phone earlier, Colleen?"

It was "Colleen" these days. Not "darling" or the nickname he coined which for years had been the only name he used, *Hong Qi*, "red flag," because of her hair.

"Your friend Gail." She laid heavy emphasis on the "your."

He brightened. "She's still coming to visit, isn't she?"

"Oh yes. Of course. Why, she wouldn't miss it for the world." But his enthusiasm daunted her, and she found it difficult to contain the sarcasm.

She was standing by the sofa, staring absently at the phone. The cigarette still burned in the ashtray. She saw him glance at it, and knew he wouldn't say a word. If she had insisted, he would have let her smoke, defended her right even to his mother. But she had promised herself: she would remove this ugly, unladylike habit out of his sight, out of the sight of his family. From the beginning it had been her, not him, who demanded perfection.

He came to her, encircled his arms around her waist. "Is everything all right?"

"Why shouldn't it be?" She snapped, too abruptly she realized, as he let go of her.

"Xiang wen hou ni." Just asking — inquiring after your well being.

"Mei you wen ti." No problem.

Kwok Po continued standing next to her, the back of his fingers stroking her arm. "Gail's just a friend," he said in English. "You know that."

She would not look at him. "I know."

"And I love you for being good to my friends. I know it's an imposition on our own holiday."

She bit her lip, forcing back the unwelcome surge of emotion. "Get some sleep. You have an early flight tomorrow," because she was taking a later flight to join him for the weekend's social obligations with his business associates.

"Come to bed with me." He ran his fingers down her back, rubbing his knuckle into that point near the base of her spine, brushing his lips against her neck.

An uncontrollable response. Yet she wouldn't give in, holding herself rigid to his touch.

He headed for the bedroom. At the doorway, he hesitated and watched, waited. But she did not go to him, at least, not right away, not till he came over, took her in his arms and let her cry until she couldn't any longer.

Vince ducked into the spacious, multi-storied bookstore. Reprieve from the afternoon shower. Walking in Singapore was unexpectedly different. In Hong Kong, nothing was as far as anyone said it would be; here, everything was further. The flat, open roads of the city made destinations look deceptively close. And the rains. Jake Wu had warned — you'll need an umbrella every afternoon. Jake, who loved to throw him these last minute assignments, these "can-you-jump-on-a-plane-to-Singapore-today" kind of jobs. Bloated marketing budgets and scrambling urgency meant fat fees. Didn't care. Nature of the hand that fed. Could use the money for his trip to see Katy.

He saw her standing by the cash register. She caught sight of him before he could disappear down an aisle.

Colleen looked perturbed, almost askance at him. "Oh, you." She bit her lip.

"Like a bad penny." Easiest thing to say.

"Not so bad."

Keep things light. "I guess I should have called."

"Not really." She appeared calm, and seemed a little thoughtful. "I don't deserve you."

Was she playing more games? He was wary of engaging her, of prolonging their connection. He should cut short this encounter right now, before it was too late.

She spoke into his silence. "I don't want anything." Then, a touch of mischief crossed her lips. "Scout's honor."

"That's my line." He smiled in spite of his unease.

"So what are you doing in MPH?"

"MPH?"

"This bookstore."

He told her. Their conversation took a peculiarly normal turn. Outside, the rain continued through sunshine. The subject of Albert came up.

"He says . . . things," Vince remarked.

"It's a game he likes to play." She was unsurprised.

He recalled one comment. "Something about . . . dull roots. He glanced at this huge flower arrangement and said that."

Her brow furrowed briefly, and then. "Was it April?"

"Yes. How did you know?"

"He was quoting T.S."

"T.S.?"

"Eliot. The poet. Albert's a well read snob, and likes to pose. He quotes Li Po and Stevens to me in the same sentence."

"Stevens?"

She laughed, and Vince thought that she looked radiant, beautiful. An open glow transformed her. It was remarkable. Before, she had been merely sexy. "What's so funny?"

"You knew Li Po, but not the American," she replied.

"My first wife, Ai-Lin, read Tang poetry to me so . . . ," he cut himself off, embarrassed.

She glanced at the doorway. "My car's here."

The rain had stopped. Vince glanced at his watch. "I've got to go too."

"So." She stretched forward, standing on her toes — even in heels she was tiny — and pecked his cheek. "See you sometime."

Startled by the naturalness of her gesture, Vince didn't respond.

She started to leave. He followed. At the entrance, she pushed the heavy glass door, paused. "By the way, a friend of yours is coming to stay with us." She didn't wait for his query. "Your girlfriend, Gail Szeto."

And with that she exited, stepped into her car, waved and was gone.

Was this the end? And that remark about Gail — what was that all about? Yet another Colleen surprise, as if he needed more. Even between two cities, two countries, he was in a small town, at least for foreigners like him and the privileged local world that kept up this Asian economic boom. People like his brother and Ai-Lin, Albert and Colleen. Or Gail. Perhaps even Ai-Lin and Gail knew each other.

It was all ridiculously unreal.

He stepped outside. The raindrop puddles were evaporating in the sunshine.

In a couple of weeks he would be with Katy, back home where life was real. Right now, he had a job to finish.

15

The incessant knocking at her bedroom door finally forced Andanna out of bed. "What?" She complained through the closed door.

"Telephone."

"I'll call back."

"It's your friend Clio," continued the maid, mispronouncing it "Clee-o." "She said she wasn't hanging up until I got you to the phone."

She glanced at the clock. Almost lunchtime. Unlocking her door, she stuck her hand out, grabbed the portable handset and closed and locked her door again.

"What's with you?" Clio exploded. "You haven't answered your pager in weeks. When I finally got a hold of Michael, he said not to ask him where you were and hung up on me. What's going on for heaven's sake?"

"Nothing. I just moved home for a bit."

"I gathered that. Why haven't you called me anyway? What's going on?"

"I'm breaking up with Michael. I don't want to be a jazz singer anymore." She yawned. "Hey, want to meet for dinner? My treat. I have money again now that I'm living at home." She could picture her friend going into mild shock at her office.

"Are you crazy?"

"No, just lazy. We could go to the Grand Hyatt coffee shop, and afterwards to JJ's."

"You loathe JJ's."

"But you don't." Andanna knew Clio wouldn't pass up the invitation.

That evening, she got out without running into her parents. The disadvantage of coming home was having to listen to her mother nag about staying out late, and her father complain that if she wasn't going to do anything with her life, she ought to get married before her looks vanished.

When she arrived at the Grand Hyatt, Clio was already there, sitting meekly at one of the inside tables. Andanna signaled the maitre d' and demanded a window table. It didn't hurt to be recognized. Her latest modeling stint for a major fashion label had her plastered on posters all over the stations of the MTR. They got a window.

Clio gaped at her. "*Wei,* Andanna. *Gaau mat gwai a?*"

Andanna anticipated her surprise. Instead of her usual black jeans and black T-shirt — "that movie kick fighter get up" as her mother called it — she was actually wearing a dress. "Quit gawking. I got it as part of the promo, and the deal is I'm to wear it when I'm out and about at the "in" places. What, you don't think I paid for this, do you?" Clio, she knew, recognized all this fashion designer crap.

A group passed by, Jake Wu among them. Clio's eyes widened in recognition at two of the others, a local fashion designer and an up-and-coming Canto-pop singer. Jake waved at Andanna who puckered her lips into an air kiss while pointing at her dress.

"Jake's younger brother, the one in the green shirt, he's straight and has the most absurd crush on me." Andanna spoke without looking at Clio, never dropping the bright smile she flashed at the passing group. "He sends me flowers every week, imagine. I've told him he can stop sending them unless he introduces me to that music promoter cousin of his." She turned back to her friend once the group was out of visual range. "Hey, I've decided to become a Canto-pop singer. What do you think of that?"

"And that's why you're breaking up with Michael?"

Her friend's tone arrested her. She had expected Clio to be awed, impressed, to ask a million questions the way she always did whenever she announced something new, like when she declared she would become a jazz singer a couple of years ago. Instead, Clio appeared annoyed.

"Not exactly. He and I don't *'fit'* anymore."

"Oh yeah, sure. You'll hate it when he finally leaves, and he will, you watch."

"Let him. I don't care." But she cared, though she'd never admit it. Clio was possibly the only person in the world who understood this.

Abruptly, Clio asked. "You're not still sleeping with him, are you?"

"Him who?"

"You know who."

Her friend's faint sneer intimidated. "Oh, him. He was just a one-night stand."

"Sometimes, you have the most awful taste, you know?"

Andanna bristled, but held back a retort. Why was her friend being such a pain? Clio could be stubborn, but this challenging attitude was new. "So, are you looking forward to the holidays?"

Clio shrugged. "It's a bore, 'crossing the year.' I'd sooner work. Next year, I'm going to take a tour somewhere, maybe Bangkok or Bali."

"Won't your parents object?"

"My father might, but even my mother suggested it would be a good idea to get out of Hong Kong during the long holidays. Well, you know what a problem Dad's family is."

She knew. The politics and bickering in her friend's extended family weighed heavily. Andanna's family turned into a carnival every Chinese New Year. She was always most homesick around this time when they had both been away in Vancouver. It was fun watching her young nieces and nephews have a good time, because it reminded her of her own childhood.

"I'm real lucky," she said suddenly.

"About time you realized it," Clio declared. "Isn't that what I've always said? You're the worst Hong Kong princess. You don't even have to work."

Her friend was just teasing, but the remark bit. Since moving home, she'd quit all her piano gigs and only accepted modeling jobs that appealed to her. An awful realization dawned. Clio wasn't interested in her anymore. She had a real job, an actual career, her own friends and a whole other life that excluded Andanna. When had that happened? Worst of all, she no longer impressed her, perhaps, even bored her. Clio was merely indulging her notion of what she planned for her life. Yet they were best friends, sisters since that instance when, as children, they discovered neither had siblings and "adopted" each other.

They ate. Towards the end of dinner, a waiter brought a note to Andanna. "It's from Jake's brother," she read. "He wants to invite 'you and your friend' to JJ's tonight. Hey, we won't have to pay."

"You go. I've got a date for karaoke."

"Who with?"

"No one you'd want to know." Her friend looked pointedly at her. "You're not the only one with boyfriends."

"I didn't say I was," she replied rapidly. But she was stunned by the accusation, and hurt that her best friend never even told her about a boyfriend. Of course, what did she really know about Clio's life outside of their private friendship, since they no longer hung together much anymore. Clio seemed unperturbed, however, and they parted company as if life would go on as usual.

That night, Andanna kept ordering round after round of drinks, taking only a few sips of each one. The music at JJ's was loud. She danced with Jake's brother, and took center stage. Before that, she elicited an appointment out of him to meet the promoter cousin. Clio had said, during dinner, that if she really wanted to sing Canto-pop, she ought to go to karaoke and learn the music instead of turning her nose up at it, and that it was a waste of time chasing connections. After all, didn't Michael prevent her from performing because she wasn't good enough? Andanna's one consolation, the one she focused on, was that jazz was difficult, especially the way Michael wanted things done.

The trouble was, Clio might be right. It wasn't as if she had any experience singing Canto-pop, although most of the songs sounded easy enough. How she hated her friend's smug attitude. How she hated the unspoken insinuation that she would never amount to anything, and worse, that she could be a dilettante because she had money. It was what Michael thought also, acting as if he were her only hope.

As Andanna commanded the dance floor, aware of the admiring audience, she danced rings around her partner. Jake's brother was such a geek! Oh he was good looking and smitten and all that. Her parents would say he'd make a good husband because he had a promising career at Hong Kong Telecom and came from the right kind of family. But surely there was more to life than that.

She'd show Clio somehow, and Michael. They were both scared of their own shadows, trying too hard, thinking that being "good enough" at anything ought to take forever. It was incredible how much time they both spent worrying about their careers. They believed too much in success, which, she felt, only required some talent, a little luck and lots of connections. Her life wouldn't be wasted. As long as she didn't give up, she knew she was meant to be a star.

The volume of the music increased as the club got more crowded. Andanna wouldn't stop dancing, even when her partner asked to quit. You go if you want, she told him, knowing full well he wouldn't dream of leaving her there alone. He hung on, mostly because he knew perfectly well that she could have cared less what he did.

"You could have made a lot of money with those pictures." Albert Ho, having ordered lunch for them at the China Club, challenged Vince. "My office still gets calls about the club opening from the media everywhere."

"Hey, we had a deal."

"We did."

It was the day before the holidays. Vince had agreed reluctantly to see him. Albert had a thing about meeting on Sundays. People here liked to push things to limits, stretching time to fit one more meeting.

Commotion at the entrance. A Chinese man, brandishing a cigar, commanded the surroundings as he was ushered to his table. Other diners turned to look. He waved at Albert who waved back.

"Do you know who that is?"

"No, afraid not." Not that he cared, but in this town, everyone else did. Appreciated Albert's manner of polite inquiry. Unlike Don and others, who expressed a tiresome astonishment that he didn't know so-and-so or such-and-such. Wasn't that important to have to know, wasn't part of such an elevated circle. By now, though, discovered people made themselves matter or, as Ai-Lin once remarked in all seriousness, "to strategize image as a natural extension of self works best when launching a long-term PR campaign" and Don had beamed at her while he cringed.

"He started this place, and owns that store 'Shanghai Tang.' Do you know the one, on Pedder?"

A bit like Manhattan, where any minute now, some celebrity would appear. The world was running out of fifteen minutes. But he knew the place. Shanghai retro, Jake Wu described it — *gwailoes* love it; locals think it sucks. A little like this club which felt borrowed from another space, another time, not Hong Kong. At least, not the Hong Kong he'd seen so far, of glitzy malls, designer labels, chic restaurants, clubs and Canto-pop in karaoke lounges. The trouble with agency work, both during and after hours, was the world it forced him to inhabit. In Manhattan, he could escape back home to Brooklyn, because food photography was just a job and not a way of life.

"Anyway," Vince continued, "why are we here?"

Albert smiled thinly. "That's what I like about you. You don't waste time."

Didi's voice, from some forgotten quarrel. *You've wasted my time for the last three years. What d'you hang around for?*

"Do you take art photos?"

Unexpected request. "What do you mean?"

"For exhibits."

"What kind of exhibits?"

"You know, art galleries. Like in Soho."

Again, struck by Albert's veiled meanings. Like the first time when all he could think was: he can't be serious. Yet now, deathly serious, as if all life depended on it. Did money eradicate humor? Just like Don and Ai-Lin, on their financial uphill trek, utterly humorless. Or had they always been that way and he just hadn't known?

"Why?"

Albert seemed slightly uncomfortable. "If you'd rather not . . ."

"I don't know what you're asking."

He let out an audible sigh, and then appeared to come to a decision. "I know this young woman, a cousin actually, who's a sort of dilettante singer cum model. She doesn't know what to do with her life. She is extremely photogenic, and has a wonderful figure. It's not that she's all that beautiful, but the photos I've seen of her . . . well, I just think it would be marvelous to have some shots of her."

"You mean nudes?"

"Possibly. Suggestive, in any case."

No one had ever asked him anything like this before. "Why me?"

"Why not you?"

"And this cousin or whatever of yours wants to do this?"

Albert's pause was very slight, barely perceptible. "She doesn't know what she wants."

He could push limits too. "But you've talked to her about this, right?"

"Not exactly."

"Wouldn't she rather just have portfolio shots? That's what all these aspiring young stars want."

"Perhaps. You ask too many questions. I'm just asking you to do a job. Stop being so American."

"I am American." Too ridiculous. Ought to turn this down because it made no sense.

"I'd pay well." Albert paused meaningfully. "Extremely well. Look, this isn't pornography."

"Isn't it?"

"Really Vincent, she is my cousin, after all." Almost coy.

Vince remained half convinced. Something Ai-Lin told him years ago about Chinese cousins —*there are numerous ways to say "cousin" in Chinese, because the extended family crosses many boundaries.*

Their food arrived. *Dim sum* bamboo steamers and bowls of dumplings in a broth. Portions like French haute cuisine. If nothing else, could always count on good food.

Albert gestured towards their meal. "Eat. You're a strange one."

"It's not what I do, you know that, right?" Vince positioned his chopsticks. The steaming aroma exuded a delicate ginger and other less familiar flavors.

"You're too modest. Your work stands up to anyone else's here."

Odd compliment. Subtly backhanded, except that Albert appeared entirely sincere. Couldn't tell with him. "I'll think about it."

"Please do it, Vincent da Luca."

"That's what you said the last time."

"And you did it."

"Yes, I know I did." He could have sworn Albert was gay, so what did he want the shots for? Discomfiting, this whole thing. Didn't understand what he was being drawn into.

Albert began talking about photography, about which he seemed knowledgeable. When Vince asked him why he knew so much, he admitted that his half brother was a professional photojournalist, and also a painter. "Perhaps you know him? David Ho."

"We've met. You guys don't look like brothers." But what pleased him was the fact that he felt suddenly connected, that the time spent speeding through almost two Hong Kong years had not been a complete blur, although it often seemed that way. Some things clicked, and they didn't all have to be some forgettable fuck, or another Don and Ai-Lin introduction. Albert had been his own "find." Putting pieces of this city together, slowly. Lucky gold coins on the streets for the picking. Like Dick Whittington. Only missing a cat.

Andanna considered calling Clio, but held back. It was Sunday evening, the eve of the new year. Clio would be home with her family. Even when it wasn't a special occasion, she always ate dinner at home on Sundays. Funny how well she knew her routine.

Since Friday, Andanna's mood alternated between wanting to dismiss Clio and a nagging sense of loss. She lay on her bed and lit a cigarette, wondering why she felt so weird, why she simply couldn't get on with things the way she usually did. But everything in her life was upside down. It was bad enough that Michael treated her like she no longer existed, but to get the cold shoulder from Clio was different.

The day she met Clio, they were in Primary 3. It was recess, and they were at the tuck shop counter. Clio was trying, unsuccessfully, to get the sales clerk's attention. Andanna watched her a minute and then pushed them both forward saying, here, this is how you get what you want. Seconds later, the clerk took Clio's money and sold her the packet of fried dough she pointed to. Clio opened the packet and offered her some, but Andanna wrinkled her nose exclaiming, how can you eat that junk, but their friendship was sealed from that moment onwards.

"You Fun, time to eat."

Her mother irritated her a lot these days. "I'm not hungry."

"You never eat. You're going to make yourself sick."

"I'll eat later."

"For heaven's sake. It's 'the annual night of the thirtieth.' What will your father say?"

She stubbed out her cigarette. What was wrong with her? Try as she would, she couldn't rouse herself to go to her family, to do what she normally loved. When she lived with Michael, she always came home for the new year. Yet now that she was home, everything about it repelled her.

Andanna lay in silence.

"Don't you want your *faat choy?*"

Even the idea of her favorite fungal delicacy didn't tempt her. She lit another cigarette.

Finally, the resigned sigh. "What did I do to deserve this?"

Turning up her CD player, Andanna drowned out the sound of her mother's voice.

16

Kwok Po addressed Gail. "So will you stay on?"

The late morning sun was hot, but not scorching, and a light breeze made their day's outing on the water pleasant. It was the third day of the new year. In two more days, Gail's vacation would be over.

"You mean in Hong Kong?"

"Or China."

"I don't see why not."

"Glad to hear it."

The 1997 question, as her American boss liked to call it, dominated *ad nauseum.* Gail was grateful for Kwok Po's understanding. Hong Kong was home. The handover was no big deal. All that mattered was having a decent enough job to keep her going.

Gail luxuriated in the sun. *This* was the life. This was bliss: to forget entirely about work, to be away from the office on a "local" public holiday and temporarily unreachable by email or phone, even cellular. The trouble with global finance was that somewhere in the world, some market was open. But during the lunar new year, enough of Asia shut down to enable reprieve from the reaches of New York.

Colleen came around to her side of the boat.

"How's your brother?" Gail asked.

"I haven't seen him in a long time," Colleen replied.

"Danny likes to be different." This, from Kwok Po, who was handing drinks around.

Gail thought Colleen looked slightly put out by his remark. What little she remembered of Danny was Kwok Po saying he wished his brother-in-law would grow up and get himself a proper job. Funny, but he would never think Colleen needed to do this. Men. Even the most enlightened preferred just a wife.

Off the side of their anchored vessel, Gu Kwun was splashing happily, secure in his life belt. The boat boy followed him around in a rowboat. Hearing her son's laughter, knowing he was safe, meant she could relax. She needed more vacations like this.

"Are you seeing anyone?" Kwok Po sat down next to her.

Gail sat up and sipped her lemonade. She was suddenly conscious of her uncovered skin. Not that she and Kwok Po had ever . . . but something about being the odd woman out, this condition seemingly without end. "Oh, not really. I'm getting too old for that sort of thing."

"Don't be ridiculous. You're young yet, and an attractive woman."

His compliment touched her. She had always liked Kwok Po's open manner, his unpretentiousness. And it was good to know he could still find her attractive. She saw Colleen glance at her husband. Surely, not jealousy?

"Yes but you're married, like all the guys who say that."

"I just got lucky." He took Colleen's hand and squeezed it, smiling broadly at her. "Very, very lucky."

There was true love between those two, even after all their years of marriage. For one brief instance, Gail felt she would give up everything, even Gu Kwun, for that kind of love. "Besides, there's Gu Kwun. Men don't like ready made families."

Kwok Po snorted impatiently. "And if you met someone who liked kids, you'd make some other excuse. Like your job, or your mother."

"What about my mother?"

"Gail, you have to ease up on yourself. Have you ever considered a home or private care or something for her?"

She clenched her teeth. "I couldn't do that." Her friends knew her mother was widowed and somewhat senile, but no one knew the whole story.

"I mean, it's not as if you wouldn't still spend time with her."

"Would you do it?"

He seemed embarrassed and glanced at Colleen who immediately spoke up. "Well, it's different for us. We don't have children." She smiled sweetly at Gail.

The conversation moved on. It was strange comfort being with friends, well, with Kwok Po; Colleen was still a stranger. Surely he didn't expect Colleen to look after his mother if it came to that? Although perhaps she would. She seemed a timid, dependent sort of woman, someone who would be quite lost without him. But they both didn't understand. Her family was her responsibility, period.

Gail leaned back on the sun chair, and stretched her legs. She still had a passable figure for her age, although the thighs were thickening, and she'd seen the loosening of skin around the upper arms. Gu Kwun emerged from the sea and began shaking water over her. Yet she didn't bother telling him to stop. Kwok Po played with him, fooling around with Kung Fu kicks. Her poor son looked bewildered.

Strange comfort. How well did she know even Kwok Po anymore? He virtually ran his family's business while she was just another drone in the hive. When had their ambitions diverged? Once, they both saw all life after the MBA as scaling Corporate Everest. He insisted he'd never be just another Hong Kong family businessman, living off the fat of his family. She said she'd never give in like other women who expected a "mommy track" to yield the same amount of power as the traditional, expected climb. Somewhere along the line, everything changed. Downsizing meant security for the indentured enslaved, and loyalty begrudgingly given to a paycheck. Now, corporate "power" meant little more to her than either working for as humane and decent a boss as possible or negotiating sufficient authority and compensation to grit her teeth and stay off the more desirable mommy track a little longer.

Salty sun rays warmed her whole being. As long as she could have moments like these, life was simply the inescapable, inevitable progress of the day-to-day, until the next definable passage.

It was annoying the amount of respect Kwok Po accorded Gail. She was such a girl scout, self-righteously condescending and tediously proper. Colleen believed in being polite and all, but Gail took herself altogether too seriously.

As the boat headed towards shore at sunset, Colleen overheard their conversation about children, and her husband telling Gail in hushed tones about how "unfortunate" things were. Gail was suggesting adoption. She would. Girl orphans in China were her favorite cause. No matter how well Gail thought she knew Kwok Po, she really was quite clueless about him. Adoption in the Tang family? No way. Besides, her husband was guilty of a little hypocrisy in this matter.

If only Gail knew the truth.

When she turned twenty-one, Colleen had demanded, and gotten, a tubal ligation. From the time she was a child, she had never wanted children. Her mother had told her then that this wasn't the thing to say. By the time she was a teenager, she discovered how right her mother was.

Only Danny knew. Even with Kwok Po, she had lied and told him she simply couldn't have children, but waited till they had been together two years. At the time, it surprised her how little that seemed to bother him. When did she know that the real reason he could marry her was because he need never divert his attention from business to children, and could deflect all grandchildren demands acceptably? It also avoided the controversy of a mixed race child in his family. As for adoption, the idea that the Tang family wealth could go to any but their own bloodline was laughable.

The truth was that less people wanted children than would admit it, Kwok Po included.

That brat, Gu Kwun, was hyperactively running around the boat .
"Hey kid," she called out loudly in English. "Don't you ever get tired?"

He stopped running and stared at her thoughtfully, mulling this
over. "Sometimes I think I must, Auntie Colleen."

She burst out laughing and said, in Cantonese. "'Silly melon', that
was a joke."

"Oh." He looked perturbed for a moment, then started giggling, and
erupted into laughter. He ran over to Gail. "Auntie Colleen says funny
things," he told her.

Gail smiled and called across the boat. "You do wonders with my
son. He's usually terribly over-sensitive."

"It's nothing. He's just a kid." Colleen gazed at the horizon, wanting
a cigarette. It had been an idle thing, yet Gail seemed unduly pleased.
The brat *was* freaky, so serious and intense. He reminded her just a
little of Danny as a boy, except that her brother hadn't been as preco-
cious. She glanced at her husband for affirmation. He caught her look
and smiled, stilling the noise in her brain. In her life, in her real life,
there was only this man.

A long time ago, she had no real life.

"Where the heck did you learn all that?" Kwok Po, a year and a half
into their relationship, still reeled from her sexual acrobatics.

She kissed his forehead and lit a cigarette. Back then, she had
smoked openly. "I was a gymnast, remember?"

"You didn't practice this stuff on the parallel bars."

A New England fall morning, late in the season. Outside her apartment window, Colleen glimpsed the fading autumnal palette. Soon,
the cold would be menacing. She hoped the boiler wouldn't die again
this winter.

They made love only in her apartment, never in his. He lived alone,
but in a building among several friends from Hong Kong who had

Chinese girlfriends and wives, or at worst, a Chinese-American. By some tacit understanding, he treated her almost as if she were a mistress, even though he had no reason to do so in Boston. She knew. It was her job to know.

Colleen turned on her back. "I've got to move." Smoke snaked above them. Sundays in bed were the best times imaginable.

"Why *Hong Qi?*"

"The rent's going up, and I can't run my trust fund down too low. We don't all have high paying jobs like you."

"I'll help."

"No. Not as long as we're not living together."

"But I'm here most of the time."

"It's not the same."

Every four months or so, she would accuse him of being in love only with her body. He would protest his denials; they would argue and end up in a weepy scenario where she'd say perhaps this relationship ought to end because it was never going anywhere, after which he'd plead for her patience to continue and they would make up over several rounds of passion.

It was four months since the last argument.

"There's this guy," she said.

He stared at the ceiling, unmoving.

"He's not like the others." It was an unspoken pact, begun early in their relationship, that as long as he kept her hidden from his Chinese life, she was free to date others. She had wondered at first if he was a truly non-jealous man — she'd never known one — because he maintained a stoic calm through all her affairs, tolerating them, so that, sometimes, she wondered if he were a voyeur, thrilled by the vicarious.

After a long silence. "What do you mean?"

"He wants to marry me."

That was when he left her. The moment was neither dramatic nor emotional. All he said as he got dressed was, "It wasn't just about sex, you know, not ever."

His absence in the days that followed created a void she'd never experienced. They spoke on the phone, but he did not come to see her. Each conversation was about inconsequential things — current news, the weather, what each had for dinner the night before. She found she did not need to weep. In the meantime, her other lover rejoiced, believing she would now marry him.

After a week of this, Kwok Po said to her, in Chinese. "You've never tried to leave me before."

Her American voice persisted. What's he talking about? *He left, not you. Don't let him pull that Chinese circular logic crap on you.* But from that other space she'd nurtured since girlhood, the one that declared, *I am a Chinese princess,* she summoned the alternative interpretation. *You were trying to leave him. You've never made anyone else propose to you before,* and then, an explosion of light, and she declared, in Chinese. "Kwok Po, *wo ai ni.*"

"You've never told me you loved me before," he said, in English.

And that was when her real life began.

**

Don was wrong about nice girls and introductions. These days, accidental strangers in the right class would do. On his flight back from New York, Vince had been upgraded to business and was seated next to a nice Chinese woman who perked up when he said he lived in Hong Kong. He knew that had he wanted to, he could have her easily enough. Didn't do the old ego any harm, knowing he still had it. No desire though. Fatal flaw. Summarizing the story of his life, said he drove his first wife insane and the second into the arms of a younger lover, at which the nice woman gave him a look that said — *you can't be serious* — ending that conversation.

Fateful flight. At Kai Tak's arrival hall, leaving the immigration line at the same time as him, were Colleen and her husband.

Couldn't pretend. She looked more stunned than him. Nice to

know she didn't always have the upper hand.

"It's Kwok Po, isn't it?" Addressed hubby first, giving her time to collect herself. "You probably don't remember me." He didn't but memory jogged, quickly enough, by recalling Albert and the Shanghai party. By then, Colleen could say calmly, "Vince, what are you doing with yourself these days?" "Oh, this and that, keeping busy. You know how it is, the workaholic bachelor life." Feeling wicked, added. "In between assignments, I try to date the occasional girlfriend."

Kwok Po said. "You must keep in touch. We're moving back home to Hong Kong, very soon as a matter of fact." He beamed at Colleen as he said this. "By the way, here's my card."

Did the card exchange and Vince disappeared first since they had luggage and he didn't. Colleen barely looked at him. Women. What did she want out of only three encounters in almost a year? Besides, after their last, accidental meeting, he had had the distinct impression she wanted nothing more to do with him. But an instance of fleeting jealousy — glanced back and saw her husband's arm encircling the small of her back, and his hand that wandered possessively into private territory. Jealous, not of her, but of both of them, of their skill at the marital art.

Their return to Hong Kong had been quite unexpected, because Kwok Po's father had taken ill suddenly with liver cancer, and was now hospitalized. An unlikely disease for this otherwise healthy man; earlier medical check ups had given no signs. When Colleen had spoken to her number two sister-in-law a few days prior, the woman had made some comment about cancer not discriminating in favor of a lack of vices. Appalling, this shocking callousness. No wonder she was *laih-lai's* favorite. No contest against the unfeeling.

"You want to go over there tonight, don't you?" she said to her husband when they checked into their hotel. She had suggested staying at his parents, but Kwok Po always preferred some distance. "Go ahead.

You know I don't mind."

He hugged her tightly; his relief coursed through her. "It's awfully late, *Hong Qi.*"

"You only have one father," she said in Chinese.

He left for the hospital, promising not to be long, but saying that he would call if he decided to spend the night there. Colleen knew he wouldn't be back till morning. Tomorrow, she would go see *laihlai* and make sure she was all right.

Five minutes later, the phone rang.

"So your husband's going to be the new overlord?"

"Danny! How did you know we'd be here?"

"Saw it in the *Ming Pao.*" Her brother read several of the Hong Kong and mainland newspapers regularly. "Your pop-in-law is enough of a big shot, and it was sudden. There wasn't foul play or anything, was there?"

"What are you on about? He's got cancer."

"Just wondering. So, your ascent's assured, the way you planned."

"It's not like that at all. Stop being such a lion."

She recalled their childhood and their imaginary China, where they fought battles against loud and overbearing lions. The lions had been Colleen's discovery, when, after a visit to the zoo, she had declared to her brother that lions were the silliest animals she'd ever seen. All they seemed to do was eat, lie around and make a lot of noise roaring. So Danny promised he would slay the lions — his idea was to creep up behind them when they were sleeping and catch them by surprise, but Colleen had objected, saying no, it had to be when they roared because that was when they were the most tiresome.

This game had gone on for several months until one day Danny had come to Colleen in tears, saying they couldn't play the game anymore because Mother said there were no lions in China! No lions! Colleen comforted her little brother the best she could, but he was quite inconsolable. Finally, she found the solution. *Then, Danny, we'll just have to send some lions to China, won't we?* That way, their game could go on, uninterrupted.

Now, her brother was not nearly as easy to love.

She continued. "You probably want something."

The wounded tone in his response was unmistakable. "Can't a brother want to say hi?"

"I suppose."

Danny told her he planned to remain in Hong Kong, at least till after the handover next year. They chatted a little longer about their mother. Colleen begged off because she was tired. Afterwards, she wondered if her brother had been lurking nearby, watching for Kwok Po to leave before he called.

She lay on the king sized bed, craving a cigarette, knowing full well she had insisted on this non-smoking room. Unfamiliar desire. After that evening when she had smoked in front of him, she had vowed to quit for real, to stop this piece of playacting. When she declared this to Kwok Po, he only remarked that it would be better for her, but not to drive herself crazy over it. Exposure made the addiction real. Before, it had been a game.

The mattress would not yield to her. Lately, nothing yielded. Everything demanded investigation, analysis, concern. Something was happening. The men and affairs had been easy to eliminate, but the growing emotional turmoil that stirred her was new.

She tossed around, trying to get comfortable. Her thoughts went to her father-in-law, that imperious, clever old man, the original *Shizi Wang* himself. She had told him once, at a family dinner when he was barking about the business to his sons, that he was noisier than a "lion king." In the dead silence that followed, everyone, even Kwok Po, looked at her in mild horror. Colleen caught her breath and uttered into the silence. *"Shizi bu tu."* A lion shouldn't hold back even in combat with a rabbit. The old man had arched his eyebrows, tilted his chin forward and suddenly roared with laughter. Kwok Po grinned broadly. *Laihlai* was pleased, delighted that this youngest daughter-in-law could make the old man laugh. The others shot her envious glances.

Danny had it all wrong. Of course she wanted her husband to succeed and take over things eventually. But not yet, not just yet. There was life in the old man still, life with spunk and meaning. He deserved what he earned. More importantly, Kwok Po needed more time with his father.

She wept a silent plea into her pillow.

17

On the ninth anniversary of her grandmother's death, Andanna missed her cousin Siu Mei among all the relatives.

"Where is she?" she asked her mother.

"She's in a home now."

"When did that happen?"

"Oh, a few years ago. I'm not too sure." Her mother turned away to chatter with some other family member.

Why hadn't she observed the movements of her family. When was the last time she'd seen Siu Mei? Surely not at *pohpo's* funeral?

Siu Mei had been there in her wheelchair, laughing and smiling to herself, wheeling herself backwards and forwards in a repetitive dance. One uncle wanted to send her out of the hall where the mourning took place, because her behavior was "inappropriate." Siu Mei's mother cried — she had always been hopeless at dealing with her daughter in public around the in-laws — and Siu Mei's father conveniently disappeared the way he did whenever things got "complicated" among the relatives.

Andanna looked around for "Prince Frog," Siu Mei's brother. He pointed at his sister and shrugged, mumbling something about how she couldn't help it. Andanna felt an exasperated impatience: what was wrong with all her relatives anyway? She marched over to her cousin. If she could catch her eye, she could somehow make her understand the situation. Andanna didn't know exactly what made her do this, but she could recall the incident as if it had happened only moments ago.

She had placed her hand on her cousin's arm, forcing eye contact. Siu Mei halted in the laughter of her happy world and stared back. "*Pohpo's* gone now," Andanna whispered. "*Pohpo* doesn't live here anymore." Siu Mei continued to stare, and Andanna felt silly, hoping that none of her relatives would notice otherwise there'd be all kinds of talk and trouble later.

Suddenly, her cousin reached out and grabbed Andanna's hand, locking it in a tight grip. Her lips struggled to force the words out. Andanna watched, amazed. Her cousin never spoke. Siu Mei exerted extraordinary effort; her face contorted in a frightening way. In a very hoarse, barely audible croak, in a voice that seemed to rise from her belly, she demanded. *No more pohpo? No more pohpo?* All the time, she gripped Andanna's hand. Other relatives had gathered round to watch, startled by the sound of Siu Mei's voice. Andanna was a little scared, unsure of what to do. She continued to hold her cousin's hand, squeezing reassurances.

And then, Siu Mei stopped smiling, and tears began to slide down her face. Her body shook in silent upheaval. It was painful to watch. The relatives edged away, unwilling to deal with her.

Come back, Andanna wanted to shout at them all. Siu Mei needs you now. *Pohpo* would want you all to take care of her.

But no one came over while her cousin cried. Agitated, Andanna had wrapped her arms around Siu Mei in an embrace, and soothed her till she calmed down. "*Pohpo's* happy now," she told her. "You don't have to cry over her anymore."

After that, the complaining uncle shut up, and everyone left Siu Mei alone.

"You Fun, it's your turn," her mother was saying.

She hastened in front of her grandmother's photo on the Buddhist altar where the urn of ashes sat, and bowed three times. This was the first time she'd noticed Siu Mei's absence. Andanna came every

March, except while away at school in Vancouver. During those years, she'd pay her own visit when she came home for the summer. That was probably why she'd overlooked her cousin, because *pohpo* died the year before she left for Canada. Still, it was remarkably careless of her. After all, she should at least have noticed after graduation when she came home to live. Was she really so thoughtless?

She moved on so that the next person in line could pay ancestral respects.

The chatter among the relatives was at an infectious pitch. Normally, she would have joined in, catching up on family gossip. But remembering Siu Mei, whom everyone seemed to have forgotten, bothered her. She sidled off alone to a corner.

Albert Ho was among the guests who had come to pay respects at her uncle's home.

"*Wei, leng leui,* what's this? Circles around the eyes? Aren't you getting enough beauty sleep?"

Her mother breezed past and onwards. "There you are. Even your *tohnggo* sees how ugly you look. Albert, tell her to get more rest. Maybe she'll listen to you. She's out late every night, and won't listen to me."

Andanna flipped her gaze over to the large photo of her grandmother in the living room. Her hair was drawn up in a tight bun, and her *cheongsam's* high collar choked her neck. It was a severe face, although it sported few wrinkles. Up till her death at eighty-five, *pohpo* had remained the matriarch.

She pointed at the photograph. "I have good genes. If I have twice as many lines at her age, I'll consider myself lucky."

"Then don't look so sad." He picked up her elbow and escorted her towards the dining room where the table was piled with sliced roasts and other delicacies. "I hear you're 'on the scene' these days, with all manner of 'friends.' What happened to the boyfriend?"

She flicked her long hair over her shoulder. "Oh, you know how it is."

"*Mang ci zai bei.*" Prickles stuck in your back. He ran his fingers lightly across her shoulder blades. "Is Michael your Han dynasty Huo

Guang, my little empress?"

"What *are* you talking about?"

He sighed. "Don't you kids read history anymore? But never mind. Come to karaoke with me later. I want to hear you sing, but only Chinese songs."

She made a face.

"So ugly, You Fun." He made a face back at her. "One of my producer friends will be there."

"Now why didn't you say so?" She slid her arm through his and led him to the food.

At the Dynasty Club in Wanchai, Albert directed her towards his private room where some fifteen people were singing. Andanna's ears hurt from the drunken, off-key caterwauling. The group was older, all over thirty and a few as old as Albert. She lit a cigarette and inhaled. It was going to be a long night.

One guy grabbed a microphone and began singing a current pop number. He wasn't too bad. Andanna only half knew the song because she seldom paid attention to the charts although she knew she should. But they were pretty much all the same, with dead easy melodies in uncomplicated keys. After listening to Michael's jazz collection, coupled with her classical training, everything else was simple.

"*Leng leui,* you sing." Albert handed her a microphone.

She put out her cigarette, feeling a little nervous. It was one thing to hear how bad everyone else was, and quite another to do a better job. The guy ahead of her wrapped up. "What do you want?" He indicated the selection chart. She shrugged. "Whatever. I don't know many songs."

"Come on, you have to choose something."

An image of Siu Mei just a few years ago — where had it been? Her cousin had been glued to a Walkman, and handed Andanna the earphones when she saw her. Siu Mei had been listening to a popular

Anita Mui tune, and was clapping her hands.

"I'll do one of Anita Mui's."

He punched in her selection and several others.

"Stand up." Albert gave her waist a nudge. "You'll have more room to move."

The music had started and she listened. There were maybe two chords in the entire piece. As the lyrics appeared on screen, she launched into song. The group stopped chattering. Not knowing the words, she kept her eyes glued to the screen, following the beat of the characters as the color streaked across them. By the second verse, she was more comfortable, and could concentrate on phrasing as well, mimicking the original rendition. At the end, everyone applauded and Andanna made a little bow. Then, seeing the title of the next song "There's Bridge in My Heart to You Forever," she spoke a transition into the mike, the way she'd seen the local pop stars do, sentiment in their gazes. She was only fooling around, but the group seemed quite impressed, so she launched into the next number somewhat more dramatically, striking an on stage pose.

There was no mistaking the enthusiasm in the resounding applause as she returned to her seat.

"You're my little star, *leng leui*." Albert smiled broadly.

"Just having fun." The intensity of his stare bugged her. She leaned away from him against the sofa. He leaned towards her, his arm a cage around her.

"You have to do this seriously."

She wiggled herself into an upright position, forcing him to back off. "Anytime you tell me, *tohnggo*." Extracting a card from her purse, she extended one towards him between two fingers. "In case you lost the last one I gave you."

"*Wei*, what about an introduction?" The guy who preceded her was standing next to them. "This is your niece, right?"

"Cousin." Albert responded sharply.

"Want to do a duet?" He was looking at her, without a second glance at Albert.

"Sure." She jumped up and accepted his hand. He was tall and rather good looking, built like Michael.

"Cantonese opera, okay?"

Andanna hesitated. She wasn't wild about singing opera, but he was already programming something. The group approved loudly.

Andanna had heard many of the pieces, although she didn't really know them. Her mother watched these all the time. In high school, she and Clio fooled around singing these, and she always did the man's part. Now, she had to concentrate to get the woman's part right.

By mid-song, she could get through the lyrics and even ham things up a bit. The group cheered. She was entertaining them. This was fun. Her partner smiled encouragingly at her. Michael's scorn disappeared far into the background. Being an entertainer didn't have to be the way Michael made it sound. It could really be fun.

From the corner of her eye, she saw Albert blow smoke rings towards her, his eyes narrowed like a cat's. He seemed pleased. Good. She hoped that now he'd come through with his promise of help.

She launched into the finale.

**

Clio's eyes widened in amazement. "Hey, you're not serious about those photos, are you?" Sprawled on her bed, she was snacking as she talked.

The packets of fried dough Clio devoured regularly were stacked on a shelf. Andanna counted half a dozen. "You'll get fat," she remarked, indicating the stack.

"It's just dough."

"Yeah, deep fried in too much oil. You eat junk, you know that?"

"And your Diet Cokes? What do you call those? At least I drink tea."

On afternoons like these, Andanna understood perfectly why she had to be with Clio. No one knew her as well. Once when they were kids on the playground, an older girl had knocked Clio over and she started crying. Andanna had gone up to the girl and kicked her leg. She sometimes felt Clio still needed looking after.

"Why not? They're art photographs, and I get paid for modeling."

"They're dirty pictures."

"You're the one with the dirty mind."

"Come on 'silly melon,' what will you do if the photos get published somewhere? What if your father sees them? How will you face anyone?"

She dismissed her friends' worries. It didn't matter to her why Albert wanted those photos, or what he planned to do with them. The night she'd gone to karaoke with him, he had asked if she would pose "for my private collection." He'd promised to fund a professional quality music video demo for her if she did. Plus he would pay for modeling. What more did she need to know?

But it was already almost a month later and Albert still hadn't called.

"You know, you really are looking pretty awful." Clio had opened a second packet of dough.

"Dry up. You sound like my mother."

"Are you still seeing Jake's brother?"

"I'm not 'seeing' him."

"Well, excuse me if I can't keep up with your social life." She rolled over and jumped out of bed. "Hey, want to come to karaoke tonight?"

Andanna hesitated. She didn't want to admit that she felt silly doing it, even if it did give her a chance to practice singing. "Who're you going with?"

"Oh, my usual crowd. They'd like to meet you, you know. Besides, it's not like you're doing anything else."

"How would you know? You're not my social secretary." But she was going out less these days, mostly because she found the scene repetitive. For a couple of weeks, she'd dated that good looking friend of Albert's, the one who'd sung with her that night. But he started to get serious, so she dropped him. Besides, he wasn't in the entertainment business so it wasn't like he could do anything for her.

"So are you coming?"

"I don't know. I'll decide later."

"No you won't."

Something in her friend's voice startled her. "Chill, will ya? It's not such a big deal."

Clio turned away and began applying her make up. "You'd rather sleep with that Tai Jai then go out with normal people. What's the matter with you anyway?"

"I'm not sleeping with him," she lied.

Her friend shrugged. "Suit yourself."

"What's that supposed to mean?"

"Honestly, Andanna. Don't you think he'll talk some day? Won't that be embarrassing? He's so nasty, like some triad thug. You're not in love with him, are you?"

"Course not." But she wondered sometimes if there wasn't something wrong with her, because she was obsessed by the way he made her feel. "Besides, now that I'm not with Michael anymore, it's not like I'm seeing Tai Jai or anything."

Clio spun around and glared at her. "And that's the other thing. How could you be so mean to Michael? What did he ever do to you? Even if you didn't want to stay with him, did you have to be so . . . oh, I don't know. So selfish, I guess."

"Quit it, will you, or I'm taking off."

"Go if you want." And she calmly returned to her makeup.

Andanna stormed out of her friend's home. By the time she reached the subway, she already regretted it. Never mind. She'd call and say sorry and everything would be like before.

Saturday evening. The MTR was crowded. Andanna wondered what she should do. Going all the way home was a pain. Visage wouldn't be open till much later, and she didn't like hanging out there nowadays in case she ran into Michael.

The train arrived at Admiralty, the interchange for Kowloon. She might as well head back, she decided, and crossed the platform towards the Tsuen Wan line.

"Long time no see. Where've you been hiding?"

It was that American photographer, the really old looking guy. "Oh, hi. What are you doing here?"

He looked amused. "Same thing you are, I suspect."

"You mean you're going to Kowloon?"

"There's no law against it, is there?" Vince held the door to the train and gestured towards the cabin. "Coming?" She followed him in.

He was at loose ends. Don had cancelled their dinner date only half an hour earlier. But he was already geared to go to Kowloon, and decided to play tourist for an evening. "Don't you have a date tonight?"

This guy was nosy. "Maybe, maybe not."

"So why are you going to Kowloon?"

"I live there."

"At home?"

"Of course at home."

"I meant, with your parents?"

"Yeah."

The kid was an airhead, and she didn't seem too comfortable conversing in English. Vince folded his arms and leaned back against the slippery metal seat in silence.

Strange guy, he didn't seem to know whether or not he wanted to talk. Andanna searched around for something that might interest him. "I gave up modeling."

Her remark startled him. "How come? I thought you were doing well."

"Oh, I get bored." She didn't want him to think she needed work.

"Too bad. I thought you were pretty good. My daughter wants to be a model."

She sat up. "You don't look married."

He tried to stop himself, but laughed anyway. She probably hadn't meant it like that.

Andanna knew she hadn't said anything amusing. Baffling the way these *gwailoes* behaved. She would never have known he was married, considering the way he carried on. Chinese guys were more discreet.

The train stopped at Tsimshatsui. "I get off here. Want to have dinner?"

"Now?"

He rolled his eyes. "Yes, now. You coming?"

"Sure. Okay."

That was amusing, Vince mused, as he headed home after dinner. Her disjointed chatter had passed the evening pleasantly enough. Did get tiring though, especially after the ninety ninth exclamation of "cool" and "really?"

Impressed her with the restaurant, a Korean dive from way back when. Had she really *never* eaten Korean barbecue? Liked his Shanghai stories, and the romance of his first marriage. Left out the later part about Ai-Lin and Don. Funny though, how pained she looked when he said he couldn't be with his daughter right now. Didn't expect a glamour type like her to give a shit about family stuff.

But the big surprise — when she offered to pay her share. Shocked him, although it shouldn't have. Lots of women did. He'd refused of course, pulling rank on account of age. She'd nodded seriously and thanked him.

Confident kid though. Had to give her that. Going to be a Canto-pop singer. Liked the way she said that, stars shimmering in her eyes. Reminded him of Don at her age, full of hope for his career, certain he would succeed somehow. Perhaps she could do it, perhaps she couldn't. Didn't matter. The one thing he felt quite sure of was that she wouldn't give up trying, because she wanted it badly enough. That counted, sometimes even more than hard work or talent, even more than all the luck in the world. Thank god for the young.

18

Vince confronted the evidence of his dream, disturbed by the ringing phone. Unfortunately, Colleen was not a forgettable fuck. Magazine photo of her, some social thing, the one he'd come across by accident. Blatant reminder. She and Didi illuminated by the tiniest flickers.

Memory desired release.

"Aren't you up yet?" Bright eyed bushy tailed Don. Goddamned chipmunk.

"It's only eight. Worked late last night."

"You work too hard."

Right. Don worked when he played. Every lunch a discussion, every cocktail a network, every dinner a deal. Ai-Lin scheduled the power breakfasts.

"We need you up in Shanghai next week."

"No problem." Easy doing business with Don. The man didn't waste time. Eating humble pie not the worst thing. Not that his brother copped an attitude or anything. Still.

He made coffee.

In this apartment, a split type A-C worked. Quietly, cleanly. He wasn't bathed in sweat every morning. Large paned windows opened a vista to the harbor and sky. Made a difference to the day-to-day. So what if it wasn't the right kind of address.

Face it. He wasn't, would never be, didn't want to be a "local" even if he continued living here. Wasn't *that* why Don and Ai-Lin worked as a couple? Here, Don could be a successful architect, satisfying his ego and ambitions; back home, he was merely talented. Money went further with the overseas federal tax exclusions and low Hong Kong taxes. Here, life was all about, only about money, about endless consumption. It did for some.

The coffee percolated perfect aromatic pleasure. Stronger, better than Didi's watery stuff, or Ai-Lin's inept attempts. Finally, the way he really wanted it.

That afternoon, standing in the elevator lobby at Central Plaza, he was startled by Gail's voice beside him. "So what have you been up to since the Harvard Club?"

Taken aback. Surely he wouldn't have forgotten if they'd run into each other in New York? Or had he? Immediately embarrassed — that he hadn't called when he said he would, but too many divorced women in this town, making demands. All the same, courtesy counted for something. "Did we . . . ?"

"I saw you, but you didn't see me."

Big smile. Upbeat superwoman. Wary, not sure he needed this, her. "What were you doing there?"

"Meeting someone. What about you?"

"Wouldn't know, depends which time you saw me." That should shut her up.

"So how come I didn't know you at Harvard?"

Annoying, this probe. Who did she think she was? "Wrong discipline."

"Oh?"

The inquiring smile. She actually believed . . . "Religion."

Frowned slightly. "Then, you must know _____, " she uttered the name of some professor.

"Yeah, sure I do."

Elevator door opened. She stepped forward, held the door, glared at him. "If you don't care to be sociable, just say so. But don't lie and treat people as if they were complete idiots. It's unnecessary." The door closed in his face.

Instantaneous guilt. What moral outrage propelled this woman? Why did he lie to her? She wasn't being nosy, or even smug. Just sociable. Where were his manners? Mama would've sent him to the corner and confessional for this one.

Got back a couple of hours later and called her direct line, the one she'd written on her card, saying, you can bypass the operator this way and if I'm not there my secretary will pick up. Over eager to connect.

"It's Vince. Listen, about earlier, I apologize. It was unnecessary."

"Well, all right." Still a little miffed.

"We had a dinner date."

"Only if you want to. It's not like we owe each other anything."

Points for candor. Admittedly refreshing. "No, but this way I get to tell you what I was really doing at the Harvard Club."

"I already know."

"This I want to hear."

She hadn't pegged him for one, Gail thought after Vince's call. But her half brother Gordie was, and he used the club as a meeting place regularly, impressing people who didn't know any better. Gail understood more than she cared to about con men and scams. Vince wasn't one, though. His problem was different. It had nothing to do with his not having gone to Harvard.

It had been a surprise, seeing him there. She had almost gone over, but then Gordie had already arrived and she was running late. When she'd left the club, he was gone.

New York was not her kind of town. The trip had been tiring, way too long a distance to fly for such a short time. She didn't like being far away from Gu Kwun, in an upside down time zone. Even though Conchita was an excellent caregiver, a maid was not a mother.

Her company had indicated that they might restructure and bring

Research to New York, and asked if she would move. This troubled her. They told her in confidence that Project Finance and Marketing would be dismantled, because those departments were expensive and not delivering results. She believed the directors probably deserved to be dumped, but she hated the idea of layoffs, especially for the secretarial and support staff.

On the flight back, she had worked out a counter proposal to keep Research in Asia, which would help save some of her staff. Her firm needed her; it made more sense than relocating to New York and travelling back to Asia constantly. Besides, in Hong Kong, Gu Kwun's father was close at hand, even if he didn't bother much about their son. Like her mother said, if she made it easy for him, he might eventually have a change of heart.

The one bonus of the trip had been that she could look up Gordie, which Mom liked, when she remembered who he was.

"It's your son." Her secretary's voice floated through the intercom. Was it already that time?

"Mom, I can't get Uncle's car to work."

Gordie had given her a battery powered Lamborghini as big as Gu Kwun's head to take back as a present. "Do you have the batteries in the right way, sweetie?"

"Grandma put them in for me."

Her mother probably put them in the wrong way. "Ask Conchita to take them out and put them in again. Sometimes, that makes things work." It would not do to undermine grandma in his eyes, but she could count on Conchita to do it right.

"Does Uncle Gordie have a real car like this?"

"No hon, he has a Jaguar."

"What's that like?"

More than he can afford, she thought. "I'll ask him for a photo, okay? Or maybe you can write and ask him to send one."

"Yeah!"

"Now do your homework like a good boy."

"Okay. Will Uncle Gordie come visit soon?"

She hesitated. It was best not to entangle Gu Kwun too closely with Gordie, even though her son adored him. Gordie was difficult to dislike. Despite his flamboyance and transparent use of people when it suited him, he had something resembling a heart. Perhaps he simply wanted to honor their father's memory, because he chose to stay in touch, yet never demanded anything from her. He had told her once that she was very much like their father, which she hadn't known whether or not to believe. "Maybe, but he's very busy in New York you know, and he can't ever stay long in Hong Kong."

"Yeah. He has to blow this pup stand."

Gail tried not to laugh. Gu Kwun got very sensitive if he thought she was making fun of him. "No, hon. Your uncle likes to say he has to 'blow this *pop* stand.'"

After the call, she turned back to her never ending pile of paper. Her in tray, she decided, was an over-fertilized paper tree. There were times she wished . . . but as Gordie said, her pragmatism was her greatest asset, because she had used her inheritance well while he had blown his. Of course, any inheritance made all the difference in the world if you were only the concubine's child.

**

Standing by the window, Vince contemplated the list of twenty five items headed "Vince's Stuff" faxed to him by his wife. His almost ex-wife. Didi had boxed up his worldly possessions, numbered and labeled the boxes, and sent them to the Da Luca family homestead where his third sister now lived with her two children. His divorced sister. Better than being the only prodigal even if neither parent could bear witness to their sins.

It was one thing to know a woman, but quite another to persuade her to do what you wanted. When he thought about Didi now, he understood that he knew her only too well. She would worry about his stuff, making sure she wrapped his mother's photograph in bubble wrap. She would even worry about his family, babysitting his sister's kids if she needed help, making sure Katy wouldn't want for cousins and a connection to her father's world. And he had depended on her being there, liked the stability of a home that worked. It was easy being with someone who lived up to the responsibility of marrying into everything about his life.

As long as it was what Didi, Deanna, also wanted to do.

But once she decided, once she knew what she had to do, that was it. Had she always felt taken for granted?

I'm not looking for apologies, Vince.

Seeing her again in New York, he wondered how they had ever been intimate. Her face had originally drawn him, with her soft eyes and open smile, a face that told him she wanted his baby. But her model-like height and posture, the pronounced breasts that turned guys' heads, these did little for him. In his dreams, Colleen's tight, small body and Didi's face. He craved Colleen, or even Ai-Lin, the woman who haunted him, the one who had once told him she hated him, the Ai-Lin that used to be, not the woman married to Don.

Didi was right, there was no point in apologizing. He couldn't say sorry for not truly wanting her, for taking advantage of her generous nature in between the selfish women he desired just because she craved marriage and family. Why wouldn't she look for love elsewhere? Marriage and love weren't only about his ego and pride.

The glass pane was cool and hot to his touch in its dance between air conditioned ice and the heat of the afternoon sun.

Only May, yet already too hot.

Had to go to Central, with a quick stop first at Pacific Place. Life hung suspended between the two ends of the northern shore of this island, along the stops of the subway. Small town, at least in his operating sphere. Even his regional travel, to China or Singapore, was along a safe air passage of "global" life.

His last Shanghai trip. Two nights in a big hotel where people spoke English. One day and evening consumed by the ad agency. Another day shooting his brother's project, accompanied by a young woman, a "public relations executive" eager to practice her English, to gain entry into his world beyond her country's shores. Hong Kong was like that too. He could live here the rest of his life and never learn the language.

Wasn't there something just a little bit phony about this so-called life?

He descended into the subway, emerging ten minutes later at Pacific Place. Ran his errand, decided to walk the rest of the way to Central. Stopped at the light, on a blind curve facing I. M. Pei's blade tower on Queensway. Once the divorce came through, in another six or eight months, no turning back on a future alone. But where? Here in Hong Kong, where he could be reminded of his first failed marriage, or New York, to be reminded of his second? And Katy. When he saw her, Katy was happy and excited. But what she kept telling him about was that Joe had given her a toy panda which she loved because it was just like the giant dancing pandas at the "City Radio" show.

Thank god for weekends, for Saturday nights. Leave enough space for a nice dinner tonight, maybe even a bottle of wine. He had a date, a long overdue one, with that superwoman. Learning to date all over again. Weren't they the real children of divorce?

Gail dressed meticulously, and then undressed and started all over again. It was five o'clock. She had promised to meet Vince at eight.

At seven thirty, Gu Kwun refused to eat dinner, despite all Conchita's good natured pleading, until Gail raised her voice and told him to stop behaving like a spoilt brat. That took ten minutes. Then, her mother suddenly emerged from her room after sleeping all afternoon, and declared that Uncle Mark was coming in fifteen minutes so Gail should go to her room. It was another ten minutes to get her settled.

Unable to get through to a radio taxi, she headed out to the street and chance. There were no taxis in sight for five minutes, so she decided to take her car instead and park at the government car park on Lower Albert Road, from where she could walk to Lan Kwai Fong.

Her right heel wobbled as she stepped out of her car, and for a minute she thought it would come off, but it held firm. Wishing she'd worn a less uncomfortable pair of shoes, she rushed as quickly as she could towards the restaurant. It was eight fifteen when she walked in.

He rose and held her chair, and kissed her cheek in greeting. The gesture caught her off guard. He brushed aside all apologies, and poured her a glass of Pinot. When she suggested ordering, he told her it was done, and trusted she liked pomelo in her salad and fish in a pseudo-Asian sauce, since the cuisine was "imitation Thai." She glanced around the bare interior with its turquoise and pale yellow walls, the diners seated at precariously stylish tables, this young and principally foreign crowd, and wondered, why was she here rather than someplace older, less trendy? Yet even as she wondered, she knew. Her generation in Hong Kong didn't "date"; the singles joined married couples in group activities where women invariably outnumbered men. They congregated at homes or private clubs, and only frequented restaurants on expense accounts or during formal occasions.

Vince wasn't as handsome as she recollected.

"You look nice," he said.

Some instinct had told her to wear a plain blouse and slacks, which she seldom did because she liked showing off her long legs. She wore understated but expensive jewelry. But her lipstick was a deep plum color, an unusual choice, something she'd recently acquired which made her look younger. That somehow uninhibited her. She knew he was looking at her face when he spoke. "Thanks."

"So," he smiled.

"Yes," she replied.

"Is the wine okay?"

"Oh, excellent."

A waiter waltzed by to pour. Had she *already* drunk half?

He held up his wine glass in a toast, and leaned towards her in an exaggerated pose. "And now, just as I start to tell you how beautiful you are, the waiter comes by and spills soup on my head."

She laughed, and he followed suit, and suddenly they were talking again, as if they really were friends, about everything and nothing, about life.

By the entree, the waiter was opening their second bottle when Gail exclaimed, "I can't, I'm driving."

"Take a taxi," he said, gesturing at the waiter to pour.

It was that simple, she decided, as she cut into the perfectly poached salmon. Hints of lemon grass and coriander delighted her tongue.

He said. "About the Harvard Club, I was meeting a friend who really did go to Harvard."

"I assumed something like that." She had almost forgotten.

"You might have heard of him. Jim Fieldman? He's a psychotherapist. I gather he generated some infamy at college."

The name clicked. He had been legendary during her Harvard days for his radio program "Psycho On Call" where he gave outrageously funny advice to callers. She hadn't known much else about him, or that he'd gone on to practice seriously. "By reputation, a long time ago. How do you know him?"

"I used to be his patient. But we wound up as racquetball partners and I got to listen to him gripe about his wife instead. He's divorced now too."

"Infectious, isn't it?"

He laughed. "I guess."

But what startled her was his admission of psychotherapy. Did people tell things like that? Of course, Vince did seem fond of disclosure. Among her circle of Hong Kong friends, mostly Chinese former classmates plus a few Americans and locals met through work, she knew which doctor, dentist, pediatrician, Chinese doctor, fortune teller, masseuse, hair dresser and interior designer everyone used. No one ever mentioned a psychotherapist.

"You should look him up if you have some free time in New York the next time you're there," Vince was saying. "He's very interested in visiting Hong Kong and China."

"I will."

That night, he insisted on taking her home by taxi.

"It's a long way," she objected. "And you'll never get a taxi back easily." Plus, she knew, she couldn't invite him up.

"I'll keep ours."

As he pecked her lips goodnight, and then waited to make sure she got into her building safely, Vince mused that he shouldn't make the same mistake twice. When he'd called to ask her out, her tone had been a little wry, but pleased.

His taxi sped away into the night.

Dinner was expensive, nearly three hundred American, more than he'd ever paid for a date. Previously, with his advertising acquaintances, the bill had always been on someone else's expense account. Should've checked. Not that he minded all that much or anything, but why pretend to afford what he really couldn't?

Perhaps, this was penance for Didi. Gail was Didi all over, the woman he shouldn't pursue. It had been a civilized encounter, better than the twenty-something English party girls he slept with, who indulged in drunken tears and went with anyone who was buying a round. He never even asked for their phone numbers.

With Gail though, at least they could talk, although she diverted all talk away from personal stuff. What was she hiding? The only feeling she revealed was how badly she wished she'd had a daughter. Passionate about that.

But the *real* trouble was that she'd be good in bed. Satisfyingly good, not like Colleen. Gail was that kind of sexy. And easy to wake up to in the morning. Just like Didi.

He neared the turnoff for his street. Would maybe Jim like her?

Gail pushed the button for the lift, watching the taxi pull away. How strange his kiss felt. The first time she remembered her father leaning over to kiss her, the sensation remained on her cheek for weeks afterwards. It had been the foreign-ness, the fact that he wasn't Chinese. Gail was conscious of it then, as she was with Vince now.

She had never slept with any man other than her ex-husband. It hadn't been either a deliberate or moral choice, but first there had been school, and then her career, and somehow, men didn't present themselves in her life. When she met her ex at a party of the Harvard Chinese students society, she was already thirty-two, and he six years younger. In retrospect, her citizenship may have been the real attraction, given his desperation to live in America as his medical internship neared its end. Perhaps by then, it had already been too late to make up for everything she had missed.

But what Vince's kiss left her with now was a desire for more.

Did she feel American, he had asked, because she had disclosed her U.S. citizenship, saying as she usually did, that her father died when she was young. Yes, she replied, at least in terms of her preferred way of working, her American education, and the fact that she had lived in the U.S. for several years. "So you're not one of those passports-of-convenience types," he'd remarked. "That's refreshing."

She had accepted the compliment, but truthfully, it wasn't something she thought about anymore. That citizenship had once been all important, conferring as it did a legitimacy she craved after years of secrecy. In secondary school, she had lied to all her friends, pretending she was American and would one day go where "my father's relatives will look after me." It was what her mother taught her to say. The panic she'd felt as time passed, and nothing of the sort materialized, was something she never dared give voice to. Her fallback was to score top marks in all her exams, hoping that this way, she could win a scholarship to an American university, and no one need ever know.

The lift doors opened and she stepped in. She looked blankly at the buttons, and, for a moment, forgot what floor she lived on. The one thing she had expected to know out of this evening — whether or not she really liked Vince — still eluded her. The desire he incited lingered, like the impression of his lips. Or was she just imagining it all, helped by the wine?

But the single, hard fact she couldn't deny loomed large: he hadn't, and more than likely wouldn't, suggest another date.

19

It wasn't going to be a large party, Gail told Andanna, but since Sylvie was the reason they met, and the party was a department farewell for her, would she like to come along and bring her boyfriend if she liked?

"We broke up."

"Oh, I am sorry to hear that." Gail surprised herself; she meant that, sincerely.

"It's okay." On an impulse, Andanna asked, "Can I bring my friend Clio? She works for Citibank," she added quickly, thinking that Gail would be looking for her cousin's replacement. Besides, this might get her back into Clio's good graces.

"Of course. Then, I'll see you?"

"Yeah. See ya."

Andanna rolled out of bed. It was past eleven. She really must stop sleeping so late, but it was hard when she didn't get to bed until three or four.

"You Fun, you look awful," her mother declared over lunch.

Andanna didn't reply.

"If you're not careful, you'll have lines on your face by the time you're thirty."

She continued eating in silence.

"Well if you're not going to be conversational, at least tell me whether or not you want to come to Europe with me this summer. My agent's been holding your booking open, but she must finalize it. It'll be much better if you do, because then you can translate. You know how I hate having to speak English."

This was her father's defeat. For years, Mother had nagged, wanting the same shopping trips and spa visits abroad enjoyed by her in-laws. For years, her father had said all that would be no problem as long as she didn't expect him to come along, knowing she'd refuse which meant he wouldn't have to spend the money. When her mother had surprised him by finally saying yes, with a proviso that Andanna could come along if she wanted to, her father had been silenced into paying.

"Besides," her mother added, "it'll be good for your singing career."

"Everything for my career is right here. I don't need to go to Europe."

"But it could be interesting."

"I'm not interested in Europe."

"You've never been. How would you know?"

"Mother, you go and have a good time. The travel guide can translate for you. You know I can't stand speaking English either."

Her mother sighed. "You young people. I just don't understand. We send you to Canada so it'll be easy for you to learn English. If I had half your opportunities when I was your age . . ."

Andanna shut out the rest of her mother's complaints. All the ancients complained that she didn't appreciate her "opportunities." They had it all wrong. Even Clio thought that all it took to become a star was just to practice singing a lot. It wasn't like that at all.

Yesterday, Michael had called to say goodbye. He'd been accepted at Berklee, and planned to go to New York in August before starting school. She had been surprised, having never thought it would actually happen, but what sentiment she felt quickly turned to annoyance when he invited her to his farewell gig at The Jazz Club at which "this German gal who sings and scats really well" would be sitting in. In all the time they'd been together, Michael had never once invited her to sing with his band at The Jazz Club, limiting her performances to inconsequential party gigs. Well, she wouldn't go. He didn't mean anything anymore and she was glad to be rid of him.

But listening to her mother carry on now about everywhere she planned to go, she felt empty. Everyone was doing *something*, except her. Damn that Albert, and Jake's brother. Neither one had come through, which meant her career was going nowhere fast.

Later, Andanna rang Clio to invite her to Gail's. "You might be able to take Sylvie's job if Gail likes you."

Her friend only seemed to be half listening. "Well maybe. I don't know about investment banks. They're not as stable as consumer. Besides, I'm up for a promotion. How much does Sylvie make?"

Andanna had no idea, and repeated her invitation. She was put out because Clio was singularly unimpressed. Even before she could finish, her friend interrupted.

"I've got some news."

"What?"

"I'm engaged."

The announcement so stunned Andanna she didn't say anything.

"Aren't you going to congratulate me?"

"But who . . . how long has . . . ?"

"Oh, we've been together more than a year now. I've told you about him, not that you ever listen. Of course, we're not going to get married for at least two or three years, until we can afford our own place. But our parents met. My friends all like him."

"So how come I didn't know till now? How come I haven't met him?"

An uncomfortable silence followed. Finally. "Well, you're always busy with your own life, and I didn't think you'd find what I was doing all that exciting. He's more like me, pretty boring, an internal auditor in an insurance company who goes to karaoke in his spare time. But he's very devoted and sweet. Hey, we can't all be like you."

"What's that supposed to mean?"

"Oh you know. Modeling, singing, hanging out at clubs. And all your admirers. First Michael, then Tai Jai, plus all those others you dangle along."

She was fuming, but held her tongue. "Hey, something new all the time. Congratulations. I hope I get to meet him."

"You can, at Michael's farewell gig."

"Are you serious?"

"Of course I am. Michael introduced us. They were classmates. Really Andanna, don't you ever pay attention to *anything* I tell you?"

Had she dared, she would have slammed the phone on Clio.

Andanna chained smoked and downed Diet Cokes. What was wrong with her? Surely she wasn't jealous? But that crack about Tai Jai . . . it was all too much. Why did she have to keep bringing him up? She wished she'd never told her about the first time. Although she denied seeing him again, Clio guessed. The truth was, she'd seen him twice since, both times because she, not he, had instigated it.

The last time had been almost two months ago. They had gone to a motel room which Tai Jai paid for. It was four in the afternoon. Afternoons, he claimed, were for sex and siestas.

"Astronomical gravitational pull." He rolled over on top of her. "Just like those galaxies no one can see."

She lit a cigarette. "Why are you always going on about that astronomy crap?"

"I study stars, like you. *Lei You Fun,* Canto pop star."

It sounded real the way he said it. Authentic. "You think I'm going to be a star?"

"You already are. But not if you kill yourself with these first." He took her cigarette and put it out, and climbed back on top of her.

"Man, don't you ever stop?"

"You want it."

And she did, until six thirty when he stopped, because he had to go.

After he left, Andanna had sat naked on the bed, smoking. She couldn't do this anymore. It was humiliating. If Clio or Michael could see her, they'd be so damned critical. Tai Jai might have been his childhood friend for whom he'd do anything, but Michael still considered him uncouth and wouldn't hang out with him. She couldn't ignore the signs of his triad connections. It wasn't like they loved each other or anything. Worse, if her parents found out, she might be disowned. What was wrong with her?

We can't all be like you. Clio's words fused into Michael's scolding. Ghastly mixture.

She had remained in the room, in a sort of trance, until the knock. "Five more minutes." Andanna lit another cigarette. Chain smoking was bad for her. She ought to stop. Tai Jai said she reeked like an ashtray. "Go away," she called out. "I'll pay for another hour."

She slid the money under the door. Things usually sorted themselves out, but right now, nothing did. Michael was angry at her, Clio didn't have time to talk when she called, and Tai Jai was only willing to see her because of the sex. Andanna had sat there alone, smoking and thinking for the next hour. If only, even though it wasn't like her in the least, if only she were able to cry.

**

Gail surveyed the final preparations for the get together.

"Everything looks lovely," Colleen said. "You're so talented."

Had it been a good idea to ask Colleen along? The gathering comprised mainly her staff and one or two other colleagues. The Leyland-Tangs had just moved back to Hong Kong, and Gail knew Kwok Po was out of town. Colleen didn't seem to have a lot of her own friends, so Gail originally thought this seemed like a good idea. She had sounded enthusiastic enough, and even offered to come over early and help.

Yet Gail felt, again, the gulf that separated them. No matter how hard she tried, she simply couldn't like Colleen. She was harmless enough, a bit fawning perhaps, but altogether too frivolous. When she had been playing with Gu Kwun earlier, she made jokes about "all the girlfriends you're going to have when you grow up." Imagine talking about girlfriends to an eight-year old. How ludicrous.

The bell sounded, and several people arrived at the same time, including Sylvie. A few minutes later, Andanna and her girlfriend showed up.

It was mid way through the evening before Gail had a chance to speak to Clio.

"Andanna tells me you work at Citibank."

An American colleague joined them, and the conversation switched to English. Clio's command of the language was impressive. How unlike Andanna, whose spoke appallingly for someone who'd studied abroad. This smart and ambitious young woman seemed interested in the world around her, and not just in herself. Also, she listened when others spoke, a rare trait among the young.

From across the room, Andanna watched her friend engrossed in conversation. Clio looked poised and well dressed. Her own casual black slacks and shirt made her feel under dressed.

She was bored. Gail rushed around, being the dutiful hostess, and hardly said two words to her. All the conversation was about business. No one recognized her, as it had been a few months since she'd done any high profile modeling. Gu Kwun was nowhere to be seen; she would at least have enjoyed playing with him. She suddenly remembered she'd never followed up on taking him to Ocean Park.

She glanced around the flat. It was as unexciting as this party.

On the sideboard in the living room were three, porcelain, Lladro figurines. The general decor was an extension of those figurines, pretty and inoffensive, in pale pastel colors, matched by unimaginative Western style furniture. The pictures on the walls were soothing land-scapes of waterfalls or flowers in meadows. It was a look that belonged in a shopping center showroom of an average, middle class neighborhood like say, Taikoo Shing, designed to please the broadest spectrum of consumers. It didn't belong in this expensive area.

Andanna thought about her parents' home with its rosewood Chinese living and dining room sets, Italian bedrooms and American kitchen. All custom designed by a top decorator. Mother had never been afraid to spend the wealth she'd married into. More important, she had taste.

"Neih dim sik Gail a?"

She was surprised to see that American woman, Gail's friend. "Oh, you speak Cantonese."

"Siksikdei, gau kinggai." I know some, enough for conversation. "How do you know Gail?" she repeated.

"Through Sylvie," and she explained.

"You don't look like you belong here."

"Well, I'm a singer actually. This isn't my kind of scene."

"A singer, how marvelous. Do you have an album? And a stage name?"

"As a matter of fact, I'm hoping to make a video any day now, but I want to use my own name, *Lei You Fun.*" And she started telling her about Albert and Jake's brother, all of which Colleen listened to, fascinated, asking her lots of questions.

Answering Colleen's questions was unlike talking to Gail. Gail was nice enough but dull. Colleen had a lively, playful manner, and didn't act older, even though she was. She also talked about relevant things, and knew many of the local artists.

"You need an angle, what we Americans call a 'gimmick.'"

Andanna frowned. "I don't understand."

"You know, something to set you apart from other Canto pop singers, so that the public will notice you. That's the way to stardom."

"Well, I did play classical and jazz before, but they weren't my scenes."

"You mean you studied?"

For the first time, she wasn't sure what to say. Previously, she always told people she'd studied music. But something Tai Jai said to her stuck: that Michael studied the heart and soul of music while she was happy just making sounds. She wasn't sure what he meant, but ever since he'd said it, she was uncertain of her own relationship to music. "Well, kind of. I mean I got a degree but I haven't exactly been a serious musician. But I'm not bad," she added quickly.

"Oh, I know exactly what you mean. I haven't had the right opportunity to really use everything I've studied properly either. But you know, you could create a kind of classical pop, Canto style, or something like that."

That was it, she thought. Andanna felt as if a burden had been raised off her. Colleen made sense. It was all about the right opportunity. In school, she had frankly gotten bored practicing classical piano, and being with Michael showed her jazz was all wrong. Singing foreign songs just didn't feel real. It wasn't as if she weren't willing to work hard or anything, but somehow, what she did had to be right for her, otherwise, there wasn't any point.

There was definitely something special about Colleen.

It emerged that she knew Albert. By the end of the evening, Andanna had promised to come visit Colleen, who in turn promised to organize something with Albert since they all knew each other.

Now, Andanna wasn't bored any longer.

"Small world, Hong Kong," Colleen said. "It's easy to know who's worth bothering with. Rather nice that way."

Gail had listened to Colleen's account of meeting Andanna, and wondered at her assertion that Kwok Po would find the young woman "entertaining." Was it only because of the family she came from? "I suppose. But it gets a little claustrophobic."

"That girl's going to be a star, I'll bet."

"How do you know? You haven't heard her sing."

"She has the will to do it, and some musical training. It's enough to get started. Besides, she's sexy and attractive. You know, that model look."

Gail listened to Colleen's chatter. How unusually animated she was tonight. Gail couldn't recall when she'd ever heard her express an opinion. Colleen was generally demure and quiet in company, while she and Kwok Po could talk up a storm. It was as if Andanna had ignited some flame, made her sure of herself. Colleen wound thick strands of hair around her wrists as she spoke, twisting them into knots which she would let fall dramatically, her hands waving gracefully in the air. She seemed unconscious of the effect she created.

"In fact, I'd like to help her," Colleen was saying.

Gail almost said, and what do you know about Canto pop music, but stopped herself. If that was what Colleen thought she could do, who was she to object? These two spoilt princesses deserved each other. Just as well they met.

Right now, though, she was tired, and began to lose patience with Colleen's frivolous nonsense. As politely as she could, she ushered her out. Her little farewell party for Sylvie had been a success. Too bad she was losing her, but then, these girls were in such a hurry to give up everything they worked for, in this case, not even because she was pregnant. To each her own, however much she disagreed. It wasn't her life.

Clio looked rather happy as they left Gail's.

Andanna asked. "So, did she ask you to apply for the job?"

"Job? Oh that. No, she isn't replacing Sylvie."

"How awful." It horrified Andanna that anyone could be dispensable.

"Why? Your cousin was just passing time, and companies often downsize by not replacing support staff. That's why I prefer being a line staff. But I liked Gail. She's quite amazing. Did you know she got her MBA at Harvard while working part time? And her job's super. She travels everywhere, and is in charge of all Asia. She's even been to places like Laos and Myanmmar. Isn't that something?" Clio talked on about Gail, and it was clear she had discovered more about her in one conversation than Andanna had from spending a whole day with her.

This silly hero worship annoyed her. "I bet you didn't know her mother's a bit off her rocker."

But Clio shot her down. "That's private, and you shouldn't be such a gossip. She's worked hard to get where she is, because her father died when she was young and they didn't have much money."

"Really?" Andanna's eyes widened. "I thought she was, you know, rich or something."

Her friend giggled, then stopped.

"What's so funny?"

"You. You sure don't get it, do you? How come you're so clueless?"

Andanna shrugged. "I don't have time for all that crap. Now listen, are you really going to Michael's farewell gig?"

After they parted, Clio's comment rankled. So what if she didn't know all that dumb stuff about Gail? Clio would never have met Gail if she hadn't brought her along. But what she was trying to decide was whether or not to see Michael again. Perhaps she should. The idea that some foreign girl would be singing with him pissed her off, though. He was probably just trying to get back at her for dumping him. It wasn't her fault he was such a bore. Why on earth did he have to take off for Boston anyway?

Colleen's remark tonight — that the twenty first century belonged to China, and Hong Kong would be a part of that. Also, she said more people in the world spoke Chinese than any other language. Now, that was deep. She liked Colleen's attitude. There she was, a *gwaipo,* yet she could speak *Putonghua* and even Cantonese, and read Chinese as well. Why did Chinese people have to learn English? One day, things would be the other way round, and then Clio and Gail and Michael would see how wrong they were.

She felt better, less bothered by Clio. If her friend wanted to keep her life separate — she still hadn't bothered to introduce her fiancé — that was just fine. She didn't need her. As for Michael, perhaps it wasn't such a bad idea to go. After all, Albert hung out at The Jazz

Club, so he might even be there. Perhaps she could invite Colleen so she wouldn't have to go alone. Now *there* was an idea.

Gail lay in bed that night, unable to sleep. This recent insomnia was unlike her. She had been quite exhausted earlier after the party, but now, as morning threatened the horizon, she had hardly slept at all.

It had been over a month since her date with Vince, and he still hadn't called.

Perhaps there was an etiquette she didn't appreciate. When she'd lived in Boston, she never paid attention to the way her American girl-friends carried on about dating. Now, she wished she had. It was just that at the time, she found American women obsessed with the idea of men to the exclusion of all else.

Well, she wasn't all that different these days.

Gail sat up, gathering her knees into her arms.

Just before the dessert arrived, Vince had stretched across the table and taken her left hand in his. "What d'you do with the ring?"

She had looked at him, perplexed.

"The wedding ring."

"I didn't have one."

"What about an engagement ring, a diamond?"

"Didn't have that either." No one had ever asked her about this before. "It isn't a custom among Hong Kong people."

"What're you talking about? The girls I work around all show off their engagement rings. Your ex was a doctor, right? Babes, you were shortchanged."

His abruptness startled and annoyed her. But as she thought about it now, of course he was right. Sylvie had worn a huge rock, and recently, she'd noticed a discreet diamond on her secretary's hand. Even that young woman tonight, Andanna's friend, she had been wearing one.

Why was it that she, with all her education and intelligence, could be so dim about such a simple thing? And did she simply demand too much of what didn't matter, and too little of what did? Perhaps she was, as her mother was fond of saying, too *"ngaahnggeng ngaam"* — "strong-necked right," stubbornly right, because once she had a notion in her head, she wouldn't let go. In particular, when she'd talked about equality between the sexes, her mother had said she was ridiculous and naïve, with no sense of the world. Right and wrong were arbitrary concepts. As long as a woman was beautiful, that was all a man cared about. Over the years, Gail had written off her mother's attitude as sexist and outdated.

Until her ex left her.

It had been a long time since she allowed herself to think about him. Vince had been quite curious, since he was plenty open about his own two failed marriages which he called "bad investments, the diamonds, I mean." She had dodged his questions about her own marriage, finding them too intimate, thinking it really none of his business, choosing instead to tell him about the daughter she wanted but never had.

Perhaps it wasn't his business, but sometimes, she didn't even make it her own.

When her ex left, one of the things he accused her of was that he was tired of always being wrong. She had demanded to know what he meant, and he had shrugged and dismissed her question with something like oh, it doesn't matter, you're always right anyway, aren't you? At first, all their mutual friends ostracized him socially, sympathizing with her because of his unforgivable behavior. But at what point had she become aware that there were fewer and fewer invitations, except from a handful of her friends? Quite recently, she'd learned that her ex and his new wife were at an anniversary party given by a couple who had roundly denounced him before. It was a huge social bash. She hadn't been invited.

What good was revisiting all this? It would only depress her. He was still an awful father, while she was stuck with all the responsibility. True, she had demanded custody, and limited his visits at first. But how could she have Gu Kwun spend time with his father and that woman? It simply wouldn't be right.

She lay down again, trying to clear her thoughts. Vince wasn't all that special; why was she so taken by him? As for her ex, perhaps she did hold a lot over him, but wasn't that all his own fault anyway? Wasn't it?

20

"Is Miss Szeto so much better an employer than me, Conchita? I need you back." Colleen was mildly irritated. Surely she wouldn't have to go through another Rosa experience again back here in Hong Kong. But Conchita was being stubborn, as Colleen knew she was capable of being.

"No, Mrs. Tang, it's not that. You know I like you very much, like sisters we are. And we were together a long time, seven, no, eight years. Miss Szeto, she can be very bossy sometimes."

Colleen downed a Tylenol and continued her telephonic persuasion. "So why won't you leave her? I'll pay more if that's what you want. You know how much Mr. Tang thinks of you."

"Not the money, ma'am. Miss Szeto, she pays me very well. It's her little boy. I have to take care of Gu Kwun." It sounded like "Goojuwen" the way she said it.

"Her mother lives there, doesn't she? Surely his grandmother loves him and he's getting all the care in the world?"

Conchita sighed. "Difficult to explain, Mrs. Tang. They're a very strange family. Sometimes," she lowered her voice, even though no one was home to overhear, "I don't think the old lady is completely, you know, right. Like maybe she's getting too old? But please don't tell Miss Szeto I said so."

It was useless, Colleen knew. Despite Conchita's promise to "think about it," the woman wouldn't budge. She had a mission now, to "save" Gu Kwun. How she wished she had sent Conchita off to that Englishwoman instead, the one who was returning to England next month. That way, she'd have gotten Conchita back no problem. Gail had just been so enthusiastic, and of course, there was the friendship with Kwok Po which she couldn't jeopardize. *Aiyaa!* The sacrifices she made for her husband.

The phone rang, and she picked it up absently.

"Sis? Heard you were back."

She almost cried out in relief. "Danny? Oh sweetheart, where are you? Why didn't you call me earlier? It's been months."

"Happy July 4th, sis. You okay?"

"Of course I am. Are you coming to see me?"

"I might. Oh, you know I will."

"Right now? This very instant?"

"Sure."

Barely fifteen minutes later, the tall, lanky boy-man ambled through her door and leaned forward to give her a hug. Ethereal Danny. Thank god he'd given up the snake, a thirteen-foot python he used to carry around his neck everywhere he went.

"So?" Colleen looked questioningly at her brother.

"I'm working for them."

Colleen closed her eyes into a frown. "Danny, the Chinese don't know the meaning of democracy."

His lips pursed. "Everyone knows the meaning."

"You could get into trouble, even get deported. Things are different now that it's almost '97. Don't you want to be able to keep going to China? Isn't that the most important thing?"

"I'll take my chances. Besides, the new Hong Kong government will only be a figurehead. You know China could take over any time. Beijing isn't going to care about someone like me, and no one here will bother as long as I'm in the background."

"But you're running with a noisy crowd. Face it, Martin Lee's a lion." She referred to the leader of the local democracy movement.

Danny didn't reply. He strolled towards the verandah and stared at the view below. They were high up on Stubbs Road, in a top floor flat next to the one where Kwok Po's parents lived. "You know, sis, life isn't just about being comfortable." His back was towards her. "You live with your Filipino maid and driver, never having to care about a thing, jetting off on glamorous holidays all over the world. Your biggest worries are whether or not next season's fashion color and style will suit you, or who to invite to the next dinner, next ball, next event."

"You're not being fair."

"Are you?"

She came up from behind and locked both arms around him, recalling their wagon train games where he was the captured Indian warrior, and she the brave pioneer woman who set him free.

He pulled roughly away. "We're not kids anymore, sis."

"How are you going to live?"

"I have some money from the trust."

"Still?"

He turned around and smiled. His face dissolved into a gentle softness that resembled their mother's. "Money goes a long way when you don't buy anyone's labels, and if you replenish it occasionally by earning some."

Her own money — they had gotten equal shares — was long gone, spent during her early travels to Asia and later in Boston where she dragged out her university years, prolonging the degree program in Chinese Studies, until finally, time expired on her Ph.D., but by then, Kwok Po had already proposed. In thirty eight years, she'd never held a real, full-time, paying job.

"I love Kwok Po." Her declaration slipped out in this unintended instance.

Danny cocked his eyebrows. "Do you know, you've never said that about him before? At least not to me."

"Well," her voice became lighter, less serious, "it's good to know I haven't become entirely predictable."

"Are you sure you're okay? I mean, you're not . . ."

Danny guessed about the affairs. He was the one person in the world from whom she couldn't hide a thing. He had watched her bring home one guy after another through all her teenage years, smuggling them in and out of the house without their parents knowing, and never judged her for it.

"And even if I am?" She glared at him, defiant. Their eyes locked in sibling history. "Isn't that my choice?"

He shrugged. "I guess."

"That's democracy for you."

Danny did not stay, despite her offer to put him up. She'd never known where he stayed or how he lived. It wasn't something he shared, and she preferred not to ask. For years, she simply waited for his call — it came, it always came — to let her know he was alive, that he would come see her for a brief while, nothing more.

Yet this time, she had the feeling he was leaving her. It wasn't that she'd never see him again, but he was different, less ethereal perhaps. She couldn't name the feeling. He strolled towards the door, his long dancer's legs commanding a perpetual grace, an unmistakable deportment. Were they really related? Astonishing the realities that separated them.

"You know, you're wrong," he said as he opened the front door.

"About what?"

"Lions. Sometimes, they have to roar."

Andanna waved to Colleen who spied her on the slope.

"Am I late?"

Andanna brushed aside her concern. "Not at all. Come on, they're about to start the first set."

Inside the darkened club, she led Colleen towards sofa seats against the wall, as faraway from the stage as possible. "It's better in the back," she explained, "I don't want to be too obvious about being here."

"I understand."

Their drinks arrived. "Let me," Colleen reached for the bill.

"Oh no, I should invite because I asked you here."

"Come on, let me be the 'big sister.' You wait till you're a star."

Andanna gave in. Colleen *was* like an older sister, full of good advice, yet was someone who understood what she needed and let her be herself. She had spent one afternoon at Colleen's home, hanging out. When in public, always be public Colleen had said about the way she dressed. She had begun to be more selective, finding off beat but expensive designer clothes that made a statement. Colleen even had given her some of her things, saying her husband had no eye for color because he kept buying stuff better suited to a Chinese complexion. Andanna had laughed saying, men, they try but they can't help it, can they? And then she'd told her all about Michael, although she didn't say anything about Tai Jai. Besides, he was in the past and she had no intention of seeing him again.

Right in front of center stage, Clio, her fiancé and a bunch of friends occupied a big table. She had waved when Andanna first came in, but didn't signal her over. Their table was quite noisy. Poor Michael. He hated groups like that who didn't listen to the music, and this would be doubly hard because he had to pretend to appreciate their presence. If Clio had any idea what Michael really thought of her, she'd be hurt. Oh well, that wasn't her concern now.

Colleen said. "By the way, Albert said he'd stop by."

"Thanks. That's so kind of you." She was genuinely pleased.

"Don't be silly. We girls have to stick together, you know?"

The band played a couple of instrumental numbers which Andanna vaguely recognized. And then Michael invited the singer to join them. The fast paced intro for "Autumn Leaves" came up and the woman began to sing.

Andanna held her breath. A weird sensation went through her.

The singer didn't have an exceptional voice, but Andanna heard the phrasing in what she rendered. As she listened, years of Michael's carping flashed by. *You don't have any imagination. You have to feel the music.* And he would play the CD of some famous singer's rendition and tell her to study it.

But what she realized was that this woman was doing what she herself resisted doing all that time. The singer owned this song for the moment because she made it hers. What was also evident was that she captured the "swing" Michael said she, Andanna, never could. For the first time, she heard what he meant.

As the pianist went into his solo, Andanna suddenly felt herself freed from Michael and all that life. It didn't matter that she couldn't be what he wanted. She was right to have left him, right to have gone back home. Now she could become her kind of singer, here in Hong Kong, instead of running off to sing a foreign music in a foreign land. At the same time, she felt a small sadness. Michael had once made her feel important, loved, worshipped and cared for. He taught her independence from her parents. Even though that wasn't the life she wanted, it made her appreciate what she now had more than ever. A pang of shame: she really ought to be more respectful towards her mother.

The woman returned after the solos and brought the song to its close. There was only half hearted applause from the audience, most of who talked noisily through the performance. Andanna felt a little sorry for Michael, but it was his choice to perform this difficult jazz that took even her, a singer, so long to really hear.

"*Wei, leng leui.*" Albert's voice floated towards them during the break after the first set.

"*Bu jiang Guangdong hua.*" Colleen's command that he not speak Cantonese.

"*Meih dou gau chat.*" '97 hasn't arrived, he declared in Cantonese. "*Putonghua hai bu shi Xianggang de mu yu.*" *Putonghua* isn't Hong Kong's mother tongue yet, he added, in Mandarin.

Andanna understood the exchange, but felt a little awkward. When she'd visited Colleen, the latter declared that if she didn't speak *Putonghua,* she really ought to take classes, especially if she wanted to sing. Many of the big name performers could handle both dialects. Some of the Taiwan and Mainland singers even sang in Cantonese now.

Why did things always have to be *difficult?*

Andanna slipped a cigarette between her lips, barely glancing at Albert. "You never got back to me. You're very bad."

"Life gets in the way of pleasures sometimes, 'little sister.'"

"Now, now. That's all going to be fixed, isn't it, Albert? You did promise You Fun you'd take care of her, didn't you? So you should."

"I suppose now that Mrs. Tang is looking after you, I don't have a choice."

The bantering continued. Albert bought a round of drinks. Andanna wanted to say something about the photographs, but with Colleen there, she didn't dare. She didn't think there was anything wrong in doing them, but wasn't entirely sure what it all meant.

It was disconcerting when Albert brought it up.

"You Fun's going to pose for my collection."

A wicked smile crossed Colleen's face. "Naughty pictures?"

"Not exactly," Andanna said quickly.

Albert winked at Colleen, and she laughed lightly, saying, "You are a bad girl, aren't you? Why You Fun, I wouldn't have guessed."

Andanna blew a thin line of smoke at the ceiling, feigning disinterest. But secretly, she was worried. It wasn't as if she'd given the idea much thought, but she also hadn't told anyone except Clio. This was becoming too public already. Who else had Albert told?

The band came back onstage for the second set. Andanna saw Clio look their way, and noted the envious glances from her table. Colleen

Tang, she was discovering, was almost as recognizable socially as Albert. Well if Clio wanted to get engaged and end her life, that was her problem. Just wait. She'd win Clio's affections back. No man was going to come between them, not for long.

**

Hong Kong was going to be her home. The finality of this revelation struck Colleen with renewed certainty. Tomorrow, Tuesday, August 27, 1996, would be her tenth wedding anniversary, a week prior to the tenth anniversary of their having moved here.

Before Kwok Po apologetically took off for Singapore last night, he had promised to be back Tuesday afternoon so that the rest of the day and evening would be theirs. This Monday wasn't a public holiday in Singapore like it was here, and he wanted to take advantage of that to get some work done there, without his office bothering him. Of course she'd said, as usual, "no problem."

"Yin Fei, puih laihlai hui geen Loh saang, hou ma?" Her mother-in-law on the phone, wanting Colleen to accompany her for a visit to her jeweler Mr. Lo, and she had to remind her it was a public holiday. Mrs. Tang always called her by her Chinese name, Yin Fei, meaning swallow in flight. Colleen knew she was her *laihlai's* favorite daughter-in-law even though she wasn't Chinese and hadn't borne children; but the wives of Kwok Po's brothers were those "liberated modern working mothers," something *laihlai* abhorred. Besides, she spoke the Chinese that mattered better than either of her sisters-in-law. So she ranked right up there.

At loose ends today, because his trip had been unexpected. Not a good day to visit the jewelers, to *yum cha* with *laihlai,* or to go shopping on her own. Even her charities were on down time.

Perhaps it was time to re-design the bedroom.

Such frivolous thoughts, although if she had chosen to present her husband with the idea of re-decorating, it would have been only as a well considered proposal which he wouldn't turn down.

She went to light a cigarette but stopped herself. Lately, nothing seemed to satisfy, except maybe Kwok Po's presence. Coming back home — Hong Kong was home now, really, truly — had meant improvements in the marital bedroom. She'd managed more or less to forget about Vince.

So what was eating at her?

"*M'arm,* can I talk to you?"

"What is it, Jacinta?" Another Rosa, except that this one was less fulsome and tedious. She was educated, like Conchita, and was much brighter than Rosa.

"I need to go home."

"When?"

"Early December, before Christmas."

Jacinta was from Manila, which meant her trips home would be less complicated than Conchita's used to be. Women like Conchita from the remote villages needed more travel time. "For how long?"

"Can you let me have two weeks? I'll come back for Christmas."

She chose not to question her good fortune. Christmas generally meant the flight of the Filipinos back to their Catholic home country. Besides, the reason was bound to be complicated and more than she cared to know. In dealing with maids, *laihlai* had said — don't get involved in their personal lives, it'll only be trouble. Colleen heeded that bit of advice now, although things had been different once. A long time ago, during her early years in Hong Kong, Conchita had been the only friend she had. She'd never admit that to *laihlai* though. Her mother-in-law was generally quite bossy and even cruel towards her maids, treating them like indentured servants. But she also assert-ed that being a Chinese wife, however privileged, was an equivalent servitude.

"No problem, Jacinta."

"I'll confirm the dates later, *m'arm.* Thank you." If she felt either relief or gratitude, it wasn't apparent. She headed towards the kitchen to make lunch.

At least her domestic had the right idea. Going home was Jacinta's right and hardly a privilege. No gratitude to a mistress was required. *Laihlai* and many others, she knew, would say otherwise. Colleen had listened often to *laihlai's* complaints that her domestics were rude and disrespectful. It was only because they were frightened of her, because Colleen and Kwok Po never had any problem. Life in America had softened the attitudes her husband learned from family. By now, though, Colleen knew better than to argue. Hong Kong *yan* had their own definitions of democracy. She suddenly wondered what Danny would think of all this. Not much probably, since he held his own principles in higher regard than the will of the majority he professed to serve.

It was noon. Colleen shook off her earlier unease and checked the notes in her diary. Might as well get on with the day. She called You Fun. "Aren't you up yet?"

The voice that answered was thick with sleep. "It's still dark."

"For god's sake, You Fun, go pull the curtains and open your windows. It's late." The girl had confessed that she kept her windows shut all the time, and lived in air conditioning. She claimed the air was too dirty. The girl lived a way too insular life, never leaving her room except at nights when she flitted into the club scene like a bat. And she ate hardly anything, substituting Diet Cokes for food. It would be hard work getting her into shape as a real performer, even if she did have star potential.

"Did you want something?" An insolent tone underscored Andanna's question.

"I got you that audition you wanted."

She could almost hear her sit up.

"What did you say?"

"You heard me. You've got a week."

"But I can't possibly be ready, I . . ."

The girl was a wimp. "Listen, do you want to become a pop singer or not?"

"Of course."

"Then get your body out of bed and start rehearsing."

Colleen agreed to help her out over the next week and even attend the audition with her. Afterward, she wondered if she had shouldered too big a burden, although it was better than this unaccountable boredom — there really was no other way to describe how she felt — and unless You Fun proved too much of a brat, she planned to take her as far as she could.

21

The large manila envelope, fortified by cardboard and tied with a pink ribbon, slid unopened into Gail's in tray. "Ariadne, what's this?"

Her secretary blinked through her glasses. "It's marked 'personal,' Ms. Szeto, so I didn't open it."

Gail began slicing with a letter opener. "When did it come?"

"Late yesterday afternoon, after Reception was closed. If I hadn't happened to be on my way to the toilet, I wouldn't have seen him knocking on the door."

"Who? The messenger?"

"No, the *gwailo,*" Ariadne corrected herself quickly, "I mean, *saiyahn.*" Westerner. Gail strongly preferred the latter, and insisted on its use.

No curiosity, Gail reflected, as Ariadne returned to her desk. Back in her Boston work life, such an unusual delivery would have caused a buzz around the office, hierarchy notwithstanding. Yet here, her secretary wouldn't call her by her first name, and if she experienced any curiosity whatsoever, she never let on. Gail had respected that distance from the time she first interviewed Ariadne for the job and asked why she chose an English name out of Greek mythology. Her then secretary-to-be had blinked, and with a perfectly straight face said, "I had no idea it was," with a finality that implied, and nor did she care. Ferocious efficiency made up for the lack of personality.

A black and white 8" by 10" photograph of herself confronted her. Gail recognized the setting. Last week, she had been the keynote speaker for Forex Asia at the Convention Center. The shot was taken as she descended from the stage. She had been in good spirits, because her talk had been well received. A mild exhilaration colored her countenance as she shook hands with the organizer. The angle flattered her.

She turned over the picture. On the back was scrawled "Photogenic? *Moi?*" and she laughed out loud, because that was what Vince had said when she stated that she wasn't the very first time they'd met.

Ariadne was hovering in her doorway. "Is everything all right?"

She looked up, surprised. "Yes, what makes you ask?"

"You . . . laughed."

Her secretary's face was so pricelessly serious that Gail burst out laughing again. Her whole body shook, and try as she would, it was impossible to stop. Ariadne would think she had lost her marbles, which only made her laugh harder until even her secretary couldn't help smiling. It wasn't till Gail calmed down several minutes later that the truth of Ariadne's bewilderment struck her: during four years in this office, no one had ever heard her laugh out loud.

All summer long, she had waited for Vince to ask her out, hoping against hope. After their date in May, she'd broken down and called him twice, once in June and again a month later. He was friendly but distant, and somehow, their schedules always clashed. In August, she tried to forget about him and concentrated instead on enjoying life with Gu Kwun during his holidays.

Having resigned herself to his lack of interest, this unexpected gift delighted her. Without hesitation, she reached for the phone and dialed Vince herself. "Dinner's on *moi.*"

"You liked it? I wasn't sure."

"I'm very flattered, especially that you managed to take it without my knowledge. And I am serious about dinner."

"I'll have to take a rain check. I'm going to Shanghai tonight for at least a week."

"What a coincidence. So am I." Gail flipped open her trip file. "I'm at the Portman Shangri-la. Where are you?"

"Same."

"See you there, then?"

"Sure."

That was awkward. Hadn't counted on this. Only meant to make a friendly gift, nothing else. It was a good shot of her. Couldn't he be "just friends" with women?

Last week, when he'd casually mentioned Gail to Don and told him about the photo, his brother encouraged him to send it. "You should get to know some nice women your own age," he told him. "Those twenty-somethings will be the death of you. You have been tested for AIDS, haven't you?" Not what he wanted to hear. Ignored Don at first. And then, yesterday evening, in a moment's impulse, packaged it up and dropped off the photo himself. What made him do it? Loneliness and a small block of free time. Deadly combination.

The rest of the day was a mad rush to get ready for his trip. More work for Don. Just as he was about to leave for the airport, his brother called for the fifth time that day asking if he remembered about the black and whites they wanted. That was when he lost it. Told him if he called again he could find another photographer. Don retreated, cowed. Patronizing, this obsessive attention to detail. How much longer did he want to work for his brother?

That night at *Hong Qiao* airport, the taxi driver stared blankly and demanded, *"qu nali?"* his voice loud, trying to force comprehension. Vince repeated the hotel name to more incomprehension. Finally, in frustration, began to disembark when the taxi driver said, "hotel!" and produced a dog-eared list of the major Shanghai hotels in Chinese and English, and then they could go.

Gail was checking in when he arrived at the reception desk. "We have to stop meeting like this."

Vince froze a polite smile. Already, the gal behind the reception desk was giving him a sly look, asking, "together?"

"Yes, I mean, no." Too loudly.

A glint in her eye. *Shit*. Away from home, she'd be uninhibited. Women. All the same when the hormones raged.

"Got any appointments tomorrow evening?"

She wasn't wasting any time. "No, I mean yes." Couldn't think straight. Wished he hadn't had that beer on board.

"You're not very decisive tonight, are you?"

"Sorry, tired."

Finishing her check in, she picked up her briefcase. "I'm in 653. Give me a call tomorrow when you've decided."

Glad to be rid of her for the moment, he proceeded with registration. Tomorrow could wait.

When she hadn't seen him on board her flight, Gail thought perhaps his plans had changed. Seeing him lifted her spirits. If only there were someone to tell.

Before she'd left for Shanghai that evening, she had tried to tell Mom. She made it a practice to leave for trips from home rather than her office, because that way, the absence from her family was a little easier to bear. "He's an American photographer. We've been out a couple of times."

"Uncle Mark is not a photographer."

"I'm not talking about you and Uncle Mark. I'm telling you about my friend."

"A boyfriend?"

"No, not exactly. But maybe he could be."

Her mother laughed harshly. "Don't be silly. You're married."

She was about to say, no mother, I'm not anymore, but her mother had wandered absent-mindedly back into her room. Why had she even bothered? Way back, long before the memory lapses when Gail had called to announce her engagement, all her mother cared about was whether or not her husband-to-be had money.

The hotel had upgraded her to a superior room. She unzipped her garment bag and hung her suits in the closet. Slipping off her pumps, she unrolled pantyhose and dug bare feet into the deep pile, delighting in the air conditioned luxury.

Gail removed her pearl earrings, and laid them on the dressing table. Unbuttoning her blouse, she unhooked her bra and lifted it up so that her breasts confronted her in the mirror. She undid her skirt and let it fall to her feet. She faced her almost naked body.

The first time she and her ex made love, he accused her of being ashamed of her body. She had been a little shy of removing all her clothes, and would not do so till he turned out the lights. Her shyness embarrassed her, because at thirty-three, she was self conscious of the fact of her virginity, feeling that she might have left this too late.

She had approached sex the way she did everything else in life, through careful, analytical research. Having read all the established authors on the subject, she made up her mind that other than procreation, the natural outcome of sex was a mutually satisfying climax for both parties. After dating her ex for about six months, she decided that she loved him and agreed to enter into what she called a complete relationship. But before she would, she insisted on discussing with him her notions about sex. He had been bemused at what he called her repressed ideas, meaning that sex could wait until two people fully understood each other. It took a year before she was willing to make love to him.

One of the things he said when he left was that she had been "too demanding."

For the first time since the break up of her marriage, she ran her hands along her body, giving into its natural response.

What did she expect from Vince?

Love? Romance? Or just sex?

Wasn't she too old for all this?

She remembered the better times of her marriage, when they would make love almost every night. Their appetites had been gluttonous, shamefully so her husband said. But she felt no shame, no inhibition. Their love justified it. After Gu Kwun was born, they slowed down a little, but still indulged regularly. When he announced the affair and asked for a divorce, her physical self had shut down, repelled.

He had said ugly things to her through the divorce, calling her a "control freak," "self righteous," "power hungry." The worst were the echoes of her mother — "unnatural," "unfeminine," his asking, demanding "what kind of woman" behaved like her? She had tuned him out, refusing to recall any pleasures they shared. Until now.

The mirror didn't lie. She was a beautiful woman, all woman.

Ten thirty. Vince waited at the bar. What was he doing here? Her message had been a command, not an invitation. But he couldn't not show, not after they'd bumped into each other at breakfast and she was virtually all over him, verbally at least. Now what? *Mistake – Mistake* flashed like a B-movie neon billboard.

Not a drinks-after-dinner or bar type, yet it was what she'd suggested to overcome his schedule objections. Tired. Worn out by the tediousness of getting anything done in China. Didn't need this.

Gail strode in like an Amazon on the warpath. She looked harassed. "Sorry I'm late. Talking to New York, you know."

"I'm not that privileged." Seeing that she didn't crack a smile, he offered. "Want a drink?"

"I suppose."

She ordered in Chinese, bypassing him completely, eyes flashing decisively. An exquisite face. Admirable, the way she took command. More natural than her attempts to be coy or flirtatious. Her white wine arrived, and she drank with relish.

"You needed that, huh?"

"There are days."

Cut this short. "I told my friend Jim about you. He'd like to meet you." Couldn't read her face. Like a grimace, but not exactly.

"I'm not sure what you mean."

"You . . . intrigued him. I guess you're his type." He turned back to his drink, unwilling to look at her.

"And where is this friend?"

"In New York. You know, my therapist, the Harvard Club guy?"

Now, she turned to the bar. "I see. The distant type."

"He'll be here. In fact, he's planning to spend time in China as well." Embarrassed. Spoke too rapidly.

"You're suggesting I'm a candidate for long distance, uh, friendships?" And then, startling him. "What did you do? Send him my photograph as well?" Her tone vicious.

"Of course not. Gail, I didn't mean . . . "

He watched her face change, erasing the perfect contours, turning her visage into some ferocious Medusa. A photo-op instance of the soul. Immediately over, back to a blank, unreadable. In the icy stillness, he groped for words. "I told him you were attractive and intelligent, and of good character. He's divorced too, you know . . . but I told you all that before, didn't I?"

She was toying with her glass, tapping her long, perfect nails against its base. Looking up at nothing. Didn't say a word.

"I'm sorry if I offended you. I just thought perhaps you and he, well, you know how it is, being divorced and all. Hey, I have trouble dating again too, you know." The neon billboard flashed *Shut up — Shut up.* Yet. "I mean, it's not like he has any expectations or anything. But you might enjoy his company, and it's always good to make new friends." Sounded as bad as Don and Ai-Lin.

She finished off her drink in a long swallow. "Perhaps. One never knows. Well, goodnight. It was nice drinking with you." Marched off, barely glanced at him.

Shit. He'd done it now. Ordered another drink. And another.

In the elevator, Gail calmed herself down. A Caucasian in a suit walked in. "What floor?"

"Six."

"Done." He smiled at her.

She hoped he wouldn't say more. Right now, she did not trust herself to be civil. At her floor, he wished her "goodnight" and that was that. She hurried back to her room, relieved.

Gail kicked her shoes off, letting them fall in a corner by the dresser. Untying her scarf, she tossed it on the floor. She ran a bath, sprinkling the water with crystals from the glass globe on the sink. She undressed and put on the hotel's white bathrobe.

It was too late to call Gu Kwun. If she hadn't been rushing to see Vince, she could have called.

The bath filled quickly. Good water pressure, although the rest of Shanghai probably wasn't nearly as lucky. No such thing as luck, not really. Discipline and persistence got her where she was. She stepped gingerly into the steaming water, allowing the heat to rise up from her feet before lowering the rest of her frame into the tub. A large tub, it accommodated her height easily.

She leaned back against the smooth porcelain. All she needed now was a box of Pop-Pans. Her head ached. She massaged her temples, seeking the return of calm. Her anger — wasn't that what she felt towards Vince? — abated, soothed by the nurturing warmth. He couldn't know, nobody could, how much she wanted just a little tenderness. She was even willing to gamble with him. All for naught. Such wasted energies. Face it. Love, or even a poor imitation, just wasn't her fate.

Closing her eyes, she cried quietly for a long time into the water.

Vince crawled out of bed, having assured the concierge who woke him with such insistent ringing, that yes, he still needed the car. Head throbbed. Too old for this.

Missed his morning appointment. Lousy path to middle age.

Forgot to pack the Tylenol.

He picked up the phone to call room service for coffee. Room 653 glared at him from the message pad. Yesterday's disaster. Move on.

Under the shower's blast, the neon billboard blinked *Asshole — Asshole.* No use. Don't ask for forgiveness. No absolution for the life of the nearly divorced. Graffiti on the walls of marriage.

Work. The only safe harbor.

The doorbell rang, followed by a knock and the voice of revival. "Room service." He turned off the faucet.

22

"You?" Vince's undisguised surprise.

Albert looked from one to the other. "You two know each other?"

"We've met." Andanna, cool as a reptile, smiled at Vince.

Someone called Albert's name and he excused himself. Vince and Andanna looked at each other across the table at The Jazz Club.

"I thought you'd given up modeling."

"This is different."

"Why are you doing this?"

"I'm photogenic, remember? You told me that. Albert will pay."

"Why don't you act in commercials? You'd probably be good in them. They pay well."

Perhaps, this ancient had something there. It wasn't the first time she'd been told. She tapped her foot, wishing Albert would get back quickly. She would have preferred if the photographer could have been someone else. Not that she knew this guy all that well or anything, but he was kind of okay. Now who knows what he'd think of her?

Albert breezed back. "So *leng leui*. Have you coaxed your friend into doing it yet?"

"What you mean, 'coax?'"

Albert rattled off something in Cantonese. She glanced at Vince, wondering if he understood. Ever since meeting Colleen, she was more wary of foreigners, uncertain which ones knew Cantonese.

"I don't know about this," Vince was saying. "Andanna, are you sure this is what you want to do?"

"Oh yeah, sure."

"Will you look me in the eye and say that?"

How weird. What did he want? She cocked her head up and glared at him. "Like this?"

Albert snapped his fingers. "There, all settled, just like Mrs. Tang wanted for you. Is my *leng leui* happy now?"

"Wait a minute," Vince said. "I didn't say I'd do it yet."

What was this guy's problem? She was about to say something when Albert held up his hand, signaling her silence. "You run along now, 'little sister.' We 'big brothers' will talk."

Andanna stood up to leave. It was exasperating, the way Albert treated her. She wasn't a child. Why couldn't he just help her the way he promised without all this nonsense? Something Sylvie had once said about their cousin — *he likes to playact, even when he's being normal.* What was that all about? But he was powerful and well connected. He knew people in the entertainment business. If she could just keep him interested in her, whatever his motives, she had a shot at getting what she wanted.

But she remembered what Colleen had said about Albert, how he liked to think he was in charge, and that it was best to humor him. Men were like that. Flashing them both a smile, she waved "bye-bye." "You're the boss. See ya."

"What did you say to her?" Vince demanded.

Albert gave him a wide-eyed look. "Why Vincent, whatever do you mean?"

"Cut the crap. What did you say in Cantonese to her?"

"I was just giving her sage, brotherly advice, like a good *tohnggo*. You know what that is?"

"What? Some Tong triad secret?"

"Your ignorance knows no bounds." Albert laughed loud and long.

Vince watched the rippling contours of his face. Such prolonged youth. It wasn't just his physical self, but his capacity for a childish self centered-ness that kept him young. Vince suspected some rude exchange had occurred, because Andanna blanched, although she tried not to let it show. Should he put up with this man, this boy who had too much money?

"I'm being rude, aren't I? Andanna You Fun is my cousin, and very much fun to tease. It's just the way things are."

"Sorry. None of my business." Vince finished off his drink and refused Albert's offer for another. "I'm gone. Got a job."

The job had been an excuse. Had to get away from Albert. Too much time around the man, eating and drinking on his tab, smoking his pot now as well. a throwback to unfettered youth. But his patronizing goodwill assaulted self respect. Earlier, back in New York, he'd spent precious time with Jim. Jim was a buddy. They could drink together, talk baseball, city politics, women, life. Play racquetball. Neither one a natural athlete, this shared space on the court was fast, short and fully absorbing. Took his mind off life.

The trouble with Albert was that he would never be a "buddy."

Outside, the remains of daylight filtered through the muggy haze. He coughed. Blame pollution. Or quit smoking. People dodged past him, heading uphill as he went down. Friday night happy hour sirens. Didn't like Lan Kwai Fong, even though he spent enough time here. Few alternatives. Wanchai too young and Brit, not that the Fong wasn't. Different breeds of youth though. Less dancing on tables.

Join a health club. Get some exercise. Don's wisdom, haughtily imparted. Arrogance of success. Don looked good, worked hard, lived and ate well. Marriage agreed with him. He and Ai-Lin smiled a lot, radiant in their sunny optimism. Daunting, all this happiness, the pursuit of which struck him as increasingly alien.

Around him on the streets, throngs of Chinese got in his way, slowed him down.

In another life, Ai-Lin had accused him of xenophobia, of only embracing an American perspective, shutting out all other viewpoints. Ai-Lin and Don — global citizens, they called themselves. Now he wondered if she'd call him racist as well. He had told Jim that after almost two years in Hong Kong, people had become "those Chinese." Jim's response — *And what are New Yorkers? The crowd is never the individual.*

A Chinese man bumped against him. No apology.

Before Jim, in another life of rage, he would have sworn at the stranger. Ai-Lin had accused him of lacking self control. Harmony and balance ruled in this new age of Ai-Lin with Don, the way it never had with him. Yet Didi's chronic irritation through that other life — *Jesus Vince, don't you ever get mad?* Women. Couldn't please them no matter what he did.

To Jim he said — it's like this non stop movie running in my head — nothing relents, can't forget and move on. Jim's pragmatic suggestion — "acquire a life." What though? No lack of social life here. Albert attracted the party crowd, and hanging with him wasn't the worst thing in a work-hard-play-hard town. But it wasn't a life.

He changed his mind about taking the MTR and decided to walk home instead. Turned back up the slope towards the roads along the hillside. A waterfront stroll meant too many cars, construction ridden sidewalks, and only the reprieve of one park next to the Admiralty subway station. In New York, he could walk, despite the people and cars. This was not a real walking city, not the way he liked it.

At the government car park on Lower Albert Road, a solo Australian woman stopped him to ask directions to the Foreign Correspondents Club. She carried a camera and looked purposeful. Once directed, she tried to engage him in conversation. He resisted. Too obvious? Not attractive enough? Too independent a woman? Ai-Lin had accused him of sexism too. Not so insidious. From the parking lot, a car alarm tripped. The shriek crescendoed against the passing traffic, silencing their voices. He walked away.

No, this wasn't about Ai-Lin. It was guilt over Gail. Unavoidable, although he had resisted confronting himself since last week in Shanghai. Couldn't ignore it anymore, had to do something. Anticipating retribution might take too long, damning him for procrastination. There had to be an end to this thing, whatever it was, that harried him. Seemed like no matter which path he tried to take, some woman accused him, wore down his conscience into exhaustion. Gail had become a part of that road which, like an unending war fuelled by race or religion, denied itself the way to peace.

But life, that lingering desire. A duller, deeper ache than lust. In the roar of the non-stop day to day, some dream, some memory sustained him still. Nothing was over till it was over. The clarity of palpable hope. A little like childhood, a little like love.

Andanna hurried towards the Central MTR. Albert was jerking her around and she was dancing. It was dumb of her. She hated his insinuations, and the way he refused to say what he really meant. Why did people complicate things that were so simple?

The bright interior of the station contrasted with the waning daylight. She was conscious of a persistent noise cycle, of trains speeding in and out at each level. Nearing the ticket entrance, she checked her pager. Among her messages was one number she didn't immediately recognize on the display. It came quickly enough, the way numbers did. Gail Szeto. What did she want? Seeing the bank of pay phones, she hunted around her pockets for change. Clio criticized her for not carrying a hand phone, saying it wasn't professional because she might miss something important since things moved quickly in entertainment. But those were such a pain. Besides, why should people be able to reach her anytime they wanted? Her mother already left too many messages on her pager, usually about inconsequential nonsense.

The line was ringing before she realized it was already seven. Gail had probably left the office. She was surprised to get her.

"Oh, Andanna, thanks for returning my call. Listen, could you give a message to your friend Clio for me? She didn't have a card with her at my party."

"Sure."

Gail rattled off a bunch of stuff which Andanna tried to scribble down. ." . . and if you could, ask her to get back to me soon because the meetings are the first week of every month."

"No problem."

"So how are things with you? Are you working much? My friend really liked you, by the way. You know, the Boston woman last year?"

"Oh, yeah. That's great." Her time was running out and she wanted to hang up, but Gail seemed intent on talking. She dropped in another two dollar coin. "I'm okay. Met with a photographer just now to do some special shots. Hey, you'll remember him, that da Luca guy?"

"I think so."

"I introduced you both, remember? After Sylvie's wedding."

"It was a long time ago, but I think I know who you mean."

"He may be doing some pictures of me. But you know, I don't model much now, because I'm going to become a singer. Colleen Tang is managing me. She's really great."

"Uh huh."

Gail obviously wanted to get rid of her now. What a pain, right after she'd put in more money. "Well, gotta go. Bye."

"Don't forget to tell Clio soon, okay?"

How annoying and pointless. What did Gail see in Clio? An unfamiliar jealousy got her. She had almost told her to ask Clio herself, but Gail's manner pre-empted refusal. Gail was the bossy type who liked making others do things for her just to show off how important she was. Also, after asking all those questions, she wasn't even interested in her reply. What a poor memory she had, not remembering the da Luca guy. They had carried on like old friends that evening so she should have recalled.

Forget her. Gail was another Albert, pretending interest and then dropping her. Ancients were like that, although that da Luca was okay. But even he was leading her on with this "maybe-maybe not" shoot. She had thought Gail would introduce her to people, or at least send more modeling leads her way. After all, she was important and well connected. But all she'd gotten out of her so far was one lead and a dumb party. The only good thing had been meeting Colleen.

Clio could wait. She'd tell her eventually. Turning back to her pager, she ran down the list and returned her other calls. Sylvie wanted to set up dinner with all the girl cousins next month. Her mother's message was the predictable daily query: was she coming home for dinner? Andanna ignored it; the cook knew enough to leave something in the fridge which she'd microwave whenever she was hungry. Colleen had news about a back up band for her. That made her feel a lot better. Andanna didn't even mind that Colleen nagged, again, about getting up earlier and eating better. People needed to nag, and up to a point she put up with it because after that, they'd leave her alone and she did what she wanted anyway. Besides, nagging was less offensive than being jerked around.

As she slid her ticket through the turnstile slot, it suddenly struck her that Clio had no right to talk about being professional. Imagine not having any cards on her at a party. How stupid. Just because she had her bank job didn't make her smart. The trains continued their monotonous roar as she headed for the Tsuen Wan line on the lower level.

The mention of Vince had jolted Gail, and she was glad to get rid of that call. As far as anyone else was concerned, they were merely acquaintances. If only she hadn't mentioned him to Colleen. But that didn't matter. It was just face, an inconsequential thing.

Gail gathered up her things. Had Andanna called even minutes later, she would have missed her. She had to get out of here. That whole farce last week with Vince had happened because she had too little life besides work. She should have known he wasn't interested. Sex didn't really matter all that much.

But why did Andanna have to mention him and remind her?

She locked up the office, annoyed that she was once again the last to leave. Just that morning, Gu Kwun had asked her what "hobby" meant, "for real."

She had been only half paying attention, and the question surprised her. "Surely you know the meaning. It's such a simple word. Why are you asking?"

"I thought it was a make up word, like one of your *geeleegulu.*"

"Why ever did you think that?"

"Because Mummy, we don't have any hobbies."

"Don't be silly, of course we do."

"What are they?"

Her son stared at her in such complete innocence that she did not say, as she meant to — now come on, stop fooling around you'll be late for school. She groped for something to say and came up with nothing.

"We don't have any, Mummy," he repeated.

For the first time since she'd become a mother, she felt guilty towards her child. It was a startling and unfamiliar feeling. She had never sympathized with other working mothers who complained of not having time for their children. After all, her son came first and always did, despite her own career aspirations. In fact, a major reason she'd quit the first job that brought her back to Hong Kong was because she had insufficient power to control her schedule, which interfered with family life.

But hobbies!

All day long, she was plagued by the memory of her ex-husband's complaint that she saw life as only work and responsibilities. Once, she could dismiss his opinion as groundless. But here was her son saying more or less the same thing about their life. When Gu Kwun called for his daily session that afternoon, she had no better answer for him, although she had hoped she would. Now, it was no better. Enlightenment eluded her.

While waiting for the lift, she recalled an incident she had chosen to forget. The last time she and Gu Kwun's father made love, he had apologized afterwards.

It happened in Shanghai. She had run into him at *Hong Qiao* airport. By then, it had been over a year since he'd left her and they were on the irreversible path towards divorce. "Dr. Chak," she had called to him that afternoon. "Are you following me around?" In an earlier argument, he had accused her of having a detective trail him even though she hadn't.

He had been so taken aback by her presence that it made them both laugh. They shared a taxi to their respective hotels — he disembarked first — and then, from some impulse she couldn't control, she invited him to join her for dinner later. It was his first trip to Shanghai, for a medical conference he said, and perhaps the foreignness of their situation persuaded him. Whatever it was, he accepted and she knew she intended to sleep with him that night.

She got her way. It had taken remarkably little. She simply asked him how life was, much as she used to once ask how his day had been. Over their last meal together, she observed him as if he were a laboratory rat. She knew him. She knew exactly what he needed from her, what he couldn't get from that younger woman. Empathy, a real understanding found in the familiar, and not in a stranger's desire to please. *"Siu daih,"* she said, using an endearment from their earliest days, because he was six years her junior, "you're not getting enough, are you?" He smiled back over one wine too many.

He had stayed till morning. When he awoke, his startled dishevelment was so recognizably him, so integral to their marriage bed. He apologized, for their marriage's end, for his "ineptitude" as a father. She knew his acute loss of face. She stroked his cheek, promising she'd never tell his girlfriend and then dismissed him, feeling momentarily avenged. Sex had been good but incidental. A bitter amusement filled her at the irony of the situation.

But as she thought now of Vince and his humiliating rejection, what troubled her most was the hollowness of her pain. The memory ache of her husband felt the same, a pain that lacked substance, that was almost hypocritical. He had never felt about the marriage and family the way she did, never, no matter how much in the right she was. And Vince simply hadn't been interested. With everything, it seemed, she would set herself up for a fall.

Ngaahnggeng ngaam. For years, she was deaf to her mother whom senility finally silenced. *Always have to have your way. Always have to be right. Sometimes Gail, you're just out and out wrong.*

The lift arrived. Noiselessly, its doors slid open.

23

It wasn't till after the weekend that Andanna remembered about Gail's call. Clio would kill her for not telling her sooner.

The day had eluded her. Last night, she'd gone to JJ's which was dead. Sundays were bad for night life. So she'd popped back to Kowloon, and had run into Albert with a bunch of people outside the Shangri-la in *Jimdung*. Another late night at those clubs which weren't dead. Luckily, she didn't have a rehearsal today which meant Colleen hadn't called in the morning to remind her, and she could sleep till lunch time.

"You Fun, you have mail." Mother's voice outside her door.

"I'll get it later."

"Well, where do you want me to leave it for you?"

"I don't care, anywhere."

She heard the irritated grumbling as her mother walked away. The other day, Colleen had said she ought to be nicer to her parents considering she was mooching off them. She was wrong of course because they preferred having her at home. Even though Colleen was really smart and all, she could be dead wrong about things. Maybe it was because her Cantonese was off sometimes and she hadn't meant it like that, but Andanna had been a little hurt.

Her bedside clock clicked over to six. She ought to call Clio. "Got a minute? Or are you on your way out?"

Papers shuffled. "Are you kidding? I'm here at least another hour.

We have this big meeting tomorrow and . . ."

"Yeah, yeah. Listen, I've got important news."

"Hey, don't interrupt. My stuff's just as important, if not more."

Her friend could be big headed. "Listen, do you want to know why I called or not?"

"If you insist."

"Remember that Szeto woman?"

"Sure."

"She wants me to ask you if you want to be sponsored for a junior executive banker's club membership." Andanna read off her notes, making sure she got it exactly right. "What do you think of that? Pretty cool, huh?"

"Oh, that. Know about it already. It's not a membership, it's a mentoring thing. Should be good. She called Friday. I didn't know she called you. What else?"

"Nothing." She was pissed at Gail. Why couldn't she have found the number before asking her, and then, having asked her to do this, why couldn't she wait? In the meantime, Clio launched into an involved explanation about the merits of the organization for her career, telling how she and Gail talked at length at her party about banking and Sun Yat-Sen, which fortunately was her boyfriend's passion so she had a lot to say about the man. All this business crap bored Andanna no end, and the idea that they could go on about Sun Yat-Sen at a party seemed ludicrous. History began and ended at school. Clio made no secret of the fact that her interest in people began with connections, and it was clear she only talked about stuff like that to impress Gail. It didn't seem right somehow. What about friendship?

". . . oh and guess what? I got my promotion."

"Hah?"

"Well don't congratulate me, see if I care? Don't you remember? I told you I was up for it. What's the matter? Can't you share the spotlight?"

She was joking, but her hostile tone startled Andanna.

"What d'you mean?"

"You haven't listened to anything I've said, have you? Just because you introduced me to Gail doesn't mean I can't make it on my own. You know your problem? You're just not interested in anyone else except yourself and your own connections."

"Take it easy, will ya?"

Clio relaxed. She asked Andanna to join her and her boyfriend for dinner on double tenth but Andanna had to beg off because the thing with her cousins was that evening.

The phone call put her in a bad mood for the next couple of hours. Earlier, Colleen had suggested she get a professional voice coach. It made her feel stupid. Why hadn't she known to do it herself without prompting? The audition last month had resulted in the promise of a possible recording contract, if she could produce a demo tape. Since then, she had tried to be more "professional," from the clothes she wore, to the way she carried herself, to the people she got to know. And she tried to rehearse according to the rigorous schedule Colleen had drawn up for her and the band, difficult though that was proving to be. Yet what quickly became obvious to her was that she had no idea what her career required. The conversation with Clio rankled, because clearly, her friend had every idea how to advance her own future.

Why didn't anyone take her seriously anymore?

When she was sixteen, everyone wanted to be her. That was the year she started going out with Michael and sang in his band. He was a couple of years older, and had been a rock musician. Back then, his band was popular and performed a lot. They even made one CD. If only things had stayed the same.

But then there was Vancouver which might as well have been prison. When she got back, Michael had started playing jazz. Even that hadn't been so bad. Everyone thought she was cool for moving out of home and living with him. The modeling also gave her lots of status. Clio still worshipped her. Now, everything had changed and nobody paid attention to her anymore. Life sucked.

She lit a cigarette. It made her cough. Colleen's admonitions that she'd ruin her voice came back, and she stubbed it out. She couldn't just sit in her room and smoke all night. The sheet music by her bed had scattered into a mess. She picked up the pile and sorted though them. There was this one song she still had to learn. But first, a Diet Coke.

Gail listened impatiently to Andanna's rambling. It was a full week since they'd spoken, and here she was making excuses for why she hadn't given Clio the message earlier. "It doesn't matter, Andanna, really," she repeated for the third time. The girl was truly tiresome, concerned only with her own little world. She was tempted to say so but checked herself. She didn't care enough to bother.

"Well, I just felt bad but I was so busy it slipped my mind and then by the time . . ."

She tuned her out. Sometimes, she wished she didn't extend herself to people who were obviously not worth her time. That family was all the same, because Sylvie had been similarly self absorbed, although at least she was a bit more gracious than Andanna.

"Listen, I have to run. I'm sorry you can't join us on the tenth, but Clio explained you had a family dinner."

"Oh yeah, about that . . ."

It was another few minutes before she got rid of her. The best thing for that girl was a real job, instead of playing at pop music and being "managed" by Colleen.

Just yesterday, Kwok Po had reminded her of Colleen's new "venture." He had invited her to lunch to meet Albert Ho, his business partner. A useful introduction. Albert suggested that her talents would be well suited to working in Shanghai if she felt so inclined. The thought intrigued her, because the work would be challenging and, as Kwok Po pointed out, her mother would like being home. Besides, with '97 nearing, it only made sense to focus her attention towards China.

"Did my wife tell you about her latest acquisition?"

She hadn't known what her friend meant at first and said so.

"Her 'star is born' protégée."

"Oh, you mean Andanna."

"Is that her name? By the way, Colleen booked her first performance. It went well, by all accounts."

"Details please," Albert requested.

"Ask Colleen. She'll tell you all about it. Hey, maybe you can book her too, at your Shanghai club, I mean."

Gail found Albert strange. Business like and professional enough, but something of a phony. If not for Kwok Po, she probably wouldn't deal with him. But it was her friend that was the real surprise. He seemed proud of Colleen's achievement. It was such a trivial pursuit. Surely he didn't take it seriously. "I didn't know you were so interested in the entertainment industry."

"It's my fault," Albert interjected. "I like to lead my friends astray."

The laughter in his eyes was faintly mocking, but Kwok Po didn't appear offended. "Colleen needs her hobbies. She spends too much time worrying about me and my family — she's wonderful that way — and this is a nice diversion."

Had her friend changed? Gail puzzled over this Kwok Po she found increasingly alien. Long before Colleen, this had been the one friend whose judgment she trusted implicitly. Sometime last year, he told her that he never regretted coming back to Hong Kong because things were, and would always be better for "our kind" here. She hadn't fully agreed with him, and he had demanded to know why not in quite a hostile way, putting her off slightly. Then, he mellowed and apologized, saying he knew her personal life hadn't been ideal but that he was referring to their careers. Since then, she had held back looking him up. Lunch had been his initiative.

Her direct line rang, interrupting her thoughts.

"Hey. It's Vince."

A sudden panic. Calm down, she told herself. He didn't warrant such melodrama. "How are you?"

"I was wondering if you'd like the negative. For that photo, I mean."

"I know what you meant."

An uncomfortable pause, like pregnancy.

She broke it first. "If you'd like to send it." Since Shanghai, she'd left the photo in her drawer.

"Sure. I'll do that."

"Vince, why are you calling?" It had been more direct than she intended, but somehow, stating the question eased her panic.

"Because I'm a jerk and owe you an apology."

She wanted to say — you're not and you don't — in an effort to be civil. Instead, she replied, "You are, but thanks."

"It's the second."

"Second what?"

"Apology."

He was right although she'd forgotten.

"Listen . . . "

"Listen . . ."

She beat him to it. "You first."

"Okay. Listen, I won't ask you out again if that's all right with you."

He spoke in such pained tones that she couldn't help laughing.

"What's so funny?"

It was like receiving the photo all over. She laughed, and simply couldn't stop herself. Ariadne looked up from her desk, startled, and glanced into her office.

"I'm glad I amuse you. At least I do something right."

"Oh Vince, it's not you."

"That's what they all say."

"No, really. It's just that you're refreshingly . . . honest."

"So you're not mad?"

"Not really."

She wanted to say the right things so as to lessen his discomfort. He didn't owe her anything, nor did he warrant her anger. But after yesterday's encounter with Kwok Po, what she couldn't help feeling was that these men in her life demanded, and got, far more than they were really worth.

**

It was the morning of the double tenth. Yesterday, a postcard from Michael arrived. Andanna sat up and looked at it on her bedside table. "Andi — New York is incredible! Have a nice life."

She got out of bed, pulled back the curtains and flung open the windows. It was *way* too dark in here for eight o'clock. The air smelled almost fresh, or at least, it was fresher than the stale air suffocating her room. It had been ages since she'd allowed anyone in, although she couldn't stop the maid cleaning when she went out. That was okay because she did restock the Diet Cokes in her room fridge.

Last weekend, she and her band had played their first gig. It was just some society thing, but a couple of her parents' friends had been there and word had gotten back to her mother who was beside herself with delight. Colleen had arranged the gig, saying that was her job as manager. Now, she was trying to get funding for a demo tape.

It was exciting to perform again. Had it really been ten months since she'd broken up with Michael, longer since she'd last worked? She stepped away from the window and flipped the postcard over to its picture — a black and white of "a young Duke Ellington." Michael was crazy about him. She tried to recall one of his songs but couldn't. A sudden vision of Michael, somewhere in that city saying to a bunch of Black musicians — please can I sit in — doing what he said he was always going to do. And then the image disappeared. She couldn't picture New York, had never been there, or even to America, just as he hadn't till now, except that for years, Michael treasured every scrap of information he could uncover about the jazz life which meant, he claimed, that he *had* to go to New York one day. His knowledge was exhausting.

Andanna stepped into the shower. The water pressure was strong today.

Sometimes, she missed life with her old boyfriend. Despite all his nagging, and the ratty flat they lived in, his discipline kept her stable. It didn't matter how late he had been playing or rehearsing, he'd be up early every morning in time for his day job as a sound engineer. He was always doing something, and that prompted her to work also. And even though he criticized her, he sort of believed in her. At least he did love her.

Love was okay, but it took up way too much space and energy. Anyway, he was happy so everything was fine, right? Andanna stood in the shower for a long time, scrubbing every pore, ever square inch of her skin with the loofah until she barely felt its rough surface. The water pounded over her.

At the cave-like MTR entrance on Pedder Street, she stopped. Oh no. A long afternoon rehearsing and she'd completely forgotten about dinner with Sylvie and her other cousin-sisters. They'd agreed to meet at a wine bar in Causeway Bay, the one near Lei Mo Toi. There wasn't time to go home and change. She pondered this problem.

The trouble with Sylvie was that she gossiped. If Andanna showed up looking too casual, negative words would get back to the ancients. Sylvie could be a bit of a bore that way, and had her own ideas of what was what. These days, she was buying jewelry for "investments," which meant she'd be flashing her latest acquisition. She had to think of something within the next forty minutes.

Right now, she missed Michael. It wasn't like she wanted him back or anything, but the difference was, with him, something as ridiculous as this wouldn't matter. The thing about Michael — he wasn't impressed by what someone had or what they looked like. He'd shaped his own life. When they were together, Andanna felt unfettered by social and family demands and did what she pleased.

But anyway, that was over.

She considered her outfit. A black tee-shirt and a thick, cream-colored muslin blouse she wore over it, and black jeans. She knew she looked fine, but without jewelry or something to compete with that queen bee cousin, she would have to put up with her ragging. Sylvie could be merciless, and loved to invoke her seniority as the eldest female of their generation.

Walking away from the MTR entrance along Queen's Road, she wandered past several top name boutiques. Just after Ice House Street, a poster caught her eye. Brilliant! As Mother liked to say, every think-ing woman had at least one asset to flaunt.

She headed for the Mandarin Hotel and ducked into the toilet, emerging several minutes later. Then, she boarded the MTR and went to meet her cousins.

When she arrived at the Wine Bar, Sylvie was already at a table with three others, an open bottle of red in front of them.

One girl greeted. *"Wei, You Fun. Gammaahn heui wet haih mhaih?"* Hey, going out on the town tonight, are you?

"Wah! *Gam 'sexy,'*" another remarked.

Sylvie cast an approving eye. "My *tohngsaimui* is always fashionable." She emphasized Andanna's position as the youngest "sister," and poured some wine into her glass.

Andanna slid into her seat and lit a cigarette. "Sometimes, I get inspired," but privately, she rejoiced, even as her cousin waved around an obviously new jade and gold bracelet. All she'd done was take off the tee-shirt, tied her white blouse over her black bra to expose her midriff, and allowed the see-through effect to do its work. Years ago, she'd heeded her mother's advice and acquired a useful wardrobe of extremely good bras. *You need one, You Fun, remember that. You're not like that ironing board Sylvie.*

The last cousin arrived, their Wong sister. She was the only girl cousin from a Lee sister who had married a Wong; the others were all daughters of Lee brothers. She grinned at Andanna and congratulated her on her recent performance.

"How did you know about it?" Andanna asked innocently, although she guessed that word would get out, since it had been among their crowd. Colleen saw nothing wrong in taking advantage of her society connections. She was beginning to think her right about that.

"You know, people talk. I heard you did real well."

"Our *tohngsaimui* is going to be a star someday." Sylvie raised her glass. "Come on, let's toast her."

Andanna basked in their spotlight. With a family like this, she could do without Michael's love. As for her little fashion crisis, thank god for that poster of Madonna which had been her inspiration. She offered the star a private toast.

When Gail arrived at the restaurant, Clio was already there. They shook hands and once settled, Clio remarked, "You heard about the Nationalist flag, didn't you? On top of Tai Mo Shan last night?" Gail nodded. The media this morning had been full of the news.

Clio had insisted on treating her to dinner, to thank her for being her mentor. They were at the *Louhfaahndim,* in the basement of a hotel in North Point. It was a long established Shanghai place, and expensive, Gail knew. She appreciated the gesture.

"How come you're so interested in Taiwan?"

"It's because of my boyfriend's family. His father served under Chiang Kai Shek."

"Oh, I see." She was reminded of her own father, the "Flying Tiger" who helped the "other China." "What about your family?"

"They're only concerned about Hong Kong. To them, the Nationalists are a minority who belong on the outer periphery. I guess they're like most people here. They aren't about to express any anti Chinese sentiments."

"And you?"

She threw her hands up. "I don't know sometimes. To tell the truth, I'm glad I'm not with my boyfriend tonight. His family treats this 'last' double tenth like the end of the world. I keep telling him it's not, and that things aren't going to change that much after next July. Come on, let's order."

Gail let Clio do the honors, and watched her, impressed. She was bright, outgoing, natural, and not fussy like a lot of young women. Yet she had managed to cultivate an appropriate sophistication. With an MBA, she could go a long way. There was still time. Her company might sponsor her, and Gail made a mental note to suggest it.

Being with Clio brought her back to the Girl Guides. In secondary school, she had loved being a guide, initially because the activities took her away from home. What she'd discovered about herself was that she was a natural leader and a good "big sister" role model for the younger girls, many of who came to her for advice. Later, as a foreigner in the U.S., she'd found herself less able to be that. After all, she wasn't a real American, despite her passport. Here again in Hong Kong, she was back in that role. Clio was, however, the first young woman she'd met who was really worth her time and effort to groom.

Their appetizers arrived. Clio gestured towards the cold platters of jellyfish and seasoned *mo* beans in the manner of a host presenting the evening's repast. "Let's eat," she said and Gail was thrust back to childhood dinners with her mother when they would savor a Shanghainese feast at a neighborhood restaurant. Just her and her mother, with all the captain and waiters fussing over them because Mrs. Szeto was highly regarded for the years of customers she had brought. Gail had been proud to be with her then, when Mom was beautiful and impeccably dressed, a lady giving orders to the staff for the meal, and, when the food arrived, insisting on proper Chinese table manners from Gail who complied willingly, eager to please. At those moments, her missing father never mattered, her mixed blood didn't signify, the fact of her mother's profession was irrelevant. At those moments, she knew she was the most treasured and important person in her mother's world.

In between courses, she asked about Andanna. "You're good friends, aren't you?"

"Long time."

"Why? I mean, you're so different."

"She makes me laugh, because she's a little crazy."

"Is that enough basis for a friendship?"

Clio shrugged. "I don't know, but she sticks, you know. I can't imagine life without her, even though she's never around most of the time. But I have my boyfriend for that. Besides, someone has to have the guts to do what no one else does."

"She seems . . ." Gail hesitated, wanting to say "selfish," but tempered it to "self centered."

"That's how she's always been," Clio laughed. "She wouldn't be Andanna any other way."

How lucky Andanna was to have a true friend like Clio. Gail dropped some of the rubbery golden jellyfish into her bowl, and dipped mustard onto her chopsticks for flavor. The chewy strands comforted her palate. That night, she ate a well selected dinner.

24

At the end of her telephone conversation with the organizer of the Dolphin Preservation Fund, Colleen almost slammed down the receiver but didn't. Her irritation at this well meaning if rather stupid woman was unwarranted. She lit a cigarette.

Surely, surely, she was too young? She wasn't even forty yet.

Last night, it had been impossible to sleep. Fortunately, Kwok Po was out of town. She had tried reading, but couldn't concentrate. Round about two thirty, she had begun to feel drowsy. It was a mild night, but she had felt a little cool and pulled the cotton cover up. Her eyes had just begun to close when it happened.

Bristling warmth flushed her skin, as if a fire had been lit and she had just stepped out of the cold to warm up next to it. An internal thermostat raised the overall warmth to hot, an unbearably warm and cloying heat which suffused her like too many layers of clothing. She wanted to peel off her skin.

She touched her face. It felt normal. All her insides had gone up by several degrees. It was a completely foreign sensation.

She sat up and pulled off the covers. No matter what she did, she couldn't cool down. She was in the middle of a fire where flames flew around her but did not scorch. Her heart beat fast, hammering its alarm signal, forcing her to know that something was amiss. And then, as unexpectedly as it had begun, it stopped. At least fifteen minutes passed before her body felt normal again. Eventually, she fell into an uncomfortable sleep.

Stubbing out the barely smoked stick, Colleen took a deep breath and tried to relax. Perhaps last night had been an odd instance. Her mother, who would have happily lived in Neverland, might as well have never gone through menopause. As for *laihlai,* the one time Colleen had ever heard her make reference to it, she called it the "thing we don't discuss." And as openly as she could talk to Kwok Po about most things, on what he called "those female body problems," they did not converse.

Colleen had never paid attention to her periods, unlike other women she knew. It astonished her that friends could tell when theirs were due. Since she knew she couldn't get pregnant, there seemed no reason to concern herself with its schedule. It would show up rather like one of Kwok Po's regular business acquaintances whom she neither liked nor disliked. After the enforced visit, the bloody guest would disappear. Consequently, she couldn't remember when she'd last had one, or when to expect the next.

Yet the idea now that it might leave her forever was menacing.

What to do? The phone rang, and she started.

"Sis?"

"Oh, it's you."

A hurt silence on the other end. Her lack of enthusiasm was unusual.

"I'm sorry," she continued. "You caught me at a bad time. How are you, sweetheart?"

"Sis, you still know some Senate folks, don't you? I mean, from your Council of Relations contacts?"

"Maybe." Her cautionary antenna went up. "Who's asking?"

"Friends."

"Not friends of mine, I imagine."

"If that's the way you feel about it." He hung up.

Screw him. It was time she stopped worrying. This callousness would surprise Kwok Po. She thought about her mother at home under constant nursing supervision. Once Dad died, Danny had never once bothered to go see her. Bit by bit, their mother had crawled further into her shell, refusing to accept their father's death, despite that most unsatisfactory marriage. She simply couldn't, no, wouldn't cope. But Colleen visited her dutifully, twice or three times every year, and made sure she received the best care money could buy, since money was the only consolation left to offer.

Yet Danny? He just didn't give a damn about anyone except himself. She stuffed away any residual guilt.

Opening her address book, she flipped to "G," searching for her gynecologist's number to make an appointment that afternoon. Was this urgent, the nurse-receptionist wanted to know.

She hesitated. It seemed ridiculous to voice her fears, yet she did want to know. So she lied. "I think I have an infection."

"Urinary or vaginal?"

What the hell difference did it make? "How would I know? I'm not the doctor."

"I'm sorry, Mrs. Tang, but the doctor's very busy today so I need to prioritize."

"In that case, it's urgent."

She heard the unwilling pause. "Well, I suppose we can squeeze you in. Four thirty?"

For the next ten minutes, she chain smoked. What would she tell the doctor later? She had only seen this woman once before, because she had made a practice of changing gynecologists regularly. After all, it wouldn't do for any one person to have any clinical suspicion that she was extra-maritally active. Not in this small town. She'd heard doctors and lawyers talk at cocktail parties. Confidentiality was a matter of planning, not trust.

The phone rang, too loudly, making her jump again.

"Is that Colleen?"

She recognized his voice instantly, and wondered what on earth possessed him to call out of the blue after all this time. "Hi Vince. What's up?"

"Thought I'd be sociable."

Probably horny. "How sweet. Are you still seeing your girlfriend?"

"You know, she's not my girlfriend."

Men were despairingly predictable. "Oh, I didn't mean anything."

"So, how are things? You like being back?"

"Absolutely. I've been real busy, but everyone says that here, don't they? It's true though. Are you getting a lot of work?"

"Enough."

She heard his unspoken plea. Screw him too, she thought, ignoring the constraint that placed on her mental vocabulary. "Listen, you caught me right in the middle of something, so I can't talk long. But it's really nice to hear from you. We should do lunch soon."

Colleen glared at the phone. It was time the men in her life grew up.

Scratch that one. Long shot anyway. Maybe even wrong to call, morally, at some level, although why the hell not? After all, she started it. That crack about Gail though.

Facing him on his desk, the envelope he studiously ignored. Divorce judgment. *Finito* for real.

Switched on the radio to catch some news. More '97 crap. As The Year approached, it was all anyone talked about. The city buzzed its obsession like a tripped alarm that wouldn't stop.

Sunny autumn morning. No work for a change.

Over a month since the Shanghai disaster. Nemesis city, luring him with a promise of lust and lucre, discarding him when he succumbed. The first visit, a year ago at Albert's party when Colleen had appeared with her husband in the darkened club. He had been lighting a cigarette. Seeing her stunned him. Almost burnt his fingers.

Her "fruit bat man," she called him, saying what wonderful work he did. Albert within earshot agreeing. She introduced him around, taking his arm possessively, shepherding him like wildlife in captivity. Paid off in the photos. People loosened up when they saw him as a friend of Colleen's, and not only as the hired help. Albert loved his candid shots, the off guard instances of depravity.

What wasn't lost on him was the way she treated him as her equal, at least in public. His fellow-sister American. In his "friendship" with Albert, the unspoken insult — stud for sale — even though he wasn't. Perhaps that was why he still tried with Colleen, even though she played him for a patsy.

Gail, though. Not even the apology seemed enough.

He lit a cigarette, coughed violently, and put it out. First shot Jim took when they met again. *Still blackening those lungs, are you?*

Not as simple as apologizing this time. Not some bad boy prank women rolled their eyes at but forgave. Why did he do it? Revenge? Because he had the upper hand. Didn't mean to do it, but there it was. Led her on, took her out, played Mr. Nice-Guy Lonelyhearts, except that he wasn't, at least not for her. Avenging himself against Didi and Ai-Lin. And Colleen. About time he admitted it. Fucking hated being dumped.

But Gail. Didn't have to string her along until she overstepped boundaries, embarrassing herself. Could have just said no from the start. He owed her something. An explanation, offer of genuine friendship. Hell and fury his punishment. Either that or her ringing laughter, impossible to forget.

Time to talk to Jim again.

Gail's presence at the gynecologist's office disconcerted her. She was the last person Colleen wanted to see in her present state. There was no escaping it. They were pressed into waiting together, because the doctor was running late.

"Is everything all right?"

Colleen gritted her teeth. "Oh, regular check up. You?"

"Same." She slouched into her seat, stretching out her long legs.

"To tell the truth, I think I'm getting to that time of life."

"Oh." Gail's candor embarrassed her.

Yet Gail seemed determined to "talk." "Some women don't like to deal with this, but I think that's absurd. I mean, we're all going to go through it sometime."

Despite herself, Colleen asked. "How did you know?"

"I'm not entirely sure, but my body feels different. There were several experiences of what might be hot flashes. Irregular periods. You know, all the things you read about." She paused, and bent down to pick a thread off the leg of her nylons. "But you're much too young to have to think about it."

"I'm not."

Gail looked up, startled. "Oh Colleen, I didn't . . ."

"Gail, I'm scared."

She was surprised when Gail sat next to her and took her hand. It was a peculiar reassurance from a woman she couldn't honestly say she liked. Yet she accepted the comfort, because at this instance, she had come up against something she couldn't handle.

"It can happen to younger women. You're very wise to find out." And then, Gail launched into what she knew. This slate of facts she presented, rationally and unemotionally, had a soothing effect on Colleen. She began to understand some of what Kwok Po saw in her. Gail was intelligent and careful. She didn't waste time on unnecessary emotions. What you saw was what you got. Sometimes, this wasn't such a bad way to be.

"Besides," Gail was saying, "think of what you can spend with what you save on tampons and liners. I can't wait to give my last box away."

She didn't respond, and Gail changed the subject to Andanna, asking how her singing career was going. Grateful for her tact, Colleen told her the only complaint she had was that she wished "she'd be a little more enthusiastic. Sometimes, I'm not sure she wants to do it."

A few minutes later, the nurse called Gail. As she stood up, she gave

Colleen's shoulder a sympathetic squeeze. "Let's have lunch sometime. There's no substitute for girl talk, is there?" She winked, and went to her appointment.

You're too damned Catholic. Always looking for absolution.

Jim had been less than sympathetic. The problem when therapist became friend. Now, he offered opinions. But didn't mind being the excuse, relished it. Already asking for Gail's number. Men *were* animals, even eight thousand miles away.

Not that Jim was all wrong. Gail was a grown up. Win some, lose some. Women lost just as much as men in this dawn of equality. After Ai-Lin, romance, with all its unfulfilled promises, died, not even resuscitated by Didi. Sweet tempered Didi. Girl with the laughing eyes, too proud for tears, too smart for martyrdom.

When in doubt, say nothing. Yet Didi's pleas that he *say something, anything for Christ's sake,* when he lapsed into his silences and hid in the dark room for days. Cowed by the memory of Ai-Lin's timorousness when he wanted to talk, to open themselves up completely to each other, and her resulting fear when he, frustrated by her unwillingness, lost it and shouted, out of control.

The duration of memory.

He didn't owe Gail. Thought she could be a friend. Trouble with her . . . but if he'd just said, up front, I only want to be friends, she'd have been okay. She was that kind of woman, with expectations tied entirely to actions. Probably had plenty of male friends, given the nature of her work. Didn't date much though. Too responsible a mother. What had she said? That men got to be the holiday parent in a divorce, while women did the work. As long as he stayed in Hong Kong, he'd be guilty of that same holiday father thing with Katy.

He opened the large windows of his apartment. At this height, the air almost bearable. Clear day, but even so, humidity of possible rain. Never crisply clear. Never dry enough to breathe. Not like autumn in

New York. Time to think about going home.

But Gail. He hadn't played fair. That original kiss a mistake. Women magnified those kinds of moments. Expected more than he intended. Learned that much from two ex-wives. First date had been a nice evening though. What harm in that? She'd seemed okay when he ran into her the day after their Shanghai evening, as if nothing had ever happened. Even had a brief conversation while waiting for their respective cars.

Jim's response. *You're not responsible for the welfare of womankind. Quit worrying.* But one woman wasn't "womankind." Reprehensible? Maybe, yet life, or love, was not, should not be, a cycle of sin and forgiveness. Friendship, on the other hand.

The trouble with too much time. He picked up the phone to hustle more work.

Kwok Po surprised her that evening by coming home a day early.

"What's wrong, *Hong Qi?*"

She had been reading Tang poetry, trying to forget the afternoon at the gynecologist. The idea that Gail read up on menopause, as if it were a subject worthy of scholarship, still nagged. Even her doctor suggested she do that. About Gail though, she regretted now having lost her cool around her. The trouble with that woman was . . . "Oh nothing. I ran into Gail today. We chatted briefly about You Fun, you know, Albert's *tohngmui?*"

"Oh, is that her name?"

"You know, the one who wants to be a singer?"

"I know who you mean. What about her?"

The earlier anxieties dissipated as she launched into what was becoming her favorite topic these days. She needed her husband for this, but previously, the timing hadn't been right. Now, she rallied to her cause. He seemed pleased at her animated enthusiasm. The more she told him, the greater her confidence grew. This wasn't at all like one of those silly, if worthwhile causes. As much as she was willing to contribute to dolphin preservation, especially given the creature's growing symbolic significance to Hong Kong, it wasn't the same as trying to turn You Fun into a pop star.

"You're enjoying this, aren't you?" Kwok Po interrupted.

"She makes me feel young." How odd, but until she said that, she hadn't considered its truth.

"I think you'd be good at managing an . . . 'investment' in her future. What do you think?"

"Oh darling, do you really think so?" She watched her husband's eyes. Surely he guessed what she wanted was money, real money, for a professional demo tape and video. Up till now, she'd done what she could out of her regular allowance, but it wasn't enough to get Andanna to the next stage. Kwok Po knew, had always known what she really wanted, even though they played this polite game of discovery.

They were sitting at the dining table, across from each other. He got up and stood behind her chair. "Come on," he wrapped his hands around her waist. "Let's discuss this in another position."

Her nervous tension unfurled itself, the way her body would at the gym. There was nothing to worry about. Not now. She placed a palm against his side. "Darling, is there really anything more to discuss?"

Later the same week, Saturday night at Club '97 in the Fong. "Come with me to Visage, Vincent." Albert could be insistent, determinedly so.

"It's almost two."

"They'll be open. We're the city that never sleeps."

"I'm not going to change my mind, you know."

"About what?"

"Taking those photos of that girl."

Since meeting with Andanna, Albert had called three or even four times each week, just to ask if he'd change his mind. Each time, he'd said he hadn't and wouldn't, and that would end the conversation.

"Forget it. That's history. Listen, I want you to do some work for my friends in Beijing. In fact, if you make a good impression, I can set you up for some real lucrative work when the handover rolls round."

"Keep talking."

"Then come to Visage."

"Deal."

Visage was a short walk from Lan Kwai Fong. Odd Couple, Albert dubbed them.

"I am what is around me," Albert declaimed to the night sky.

Stragglers headed home, abandoning the debris of the Fong.

"Look around," he continued. "We're the center of the universe. Starry Night Vincent, *you* are what's around you too."

If didn't know better, would think he was drunk. All the man drank was Perrier and lime. "So, that makes me Hong Kong then." It was deliberate dig. Albert was fond of declaring that he, Albert Ho, was Hong Kong, an accident of geography.

Albert waved his hand languidly in a dismissive fashion. "Vincent, Vince. That sounds too much like a political statement. How revolutionary. In fact, your very presence here is a political statement."

"Oh yeah?"

"As you say, 'yeah.' All you Westerners who've come here, now, at this time, getting a piece of the action. While the sun sets on Britain, it rises in China."

"I'm not British."

"Immaterial. West is west and east is east."

"Besides, we all look alike anyway, right?"

"Exactly."

Albert's expression, impassive. Perhaps this city just wasn't about laughter and a sense of humor.

"Let me give it to you straight, Vincent, as you Americans like to say. Pearl of the Orient. *Laissez-faire* capitalism. Electric energy. City of the future. China's hope."

"You sound like the Tourist Association, or a bad journalist."

"What do you want from us?" A flash of, was it, temper? "You're already welcome on our shores. How much more do you expect us to give up?"

"Who said anything about giving up?"

Albert went silent and continued walking. Vince followed. Strange dude. His optimism, unlike many others here, was tinged with sadness. Couldn't figure that. Maybe this "geographical accident" contained something he didn't understand. Wondered what made him change his mind about those photos.

At the building entrance leading to Visage, distinguished by the wooden sign of a sheep, Albert suddenly halted. "I like you, Vincent." An unashamed stare. "You're not what is around you, are you?"

Vince threw his hands open, held them up a moment. "Guess not. I prefer being my own person."

"And you think we're not?"

"Who we?"

"All of us. We locals. We colonials. We Chinese. What's that you Americans call us? Chinks?"

"Not the ones I know."

"I daresay not, since you're all making money off us and . . ."

"For someone who claims he likes me, you could have me fooled."

Albert glared at him, as if piqued at being cut off. The glare turned into a broad smile. "I, on the other hand, I am what is around me." He spread one arm out expansively.

Quoting, always quoting. Pattern with him. "Who said that?"

"Some American insurance salesman. Come on, Vincent, let's go up."

25

Sylvie was pregnant. When she called to announce this, Mother made a huge fuss. Andanna was tired because she had been out the night before.

"Your life's too disorganized, You Fun. You're tired all the time and can't think straight. You're not even pleased by your cousin's news."

She popped a Diet Coke. "Of course I am."

"How can you drink that so early in the morning? All that sugar. Your teeth will rot."

"I need the caffeine."

"Then drink coffee. It's much more civilized. Did I tell you how tasty the coffee in Paris was? We had it every . . ."

Her mother was off again, reminiscing over her August trip. Andanna blocked out the chatter. Incredible how ancients repeated themselves. When would she shut up about it? Christmas? She let her go on until she'd covered all of Paris and Switzerland before she interrupted. "When's the baby due?"

"Baby? Oh, May, possibly June."

"That soon? She didn't look pregnant when I saw her last month. Do you suppose she'll have it July 1? That would be exciting."

"She might have the 'full month' dinner then. Where do you think she'll do that? You know, her husband's family . . ." And she took off on the latest gossip.

Andanna half listened, but wished her mother would stop so that she could call Vince. Last night bothered her a lot, although she wasn't sure why. Perhaps her mother was right when she said, as she increasingly did these days, that Hong Kong was becoming too *jaahp*.

She had gone with Albert to a *Jimdung* club that had recently opened. It was easier going around with him, because her mother thought this acceptable, which kept peace at home. Besides, he did know everyone. Jake Wu was there. He almost didn't recognize her until she called him by name. Jake asked if she'd gained weight, and said her complexion looked bad. That bummed her out.

Later, on the dance floor, some girl, who couldn't have been more than eighteen, shoved her way up to Albert and started making all kinds of sexual innuendoes, laughing and pretending to strip. She acted as if Andanna weren't there.

"Let's go," she told Albert after they left the dance floor. "This place is too *jaahp.*"

"What's the matter, *leng leui?* Are you turning into a ancient? You're much too young for that."

"The people here, they're so boring."

"They are, or you are?" Saying that, he got up and started dancing with that girl and one of her friends, both of whom giggled ridiculously.

Andanna fumed, not sure what to do. She could leave, of course. He wouldn't care. It wasn't like he was her *boyfriend* or anything. Before she could decide, she saw Jake's brother headed towards her. What was he doing here? For a long time after she brushed him off, he would moon about, telling everyone how much he loved her. It had been horribly embarrassing. She wanted to crawl under the table so that he wouldn't see her.

But he was with some model cum singer — Andanna vaguely recognized her — and walked right past, never even acknowledging her presence.

Then, she saw that American photographer guy talking to Jake.

Albert waved at them, sidled his way to the edge of the dance floor, and grabbed Vince by the arm. He signaled to the two girls, and made photo taking gestures at them, while pointing to Vince. Perhaps that American was gay, Andanna thought, although all her instincts said otherwise. Who knew for sure though?

Vince was laughing, saying "no" with his hand, and trying to get away. Albert had his arm firmly in his grip. The original girl came over and struck a fashion pose. That was when Andanna recognized her. She was that jeans commercial model who had just gotten a leading role in a kung fu movie. All the gossip columns were calling her the hottest of the new stars. She faked a couple of kicks into her dancing, showing off her long legs. How did she do it in that tight miniskirt?

Andanna pushed her way onto to the floor, hoping Vince would notice her. But amid all the crowd and commotion, she was edged out to the periphery and almost lost her balance. That was when she left, fed up. Albert, she was sure, would never notice her absence.

"You Fun, you're not listening to me."

"Of course I am." The Diet Coke revived her, clearing her head. "I'm just a bit preoccupied. Lots to think about."

"Like what?"

"You know, the usual."

"It's that Mrs. Tang. She's difficult, isn't she?"

"No, mother."

"Now don't deny it. I know when you're upset. Haven't I always been able to read your face? With you, I'm better than any fortune teller . . ."

Her mother's prattling cheered her up. It was true Colleen worked her hard, insisting on a daunting seriousness. Things were as bad as with Michael, worse actually, because at least around him, she'd gig more often. Colleen wanted her to "perform," and was choosy about when she ought to appear, demanding that she perfect her band's repertoire. The band didn't care. They were paid by Colleen to

rehearse and did their own gigs without Andanna. Right now, all
Colleen concentrated on was the demo video, which she'd hinted at
funding "when you're ready."

But she couldn't complain about Colleen to Mother who would tell
her to drop this singing thing and suggest prospective husbands.

Running into Vince brought back Albert's offer. Why didn't he
return her calls? If she could just convince Vince to take those photos,
she could make Albert come through on his promise. That way, she
wouldn't have to rely entirely on Colleen Tang.

Vince was tired, but at least he wasn't hung over. He spread out the
prints from the last fashion shoot, trying to decide which one would
work. From food to fashion. Enjoyed it more than the other work,
more than he expected. Pretend seduction. Eye candy.

Late last night, Albert had declaimed, *the city possesses you, takes you
to another level.* The man messed with his head. It was always Albert
who called, Albert who initiated, Albert who pushed the envelope on
the night. Up side — besides the work contacts — no booze or
women and occasionally, a kind of amusing insight, maybe even
enlightenment. Reason enough to hang out? Or was it just relief from
boredom, reprieve from the pollution and heat? Mid November, but
he still drowned in sweat whenever he stepped out of air conditioning.

Albert was becoming his Hong Kong.

Limited options, since the women in his life were not. Everything
else was work. Gunter spent more time in Beijing or Shanghai than
Hong Kong these days. As for Don.

For the past few months, Don had been making noises about moving
to Shanghai. The "braver, newer world" he called it. The "real thing."
Such retro cultural hype. Maybe, but what did he know? As Albert
said, he, Vince, was just another ugly American, exploiting the natives
until it was time to leave. A cynic's humor, which was more than most
people here had. Treated seriousness with the right touch of frivolity.

Don and Ai-Lin also talking children, possibly adopting a Chinese child. First reaction, whatever for at their age, and then stopped himself. Jealous? Admit it, yes, because they could still be young and adventurous at forty-plus whereas he . . . ? Don not just making money, but rolling in it. Got a gold cigarette case for his last birthday. He and Ai-Lin going on about China A and B shares. Gobbledygook.

Geeleegulu.

Gail had quipped that in Shanghai, when he'd used some Americanism she hadn't recognized. "That's what we called English language words we didn't understand when we were kids." She'd also told him that the local Cantonese expression for Eurasian was a derogatory equivalent of "chop suey breed."

Phone.

"Is this Mr. Da Luca, the photographer? I am Andanna."

Honorific shit. "He's not in, but Vince is."

"Hah?"

"Never mind."

She had left two messages during the past week. With her, lust figured strictly in the visual realm. He had deliberately not returned her calls.

"I left message for you, twice. You didn't call back."

"I was busy. What's up?"

"You decide about those photos?"

"What photos?"

"For Albert Ho, of course."

Hadn't Albert told her? He hedged. "I guess I just didn't think it was a very good idea."

"What do you mean?"

"Well, do you know why he wanted the shots?"

"None of my business."

"Of course it's your business. It's your body."

"I'm just model. Besides, I want to do it."

Should he tell her Albert was stringing her along? Too disloyal,

mustn't bite the outstretched hand. Besides, he probably couldn't see
the total picture. Girl was obstinate though. He pictured her lips pursing,
their perfect symmetry. She had this exact outline on the upper lip, as
if etched, it was so prominent. Lipstick ad lips. Thick enough to be
sinful but not vulgar. "Get someone else."

Noises. "Albert wanted you," in a tone implying she didn't understand
why but was putting up with it. "Doesn't he pay enough?"

"It's not the money."

"Oh, you're rich, is that so?"

Enough. Time to get on with work. "Look kid, I'm sorry if you want
to do it, but I just don't and that's all there is to it. Nothing personal."

Exasperation. "Okay, never mind. Sorry to bother you."

"No bother."

What lingered? "Mr. da Luca, Vince, is it . . . you're angry because
I won't have sex with you?"

Jesus Christ! What was it with all these twenty-somethings? Was he
that bad? "Andanna, you've got it wrong. It's nothing like that. I just
don't want to do the job."

Sounded as if she slammed the phone down. Vince rolled his eyes.
Who said English was the universal language?

When she told Colleen a week later, the latter smiled sympathetically
and told her the photos weren't important.

"But Albert made it sound like that photographer liked me very much,
and that if I, you know, was nice to him, everything would be fine."

"He's just playing games. You Fun, don't take him seriously."

They were in Colleen's car on their way to a recording studio.
Colleen had promised a demo tape session which was better than
nothing. The band had recorded the instrumental track a couple of days
earlier because of a schedule conflict. It would be easy, like karaoke.

"Why won't he do more for me?"

Colleen shook her head. "Stop worrying about him. You should learn to depend on yourself, anyway."

"But I don't know what I'm supposed to do."

"Did you rehearse for this?"

Andanna shrugged. "Some."

"You don't sound very enthusiastic."

"I don't think I'm much good."

They had arrived at the studio, which was off Caine Road. It belonged to a sound engineer friend of Colleen's. Andanna recognized his name. Michael sometimes worked with him. Why couldn't she have set this up herself? Why did she need Colleen?

"You're going to do badly if you keep up that attitude." Colleen waved away her attempt to pay the taxi driver. "Come on You Fun? Why are you so *saidaam?*"

Even Colleen thought she was gutless! "What's the good of being 'big in courage.'" "It doesn't get me anywhere."

"Listen to me. *Daam daaih sam sai.*" Big courage small heart. "Your problem is that everyone can read your heart. Once you allow that, you lose all power over others."

"Won't we be late?" Andanna looked away, unwilling to listen. Beyond the traffic and trees, a hazy layer obscured the blue of the afternoon sky.

"You're not listening, You Fun. Look at you. You're acting like a child. Why are you being such a wimp?"

"I'm not a wimp." She stared off into the distance. The buildings down the hillside were wrapped in the haze.

"Then stop behaving like one."

She could feel herself almost on the verge of tears. This wouldn't do. This simply wouldn't do. She continued staring, arms folded.

"Well then, perhaps you don't want to do this demo?"

She pursed her lips and didn't answer.

"You Fun, what are you frightened of?"

"That I'll fail you too." It came out unexpectedly. She hurriedly wiped away a tear.

Pulling a cellular out of her handbag, Colleen rang the sound guy, said they would have to re-schedule, and re-directed the chauffeur. Taking Andanna firmly by the arm, she dragged her to the Mandarin Hotel's mezzanine coffee shop. There, Andanna somehow managed to talk about how afraid she was of the potential failure ahead, of how her life was nothing but little successes that never amounted to much, of how Clio and even Sylvie seemed more like real adults, of how she was losing Clio's friendship since she hardly called her anymore. It was the first time she'd talked to anyone this way since she'd broken up with Michael. They talked for hours till the afternoon ended.

**

Christmas was less than a week away, but for once, Colleen's shopping wasn't done. She didn't care. She switched off the demo tape. It was excellent. Along with the photographs spread out on her coffee table, she knew she could make something out of all this work. The video demo could follow, but not till she had a signature tune to showcase. Perhaps she ought to find the girl a composer?

"So that's your protégée?" Kwok Po had wandered out of his study and picked up a photo. "She's sexy."

She glanced up at him from her perch on the floor. "Not protégée, client. You Fun and I have a business arrangement."

His smile indulged her. After all, she had no business experience. The photos had been her own work, and she was quite proud of the outcome. She laid several photographs next to each other, trying to decide which one worked best.

"You wait." She smiled back. "I'm going to make her a star."

Kwok Po lowered himself to the ground behind her. "I'm sure you will." He kissed her neck.

"Not now, sweetie."

He kissed her again, more insistently this time, his arm firmly around her waist. Surprised by his persistence, she turned around. She had forgotten it was Saturday. He rolled her gently on the floor. "Love means never saying no," he said. "Didn't you tell me that, *Hong Qi?*"

Much later, she rang You Fun to say that the promotional package was ready and that guess what, Kwok Po had agreed to give one to his lawyer friend Paul, the one who handled a leading female pop star. Oh, and, would she sing at this New Year's party they were hosting — it would give her a chance to meet Kwok Po and probably also Paul. There wouldn't be many people, maybe thirty or so, but some of them were connected to the entertainment industry.

The elated response pleased her. This was far more satisfying than all those idiotic balls she organized every year. This was much more personal, much more exciting. It didn't hurt that Kwok Po had been generous about investing, making it easy for her to set up a company and do everything right. Good thing she'd put a word in Albert's ear to give up his silly photo idea. She hadn't told You Fun, of course. No point upsetting her. That girl needed looking after. She just didn't know what was good for her.

Colleen cleared up the mess in the living room. Life was beginning all over again, the way it once had when she first fell in love with Kwok Po.

Lunch break was over. Andanna drank water. Her voice coach had only interrupted once that morning. The last six weeks had been daily rehearsals, starting early in the morning. She had cut down her smoking, stopped going out as much at nights, which Mother approved of. Following Colleen's guidance, she now had a shorter hairstyle and more colorful wardrobe.

"You have to project confidence," Colleen had told her the day she couldn't go through with the demo. "People have a kind of radar that warns them away from failures. They also smell success a mile away. You have that, You Fun, and you know it. What you have to learn to do is switch it on when you need it. Your problem is that you have too much time on your hands. Get busy, for heaven's sake. Work keeps the soul alive."

There was something to that. Her father ragged her often because she was idle. But nothing excited her, until Colleen came along. Now, her father had less complaints, because she didn't ask for as much money since she'd slowed down on the clubs. As long as she depended on her parents, no one would take her seriously. Colleen's investment, to launch her career, was different. All she had to do was perform. Colleen treated her seriously, unlike everyone else. She mustn't let her down.

Her band arrived and began setting up. The voice coach was saying it was time to work again.

FEBRUARY 1997

26

Colleen was saying something about "You Fun and that photographer, you know, Vince, the one you were dating?" Gail protested, saying she hadn't seen him for months, although he had called to wish her family a happy Christmas and New Year. Colleen made oddly sympathetic noises. Gail couldn't figure out what she was really trying to say.

They were at the Cultural Center for the international premiere of Tan Dun's new opera "Marco Polo." This last minute invitation, because Kwok Po had to work late, piqued Gail's interest. She rarely attended the annual arts festival events, because her schedule made it difficult to book tickets in advance.

"Anyway," Colleen was saying as they waited in the lobby before curtain time, "I heard he wanted her to pose for these 'art' shots. You wouldn't have guessed he was that type, would you?"

"Oh, I don't know." She was hardly prepared to defend him. She thought of her ex. Men. All useless at mid life. "She's a wild one."

Colleen appeared almost surprised. "You don't think he's interested in her?"

"Why not? Men prefer girls over women. Besides, how do you know all this?" If it hadn't involved Vince, she would have re-directed the conversation.

"I notice what people are up to. It pays to know."

The chimes signaling show time echoed through the foyer.

As the lights dimmed, Gail wondered if any real friendship with Vince could continue. It didn't seem likely. The music, a mournful and haunting wail, coursed through the silent theatre, casting its spell. Earth colors and sky lit up the stage, drawing the audience into another world. The vision of a journey.

Marco and Polo were two people.

This idea amused her. She supposed if anything were possible, such a mythical journey could have taken place. The slow drama unfolded; the spectacle fascinated but she didn't understand why. Its music was neither beautiful nor majestic, the set rather bare and not what she expected of an opera. And she couldn't always follow what was going on.

As theatrical time progressed, winter moved through spring into summer. Kublai Khan sang about waiting in a city *which is not my city / where I am a stranger also / in this city, in this place.*

Somehow, this *dungsai,* this East-West "thing" infected her imagination.

Several days ago, when she was returning from Shanghai, she'd encountered Tan Dun's welcome party at Kai Tak's arrival hall. There had been a number of young people there, holding signs for the Chinese composer, peering anxiously for the man. What would it be like, she had mused, to be a celebrity, the perpetual center of attention? She had walked, alone, down this same ramp many times, headed to the taxi rank and gone home. One of the travelling anonymous. These artists who needed to leave their mark, to make a splash wherever they went — she'd never know what that felt like.

But now, watching and hearing his creation, she felt it speak to her the way Chopin couldn't. His nocturnes soothed, but Tan Dun injected dignity into chaos, and a peculiar morality where east and west collided.

Make your escape to where you always were.

The words and music glittered like the milky way bridge, forcing her to cross over, to lose herself in its astronomical swirl.

She had come home to escape Boston, to return to a world where she could claim some roots. Yet Hong Kong had also meant the end of her marriage. When Vince had rejected her — how she despised that, how she still wished it hadn't been so — all the outrage that stormed through her when her husband first confessed his affair emerged again, unrelenting. But this time, the storm dissipated quickly, so quickly, like a typhoon on an uninhabited island, having nothing to destroy, no place to go.

She simply wasn't Vince's type.

Five years of marriage. She had known after a year that she wasn't her husband's type either. A palpable knowledge. She had married to create her own brand of family life; he to get as far away from his roots as possible, and thought a U.S. citizen wife would want to live in America. Like the move back, pregnancy had been her idea, not his. Once in Hong Kong, she had been annoyed by the demands of his traditional family, to which he responded, *I warned you — that's the way it has to be here at home.* She accepted what she could stomach, as long as their own nuclear family was the way she wanted it. He agreed patiently enough, and their lives progressed according to her design. The bottom line was, she had no reason to end the marriage. The first opportunity to escape, however, and he was gone.

It wasn't escape if it was where you belonged.

As for Vince, he had seemed open minded, tough enough to be unafraid of a woman like her. Now he'd turned into just another of life's little jokes.

Men. She just didn't belong with them.

Something Kwok Po said at Christmas, when they'd had her over for dinner, that she was escaping life by working all the time. She countered that if she were a man, that would be life. Colleen had smiled prettily and said life was what each person made it.

On stage, the journey continued.

"What did you think?"

"It transformed me."

Colleen was uncomfortable, because Gail really did seem transformed, her face radiant with self discovery. Dreadful the way some people reacted personally to the arts, dragging their private lives into their response. So pedestrian. Couldn't they see artifice for what it was? If only all her friends hadn't been busy tonight, she wouldn't have had to bring her, even though Kwok Po would be delighted by this. The idea of having Gail tag along to the cast party was atrocious, although she couldn't exactly not invite her. "Well, I'm glad you enjoyed it."

"Oh, I don't know that I did, but it was . . . revelatory, I guess."

Colleen was relieved to see Albert across the foyer and waved to him. As he walked over, she said, "I believe you know my husband's partner." Gail nodded.

Albert air kissed both Colleen's cheeks and shook Gail's hand. "Well. Was this yet another statement for 1997?"

"The question should be," Colleen replied, "is it good opera or not? He shrugged. "So, is our young star ready for her debut?"

Colleen glanced at Gail, and said, in Cantonese, "you know about *Lei You Fun,* right?" Seeing Gail's puzzled look, she clarified, in English, "Andanna Lee, from your party? She's the warm up act at a concert in the Coliseum next week. Would you like a ticket, by the way?"

"Oh, no thanks. I don't care for pop music." Gail's expression was annoyingly blank.

"Colleen, are you sure she's up to this?"

She hoped Albert wouldn't be difficult. The real star of the evening was his personal friend. "Have a little faith, my dear. She's your cousin."

"But so young and innocent."

He was deliberately provoking her. She wished Gail wouldn't just stand there, looking obtuse. Managing You Fun was just good fun, but Albert was taking it all too seriously.

Gail winked at her. "Hardly innocent, at least, not from what

Colleen tells me. And she's obviously far better connected than I imagined." She gave a knowing glance at Albert, who smiled.

"She *can* sing." Colleen hoped Gail wouldn't say anymore. It wouldn't do to get caught out in her lie about the photographs in front of Albert. Damn Vince. How did he manage to keep popping up in such an inconvenient fashion?

Fortunately, Gail begged off going to the post performance celebrations, and bid them goodnight. Colleen slipped her arm into Albert's. "Come along, dear. Let's go have a little fun now."

The elation from the opera remained. Gail had originally been afraid it might bore her, since she knew so little about the arts. In fact, what did she really know about outside of work? Her life sometimes felt a bit narrow. Hobbies. She ought to have a hobby.

At home, a surprising note from Conchita. "A Mr. Chak called. He said he was Gu Kwun's father." It did not indicate that he had spoken to their son. Only the time, around nine thirty. Wondering if it would be too late to call back, she checked Gu Kwun's room. He was asleep, and his breathing was regular. A good thing, since he hadn't been feeling too well lately, and she worried that he had caught something.

The last time she had spoken to her ex was around Christmas, when he had been two weeks late on alimony. Since they'd split up, this was only the third or fourth time he'd actually called. It was also unusual that he called in the evening, at home. His wife would hardly approve. Gail was tempted to call now, regardless of the hour, just to be rude. Even as she dismissed the thought, the phone rang. It was him, with the excuse that her maid had told him she'd be back late, and he assumed she wouldn't mind. They talked briefly. When she hung up, the earlier mood remained, and she experienced a strange joy, even though she felt she ought to be angry at him. How presumptuous of him to be apologetic now, wanting to be a father again, promising to see Gu Kwun regularly if she would "allow" it, as if it had all been her fault. And he'd waited till after Christmas and Chinese New Year, times that would have mattered, when their son needed more because all his friends had family devoted to them. Late though, was better than never.

But the strange joy persisted. Did the opera — all that music and drama played out in a make believe world — have such power to move her, to ease worry over life's traumas? Whatever it was, she went to bed in a peaceful mood and slept soundly. When she awoke, refreshed, she saw that she'd overslept, and immediately knew she'd missed an important meeting. No panic overtook her. Somehow, it just didn't seem all that big a deal.

When Albert dropped her off that night, Kwok Po was already home. Colleen invited him in.

Her husband kissed her. "Did I miss much?"

"Depends," she shrugged. "Maybe, maybe not."

"How unlike you," Albert declared. "I thought Mrs. Tang always pronounced on new artistic endeavors."

"Not when in the company of your superior sensibilities."

"You've kept her in Hong Kong too long," he addressed Kwok Po. "She's learned not to express an opinion until the universal consensus is out."

Pompous ass, thought Colleen. "In that case, I'm keeping the right company." She smiled mockingly. "Tea?" As she headed towards the kitchen, she heard Kwok Po bringing up one of their joint real estate ventures in Shanghai.

She put the kettle on and took the teapot and tin of jasmine tea leaves out of the cupboard. Only a tiny bit left. She must remind Jacinta to get more. Arms folded, she waited for the water to boil. That would give her husband time to talk with Albert.

There were times she simply didn't trust Albert. At the cast party that evening, he carried on the way he usually did, flirting and teasing as if he were a playboy. Yet she'd never, ever seen him with a partner, male or female. She wondered when and if he slept. Andanna told her how late he stayed out at the clubs, but she knew from Kwok Po that Albert always showed up for business appointments on time, even early ones.

Something he'd asked earlier — should Vince take some promotional shots of Andanna, which he'd pay for? As a contribution, he insisted, because she was family, and after all, he had agreed not to push those "other" photos? It troubled her, but she accepted. Then, he remarked on her and Vince, saying what a coincidence it was that they'd met in Subic Bay. She replied cautiously, and was annoyed when he continued to press the issue, wanting to know more, ferreting around the circumference of her secret existence. It wasn't just sex gossip he was after; he was trying to force her soul. Moments later, he dropped the subject and carried on as if he'd never mentioned it.

In retrospect, she might have been better off with Gail at the party. At least the woman was up front, even if she were a crashing bore.

The kettle whistled.

"Heung Gong bu shi Shanghai," Kwok Po was saying when she emerged.

"Darling, you're mixing up your 'Chinglish' dialects," she said in *Putonghua.* "Why isn't Hong Kong like Shanghai?"

Albert was laughing, although it was more a smirk than a laugh. "Your husband puts far too much faith in our future leaders."

She smiled. "And you don't?" Albert consorted with an influential China crowd, and his almost perfect Beijing accent put Kwok Po, and most other Hong Kong *yan,* to shame.

"To survive, we Hong Kong people will do most things. Faith, however, should be reserved for a different sensibility. It's rather like American individualism, which your people pursue with remarkable persistence."

"That isn't strictly American."

"Enough, you two. Drink tea," Kwok Po declared.

Colleen watched her husband pour him a cup. Quite a change since the Boston days, when he shunned people unlike himself. It wasn't out of snobbishness, but ignorance from his narrow minded upbringing. These days, she had to remind him not to be too friendly with any of their hired help in his family's presence.

"How did you two end up together?" Albert suddenly asked.

Her husband grinned. "She pursued me."

Colleen let him tell his version. It was one of his favorite anecdotes, and the one he called up when relaxed. Her earlier anxieties abated. There was a unstated protocol and civility both men observed that she found reassuring. There was hope for Albert yet.

Her version wasn't very different from his. She had gone to a party given by one of the Sino-American organizations at her university. It was at some hotshot China watcher's home. Her date was a classmate, and an even worse Sinophile than herself. All night long, he had bored her with his need to impress everyone with his Chinese language ability. Yet he kept quoting four-character *cheng yu* quite inappropriately.

Kwok Po had been standing alone near the bathroom where she'd gone to escape her date.

"Are you waiting?" she asked in English, pointing at the door.

He'd stared through her as if she were invisible. "No, but it's occupied. There's another one in the bedroom."

"Mei wenti. Keyi deng."

"Huh?"

"Oh forgive me. You're from Hong Kong, aren't you?"

"Yes, I'm afraid so."

It was '83. China was in. Universities invited "students" to America, the aged and young offspring of cadres in a newly enlightened Communist party. That night's crowd was evidence of the social fallout: Cantonese speakers were in the minority. "Don't say that," she told him. "Hong Kong's lovely."

That was when he looked at, and not through, her. "You've been there?"

"Oh yes." And she told him of her trip, on her way back from China. About how much she'd liked his home city and looked forward to going back.

"You liked it more than Beijing?"

"Heaps more. Beijing is historically significant, but Hong Kong, that city's alive right now. China may be the middle kingdom and all that, but to the rest of the world, your home's still the most exciting port of call."

His date emerged from the bathroom. Colleen recognized her as one of the Mainland students, a real airhead with tits. Guys went for those. She spoke to Kwok Po in English, saying "thanks for waiting." Seeing Colleen, she slid her arm through his and tried to move them quickly away. But he managed to tell her his name and where he worked.

". . . and she tracked me down and invited me out for a drink," her husband was saying. "Wouldn't take no for an answer."

"I guess it pays to be a persistent American." Albert's tone was almost sincere.

They conversed till quite late over tea.

27

Vince switched off the radio. The handover again. It was all anyone talked about these days. Since the start of the year, the entire world was going nuts. Even Didi, Deanna, who didn't read newspapers and hated news broadcasts because "they never have anything good to tell you" during the last phone call had asked, "so, are you're really going to stay on in China? I mean, isn't it like this big takeover over there?" No point explaining. Her interest was fleeting at best. Would he have married her if she *hadn't* been pregnant?

"You are privileged to be here at this moment of historical change." Albert declared, the last time they'd met. He often spoke as if he were some kind of elder statesman for Hong Kong, with a possessiveness that conferred distinction to utterances from on high. "In a way, Vincent, you are in a slightly better position than some to appreciate it because you originate from a city that once almost defined a new order for what a city was and should be. Of course, New York is some- what passé now."

Proclaimed not as an opinion but as a fact.

Hadn't bothered challenging him that time. Why argue with the converted? For himself, he'd stay in Hong Kong, see the handover through, make more money, and worry about the future after July.

It was only eleven. He had to go see his trombonist friend at the Conrad Hotel around one. Amazing how successful that guy had become, gigging all over Asia at fancy hotels now that jazz was in.

Didn't hurt that he was African-American. Authentic in the eyes of the locals. Like himself, when he said he was from New York.

Real Thing.

Albert could say what he wanted.

Each party of the bridal entourage appeared to have her or his role. Two women took care of flowers, another ensured the bridal train did not get caught as the procession moved towards the fountain. One man played photographer while another ferried props from the car for the shot. Only the groom seemed out of place, waiting to be directed, hot and uncomfortable in his tuxedo.

Normally, Gail wouldn't have stopped. Countless weddings took place amid the man-made landscape of Hong Kong Park, where the marriage registry was located. But the groom's aspect arrested her. He appeared a timid man, while his bride held court in the center of her universe, the way Sylvie had.

Gail watched the spectacle. It was late afternoon.

The bridal party descended towards her down the stone steps by the fountain. The girl bearing the train clucked excitedly. Everyone was in too much of a hurry, slow down, she said. And the groom, directed by one of the flower girls to look sharp, to stand next to his bride. She tilted her head. A graceful movement, regal demeanor. Not a single bead of sweat spoiled the white lace and tulle vision she presented on this warm March afternoon.

Gail felt a stab of empathy for the groom.

Her own marriage had happened without ceremony at the registry in Boston. No friends or relatives, with strangers for witnesses. Life shouldn't be about such a lot of fuss. When her ex re-married late last year, she'd heard they had a wedding banquet with over forty tables. A grotesque waste of money.

She was about to walk away when she saw Vince, camera poised, shooting the bridal scene. Should she bother? Without too much thought, she went up behind him. "Are they friends of yours?"

He spun around, startled. "Oh, hey, how's it going?"

His face was tired. Too much work, not enough routine, probably. Hong Kong was rough on his brand of expatriate, the ones who weren't in the business safety net of bankers, lawyers and corporate soldiers. It was what attracted her originally. He wasn't like everyone else she knew.

"Not too badly. Are they friends of yours?"

He grinned like a school boy. "Stole someone else's history."

"How very revisionist."

"They're happy." His face became serious, the playful instance over. "How 'bout we talk?"

She hesitated. "I don't know if we should."

"So why'd you come over and say hello?"

It riled her, this ability he had to come straight to the point. She didn't know why she had. She could have walked away easily enough, and not gotten herself into this. But there was no reason to be afraid.

She glanced at her watch. "When?"

He didn't look at his. "Right now? Coffee? Or whatever."

"Sure. Whatever."

He suggested Dan Ryan's, the standard American hangout. It seemed to please her. Face value, don't speculate. They headed to the bar.

"You seem in reasonable spirits." Vince raised his beer.

She clinked her glass of wine against his. "I am."

"So why were you watching?"

"What?"

"The wedding."

"I don't know. Bored, I guess."

"How come you're not at work?"

"You ask a lot of questions."

"Can't help it."

"I know," she said.

Her manner neither imperious nor sharp. Liked her better this way, as if some barrier between them had been removed. He was reminded of their first meeting, when he had quite naturally pulled out Katy's photo and said, "she's my princess," and she had reciprocated with her prince and there had been a flash, a moment, a communion of souls.

"And what have you been up to?" A glint in her eyes. "Breaking more hearts?"

"It's that what I do?"

"Not exactly. A kind of . . . cheap imitation?"

"Boy, you sure hold grudges, don't you?"

"Don't we all?"

"No. I can't be bothered."

She didn't respond.

Maybe, he decided, nothing more needed to be said. Long, neatly manicured, pale pink nails tapped her wine glass. Caught the light and glimmered. A pink tourmaline set in silver circled the ring finger on her right hand. Only the veins told her age. He wanted to take that hand, to tell her to let go. Why this odd sympathy? She seemed like someone cheated out of life. But he didn't know for sure.

"So, should I shoot the handover?"

"I didn't think you were a news photographer."

"I'm not. But the whole world's descending on this town. Thought maybe I could sell a shot or two. Really, though, it's to hang onto a piece of history. "

"Don't bother."

That surprised him. "Why not?"

"It isn't worth it, except for a moment."

"Guess I thought you cared about Hong Kong."

"I do. Certainly more than you."

"Isn't its history important to you then?"

She was silent a long moment. "No." And then, after another swallow of her drink, "well, that's not strictly true. Like most people, I don't care that much about history, not really, except in how it affects me personally. I'll write the market reports for my job, and crib from all the over-reporting that's already happening, which will be plenty good enough for my American employer."

"You're really that uninterested?"

"Making money here is what counts, so that I can fulfill my responsibilities to my family and society. That's fair enough, isn't it? I've been fortunate, and done better than many others, so I like Hong Kong pretty much the way it is. The politicians can say and do what they please as long as my life's not disturbed."

"That's the way life is here, huh? No one gives a shit about anyone except herself?"

"It's honest." She hesitated. "Maybe, more moral than pretending otherwise."

"Morals? In this town?"

Mocking smile. "We have a few."

"But you're going to become a part of China."

"So what? We always were. It's only the rest of the world that thinks we're not. What do you think? That Hong Kong will disappear on July 1st?" She flashed a mildly tipsy look at him and got up. "I have to run."

Wanted to stop her, afraid suddenly of yet another lost connection. Just to do right by one woman. Wasn't too much to ask. "My friend Jim might be coming for the handover." He watched her face. Either put his foot in or . . . she sat down again.

"You know, you're really something." But she began to grin.

"You're not mad at me?"

"At you? Why should I be? You sent me a beautiful photograph."

"So, can I send him?"

She laughed. Music to his soul. "You're not joking, are you?"

"Nope. I'm the eternal romantic."

"Would you care to define that?"

"Goes something like this, I think. Beautiful woman like you deserves better than the likes of me. Least I can do is help out my friends."

She smiled from somewhere deep inside.

He offered a handshake. "Friends?"

"Friends." Silent laughter as she departed.

Yeah, Jim would *definitely* like her.

At the top of the escalator leading down to the subway beneath Pacific Place, Vince paused briefly. The late afternoon sunlight danced layers over the skyline. Unbeautiful city, he had often told himself. Yet at this moment, in this perfect light, it was spectacular.

Gail was part of his Hong Kong now, and it somehow made him feel less of a stranger. He roamed the city, photographing, delighting in its warmth. Seeing familiar sights as if for the first time. Storing images as keepsakes to bring home. When had he begun to think in terms of going home?

Last week, Jim had called to confirm travel dates. The conversation turned down the usual path of their lives and loves, or, as Jim put it, their lack of love in the midst of what passed for living. *Sometimes, I think we'd be better off celibate,* he declared. *Celibates know the meaning of love that's divorced from the physical, that exists in an easier place. At least the ones I see in therapy seem to.* Vince thought of Albert. For an instance, he almost agreed.

In Wanchai, he stopped along Lockhart Road, in the heart of the red light district. He still thought of it that way from his previous encounter with this city, even though the area was now as much the yuppie club scene as whorehouse row. Across the street, he spied three women, two Chinese and one Caucasian, well dressed and attractive. Everywhere he looked, beautiful women provoked seduction, hinted at the promise of love. His dual preoccupations on landing here — my brother might be sleeping with my ex-wife and my present wife is sleeping with our contractor — had stifled hope, turning him into a clumsy imitation of himself. Time dulled but did not erase the pain of life without intimacy. This duration of loneliness all came back to sex and love. Life had to be more than that.

Home's where life should be. Who was he hearing? Not Jim.

The idea of home hung in limbo. No shame in failure, no sin in divorce, even the second time. Hong Kong merely a shelter from the typhoon, until the winds subsided.

The trouble with therapy answers were that they were equally as seductive. Offered hope, sometimes too much. The one thing this place made him confront was the illusory quality of hope. One of the ad guys once, bitching about market research results of some new product. *Nobody has strong opinions about anything here — on a scale of one to ten everything comes up five.* Life is neither bad nor good, he could hear a Hong Kong chorus chant. Life, if he could only accept it, was simply what it was.

Much later, back at the apartment, a message from Didi. "Call us please. It's Katy." Panic, and then the fight to remain calm.

"What's wrong?"

"It's nothing, she's okay. She's just been crying something silly because she wants to talk to you." He heard her call their daughter. "Calm her down, please?" Across the world, his Katy was telling her mother that she couldn't listen because this was a "private conversation with Daddy."

"What's the matter, princess?"

"It's Caitlin." Her best friend of the moment. "She said you're not really my father."

"Why did she say that?"

"Because her parents are divorced too, but she gets to visit her dad every week. Why can't I visit you?"

"You can."

"I can?"

"Sure. You get on a plane and fly out here."

"Doesn't that take a long time? Mommy says you live very far away."

"About eighteen hours."

He heard her think.

"That's longer than it takes to go to Grandma's." Didi's parents lived in Brooklyn's Bay Ridge, less than a half hour away.

"Yes it is."

"Then, that's way too far. Mom says we can't go to Grandma's every week because she's too faraway, so I can't take even longer to go see you." Petulant pouting tone.

"Tell you what." "What?" "How 'bout I come back to Manhattan?" "Is that far?" "No. It's where Radio City Music Hall is. Remember that? Where Joe took you?"

"Can you come back at Christmas and take me there?"

The urgency in her voice, the eager excitement. Anything not to let her down. "Sure."

Caitlin forgotten, Katy chattered on and on until Didi finally stopped her, saying it was late over there, and she said goodbye, reluctantly.

Vince looked at his daughter's picture by the phone. Katy was life. He had to continue believing it, because perhaps then, there was hope for the idea of home.

28

The MC announced her name, and Andanna heard the welcoming applause. Colleen squeezed her hand. Her voice coach gave her a thumbs up, signaling her forward. She drew a deep breath. It was now or never at all.

Andanna emerged onstage, in time to the music.

She was only the opening act for a famous female singer, but if it hadn't been for Colleen's and Albert's connections, she wouldn't be here at all. She couldn't let them down. She sang.

Afterwards, a sea of congratulations, even a nod from the star herself.

Her mother was talking to Albert, delighted by all the attention Andanna was getting. "You're so good to her. She's lucky to have such a generous *tonggho*," she heard Mother say, which Albert waved away, saying, "my cousin is special. I like to showcase talent."

Colleen, she noticed, was chatting up the star's manager. She could hear words like "duet" and "unique, classical-pop talent."

Clio had found her way backstage, fiancé in tow. "Hey Andanna, you were really terrific."

Andanna gazed at her friend, shocked. It had been months since they'd spoken, longer since they'd seen each other. She had been almost convinced their friendship was over. Yet here was Clio, beaming and laughing, delighting in her success, as if their long separation had never happened.

"What're you doing here?"

"Came to 'hold up your platform' of course, 'silly melon.' You don't think I'd miss this, do you? Hey, are you going to record a CD? You should, you know."

"You're the 'silly melon.' Why didn't you tell me? I would've gotten you comp tickets."

"Doesn't matter. Besides," she inclined her head towards her partner, "he paid." Her fiancé stood there with the obliging air of a sheepdog. Clio abandoned him to follow Andanna into the dressing room.

"So you did it." Clio glanced around the tiny, makeshift dressing room. "Pretty nice."

"It sucks."

"You've got to start somewhere."

She shrugged. "You really liked it?"

And then, Andanna saw the adoration in her eyes. It was what bound her to Clio. She hadn't thought she'd ever know that feeling again. For a second, Andanna nearly cried.

Her friend was exuberant. "You did it, didn't you? You're really going to be a star."

Colleen watched You Fun exalt in the moment. A funny thing, this manager business. It was a little like looking after a rare flower, ensuring its health and bloom each season until it was time for the next flower show. A little like looking after a husband.

Kwok Po hadn't attended because of work, and truthfully, Colleen preferred that. She needed to do this alone. He'd be proud of her, however great or small a success she was. But he'd be proud of anything she did because he loved her. It was a certainty she could count on; whether or not he had time to be with her was immaterial. This was the way marriage was supposed to be.

"Madame Tang, you're looking thoughtful." Albert handed her a rose plucked from You Fun's bouquet. "Your protégée has launched wonderfully."

She held the flower to her nose. It was devoid of fragrance. "She works hard."

"And will she continue to?"

"I don't know."

Albert affected a cunning grin. "Why, is this a shooting star that's already fallen to earth?"

Colleen glanced at You Fun who was laughing noisily with her cousins and friends. A gaggle of girls, carousing in Cantonese. Just like her first trip to Hong Kong years ago, long before this life with Kwok Po. At the airport, the friend who was supposed to meet her had been late. While waiting for him, several young women were shrieking together the way Andanna's group was doing now. Having just left Beijing, the unmusical Cantonese tones hurt her ears. But as she watched the faces of the chattering crowd, a distinct image of this world she had just entered crystallized, and she remarked that this place, peopled by these cacophonous beings, was not China. They inhabited a world that had drawn its own boundaries, within which a delirious energy could flow. Entry was barred by an invisible wall, unless one insisted on intruding. Otherwise, the delirium engaged anyone who chose to be a spectator. Then her friend arrived and the image vanished.

Colleen lightly struck Albert's arm with the rose, waving it around like a wand. "Stars and their light years aren't always visible to the rest of us."

"So," Albert countered, "we'll simply bathe in their illumination while we can."

The last people straggled off. Andanna slumped into a convenient chair. Her feet hurt. Mother had gone home over an hour ago, telling her not to stay out too late.

"Can I give you a lift home, You Fun?"

Colleen looked exhausted. Not smoking was getting to her.

Andanna stretched a hand out and lightly squeezed her shoulder. "No thanks. You're near the tunnel here and it'll be out of your way. I'll get a taxi."

"C'mon, I'll walk you out."

Cradling her roses, Andanna picked up her things and followed Colleen. The cleaning crew had already begun their work at the Coliseum. She glanced once more at the stage. How *huge* the performance had been! The Jazz Club, which Michael magnified in her earlier life, was puny by comparison. Had she been nervous, Clio had asked. Just a little, but the minute she walked out there, the audience ocean glistened before her, and it was the easiest thing in the world to plunge into its inviting depths, unafraid.

To be a star, you have to change your life. Colleen had told her that the day she couldn't face the demo taping session.

"*Wei, gihng a!*" The voice in the darkness of the doorway startled them both. A man handed Andanna a bouquet. "For your starlight. See you again soon."

They watched him depart. "Did you know him?" Colleen asked.

"Oh, just an acquaintance." Andanna deposited his bouquet atop the nearest trash receptacle.

Colleen saw her off into a taxi before stepping into her own chauffeured car. Andanna leaned back against the seat. It had been months since she'd had any contact with Tai Jai. Why had he come by? And what did he mean about seeing her again soon? She was worried for a moment, but dismissed her fears. He probably only meant to wish her well, and had been too embarrassed to go backstage. That was all. That must be it.

The taxi drove down the slope in Hunghom where the Coliseum was located. It sped past what she thought of as funeral parlor row. At the end of that street was the Kowloon Mortuary. Andanna didn't know this area very well, but she did know the funeral parlors that stood next to each other. Grandmother's wake had taken place there, as had those of other relatives. The driver was going a long way around. She ought to say something, but right now, she didn't want to argue. Besides, what did a few dollars more matter?

She closed her eyes and imagined herself back on stage, the feel of the mike in her hands. The bare stage, with the orchestra set far back, gave her ample room to move around. A natural dancer, Andanna never found movement difficult. The few times she had done any cat-walk modeling, she had been complimented on her grace and posture. As for the music, as long as she'd rehearsed the songs, the performance was easy.

All that time wasted with Michael. He had made her feel like she'd never be good enough for any kind of singing career. She didn't get the "swing" feel, she didn't concentrate, she couldn't pronounce the lyrics properly because her English sucked. The problem with Michael was that he couldn't see what she needed to be doing with her talents and wanted to make her what she was not. Tonight was far more natural. Nothing worth doing should be as hard as Michael demanded. This was Hong Kong. Why sing in any language except Cantonese? And why bother trying to "swing" if nobody else did?

When Michael tried to get gigs, he had to suck up to club owners, sweet talk idiotic hotel managers, and worse of all, he had to be nice to all the foreign musicians so that they would let him play with them. Most of the time, the club owners or F&B hotel managers didn't even return phone calls, and he had to persist and follow up everything. When she tried to arrange gigs on her own, the whole experience had been so humiliating that she refused to ever do it again. Even getting paid was a chore. Those hotel people, and even some of the foreign musicians, paid him as if they were doing him a favor. Michael kow-towed to all of them because he never thought he was good enough.

Tonight had happened far more easily. Once Colleen decided she was ready for a big debut performance, she had called her contacts to figure out the best forum for her. Colleen thought big. She chose a well established singer who wouldn't feel insecure with a newcomer. In fact, the singer was so big she even did tonight's show backed by part of the Hong Kong Philharmonic's orchestra. It had been a kind of classical pop, perfect for someone like herself. A classy act. Besides, the woman was a personal friend of Albert's, and therefore agreed to do this. Everything had gone smoothly.

Now there would be interviews with magazines, and maybe a TV appearance.

It made a difference having a manager. Even though this performance hadn't meant any money, and had in fact cost Colleen, it was a way to get started. And the audience had been so welcoming.

Wouldn't Michael be jealous if he knew? Of course he'd hear from their mutual friends. She knew he would only laugh, thinking the whole thing a big joke. What did she care what he thought anymore?

They were finally headed in the right direction towards her home. A motorcycle roared by, overtaking them in their narrow lane on Wylie Road, almost cutting off the taxi. The driver swore at him. For a minute, Andanna thought the motorcyclist was Tai Jai. What a creep. But it couldn't be, surely it couldn't be.

She ejected the idea of him to the furthest galaxies.

Tonight was the beginning of her new life, and no one, not Tai Jai, not even the memory of Michael could spoil it.

She cradled her drooping roses.

Vince was propped on a barstool at The Jazz Club when Albert walked in during the last set. "Perrier and lime?" He offered.

Albert nodded. He signaled the bartender to put it on his tab, but Vince beat him to it. "What's this for?"

"What? Can't I buy you a drink?"

"If you insist."

"So how did your cousin do tonight?"

"She was fine."

"You don't sound too enthusiastic."

He shrugged. "What can I say? I was born in a different time and place. It's not my kind of music."

"But it's popular in Hong Kong."

"These days, it is."

"Admit it, you're just an aging, decadent colonial."

Albert lapsed into silence. Vince occasionally saw him in these moods, when he seemed malcontent with the state of things. At these moments, Albert seemed most like a friend, unaffected and open, willing to question the perfect image he posited of his world. It was better than all his posturing.

At Albert's suggestion, they took their drinks next door to the music room where the house band was playing.

"Listen to him." Albert pointed at the trombonist. "How does he do it?"

Vince shrugged. "I've heard better in New York." The guy was good but not exceptional. Except for their friendship, Vince wouldn't bother coming to hear him.

"No one else in Hong Kong can play like he does," Albert continued. "But does anyone care?" He gestured at the room, empty except for two other tables. "All performers need an audience."

"So book him at your Shanghai club."

"I already have."

This strange friendship had its moments. Albert had a remarkable face. Unlined and smooth skinned. Hard to believe it belonged to someone who was almost fifty. Next to him, Vince felt old. First time they'd met, here in The Jazz Club, Vince thought of him as a Hollywood runaway, a Chinaman character out of the old movies.

The mellow voice of the trombone curled round the room like a smoke ring that was slowly unfurling. A member of the audience applauded a solo.

"C'mon Vincent. Let's go to your place." Lowering his voice. "I've got a joint."

Albert called pot smoking "holding onto my America." Vince shook his head, and indicated the stage. "Can't. Have to talk to him when he's done."

"Come to my place then, when you've finished."

"What's this, some kind of belated April's Fool joke?" Because it was past midnight.

"What do you mean?"

"No idea where you live."

"Really?" He seemed genuinely surprised.

"You've never invited me over before."

Albert scribbled an address on a napkin. Walking distance. Round the corner on Wyndham, near the gay bar. Explained why he always liked to meet here in Lan Kwai Fong. Albert was cryptic by accident only. Vince stuffed the napkin in his shirt pocket. "Catch you later."

Albert's fingers worried his shoulder. "Make sure you do."

Lonely hearts club tonight. Why didn't Albert come out gay? Convinced he must be. Either that or a true asexual. Albert pronounced on many things, but sex was the one subject he deliberately kept vague. Jake Wu called him sexually undefined.

About to order one more beer. Didn't. Don controlled consumption. Guardian angel or nagging shrew? One body; two voices, faces, moral codes. Image manipulation.

What would Jim think of Albert?

One passport two countries. Albert's little joke last week when the conversation turned, as it did incessantly, to one country two systems. Albert had a green card, acquired through his half brother. Had it for years. Wouldn't get a passport though. He was, he insisted, a citizen of Hong Kong, not America, although he increasingly spent time in Shanghai these days.

Yet tonight.

Perhaps it was the proximity of change.

By an accident, fortuitous or otherwise, he, Vince da Luca had fallen into the middle of an historical instance, amid a society he would not ordinarily inhabit. Something in what Albert said, about being forced through the maze simply because he was there.

Felt the napkin in his pocket. Flattered.

Might even miss this town.

The last number, an Ellington tune, pulled him back into his own world a moment longer.

29

"Gail's changed."

"How so?" Colleen asked. Her husband's declaration over breakfast surprised her.

"She's moody. When I called her at work yesterday, she wasn't her usual self. You know how she's always bright and cheerful?"

Pollyanna-ish. "Oh yes. She's such an optimist."

Kwok Po nodded agreement. "Exactly. That's why she surprised me when she said she'd rather not come to our handover bash. Didn't even offer a reason."

"Well darling, I don't mean to be indelicate, but she is around . . . that age, you know."

He looked baffled at first, and then uttered an "oh" of comprehension.

"Besides, she's not exactly the social type like we are, is she?"

"Perhaps not." But he sounded unsure.

Later that morning, Colleen rang Gail. "I'm sorry to hear you won't be able to make it to our party. Are you going to be away?"

"No, I don't plan to be."

"Oh, you mean you haven't made plans yet?" The woman was absurdly obtuse.

"What's your point, Colleen?"

Gail's irritation daunted her. It was unexpected. "I didn't mean anything by it. It's just that you're such a close friend of ours that I wanted to emphasize how much we'd like you to be there."

Her voice was cold. "I know Kwok Po's my friend."

"Well, in case your plans change, call me and I'll make sure you're on our guest list. Vince will be there. He's doing the photographs."

Silence on the line. Was she offended? "

Gail spoke slowly, deliberately. "You know Colleen, don't take this the wrong way, but my relationship with Vince is really none of your business."

Colleen was taken aback. Before she could respond, Gail hung up.

Later, after lunch, Gail tried to concentrate on work, but her thoughts kept drifting back to the morning's conversation. Kwok Po's wife might be a tiresome gossip, but it was no reason to be rude. Was she becoming rude, or had she always been that way? Earlier, Ariadne had seemed quite upset when she asked her why the back file to some correspondence wasn't attached. She was just asking, but her manner had obviously put her secretary off.

Dismissing her worries, she headed towards the executive toilet to see the "out of order" sign on it. Annoyed, she went to the other ladies room. From her stall, she overheard Ariadne speaking to someone.

"That Szeto bitch makes me want to throw up."

"Yeah, I know what you mean."

"It's that 'A-merican' experience of hers. She's not Chinese anymore. Thinks she's 'better' than us."

"She always has to be right."

The other women laughed. "She's like a robot, completely inhuman. I've heard her say she works till ten at night sometimes. How abnormal."

"But if she makes a mistake, you'll never hear her admit it."

"I don't know how you work for her."

"You know how that goes. Besides, what choice do I have?"

The voices faded as they left.

Her first reaction, *how dare they*, and then she began to cry, weeping uncontrollably. She gulped down the tears and composed herself. Why all this emotion? Her gynecologist said she wasn't menopausal yet, even though she thought otherwise. Surely her hormones were out of sync. Or was it something else, something she didn't understand?

Ariande! What an awful betrayal. The other woman was from Private Banking, someone she considered friendly. Did the whole office think *that* badly of her? She knew she was a tough boss, but she'd always tried to be fair. That crack about American experience. Did they still see her as one of "them" and not "us."

Make your escape to where you always were.

This stolen instance shouldn't matter. She wasn't supposed to have heard. People didn't show their feelings as openly as in America. She was a Hong Kong *yan* too. Staff always complained about bosses — didn't she do likewise to her peers about their boss?

But the private banking woman was a peer.

She returned to her office, passing by Ariadne's desk. Her secretary smiled and handed her the file she needed. Normally . . . just what *did* she do normally, thank her? She thought so. Now, she wasn't so sure.

At first, Colleen was put off by Gail, but her annoyance quickly became concern. She knew how important that woman's friendship was to her husband, and didn't want him to think that she was causing Gail's distance. If Kwok Po had his way, he'd hire her to run a Shanghai office. So perhaps she was pushing it with that remark about Vince, but honestly, why the secrecy? Gail had virtually confessed she had a thing for him.

But Gail would eventually go back to the States. That brat of hers would go to college there, and maybe even high school. She wouldn't commit herself to China long term, not the way they would. Kwok Po once said that Gail hadn't resolved her American half.

Anyway, the woman was basically harmless

Danny's call interrupted her mood.

"You're leaving? Why?"

"It's too small here."

"You're not making sense, Danny. Of course it's small. What's that got to do with anything?"

"I mean, it's too insignificant for democracy to matter. Once this becomes China, it'll just be a matter of pleasing the new 'sovereign.'"

"So where are you going to go?"

"Back to China. Maybe Shanghai. I know some folks there who send news about dissidents out over the Internet. I can help them with their English."

Colleen pictured Kwok Po's irritation. Still, she'd rather know than not know what her brother was up to. "When are you leaving?"

"Tonight."

"Stay in touch, okay?"

"Sure sis, sure."

If she could re-order her world, Gail would come work for Kwok Po and her brother would return to the anonymity of America. At least Gail was a useful business contact for her husband. Yet despite her discomfort, she knew that Danny's idealistic fervor balanced out her chosen life in some kind of karmic retribution. He could prove embarrassing, or worse, end up in jail which would mean her having to campaign publicly for his release. It was so painful it was funny. Wouldn't the Tang family love that!

For the moment, however, she had an invitation list to complete.

Along the empty beach at Shek O, Gail chased Gu Kwun. Her son laughed to the waves. Sheer cliffs surrounded them. It was the last day of April, and the city's swimmers had not yet begun to brave the waters. In the distance, a lone figure surfed towards the shores. A golden Labrador ran across the sands, followed by his jogging master.

Her mother sat on a blanket, far back from the shoreline, guarding the picnic basket. Gu Kwun raced towards her. "Look grandma, I'm an aeroplane, I can fly!" He spread his arms out. The sound of her laughter echoed across the emptiness around them.

Gail inhaled the salty sea breezes. If she closed her eyes, she could pretend she was in Maine. Almost perfect day. If only she could forget yesterday's overheard conversation.

She stood at the shoreline, watching her family. Debris and garbage rolled in with the waves. During her childhood, the waters at all the beaches had been clean. Now, she didn't dare go in, not since a bad earache after her last dip in the sea six years ago. Sad, this uncontrolled pollution. The water splashed against her bare feet. Lukewarm, not even slightly cold. Certainly not the clean, bracing foam of New England. It was easy to lose track of the seasons here. Since she'd been back, she had only worn her winter coat in China, Korea or Japan, never here.

Gu Kwun's voice called to her. "Mother, you be an aeroplane."

"Okay." She spread out her arms and buzzed her way towards him. He clapped his hands, along with his grandmother. Her two children.

"Mother, I want to take an aeroplane to go see Uncle. Can we, please? I'll practice till my English is well enough, I promise," he said, in English.

She tousled his hair. "Till it's good enough," she corrected, but added, "okay."

He sat down happily next to grandma and began building a sand castle, although Gail knew it would probably turn into a tall, square block, the way his castles usually did.

Cautioning him to stay close to grandma, she headed back towards the water. The surfer had emerged on shore and was walking with her board towards the pier. She was a striking and tall Asian woman, extremely tanned, in a skimpy bikini. Her hair was dyed that popular auburn. Gail was pretty sure she was Chinese. *You've come a long way, baby,* without even having to go to Hawaii.

Shek O was relatively deserted on this weekday. Gail gazed out over the horizon. *Was* this home? In answer to Vince's question, "do you plan to stay?" she had responded with an unequivocal, "but of course, Hong Kong's my home." Yet these days, her son talked more and more about the U.S., a country he didn't know. Gordie's recent profits from Chinese shares meant he could afford to call almost weekly, and each time, he would chatter away with Gu Kwun, whom he called "Gordo's Gucko" which made him laugh. Of course she welcomed her half brother's attentions for her child. But somehow, it didn't feel . . . right? A continual unease because Gordie represented . . . oh, what was the use worrying? Gail bent down and pick up a handful of stones, and began idly tossing them one by one into the sea.

She had almost told Vince about Gordie, but stopped herself. No one, except her ex-husband, knew the truth about her family, and even he didn't know the whole story. It wasn't anyone's business. Besides, Vince was a stranger. Thank goodness they'd resolved to be just friends. It was better this way. Less complicated.

The overheard conversation echoed. If they only knew the truth of her "A-merican experience," that would be real gossip.

"Gordo Gucko," she heard Gu Kwun say to his grandma, inflecting the name with a Cantonese slant. "Uncle says I'm Gordo Gucko!" Her baby. The American boy with no English name, as his American uncle called him.

She flung the last stone into the water as hard as she could.

Gu Kwun *was* Chinese, despite his citizenship, no matter what Gordie or anyone said. Even though her marriage had failed, she had at least managed a Chinese husband and borne a son, which was more than Mom did. Startled by this thought, never before articulated, she could not suppress the anger that resulted. Gail felt her damp cheeks. Her colleagues were right: she was abnormal. Afraid to laugh and now crying over nothing. When had she become so unknowable to herself? And why couldn't she, no matter how hard she tried, ever reach deep enough inside to isolate and understand the core of her sorrow?

Gail flung her head back and inhaled the salty air. She must get a grip.

At the water's edge, the surfer was examining her board, which was propped vertically against the pier. She searched for some unknown injury, some flaw, a look of intense concentration on her face. After a few minutes, the woman appeared satisfied that everything was in order. She took her board back out to the waves, rode far from the shoreline, and then, as a wave took hold, rose up from the sea onto the crest.

Gu Kwun had come by and was asking something.

"Look out there, sweetie." Gail pointed to the surfer. The woman was riding high, her tanned, lean body silhouetted against the horizon. It was magical. As she closed in on the shore, she seemed to fly off her board into the water. Then, her head appeared, and her arm reached up around the board. Home base.

"Flying fish, flying fish!" Gu Kwun exclaimed, and ran off to tell his grandmother.

Last weekend, her mother surprised her by asking if she wanted to go back home to Boston. But Mother, she'd replied, I am home. For just one instance, her mother had looked at her lucidly and said — *I wanted him to love you too, you know, really I did* — and then she lapsed into her usual state, muttering her way back into her bedroom.

That evening, Conchita gave notice. "It's time for me to go back to my family in the Philippines, ma'am. Besides, it might not be so easy for me here after July."

Gail hoped someone she knew had another available maid. "Well, you've been a great support to my family. Thank you, and I'm sorry we'll be losing you."

"Do you want me to tell Gu Kwun?"

The question puzzled her. Did Conchita really think her incapable of breaking the news to her own son? "No. I'll do that."

She informed Gu Kwun after dinner, in Conchita's presence. She explained that Conchita had her own little boy to look after who needed her. "And I need you to be a very responsible boy and help me train our new maid."

Her son listened quietly. She wondered how upset he would be.

"Is there anything you'd like to tell me, sweetheart?'

"I don't need a maid."

This she hadn't expected. "What do you mean?"

"I'm old enough to take care of myself."

"But who's going to do the cooking and cleaning?"

"You can."

This new attitude baffled her. "But I have to go to work. You know that perfectly well."

"Auntie doesn't work."

So that was it. His father's wife. She should have guessed. Gu Kwun had recently visited her ex's home for the first time. That woman.

Conchita interjected. "Ma'am, let me talk to him." Gail nodded, more exasperated than upset. She knew he was worn out by the day. Surely by tomorrow he'd forget all this nonsense.

"Gu Kwun," Conchita said, "that's because auntie is not as smart as your mother. Don't you know that?"

Gu Kwun frowned. "Why not?"

"Very few women are as smart as your mother. She's special."

Gail watched her son think. She wanted to say something, but Conchita had taken over, and this conversation didn't include her.

"But I don't need a maid. I can take care of myself," he pouted.

"Maybe not, but don't you want Mummy to have someone help her?"

His face softened. "I guess so."

"Now say goodnight. It's time to go to sleep."

Gail caught Conchita's wink as she ushered Gu Kwun towards his bedroom, her lips forming an "O-K." Her boy was growing up, sooner than she expected. One day, he wouldn't even need his mother.

30

Colleen wondered if she should call Vince. This handover party weighed on her. What had Danny said about what he called the upcoming "red glare era"? That she'd finally be forced to know the personal as the political.

But she didn't want anything awkward with Vince.

Later that morning. "Oh dear, I've woken you."

His voice was thick with sleep. "'sokay."

"I'll call later."

"I'm up now."

She resisted the urge to tease. Something about Vince, his innocent candor, perhaps, invited it. "It's about June 30th."

"Oh, that."

"You're not, you know, bi, are you?"

"Babes, what the hell . . .?"

"Albert."

Silence. "No."

"Okay, just checking."

"Look Colleen, quit playing games. This town's too small. We're going to run into each other, right? Let's keep it cool."

"I will if you will."

"Deal."

The nice thing about most of her fellow countrymen was that they did come round to their senses eventually. Vince, she decided, was turning into quite a tolerable American abroad.

At Albert's new third floor studio above his home, Vince waited for Andanna to show up. She was scheduled for promotional shots. Agreed to Albert's request, relieved that his friend had finally given up the quest for "art" photos.

Andanna breezed in ten minutes late. No apologies. "Hiya. Give me a few minutes, I go change."

She emerged in a microscopic dress. The girl was too sexy for her own good.

"D'ya like my dress? My manager choose for me."

He focused the camera on her. "Who's your manager?"

"Mrs. Colleen Tang."

Too fast, the way sands shifted. "When did that happen? I didn't know she was in the business."

"Oh, you know her?"

"You could say we're acquainted."

"Wha . . .?"

"Never mind. C'mon, look like a singer." Natural ham, but she did look good. "How d'you meet Colleen?"

"Through friend. Oh, you know her too. Gail Szeto."

The women in his life were in a conspiracy against him, even here.

"Actually, I know you know Colleen." She giggled. "She tell me to be careful of you."

"Oh yeah?" Resisted the urge to correct her grammar.

"She say you have too many girlfriends."

"And don't you have too many boyfriends?"

"Guys no fun. They all want to be serious."

Visions of Katy as a teenager with breasts. Dating guys. Frightening. He took several more shots. What the hell, might as well be bad and shudder the grapevine a bit. "Doesn't Colleen have many boyfriends?"

Pure, unadulterated horror. "Course not. She's married."

Defining morality. Gail's voice tickled his brain. Hope for Katy yet.

"Albert say you are good photographer. Are you?"

"What do you think?"

"I guess you're okay."

"Damn with faint praise, huh?"

"Wha . . .?"

"Forget it."

Colleen was coming by to pick her up, Andanna said, because they had a manicure appointment together. No wonder she'd called this morning. Now what?

"I have to go." Leave first. Wouldn't have to see her this way.

"Don't you want to say hi to Mrs. Tang?"

"I'm sure I'll see her again."

Opened the door. Too late. She stood there, as if he'd just appeared at her hotel room.

"Hi there. You been taking care of You Fun for me?"

"Who?"

Colleen waved at Andanna. "You Fun. That's her name."

"Oh, her . . . Chinese name." Dumb, but that was what came out. Colleen had that effect.

"Her name."

The two of them made quite a pair. Andanna towered over Colleen, but the latter managed not to look short. Vince felt clumsy, a creature lumbering into the wrong species.

"You Fun, could you go down and wait for me. I need to talk to Mr. da Luca privately about business."

"Sure, okay." She took off.

Vince raised both hands. This woman might as well be armed. "Listen Colleen, let's not get started on anything."

She propped herself against the studio wall, her body closed and uninviting. "I wasn't trying to."

"So what d'you want to talk about? Haven't you said it all?"

Colleen glanced around the room. She looked uncomfortable. "I love my husband."

Her voice was so soft he had to ask her to repeat herself.

He asked. "And . . . this is a revelation?"

"No. What I'm trying to say is that I am really happily married. I just have . . . used to have . . . lapses."

"We had a deal, right? What's the problem, Colleen?"

Right now, this was not the woman he knew. Her petite frame appeared more diminutive than it really was. Wouldn't look at him, spoke in a sideways manner. And the sexual challenge she embraced, the one that tinged her voice, her movements, her every look, might never have existed. Another being had taken over. He wondered if she were slightly schizo. Should talk to Jim about her.

Then her demeanor changed, and the softly wicked smile returned. "No problem, I guess, now that we understand each other."

Before she left, she kissed his cheek in a friendly way, saying she looked forward to seeing him again. Then she ran down the stairs.

Strange fruit, Colleen. Should have left her in Eden, among the fruit bats.

From the window, he could see the two of them walking towards the taxistand around the corner. Radiant, magnificent beasts, aware of their presence, ignoring the glances of the throng. Hunting down, and vanquishing, the real "second" sex.

"You like that da Luca guy?"

Andanna was trying to hail a taxi. "Oh sure. He's okay."

"Not your type?"

Her look of disgust took Colleen aback. "Yuk! That old *gwailo?*" And then suddenly, catching her *faux pas,* "oh sorry, I mean not that he's like, old, but you know, some people remain young much longer. Like you."

"He probably likes you."

Andanna laughed. "How funny! You think so?"

"Oh come on, You Fun. It's not like you're a girl. You know what all that's about."

A taxi glided to a halt in front of them. Andanna busied herself getting in, giving the driver instructions, setting down her bag. She didn't want to talk about Vince or sex, Colleen realized. Not pushing it any further, they chatted about other things.

At the beauty parlor, Colleen began to relax. Her manicurist showed her a range of colors, and she selected a golden red flame. It made her think of foliage, of the movement of the seasons. There was no reason for concern. She knew she shouldn't have come up to the studio, but it would have irked her if Vince had any kind of thing for You Fun, even if it wasn't reciprocated. Admit it, she was jealous. If she could, she'd still do Vince. But she had meant everything she'd told him. It was just that life with Kwok Po was sometimes a little bit too predictable.

Old. You Fun considered Vince old. He was probably around Kwok Po's age. There was something disconcertingly child-like about her. With a few extra years, she could be her mother. Sobering.

That strange body heat hadn't resurfaced, thank god.

The manicurist poked the cuticle of her left ring finger slightly too hard and she winced.

"Colleen, what d'you think of this color." Andanna waved a long, pale nail that looked almost completely white.

The girl knew fashion but could be a bit more discerning. "Darker. You don't need to go the heroin route. Get some color in there. A little beige maybe."

"How about gray?"

"You Fun, you've got to get off this black and shades of black thing. It won't work on stage."

Andanna pouted, but directed her manicurist to another range of colors. Colleen saw her look, but decided to ignore it.

Was it a good idea to do this manager thing? She was spending a lot of time with You Fun. It was entertaining, but the girl had no imagination. Oh, she'd do whatever she was told, but surely she should have more of a standpoint of her own?

When she'd echoed these thoughts to Kwok Po, he dismissed them saying she expected too much and that the girl was still young. Perhaps that was true, because she wasn't even twenty five. But when she considered herself at that age, she thought she'd done much more, or at least, that she had much more of a sense of who she was. She certainly expressed more opinion. It's different in America, Kwok Po reminded her. Youth is meant for self determination over there. Among Chinese, only the old and seasoned are accorded that privilege while the young keep their mouths shut — the way they should — she knew he believed.

Colleen didn't agree. Not all Hong Kong people she met were like that, especially not among the arty crowd. You Fun skirted its periphery, giving lip service to her need for self expression. She wanted it because it was the in thing, because it made her cool, but not because there was some inner driving need to create or perform. There was also a vulnerability about her she couldn't reconcile. What bothered her most was the time You Fun seemed to waste, as if life were infinite. Had she been as callous with her own existence at that age?

Or maybe Kwok Po was right. After all, pop music was hardly high art. This star making business was fun for now. She'd see how long it would last.

In bed that night, Kwok Po asked, in English. "Things are okay between us now, aren't they?"

"What makes you say that?"

"I'm a man. I can tell." He kissed the edge of her mouth. His scarred tongue ran lightly against her lower lip. "Goodnight."

Colleen turned over, worried. Would she ever really understand him? Even after all these years, he still wouldn't come right out and accuse or blame her. As long as she stayed with him, as long as she loved him.

It was a perfect love.

And then, her body began to warm up; that strange heat filtered its way towards her face. The sensation was only slightly uncomfortable, and in their air conditioned bedroom, it felt peculiarly out of sync with the room temperature. Were these hot flashes predicated on tension? Gail's suggestion — to read up on menopause. How dreadful.

She must have shifted and disturbed him, because her husband turned around and asked. "You okay?"

It had to stop. She would not let this, or any other problem, get in the way of anything. "I'm fine. Just a little hot."

"Want me to turn up the air conditioner?"

"No, don't bother." She eased up against him. His body was cool. Her hands spread over his naked chest, and reached for the back of his neck. Kissing the point where his hair converged, she whispered in Chinese, "there's never been anybody else, you know that, don't you? I'm your *Hong Qi*, only yours. You know that, don't you?"

In answer, he faced her and ran his fingers down her spine, stopping at that point near the base. "Show me, my love," he said.

She did.

31

Michael's postcard read. "Fell in love. She's Japanese and sings real music." The real was twice underlined in bold, black ink. Her boyfriend was getting his revenge. Let him laugh. It didn't matter what he thought anymore.

Yet, his message bugged her.

Andanna was tired. The interview with that entertainment magazine yesterday evening had lasted almost an hour. Why hadn't she ever entered the Miss Hong Kong contest, the journalist wanted to know. Because she hadn't and this was a dumb question, she'd wanted to retort, but knew she couldn't. Instead, she'd mouthed some garbage about how each person had to seek her own way to self expression, and that hers didn't happen to include this. The journalist had "uh-huh, uh-huhed" earnestly and scribbled that down. And then there had been all those silly questions about which singers she admired, and who she modeled herself after? How would she know? She just sang whatever the band put in front of her, although of course, she couldn't tell the journalist that.

All this business, how tedious. She would rather have gone dancing.

It had been months since she'd been out just for fun.

These days, all her life was wrapped up around rehearsals and attending the "right" parties. Those were awful, full of tiresome types who made silly remarks about her "glamorous" life. Otherwise, she had to compete with a bunch of starlets, models and singers all vying for some producer's attention. Colleen suggested that a movie role, even a minor one wouldn't hurt. What a pain. She didn't care about acting in some stupid film.

It was tiring. She never got enough sleep, because she was up early and in bed late. And she couldn't hang out with friends, except Colleen, but then, she wasn't exactly a friend. All day, every day it was rehearsals for the handover gig, which was less than a month away. What was the big deal? Important people from China, Colleen said, intimating that this could lead to gigs on the Mainland.

Why would she want to go to China? The people were rude and the toilets filthy. And even though she had learned to sing in *Putonghua,* she still felt unnatural speaking it.

It was almost nine. If she didn't get out of bed soon, Colleen would call and ask what time she planned to come over. The trouble with Colleen was that she took all this too seriously. Oh, it was fun, but this was getting to be too much work. On cue, the maid knocked. "Phone for you, Miss. It's Mrs. Tang." Andanna moaned. "Tell her I'm in the shower."

She sat up in bed and stretched.

Last week, Sylvie had told her she could already feel movement in her tummy, and that it was really exciting but scary. She also said that there were such cute clothes to buy for babies these days and would Andanna like to come shopping with her sometime?

Babies were adorable, so helpless and cuddly. How nice it would be to have one. A girl. She wanted a pretty baby girl. Mother would like that, wouldn't she?

"This won't take long," Colleen said when Andanna arrived. The contact sheets from Vince were spread all over her living room floor. "Besides, I want to get out with my camera."

"Why?"

"*Luhk sei,* You Fun. It might be the last time we'll be allowed to remember it. Things will be happening."

"Oh." She lit a cigarette, ignoring Colleen's disapproving glare. Just because she'd quit, she now denounced smoking altogether. What a pain. When she'd first told her mother about Colleen being her manager, Mother said she was just a *tai tai* like herself. Even Clio described her as "that wife of a rich man." They made her mad, and she defended Colleen. Now though, she was beginning to think that perhaps Mother and Clio had a point. After all, if not for her husband, Colleen would be nothing, and certainly not someone to be taken seriously about anything. "Why are you so interested in *lukh sei?*"

Colleen shrugged. "It's history. I believe in remembering. Where were you during Tiananmen?"

"In Vancouver. I watched it on television."

"Did you cry?"

"Of course."

"See? It's Chinese sorrow. The democracy struggle touches everyone."

"One democracy, two systems?"

Colleen laughed. "You Fun, you're becoming quite a wit."

Andanna was glad she could make her laugh. Sometimes, Colleen intimidated her, because she made her feel ignorant. It wasn't just her language ability, but her intense interest in and knowledge about everything Chinese. "This handover gig. How important is it really?" Seeing Colleen's surprise, she quickly added, "it's just that my family wants to do a big dinner together, and my mother would like me there." She rolled her eyes as she said "my mother."

Colleen frowned. "I understand that, but you really need to think about your own life. It's not as if you can depend on your family forever." With that, she turned their attention to the publicity photos.

Andanna glanced disinterestedly at the shots. Colleen had such funny attitudes at times. Why did she keep harping on a career? This singing thing was great of course, but now that she'd done it, what was the big deal? Colleen kept talking about "launching" her by making a video for MTV and cutting a CD. She showed her calculations of how much money she could make. It was all so serious.

Besides, why shouldn't she depend on her family forever? She was one of the lucky ones. Just because other people couldn't, it didn't mean she shouldn't, or wouldn't.

"What do you mean? Of course you have to do that gig." Clio sounded almost mad.

"Why are you so annoyed? You said she was just playing at being my manager."

The two of them were riding the hydrofoil to Discovery Bay. Andanna had called Clio as soon as she was done with Colleen and asked her to take a day off. Clio had resisted at first, and then said, "oh why not, you can actually see a little sun today," and they'd agreed to meet at the pier.

"I can't believe you've never been to Discovery Bay," Clio exclaimed for the third time. "It's been there ages. Don't you go anywhere? I'd love to live out there — the flats are bigger than in the city — but this boat ride every day would be a pain. But I could skip work when typhoons hit. It would be a legitimate excuse."

"Shut up about that. Look, why should I do this gig? I really want to be with my family."

Clio poured some melon seeds into Andanna's hand. She cracked and popped the seeds into her mouth rapidly as spoke. "You can be with your family anytime."

"But this is a big, historical event. I don't want to be working."

"Give it up. Since when did history matter to you? You flunked it in School Cert."

The sea splashed the windows of their speeding vessel. Behind them, Hong Kong receded into a horizon speck.

"How come you're taking her side all of a sudden? You used to call her a *tai tai* with too much time on her hands."

"You know your problem?" She tore open a bag of fried dough, pulled out a couple of pieces and chewed noisily. "You don't take yourself seriously."

"Yuk. Close your mouth for heaven's sake."

"Why? There're no *gwailoes* around." She continued to talk and chew. "Look, *Lei You Fun,* that concert was really great. You were a star. You could have a great career."

Andanna groaned. "Not you too. Why does everyone want me to have a 'career?'"

"Because you did."

"What d'you mean?"

"You said you wanted to be a Canto-pop singer. Now that you're on the way there, you want to give it all up."

She fidgeted uncomfortably. "I'm not giving it up."

"Yes you are, just like you give everything else up." She offered the bag of dough to Andanna who shook her head. "Remember in school when we joined Girl Guides together? You lasted all of three months and dropped out. But you had to have not one, but two uniforms, new shoes to match and a whole bunch of other stuff before you even knew whether or not you'd like it.

"Then there was dancing, and the *pipa.* Your dad bought you a brand new one, and even set up a practice room for you. Oh, and acting. You went and took classes for what was it, a month? And calligraphy. All that beautiful rice paper gone to waste, and those brushes, how many did you buy?

"You never see anything through." She took a swig from her can of chrysanthemum tea, sated by the packet of dough she demolished.

"You eat too fast. You'll get fat."

"Stop changing the subject. Come on, it's true. You're lucky you got your degree in music, but that was only because that *haahmsap* teacher had the hots for you and he passed you in all his classes. You hardly turned in any assignments."

Andanna stuck her hands over her ears. "Stop. It's hurting my head."

They sat without speaking for several minutes.

"Wei." Clio poked Andanna's arm lightly. "Quit pouting."

Andanna folded her arms and stared at nothing.

"I'm only telling you what you know. It's not so bad. You've got to do something in life, and you're great on stage."

"Really?"

"Of course, really. All that stuff you did before just bored you, right? This is different. This is big time. If you stick to this, your parents'll be so proud they won't mind that you didn't come to the dinner."

"You think so?"

"I know so. Besides, your mother will sort out any problem your dad's family raises."

"I guess you're right."

"You know your problem?"

"Like you won't tell me anyway?"

"You think *way* too small."

The hydrofoil sped over the waves towards Lantau island. The sea was moderately choppy, and occasionally, the ride was bumpy. But it was a pleasant day, temperate with almost clear skies, not yet the scalding heat of mid summer.

Andanna wished she could get up and walk around the boat. Sitting in one spot so long made her antsy. Clio tore open a second bag of dough. Andanna's stomach did flip flops. Maybe one day, although it would probably take another handover, she might, if she tried hard enough, understand how her friend could eat that awful crap.

Discovery Bay had been a bore. It reminded her of Vancouver. They walked around a bit, and then headed back on the next boat. Back in Hong Kong, Andanna disembarked, wondering how anyone could live on those islands and ride a ferry every day. Clio took off back to her office.

Andanna walked from the pier into Central. Passing a newsstand, she saw a headline quoting the new governor saying something about "shedding the baggage of *luhk sei.*" No, not governor. Colleen had laughed when she called the Chief Executive that. These stupid titles didn't mean anything. They were all the same.

Clio was right, much as she hated to admit it. Well, maybe not about everything, but in general. What continued to nag was Michael's postcard. Some nerve. He thought he was so smart. She had wanted to tell Clio about it, but something held her back. Her friend wasn't sympathetic when it came to Michael.

So what. He was history.

She threaded her way across the bridge and into the concourse of Swire House. Just before she was about to go to the subway, a sudden inspiration struck. Heading into the Mandarin Hotel, she found the lobby shop and bought a postcard. It was a picture of Victoria Park. She and Michael had gone there for the candlelight vigil on this very night the year after she returned.

Having purchased a stamp from Reception, she propped herself against the phone booth and scribbled the date and a message in English. "Remember June 4th. It's not Japanese." As a final touch, she added a row of kiss marks and signed her name, in Chinese.

June 30 1997

32

From the rooftop balcony, a spectacular view of the harbor and fire-works. A plastic canopy sheltered against the rain. In the distance, beamed over satellites for the world to witness, a monarchy drowned.

On the makeshift stage, *Lei You Fun* sang. This stupid affair was pretentious. It wasn't a whole lot better than some of her hotel gigs. But the audience appeared to be listening, and, at the end of each song, people applauded, especially the Mainland guests. At least she wasn't invisible, like at the hotels.

After the first set, a man approached her and offered his card. It was Jake's cousin, the producer whom she had been trying forever to meet. She was surprised by his enthusiasm. He said Colleen had told him all about her, and he wanted to set up a meeting. She handed him her card and promised to call.

"Andanna!"

A flash went off nearby.

"Oh, you." It was that photographer guy again, the one Colleen liked.

"You disappointed?"

"Wha . . .?" This guy always said the weirdest things. "Hey, Mrs. Tang thinks you're sexy."

"How d'you know?"

"I just know. Female intuition."

"Sure, sure. C'mon, give me a sexy smile."

He wasn't such a bad guy, and he did take okay shots. With the last batch, he even blew one up and framed it for her, because she'd mentioned her mother wanted a picture. It was nice of him, and Mother loved it. But what did Colleen see in him? How naïve if she thought she was hiding anything with her pretense of "business" with Vince.

Across the room, Colleen was flirting with some Mainland banker. The woman had been such a pill before tonight, fussing about every tiny detail. This place, the Club of China, or whatever it was called, was an old fashioned room, the kind of look her parents and other ancients liked. She stifled a yawn and glanced at the time. *Too* many more hours. On TV, the governor was making a speech. It was all *so* boring. She'd rather be dancing.

At midnight, the braver guests withstood the elements to catch their personal view of history. Downstairs, Albert asked the band to play the "Internationale." The lead guitarist whispered to Andanna, asking if she could hum the first bars, while the rhythm guy searched frantically through the music books. She rolled her eyes. What a request. Why did everything have to be difficult?

Colleen held her husband's hand. A successful party. She really ought to circulate and keep things lively. But Kwok Po clasped her hand tightly. He looked almost wistful.

"No more Hong Kong," he whispered, suddenly. A sentimental melancholy tinged his voice. "It's really over."

At this most inconvenient moment, heat flushed over her body. She hoped this wasn't what she could expect from now on. Perhaps she should read up on it, as distasteful as that was. After all, there was no stopping it. A few moments later, her skin cooled. This too, like the rest of all life's parade of ills, would eventually pass.

She leaned her head against her husband's shoulder.

It was long past midnight in Sheung Wan. A moonbeam grazed the streets.

Albert said. "Let's go to the park. The one on Aberdeen Street."

Vince followed him up the steep slope, marveling at his friend's unflagging energy. He had been wiped out by the party and wanted to go home, but Albert insisted on seeing in the dawn.

"We are the unwalled city," Albert declared as he walked several paces ahead.

"Come again?"

"Don't you see? Here in Hong Kong, we were never inside the wall. We're like barbarians. Mongols at bay."

"Hardly."

"Vincent, Vincent. Have you no imagination?" He stopped suddenly in the middle of the road. "I want to recite you a poem."

"Does it rhyme?"

"Only if you want it to. Listen.

    'From a park on Aberdeen Street

    I gazed at a full moon.

    Its glow caressed skinny skyscrappers

    Desperately trying to scrape the heavens.

    This is Hong Kong, I said to the moon.

    The ugly is beautiful, and the beautiful

    Is lost forever.'"

He paused and looked at Vince. "What do you think?"

"How would I know? I'm not a judge of poetry."

"But Vincent, you have the soul of an artist. You must know."

"Then I think it's poetry."

"I like you Vincent. Come inside the wall with me." He lapsed into silence.

Vince had grown accustomed to his friend's instances of declaration and long silences. Albert seemed comfortable not speaking around him. *Was* he a friend? When had he begun thinking of him as one?

"You've been divorced twice." Albert said, suddenly.

Unexpected. Wondered how he knew. Colleen perhaps. Albert never commented on anything personal. "What about it?"

"What happened?"

He wanted to say something flippant, the way he'd become used to doing, to dismiss all of it as past inconsequence, to show he had "moved on." Baring his soul only met with no response from Gail, while giving Colleen the power to manipulate him afterwards. Also, this wasn't a guy thing, except with Jim.

But Albert's features, usually impassive, were a little sad. He looked away and said, abruptly. "Sorry, I shouldn't have asked. It was rude."

"No, it wasn't. You're just the first to . . . give a shit."

He continued to walk but did not look at Vince. "Do you think us . . . impersonal?"

"More formal than Americans, I guess."

They arrived at the park. A small square of implanted trees lined concrete paths. Vince had passed it often but never stopped. By day, it was drab and gray, lacking natural contours. Moonlight softened its harsh edges. It appeared more natural, even beautiful.

Standing by the entrance, Albert held out his arm in a welcoming gesture, like a host. "Yes, that formality, as you call it. Our talent and our downfall."

"Downfall?"

"We're too correct, not politically though." Then, laughing a little, he added. "But that does depend on your point of view, doesn't it?"

It was Vince's turn to be silent. Finally. "Marriages are like an unbalanced scale, because who you are weighs more than who you think you ought to be. Well mine were like that, anyway. Gave too much to my first wife, who didn't want it, and too little to the second, who did."

Albert motioned him towards a stone bench, and sat himself down. "And your time in Hong Kong. Has that helped you find balance?"

Vince did not sit. "You make it sound like I'm leaving."

"You get to go home. You are going?" He stared at the moon. His question was a statement.

"You trying to kick me out?"

"Just asking."

"I suppose, eventually."

Albert continued to stare absently at the sky. "You get to go home," he repeated.

He sounded almost envious.

AFTERWORD

XU XI'S HONG KONG

The Unwalled City of this novel is Hong Kong, experienced and witnessed by a cluster of characters in the years between 1993 and 1997, the year of the historic "Handover," which was also sporadically dubbed the handback, takeaway, or takeover. This is where Xu Xi's novel culminates, although the action of the novel hardly reflects the dominant story of the menacing Communist takeover of a free-wheeling capitalist enclave that the international media fed the world at the time.

Of course, it is true that for a brief while in the summer of 1997, a month or so, Hong Kong was taken over, but it was not by goose-stepping soldiers of "Red China," or the tanks of the PLA, but by the serried ranks of the international press corps themselves. They typically came here looking for a story whose plot they already knew, and the arc of their invasion ran through the hotels of the territory and the bars of the Foreign Correspondents' Club. In the event, the Handover itself was anti-climatic. Prince Charles came, attended the ceremony, and then he and the last British governor of Hong Kong sailed out of the harbor on the royal yacht Britannia. It rained a great deal.

Shortly after, the spotlight of the international media swung elsewhere, to Africa, the Balkans, the UK or USA, and the ranks of journalists took off too, back to the "real world" of their home bases, wives, children, and mortgages. For many of them one imagines, the Hong Kong story was completely dead by the time they buckled themselves into their seats. And anyway, Hong Kong had always had this unlikely, unreal quality to it, hadn't it? In the late seventies, Le Carré captured that attitude well in *The Honourable Schoolboy*, when he claimed that "When you leave Hong Kong it ceases to exist. When you have . . . held your breath as you race sixty feet above the roofs of the grey slums, when the out-islands have dwindled into the blue mist, you know that the curtain has been rung down, the props cleared away, and the life you lived there was all illusion."

The perceived unreality of Hong Kong, heightened by the stock constituents of drugs, oriental sex, political intrigue, and triads, has surfaced in so much of the English-language fiction on this quasi city-state. So many of the English-language novels written on Hong Kong, for example, from the pot-boilers of Clavell to Theroux's recent *Kowloon Tong*, have dealt in the kind of illusory stereotypes that have meshed unreality and banality in large measure.

Xu Xi's *Unwalled City* represents a very different approach to the representation of the city and its people. But initially the title had me wondering. Was there some reference here to the notorious "Walled City" of Kowloon? Until very recently, this was a rabbit's warren of slum tenements located near the old airport, by the 1950s and 1960s a no-go area with brothels, drugs, and crime. By the time it was pulled down in 1991 it had a population of 35,000, finally ejected after the Hong Kong and Chinese governments had resolved a territorial dispute over the district and demolished it. The thoroughly bourgeois milieu of Xu Xi's middle and upper class is clearly a world away.

But a walled city of a very different kind is first indicated by the Eurasian Gail Szeto in this novel when she describes herself as a *jaahp-jung*, a "mixed breed" a "miscellaneous species," who in her childhood dreams "lived outside the Great Wall, where she would knock and knock at the door to the Wall, but no one would let her in." Like Gail, modern Hong Kong itself has its own *jaahpjung* qualities. From the 1960s to 1990s, Hong Kong people emerged as a breed in their own right, part "traditional Chinese," and part "Western" (whatever that is), owing allegiance neither to the mainland nor to Taiwan, but claiming their home primarily in the 400-odd square miles of the territory of Hong Kong. The key to the puzzle is finally given to us in the last chapter by Albert Ho, on the night of the Handover, when he explains to Vince, "We are the unwalled city ... Don't you see? Here in Hong Kong, we were never inside the wall. We're like barbarians. Mongols at bay."

Xu Xi's achievement in *Unwalled City* has been to create a fictional world with a "social realism" anchored in the acute and detailed social observation of a particular group of Hong Kong people, some Chinese, some Western, some bi-racial, whose cosmopolitanism mirrors the developing life of the city at a particular, and crucial, point in its history. *Unwalled City* is Xu Xi's "handover" novel, although it took me at least until the mid-point of the book to realize how this actually works. Then it dawned on me. That the characters of the novel, the ensemble of Vince da Luca, Gail Szeto, Andanna Lee, Albert Ho, Colleen Tang, her brother Danny, and the others, were all pretty much like the people one knows here, people like us. The us, I suppose, being long-term residents in the kind of special social space that enables academics, for example, to mix socially with advertising folk, business people, entrepreneurs, lawyers, politicians and all the assorted types of people with whom we form friendships, intimacies, and other relationships, in the often improbable world we inhabit here.

In this context, the men, women, and children who live in these pages, are "realistic" in exactly the way that the characters of most Hong Kong novels are not. In the runup to "Ninety-seven," the stuff of their lives here mirrors our own. Our lives in the mid-nineties were not concerned with Chris Patten or Tung Chee-wah or some grand public drama but with work, marriage, friends, and lovers. With the possible exception of emigration, politics took place largely offstage, as it does in the novel. The media circus of mid-1997 is long gone, but the lives of people here continue. Political intrigue, as ever, continues, but, as in most societies perhaps, out of view of most of us. For the rest, we all attempt to make sense of our lives through work or love, our inner emotional life, and all of the above. The title of the original manuscript was *Lives and Loves in the Unwalled City,* and what Xu Xi does in this book is to capture the texture of living and loving in this Asian metropolis more accurately and realistically than any other novelist, at least in English, has ever done. This she is passionate about. Her passion for this city, its people, and her craft shine through this work. Just as, against the odds almost, the singular vitality of Hong Kong people shines through the chrome and concrete of this most materialistic of cities.

Dr. Kingsley Bolton
The University of Hong Kong
January 2001

GLOSSARY

In this short glossary, I include an explanation of some of the most important Chinese and "Hong Kong English" words and phrases that occur in the novel. Unless stated otherwise, the Chinese phrases are from the Cantonese variety that is dominant in Hong Kong. "Md." indicates Mandarin, the dominant variety of northern China (also referred to as "Putonghua"). There are a number of competing systems for writing Cantonese alphabetically. The system mainly used here is a modified form of the Yale romanisation system. Mandarin words and phrases are transcribed using "pinyin," the official system of mainland China.

Prologue

(p.1) *Gwailo* — (Hong Kong English) literally "ghost man," pejorative term used to refer to Westerners. Cf. gwaipo, "ghost woman."

(p.1) *Fong* — lit. "square"; here a reference to Lan Kwai Fong, the popular dining and entertainment area in the centre of Hong Kong.

(p.1) *yan* — (Hong Kong English) a human being, a person.

(p.2) *Gaau mat gwai a?* — lit. "What ghostly realm has been disturbed this time?"; here it simply means "What's going on?"

(p.2) *feijai* — "teddy boys" or hooligans, ruffians, often used to refer to "triads," members of criminal secret societies.

Chapter 1

(p.10) *siuyeh* – literally "digest the night," used to mean "late night snack."

(p.10) *Wei! Meih fanseng, sai sengdi la!* — Lit. "not yet sleep aroused softer sound," meaning "Hey! I"m not awake yet, be quiet!"

(p.11) *laisee* (Hong Kong English) — small red envelopes containing bills of money, given at Chinese New Year, weddings, or in celebrations for the birth of a child.

(p.11) *gam fit* — lit. "so fit," meaning "it fits so well."

Chapter 2

(p.15) *deihji* — address.

(p.15) *Yihdung Jaudim* — the Chinese name of the "Excelsior Hotel," which is located on the harbor front in the Causeway Bay district of Hong Kong island.

(p.18) *saigaai janhaih hou sai* — lit. "the world really very small," meaning "It's really a small world."

Chapter 3

(p.24) *pouh* — traditional Chinese wedding dress.

(p.24) *louhbaan* — boss.

(p.24) *Neih hou?* — lit. "You good?" meaning "Hi," or "How are you?"

(p.25) *Yambui!* — lit. "Drink cup," meaning "Cheers!."

(p.28) *gwais* — lit. "ghosts," abbreviation of "gwailos," i.e. "ghost people," foreigners.

Chapter 4

(p.37) *Putonghua* — lit. "common language," the official term used in the People's Republic of China (PRC) to refer to the Mandarin Chinese dialect, the national language of mainland China.

(p.37) *pinyin* — the official form of alphabetic writing used in the PRC, lit. "match tone."

(p.37) *laihlai* — mother in law.

Chapter 5

(p.42) *gammaahn dim a?* — lit. "this night how?," meaning "How are you tonight?."

(p.42) *leng leui, leng jau* — lit. "beautiful girl, beautiful wine," meaning "a beautiful girl deserve only the best wine."

(p.42) *tohnggo* — an older male cousin on one's father's side.

(p.43) *Luhksei* — the Chinese name of a club in Lan Kwai Fong called "Club 64," the name of which inscribes a reference to the sixth month and fourth day, i.e. June 4th, the date in 1989 of the protests at Tiananmen.

Chapter 6

(p.52) *wanfaan* — lit. "found back," meaning "found."

(p.52) *pohpo* — granny.

Chapter 8

(p.68) *Ni zhidao gai zhen yang baan ma?* — (Md.) Do you know what you must do? Literally, do you know what must do? The second you being implied.

(p.69) *Shizi Wang* — (Md.) Lion King or king of the lions.

(p.74) *gwaipo* — "ghost woman," Western woman.

(p.74) *muihmui* — younger sister.

Chapter 9

(p.80) *wahtdaht* — awful, disgusting.

Chapter 10

(p.85) *Gingluhnggaai* — Chinese name of Cannon Street (lit. "grand view street"), located in the Causeway Bay area on Hong Kong island.

(p.85) *Gousihdadouh* — Chinese name of Gloucester Road, which is located in the same area. Like many street names in Hong Kong, the Chinese name represents a rendering of the English sound, through the use of approximately equivalent Chinese syllables.

(p.86) *jyun jo* — turn left.

(p.93) *chengyu* — (Md.) a proverb or idiom usually written with four Chinese characters.

Chapter 11

(p.100) *heungha* — village, or "ancestral village."

(p.100) *fongbihn* — convenient.

(p.102) *daamsam* — lit. "burdened heart," meaning "worry."

(p.104) *jaahpjung* — lit. "mixed breed," derogatory term used to describe Eurasians and other people of mixed race.

Chapter 14
(p.133) *Hong Qi* — (Md.) lit. "red flag," Colleen's nickname.
(p.134) *xiang wen hou ni* — (Md.) lit. "want to ask after you," here meaning "inquiring after your well being."
(p.134) *mei you wen ti* — (Md.) "no problem."

Chapter 15
(p.145) *dim sum* (Hong Kong English) — The small dishes served at Chinese brunch or *"yum cha"* (lit. "to touch the heart").
(p.147) *faat choy* (Hong Kong English) — a fungus delicacy served at Chinese New Year for good luck, whose Chinese name is a homonym for "to get rich."

Chapter 16
(p.157) *shizi bu tu* — (Md.) a traditional saying, meaning that "a lion shouldn't hold back even in combat with a rabbit," i.e. that one put one's whole heart into a fight, however minor.

Chapter 17
(p.161) *cheongsam* (Chinese English) — the traditional, high-collared dress with side slits that some Chinese women wear on formal occasions.
(p.161) *Mang ci zai bei* — (Md. Proverb) "a thorn stuck in one's back" to describe a troublesome irritant.

Chapter 19
(p.187) *Neih dim sik Gail a?* — "How do you know Gail?."
(p.187) *Siksikdei, gau kinggai* — "Know her a little, enough to chat."
(p.192) *ngaahnggeng ngaam* — lit. "hard necked right," an expression to describe a person who stubbornly clings to his point of view.

Chapter 20

(p.199) *Wei, leng leui* — "Hi, gorgeous."

(p.199) *Bu jiang Guangdong hua* — (Md.) "Don't speak Cantonese."

(p.200) *Meih dou gau chat* — "1997 hasn't arrived yet."

(p.200) *Putonghua hai bu shi Xianggang de mu yu* — (Md.) "Putonghua isn't Hong Kong's mother tongue yet."

(p.201) *puih laihlai heui gin Loh saang, hou ma?* — lit. "accompany mother-in-law to go see Mr. Lo, okay?"

(p.201) *yum cha* (Hong Kong English) — Chinese brunch, literally "drink tea"

Chapter 21

(p.205) *saiyahn* — Western person.

Chapter 22

(p.221) *geeleegulu* — (Hong Kong English) gobbledygook.

(p.222) *Hong Qiao* — (Md.) "Rainbow Bridge," the name of Shanghai's international airport.

(p.222) *siu daih* — lit. "little brother," also means I myself, a humble form.

Chapter 23

(p.224) *Jimdung* — lit. "Tsim East," Tsimshatsui East, a district in downtown Kowloon.

(p.232) *Gammaahn heui wet haih mhaih?* — "Tonight going out to have fun, eh?"

(p.232) *tohngsaimui (tohngmui)* — younger female cousin on one's father's side.

(p.233) *Louhfaahndim* — restaurant name, meaning "Old Restaurant."

Chapter 24

(p.243) *tohngmui* — younger female cousin on one's father's side.

Chapter 25

(p.248) *jaahp* — cheap, low class.

(p.253) *saidaam* — lit. "small guts," cowardly.

(p.253) *daam daaih sam sai* — lit. "guts big, heart small," meaning "brave but cautious."

Chapter 26

(p.258) *dungsai* — lit. "east west," meaning in standard Chinese "a thing."

(p.263) *Heunggong bu shi Shanghai* — (Md. mixed with Cantonese and English) Hong Kong isn't Shanghai.

(p.264) *Mei wenti. Keyi deng.* — (Md.) No problem. (I) can wait.

Chapter 28

(p.277) *gihng* — slang meaning super or fabulous.

Chapter 31

(p.300) *tai tai* — (Chinese English) a wife, often used to mean a housewife, one married to a wealthy man; also designates "Mrs." when placed after a surname.

(p.302) *pipa* — (Chinese English) a stringed musical instrument.

(p.302) *haahmsap* — lit. "salt wet," slang meaning sex maniac.

Thanks are owed to Mr. Cedric Lee and Ms. Michelle Woo for their expertise and invaluable assistance in compiling this glossary.